Going it Alone

Going it Alone

Clare Dowling

headline
review

First published in 2008 by Headline Review
An imprint of HEADLINE PUBLISHING GROUP

1

Cataloguing in Publication Data is available from the British Library

Hardback ISBN 978 0 7553 4148 1
Trade paperback ISBN 978 0 7553 4149 8

Typeset in Bembo by Palimpsest Book Production Limited,
Grangemouth, Stirlingshire

Printed and bound in the UK by
CPI Mackays, Chatham ME5 8TD

Headline's policy is to use papers that are natural, renewable and recyclable
products and made from wood grown in sustainable forests. The logging and
manufacturing processes are expected to conform to the environmental
regulations of the country of origin.

HEADLINE PUBLISHING GROUP
An Hachette Livre UK Company
338 Euston Road
London NW1 3BH

www.headline.co.uk
www.hachettelivre.co.uk

For Stewart

ACKNOWLEDGEMENTS

Thanks go as always to Clare Foss and all at Headline. Many thanks to Darley Anderson and all at the agency. Special thanks to Sean and Ella for staying quiet during those crucial chapters, and to Stewart who was a wonderful house-husband for five years but who is now off in pursuit of his own venture, leaving me to make my own cups of tea. Good luck with it.

Chapter One

Millie's order had arrived that very morning, discreetly packaged as promised in a bland padded envelope. In fact the postman thought it was yet another free gift from Kelloggs – Millie was a great one for collecting coupons – and had handed it over with an indulgent smile, unaware that he was fingering five tubes of high-voltage sexual lubricant that swore it was convenient, easy to use and, most important, sperm friendly.

Not that the sperm had shown up yet. But they were due any minute. Andrew had phoned from the car half an hour ago to say that he was just hitting the M50.

'You do know what day it is, don't you?' Millie had questioned anxiously. She didn't want to put pressure on him. But on the other hand it only came round once a month.

'Yes, yes,' he'd said.

He always sounded very far away on the phone these days. Which he usually was. He had changed jobs three months ago to a young, dynamic company whose mission it was to roll out broadband to every far-flung field and bit of bog in Ireland. Having lounged on his backside behind a computer in the bank for the past ten years, being forced to actually work had come as a bit of a shock to him. Through his lunch break, usually. And into the evening, when *Top Gear* and his dinner waited for him at home. Last month he had spent so many days driving up and down to Cork that he declared that they might as well move down there.

There were other concerns too. 'The rest of them are all under twenty-five,' he had relayed to Millie fearfully after his first week. 'They speak in this strange, shorthand language that I can't make head nor tail of. And they can all drink fourteen bottles of beer in the pub after work without batting an eyelid. I haven't been able to do that in ages.' Years, actually.

Millie had briefly tried to persuade him to go back to the bank. He'd been happy there, leading a gentle, slob-like existence, only exerting himself to fix the occasional computer glitch or do a weekly backup of customer accounts. The job was permanent, pensionable, and with no hope whatsoever of advancement. It suited him down to the ground, and he could easily have coasted along until retirement. Look at Millie, after all. Still in the same job since school and not a bother on her.

'Exactly,' Andrew had said, superior – as though it were some kind of deficiency on her part. She worked in the claims department of an insurance company, for heaven's sake. It wasn't exactly the kind of career that propelled you through glass ceilings at a great rate. The highest she ever got was the first floor of Manahans pub on a Friday evening after work to drink pints of lager and bitch with the girls about bad pay and Paul from Personnel, who was down like a ton of bricks on anybody who left even half an hour early on a Friday afternoon. And don't get them started on the customers, even though most of them had suffered terrible misfortune, what with car accidents and house fires and burglaries every time their backs were turned. She would never say it out loud, but Millie would be secretly sorry for them.

'Our Millie was always the compassionate one,' her mother used to insist, back when she could be bothered to. This was because Millie was forever bringing home bedraggled, three-legged dogs she'd found in the park, building them little huts out the back and tenderly feeding them warm milk. More often than not they'd have disappeared by the following morning, having first dug up the flowerbeds and savaged the clothes on the washing line. She had no idea back then, of course, that that kind of ingratitude would be par for the course in her future career in a claims department.

'Just don't bring home any donkeys,' her father had pleaded. 'The garden isn't big enough.' A brief flirtation with vegetarianism at fifteen was all it took to copper-fasten her place as the socially aware one in the family.

'At least you're not the irresponsible one who went and got herself banged up,' her sister, Oona, pointed out. 'I knew it, I knew it,' their father had kept saying, shaking his head in a scandalised fashion even though Oona had been twenty-nine at the time, and married.

Now, the lubricant awaited Millie. The instructions advised her to apply it about fifteen minutes before making love. Great. That should give Andrew enough time to take off his coat and check the football results on teletext, if he had the energy. And to down a beer for courage. That used to be their little joke. But, honestly, the way he drank that beer now you would think he actually meant it.

The lubricant was cold and unfriendly, and unseemly to apply. It was a far cry from the halcyon days when she used to throw herself down in wild abandon upon the bed shouting, 'Take me, tiger!'

Still, maybe it would do the trick. Apparently one of the main impediments to successful conception was the lack of a suitable 'medium' for sperm to travel upwards after being let loose. She had discovered that fact on the Internet. You wouldn't believe how many websites were devoted to trying to conceive. They broke down into all kinds of subgroups, such as Trying to Conceive After Forty, Trying to Conceive After Tube Reversal, Trying to Conceive With a Female Partner (good luck). Millie would sometimes dip into Trying to Conceive With Prayer and have a good snigger, even though everybody knew that this was a deadly serious business, and that any kind of laughter was totally inappropriate.

It was on one of these websites that Millie first found out about hostile mucus. She had never known that such a thing existed before. It was a condition in which, alarmingly, some women's bodies took grave exception to their partner's sperm, so much so that they actually sent their mucus after them to more or less bludgeon them to death.

It seemed a terrible fate for sperm in general. Especially when the odds were stacked against them in the first place. Of the three hundred million or so that swam off, furiously doing the backstroke or the crawl, only about three hundred of them could actually be expected to make it past the finish line at all. Never mind encountering hostile mucus around every bend.

'They don't have feelings,' Andrew had pointed out.

Millie couldn't believe he was so cold about them. And he owned them!

She hoped to God that she wasn't suffering from the hostile condition. But just to be sure she had spent a fortune on the aforementioned special lubricant, which promised a pH balance that was acceptable to all parties, thus restoring peace down under. Either way, it couldn't hurt, couldn't it?

Millie had a drawer full of things that couldn't hurt: ovulation predictor kits, saliva tests, charts, digital thermometers, pre-natal vitamins, Robitussin Expectorant (apparently it served the same function as the lubricant, but all Millie had done was cough for a couple of days). She also had a dozen cheapie pregnancy tests bought off the Internet. So far none of them had been positive, even though she would take them apart with her tweezers and shine a high-powered torch on them in the vain search for a faint pink line. But there was still plenty of time yet. Oodles of time.

Actually, not really.

The horrible truth was that Millie was thirty-nine. Thirty-nine! Even though she was only twenty-six in her head, sometimes even twenty-three. She still watched *Friends*, for goodness' sake, and browsed in Topshop without anybody coming over to advise her that she'd be better off in an old folks' home. When her friends recently began to turn forty, Millie would still unaccountably think: God, they're ancient, not quite facing up to the fact that it was going to happen to her. In less than a year's time, to be precise. And if she didn't get a move on she might be joining them on the Trying to Conceive After Forty discussion forums.

Still, didn't a woman somewhere in Italy have twins last year, and wasn't she sixtysomething? And another woman had produced a baby in her late fifties. Millie was practically a spring chicken in comparison. It wasn't like before, where you were all washed up if you hadn't popped out four by the age of thirty. Women were having healthy babies well into their middle age. Well into retirement in Italy.

'No matter how young you think you are, your eggs are still thirty-nine,' her GP had intoned last week.

He was a desperately gloomy man. But possibly he hadn't heard about the woman in Italy who had produced the twins. He had then brought up the subject of her FSH levels without even being asked.

'My FSH?' Millie had said, trying to let on that she didn't know what he was talking about. FSH was something the women on the Internet forums went on about quite a lot, usually with dread. She tended to skip those bits.

'Follicle Stimulating Hormone,' he clarified, as though it were something highly toxic. 'It gives an indication of ovarian reserve. The number of eggs you have left.'

Millie didn't think that the number of eggs she had left was anybody's business but her own.

'And the quality of them,' he added heavily. 'It diminishes with age, you know.'

Well, that was enough to depress anybody. She had traipsed out past all the women in the waiting room with their buggies and bumps, feeling like an old prune. That very night she had jerked awake in bed, roasting hot. Oh God. A night sweat: one of the first signs of the menopause. She was doomed. She told Andrew that she might as well go back to taking in stray dogs. Then they discovered that the central heating had been left on full blast all night.

Andrew said she was getting too stressed out about the whole thing. He often said that nowadays. But then again he could father a child into his nineties, if he could find a woman to oblige, so why should he feel any stress at all? Men had it so easy. In her darker moments, when she was truly feeling thirty-nine and not pretending that she was twenty-three, Millie wished that their scrotums would shrivel up and fall off once they hit forty-five. That would certainly level the playing field.

You would think that she had deliberately left it late. That she had selfishly decided, 'Oh, I'll have a great career for fifteen years and drink like a fish and go on flash foreign holidays, and then when I've tired of that I'll marry someone half-decent at thirty-seven, and squeeze in two kids before everything dries up, and that way I can have it all, just like the magazines tell me.'

The simple truth was that she had never found the right man. Not that she had devoted every second of her life so far to looking, or anything like that. She hadn't conducted an extensive search up and down the country in pursuit of suitable specimens. But she had dated, of course she had. All through her twenties she had gone forth with great hope and expectation that she would meet someone nice, or fun, or even both.

Instead she had ended up with a series of losers, idiots, lunatics and men who were married but failed to mention that fact. Drunks, commitment-phobes, mammy's boys – for some reason they saw her coming, and would hunt her out like heat-seeking missiles and ensconce themselves in her life before she copped on to what they were really like. But even then she usually didn't have the heart to kick them out; the customer-care employee in her tried to change them, and when that failed abysmally, she tried to live with their shortcomings. After all, nobody was perfect. But even Millie's patience would eventually run out and she would end up having to change the locks.

'What is it about me?' she complained bitterly upon turning thirty, and leaving behind a decade littered with the corpses of rotten relationships.

'You look too nice,' Oona advised her kindly.

'What?' Millie said, hoping that this meant she was stunningly beautiful.

But Oona said, 'You're too open. Smiley. You've the kind of face that appeals to users and chancers, and stray dogs.'

'You mean I'm too soft.' Tell her something she *didn't* know.

'Well, it wouldn't hurt to toughen up a bit.'

Millie threw back her head in what she hoped was a defiant way. 'I'm not going to become all aloof and horrible in the hope that it'll get me a man.'

She needn't have bothered, because there then followed a spectacularly dry period in which she met no men at all. Not even on the bus. This went on for several years until she began to wonder whether there was some kind of world shortage, and that there might actually be none left. Not even creeps.

It dawned on her then that it could be too late. Most of her friends had been married for a couple of years at that point. She was sick of them taking maternity leave in work. Why did everybody have a husband except her?

'If you wait another year or two the first round of divorces will be starting, and you might get one second-hand,' Oona advised her. Easy for her, when her youngest had turned two the previous week. Mind you, she did look wretched. Between them all she hadn't had a full night's sleep since 2001. 'I hear on the grapevine Fiona and Finbarr Maguire are breaking up.'

'Finbarr Maguire?' Millie was appalled.

'I know, I know. But with a haircut and some new clothes . . .'

'And a face lift. And a personality transplant,' Millie said grimly.

Oona was only trying to be nice. But Millie would be damned if she was going to take somebody else's leftovers. Not until she was thirty-seven or -eight anyway, and really desperate.

Out of the blue she met Andrew at a friend's house one day, just like that. She didn't even have to squeeze into that horrible scratchy red top and cruise the clubs. Even better, he seemed like a normal, decent, sane person who could actually hold down both a job and his beer, and was reasonably attractive and personable to boot.

Amazingly, he seemed to want a long-term relationship as much as her. 'I've been fighting off a beer belly for about two years,' he confessed to her within a month. 'I'm dying to settle down and let myself go.'

Millie had laughed. But only for a minute. She had a few things to tie down, even at that early stage.

'What about children?' she said baldly. Recently she had become so broody that she went around trying to catch the neighbourhood cats just to give them a cuddle.

He froze, and gave her that rabbit-trapped-in-headlights look. Still, it was better to know now.

'I don't know what people have been saying, but I don't have any,' he blurted defensively. 'Not that I know of, anyway.'

'I wasn't accusing you,' Millie assured him, her heart rising. 'I was wondering whether you might like any. You know, at some point in the future.' The very near future, at her age.

'Children?' His whole face relaxed. 'Oh, definitely.'

They got married the following June. It wasn't a moment too soon, although nobody was so rude as to actually say it out loud. Instead of going straight for babies, they decided to devote the first year of their marriage to 'enjoying' each other, which meant loads of pints in the pub, and lie-ins on a Sunday morning, and plenty of experimental sex (which usually involved doing it in the back garden when the neighbours were away). The problem was that they enjoyed themselves so much that one year stretched into two, and it was so easy to put off making any decision to start a family.

But thankfully Millie's biological clock had some kind of inbuilt warning system, because one morning she sat bolt upright in the bed, suddenly wide awake, and demanded, 'What age am I next birthday?'

Which was in two weeks' time.

Andrew eased open one eye and croaked, 'I don't know. Thirty-nine?'

'Jesus, Mary and holy Saint Joseph.' Thirty-nine! And lounging around in the bed, actually *sleeping*, instead of having unprotected sex. 'Get your pyjama bottoms off,' she urged him.

'What?'

'Quick.'

All of a sudden Millie was focused. Fiercely focused. She went out that very afternoon and bought a book called *Taking Charge of Your Reproductive Cycle*, seeing as nobody else was offering to.

'What's it about?' Andrew wondered, having a flick and no doubt hoping to find pictures of naked people doing exciting things to each other.

He was disappointed to find only fertility charts and ways of documenting Peak Days.

'Mine is Day 14,' Millie announced to him, having worked it out. 'We have to have sex on Day 10, Day 12, Day 14, and Day 15, just to be sure we nail it on the head.'

'OK,' said Andrew, nodding very seriously, but anyone could see he was delighted at the prospect of all that sex.

Now that they had decided to go for it, Mille couldn't stop thinking about babies. She would daydream constantly about being pregnant, and what it would be like. She found herself hanging around Mothercare on her lunch breaks, fingering the tiny Babygros and socks, and lost in happy dreams of bottle-feeding some tiny little bundle that would look just like a miniature Andrew. Well, not if it was a girl, obviously. Millie told herself that she didn't mind what gender the baby was, so long as it was healthy. She even began to pick out names. She wanted something Irish, but not something too obscure and that nobody from outside Ireland could pronounce, like Ailbe or Dhoireann.

'What do you think of Sean?'

Andrew looked up from the 592-page report he had brought home for the weekend, and said, 'What?'

'As a name for the baby, Andrew.'

'Lovely,' he said vaguely. Then, 'Do you want me to take my trousers off?'

'Not now. Later.'

'Just give me a whistle,' he said, and went back to the report. It was a shame that the new job had happened the very month they had decided to get pregnant. He was distracted, to say the least, leaving her to flick through the baby magazines by herself. He hadn't even been that interested in the whole argument over what travel system to buy for the newborn. Whether to go for the 'two-in-one' or the 'three-in-one'? It was a conundrum. But a nice one, of course. She couldn't wait to get out there and start spending a whole load of money.

'Let's just get pregnant first,' Andrew cautioned. After he had finished the wretched report, of course. And then memorised most of it. He didn't want to look like a klutz at the meeting on Monday morning, he fretted. He was already at a disadvantage, joining a telecommunications company directly from somewhere like the bank. Apparently on his first day they had all gathered around his ancient mobile phone in wonderment, as some of the younger ones had barely been born the year of its production (circa 1995, an expert amongst them had correctly deduced). His ire was up after that. He went in there every morning with something to prove. 'At least once we get pregnant you can brag to them that you're fertile,' Millie had joked to him. But his head was back in the report again, his lips working feverishly, and Millie was a whole hour waiting for him to come upstairs that night.

She took her first pregnancy test the following month in full expectation that it would immediately turn pink.

It didn't.

She waited ten minutes, then an hour, and then a whole day, and the damned thing still hadn't turned pink.

'Let's write to the manufacturers,' she said a week and nine tests later. 'Their products clearly don't work.'

'Millie, we'll just try again next month,' Andrew said gently.

They did. You never saw two people try harder. They even gave it a lash on Days 17 and 18 just in case, even though Andrew had just got back from a sixteen-hour day in Galway and could barely lift up his head, never mind anything else.

The next pregnancy test was negative too.

'Next month we'll start on Day 8,' Millie vowed, disappointment like a stone in her stomach. 'Just to be sure we don't miss it.'

There was no doubt that it was a gruelling regime. Sex was all very well until you were getting too much of it. It didn't help Millie either that the person she was having sex with was so tired that he would sometimes have little catnaps in the middle of the act. But she didn't mind that so much as the expression on his face when he would arrive in night after night with some big tome of a report or other, only to find her waiting for him in her nightie.

'Just give me five minutes to have a coffee,' he would say wearily. 'That'll gizz me up.'

Millie naturally began to feel like a bit of an imposition. You would think it was all her fault. Many a night she would much rather have watched telly – a *Budget Special*, anything – than be faced with Andrew's willy yet again, but what was the use in complaining? If they wanted a baby there was only one way to make one, and it wasn't hiding under the bed and whinging.

She began to have very bad thoughts about his new job. He'd have been delighted to have jiggy-jiggy every hour of the day if he were still in the bank, she mused sourly. Who would have thought that blooming broadband would turn out to be the new birth control?

But then she would feel awful – especially as he had begun to settle in a bit. He wasn't so intimidated going off in the mornings, at least. His big breakthrough came when he won a new account for the company, having sat up till four o'clock the night before memorising a report the size of a telephone book. 'I've arrived!' he announced to Millie that night, triumphantly. But she soon wiped the smile off his face by taking her clothes off and asking for sex.

Then, last month, disaster struck. They were going to miss Day 14 altogether.

'They want me to go to Frankfurt for the week,' Andrew announced. He even had the gall to look pleased.

'What?' She couldn't believe it. She was absolutely sure that this would be their month. The statistics were on their side: well, if every couple had a one-in-four chance of conceiving each cycle, then their number should be coming up right about now.

Except that her husband wouldn't actually be in the country. Her mind raced irrationally to Thermos flasks. How long could sperm survive in the fridge?

Belatedly he realised that there might be something of a clash.

'I'm really sorry, Millie. But I can't help it. It's the first time they've asked me to go, and if I turn it down I probably won't get asked again.'

Millie wanted to give out furiously, and say feck them, what about her? But he looked so excited that she would only feel mean and small.

'Do they not have their own broadband companies in Frankfurt?' she said, rather sulkily. 'Unless you're planning to roll out broadband across the Irish Sea.'

'We're going over to meet a company with similar interests to our own,' he informed her. 'There could be a deal on the table.'

It was then that Millie realised that there was some kind of transformation afoot in Andrew. He'd never have talked about deals being on the table if he were still in the bank: a sandwich, perhaps, or a coffee, but that would be about it. And now that she really looked at him, she saw how much he had changed in four short months. For starters, he had dropped a good bit of weight from missing all those dinners. Where had his beer belly gone all of a sudden? And someone in the office – someone much younger – had obviously taken him down Grafton Street at lunch break, because he now sported an Avengers-style haircut and a couple of cool new suits.

But it was the look in his eye that struck Millie the most. It was something she'd never seen before, something alien and indefinable. Holy cow – was it ambition?

'Go then,' she said heavily, because there was very little else she could say. 'There's always next month, I suppose.'

So to cut a very long story short, here Millie was again: Day 14.

Month: five.

Lubricant: yes.

Pink sexy nightie: check.

Biological clock: screaming.

Husband: unfortunately still on the M50.

She was afraid that she'd jumped the gun with the lubricant. At least half an hour had elapsed since application and she had a suspicion that it was melting. Should she apply a second tube, or would that create problems of its own?

Then, thankfully, the front door opened downstairs. Andrew was home.

'Hi!' Quickly she got rid of the packaging from the lubricant, and dimmed the bedroom light. Best to try to keep things as romantic as possible.

'Where are you?' he shouted back.

'In the bedroom!' Honestly, where else did he expect to find her at ten o'clock at night? Outside mowing the lawn? Rustling up a batch of cupcakes in the kitchen?

'Come on up!' she added, just in case he needed a further hint.

Please God may he not be too wrecked, she prayed, as she arranged herself on the bed in what she hoped was a vaguely seductive pose. Please let him have had a half-decent day, without too much stress, and have picked up something to eat on the way home and not be so weak with hunger that he can't make love. (It had happened once before.)

'Hi.' He stood in the doorway, blinking around the room. He always had an owlish look after driving in the dark. Eventually he located her on the bed. 'There you are. Sorry I'm late.'

He was all tense-looking. The traffic must have been murder. And since getting the new company car – a very expensive black number – he seemed to have become a tad intolerant of other drivers. Millie had been most surprised during their trip to the supermarket last Saturday when the conversation had been interrupted repeatedly by him bellowing out the window, 'For fuck's sake, are you blind!' He'd never have behaved like that had they been puttering along in their little Punto.

'That's OK,' she told him, very civilly. 'Have you eaten?'

'I don't know,' he said, frowning. 'I think so. I might have had something in a garage.'

'Great!' she said.

She waited for him to notice the new pink nightie, and her Joan Collins pose on the bed. Any other man, any normal man, would be galloping to the bathroom for a quick brush of his teeth before leaping on her happily.

But Andrew was jangling his car keys restlessly, and hanging about at the door as though they had all the time in the world, while Day 14 slipped past minute by minute. At this rate they'd be into Day 15 before he even got his socks off.

'Did you have a good day?' he enquired.

Her whole day had been leading up to this very point, stupid man. But she managed a bit of a smile and said, 'Fine.'

'Good,' he said.

But he wasn't really listening. He looked completely preoccupied. Probably still thinking about some deal or other.

'Look,' she snapped, 'do you want to do this or not?'

'What?'

She abandoned her pose and jerked up in the bed. 'I know you're probably not in the mood. You're probably tired. So am I. But, you know, I had a shower an hour ago, and shaved my legs specially, so let's just quit dragging our heels and get on with it, will we?'

He really did look startled now, which made her crosser.

'All right, so I'm not exactly Jennifer Lopez, but I'm not the back of a bus either, so you can stop looking at me as though you'd rather bed down with something in the zoo!'

Something clicked with Andrew. His face cleared. 'Shit. It's Day 14, isn't it?' He slapped himself on the forehead. 'Sorry, Millie. I know you told me earlier. So much has happened today that I completely forgot.'

Millie began to feel better, but only slightly. How could he actually forget? When she had reminded him less than an hour ago?

All apologies now, he came scuttling over to the bed. 'And you've gone to all this trouble . . . you look lovely. The nightie's cute. You even smell lovely.'

'Oh, shut up.' She felt patronised now.

'Come on, Millie. I'm sorry, OK? Give me two seconds and I'll jump in the shower. I can't promise to shave anything, though.'

She didn't smile.

'Hey, Millie. Give me a break here.'

She should have left it at that, of course. He was ready and willing, that was the most important thing, right? But she couldn't let it go. 'Sometimes I feel like I'm the only one who wants a baby.'

'What? Don't be daft.'

'It's like I'm always nagging you. Reminding you. That I'm forcing you into it!'

'Millie . . .' He looked a bit irritated now.

'We didn't even make love half the number of times we were supposed to this month!'

'We'd have been dead if we had,' he snapped. 'Other people manage to get pregnant without all this planning, Millie.'

Oh! She was really hurt now.

'Well, at least I know now what you really think,' she said, icy.

'Oh, Millie.' He put his hand on her leg but she drew away. 'I just think that maybe we're putting too much pressure on ourselves, that's all.'

She tried to keep her voice even. 'You see, the thing is, Andrew, I don't really have that much time to play around with here.'

But he just swept this away with a flick of his hand. 'Loads of women are having babies into their forties these days.'

Next thing he would bring up the pensioner in Italy who'd had the twins.

'No matter what you read in the papers, my eggs are still thirty-nine!'

He looked a bit startled by that. 'Let's just try and chill out a bit, eh?'

The more people said that to her, the higher Millie's shoulders rose. There were no two words in the English language better designed to stress out a women who was trying to get pregnant than 'chill out'.

'I *am* chilled out,' she lied. 'I would just like to get on with things, that's all. I thought you did too.'

'Well, yes,' he said, vague.

'Andrew, what's going on here?'

He looked at her and announced, 'They want me to go to Frankfurt again.'

'What, *now?*' Her immediate thought was, did they have time for a bonk before his flight?

'The deal with the company over there came through. We're opening a new office in Germany. They need staff.'

Millie tried to process this information. 'You?' she said. She had an image of him on his hands and knees rolling out broadband all the way down the Autobahn. Even though that wasn't even part of his job description. If she was pushed, she realised she didn't even know exactly what his job description *was* these days. Something to do with winning new accounts.

'And a couple of other guys from the Dublin office,' Andrew said.

That look of naked ambition was back in his eye. Only now it was mixed with excitement. The combination of the two filled Millie with a peculiar sense of dread.

'What are we talking about here?' she asked, trying not to jump to conclusions. 'A couple of days a week?'

They could handle that, couldn't they? They could manage to fit Day 14 in around it.

But of course it wasn't going to be that simple.

'Monday to Friday,' he confessed. 'But I'll fly back every Friday night, Millie. Or Saturday morning,' he amended sheepishly. 'It'll be fine.'

'Fine? That you'll only be home at the weekends?'

He must have already felt defensive because he threw his hands up and said, 'I knew you'd be like this about it! Thinking about the negatives straight away.'

Millie tried to keep calm, even though she felt completely blind-sided by this latest development. 'If you have some positives then I'd like to hear them.'

'This is a chance for me, Millie. Can you not see that? I get to be part of a start-up operation. I've never been offered anything like this before.'

He'd never *wanted* anything like it, in Millie's experience. What happened to the guy who'd told her on their third date that his life's ambition was to collect a beer mat from every country in the world?

'I thought we'd decided to settle down.' It came out sounding whingy and boring. She tried to make it sound more exciting. 'I thought we wanted to start a family.'

'For goodness' sake, Millie. There's nothing stopping us.' He sounded impatient and cross, and not at all like her lovable, soft Andrew.

'What, apart from the fact that you'll be in Frankfurt?'

'Only Monday to Friday.'

'And what are we going to do if Day 14 falls on a Wednesday? Courier your sperm over?'

He looked at her in distaste. 'There's no need to be crude.'

'It's being practical. I can't get pregnant without you, unfortunately!' She didn't bother hiding her anger any more. These were her hopes they were talking about. Her dreams. 'I'm thirty-nine, Andrew! I can't afford to miss month after month because you're furthering your career in bloody Frankfurt!'

He got off the bed. 'I'm thirty-nine too, Millie. But I don't go around acting like my whole life is over!'

'What?'

He took a deep breath. 'Look, let's talk about this when we calm down.'

'I *am* calm.'

But he just grabbed up his car keys from the dressing table and made for the door. 'I'll see you in the morning.'

A moment later, she heard the front door slam behind him.

Chapter Two

'Millie? I know you're in there. Come on, get up, you lazy cow, and let me in before I freeze.'

Millie awoke with a start to bright morning sunshine. Her first thought was that it was Andrew, home. Her heart lifted. She didn't even care that he was calling her names. Naturally he would be angry: she had put the security chain on the door last night in a temper to stop him getting back in, and would have put the dog on guard if they'd had one.

But it was only Oona standing on the doorstep and peering up at the bedroom window. Her hair, normally a big ball of brown frizz, was sleek and smooth and well behaved today. She must have come from the hairdressers, God help them.

'What are you wearing that big slutty nightie for?' she shouted up cheerfully. Millie hastily withdrew from the window. All she needed now was the neighbours speculating that she'd had sex last night.

As if. Another Day 14 ruined. Another chance at a baby, gone.

She pulled on a dressing gown over the slutty nightie. Her head was screaming and her eyes swollen from all the crying she'd done last night. She quickly lashed on a bit of horribly expensive de-puffing eye cream in the belated hope of damage limitation.

He had not come home.

He had stayed out all night.

She couldn't believe he'd actually done it: well, talk about an idle threat! He didn't even have anywhere to stay for the night. The way he'd said it you would think he had rakes of male buddies scattered across the city in cool bachelor pads ready to welcome him with open arms and a nice cold beer. They were all married, like him, but with children coming out of the woodwork. The only person he could really ask was his sister, Barbara, but her new fella had moved in only a week

15

ago and they probably wouldn't be that keen to see him pitch up at eleven o'clock on a Friday night on their doorstep having had a row with the missus.

She had decided that he had ended up in the Esso service station down the road, munching disconsolately on a cold, greasy doughnut and wondering why the fuck he'd said he wouldn't be back till the morning. She savoured his realisation that he would have to check into some cheap hotel, and endure the receptionist giving him sad-loser looks. But he would never have the bottle to do that, and so was probably furiously thinking up ways of sneaking back into the house after she was asleep and pretending that none of it had happened.

She had found great solace in this scenario, so much so that around midnight she felt up to going downstairs and fixing herself a bowl of Crunchy Nut Cornflakes. She wanted to have the energy to berate him roundly when he finally *did* come back, once the Esso station closed, around one a.m. It was at this time that she had secured the front door with the safety chain. There would be no furtive entry in the small hours and a nice comfy night spent on the couch for him. No, they had issues to discuss. Important issues. None of it could 'wait till the morning'!

It was possible, of course, that he would crawl home completely contrite and with a Cadbury's Creme Egg for her from the service station, which he often did as a little surprise. And, of course, once one of them said sorry the other always crumpled like a paper bag and was sorry too, until they ended up trying to outdo each other with apologies: 'No, it was *my* fault', to which the other would reply, 'Oh, it wasn't! It's *me*, I'm terribly selfish sometimes, I never considered your feelings . . .' only to be interrupted by, 'Stop! You're the most generous person I know! If it wasn't for my complete inability to see anybody else's point of view . . . I should be shot. Really. I should.' And there would be lots of hugs and kisses and sometimes even make-up sex. What a bonus it would be if they had it on Day 14!

But there was no sense in getting ahead of herself. She would just wait to see what happened.

By three a.m. there was nothing at all happening. She took to the bed again, keeping one ear open for the rattle of the security chain on the front door.

By four a.m. she was crying: big, gulping tears that drenched the pillow and made her chest hurt. The cornflakes were churning around in her stomach sourly. It was just a stupid row, she kept trying to console herself.

But it wasn't. They'd had stupid rows before, one of them more stupid than the others. Tonight's was different. There had been a distance in him – a coldness. He had looked at her as though she were one more problem to be solved at the end of a very long day.

It was that bloody job, she swore to herself between sobs. It had taken a perfectly lovely, cuddly, bone-lazy man and turned him into a lean, mean, productive worker. What was the world coming to?

She didn't even let herself think about Day 14. It was too upsetting to imagine a little egg floating about inside her, lonely and unfertilised, and about to disintegrate and die for the want of just one decent spermatozoid.

It could have been a baby. It could have been her baby.

'Millie?' Oona called up once more. She had the kind of voice that carried. Well, she had to, with three children under seven.

'Coming!' Millie hurried downstairs.

She would have to come up with a cover story. She would say that Andrew was working or something. It certainly wouldn't be unheard of on a Saturday morning since he'd started the new job. She would tell Oona that he was off building a two-hundred-foot satellite mast. Nobody in her family had a clue what he really did, no more than she herself, and he could credibly flit from IT to closing international data networking deals or even to installing telephones in people's homes.

Downstairs she unchained the front door and opened it with a big, sunny smile. 'Hi, Oona!'

Oona wasn't a bit fooled by the sunny smile, of course, or indeed the late application of eye cream. Her big round face creased into concern and she asked immediately, 'What's wrong?'

What was it about sisters that they always *knew*? It probably came from eighteen years of looking into each other's faces at the kitchen table, over the bathroom sink, in the back seat of the car on endless journeys, et cetera. They could read every quirk of the eyebrow, every shifty little glance. They knew when you were thinking of stealing a fig roll from the biscuit tin, or when you had already stolen it and scoffed it down. In secrecy. Behind a locked door. And wiped your mouth carefully afterwards. You could keep nothing from them.

'Nothing,' said Millie, thinking that she would try anyway.

But Oona's next question was, 'Where's Andrew?'

'Out.'

'Where?'

'Building a mast, OK?' Then, to throw her off the scent, she said, 'And where's Brendan and the kids?'

Brendan was Oona's husband. The kids were Aoifa, Gary and Chloe, and all had the same unruly, frizzy brown hair as Oona.

She beamed and announced proudly, 'At home, making Christmas decorations out of Play-Doh. I know it's a bit early but Brendan wanted to get ahead.'

That explained her hairdo anyway. Recently Brendan had begun to let her take Saturday mornings off to do the kinds of things that other women with children could only dream of.

'You've had a hard week at work, take some time for yourself,' he would generously urge, before ushering her out the door in the direction of the shopping centre. 'Me and the kids will wash the windows.'

He was a gem. Everybody said it. Ever since he'd been made redundant from the garage and become a house-husband, Oona had been in clover. Especially as she herself was no great shakes in the domestic department, as anybody who had ever sampled her shepherd's pie could testify. Not that she had usually got around to making shepherd's pie, what with the washing and the ironing and the dirty dishes piling up all around her. She'd been the first to admit that the household chores had been somewhat neglected since she went back to work full time after little Chloe started playschool. It was all she'd been able to do to pack their lunches in the mornings, and sometimes she hadn't even got around to that, and there had been stiff notes home from school.

Then she got the promotion at work out of the blue. She didn't want it at all, and kept trying to give it back, but they insisted, and gave her a hefty pay rise to boot. The downside was that she rarely left the office before seven. The house went to pot altogether after that. The children grew good at picking out the least soiled clothes from the laundry bin in the mornings, and giving them a quick press with Chloe's Barbie iron. 'You're great kids altogether!' Oona would say, and guiltily resolve to get a hot meal on the table for them that evening. And she would too, but it could be nine o'clock by the time she managed that, and they'd all be fast asleep on the couch. In their dirty clothes.

By the time Brendan's redundancy from his sales job at the garage came about, one of the children had gone without a bath for nearly three weeks. Not that that worried them too much; Brendan was in shock over being let go, and had to be constantly consoled that he would find a new job in a week or two, no problem. With his six-foot-five frame, iron jaw and super-aggressive sales technique, it was just a question of time, that was all.

In those two weeks that he was home the children got washed, dinners were on time, homework was done, and packed lunches were dispatched to school every morning. It was a surprise to them all, especially Brendan, who usually confined himself to the manly tasks of mowing the lawn and changing the occasional light bulb. 'I think you should stay at home full time,' Oona had said to him, joking, of course. 'Maybe I should,' he'd said, laughing his head off too. But – the way Oona described it afterwards, anyway – didn't a kind of a heavenly light shine through the kitchen window at that very moment, bathing Brendan in a beatific glow. He was wearing an apron around his beefy middle and wielding an egg whisk at the time.

The solution to the family domestic crisis was evident in that instant, although it took a couple of humiliating failed interviews to make Brendan finally see that staying at home was not only an option, but a positive lifestyle choice. 'I never thought Brendan had it in him to become a stay-at-home dad, but he's nearly better around the house now than I am,' Oona confided in everybody, without a hint of irony.

Oona was looking at the hem of Millie's pink nightie now, poking out from under the dressing gown. 'I used to wear that kind of gear too when Brendan and me were trying,' she said nostalgically.

Oh, how bitterly Millie regretted telling her family that they were 'trying'. Andrew had been raging over it. What possible interest could they have in knowing that they were now having unprotected sex, he had asked her. Quite a lot, as it turned out. Her father would occasionally look at his shoes and mutter, 'Any news?' in a leading kind of way. Brendan kept winking lewdly at Millie and advising Andrew that zinc supplements were a great way of putting a bit of lead in the old pencil. Oona had gone up into the attic to find her old maternity clothes, and wasn't seen for the better part of a day. Then she spent hours washing and ironing them, or rather Brendan did. He had then efficiently handed them over in plastic bags colour-coded by trimester.

Millie tugged down the dressing gown over the nightie. 'Actually,' she said rather loftily, 'I wear négligés all the time.' Had she pronounced it right? To get off the subject she enquired, 'What do you want, anyway?'

'You. We're going to visit Mum, remember?'

'Of course.' Oh, the guilt: there was her poor mother lying in the hospital and her eldest-born daughter couldn't even be bothered to get dressed. 'Did Dad come?'

On cue their father, Dennis, poked his head out of the passenger window of Oona's car and waved.

'We'd want to go. The traffic's bad.'

Oona rolled her eyes. 'The traffic is fine.'

'I just heard the radio. There's a truck after breaking down,' he advised her helpfully.

'What, right in our path?' Oona said back.

He looked full of doom and gloom. 'Knowing our luck . . .'

Oona looked like she might explode. It had obviously been one of those journeys. Even though he didn't drive much himself Dennis was liberal with his advice to Oona, and liked to draw her attention to the various road signs that they passed, especially the ones with the speed limit. 'You'd better slow down,' he would guide her. 'We're coming into a sixty zone.' Oona would be wild with rage by the time they had reached their final destination. Usually she wouldn't be on speaking terms with him at all.

He would be baffled. How could she possibly take offence at someone giving her good, sound pointers on how to execute a three-point turn? And how best to cut down on fuel consumption? If she just took her car out of gear at traffic lights she would be halfway there, as he had told her many times over the years. But of course Oona's problem was that she didn't *listen*. Not to him anyway, which was a shame, as in his opinion she could learn quite a lot. You didn't get to his age without picking up a thing or two along the way, he liked to tell her with satisfaction, and then fail to notice as she slowly turned puce.

'I hope you're not going out in that thing,' he said to Millie, eyeing the nightie.

'I am,' she assured him. Unlike Oona, she never let herself get wound up.

To his credit, he wasn't a bit embarrassed by the nightie. After all, here was a man who had lived through his daughters' teenage years; he had been on the front line as they had tried to sneak out the door wearing micro-minis, boob tubes, Doc Marten boots, and bra tops. Out of the darkness he would loom, in his habitual grey cardigan, arms folded ominously across his chest, egged on by their mother, Nuala, from the living room: 'Go on, Dennis, you tell them, they won't listen to me.' She had been right too.

Then, the immortal words: 'I hope you're not going out in that thing, young lady.'

Oona would be raging. 'Where the feck does he think we're going at ten o'clock at night, only out? And why does he keep thinking we're ladies?'

He had been able to relax a bit when Millie entered her New Romantic phase (about the same time as she started bringing home stray dogs) and began wearing big ruffled white blouses and demure pencil skirts. He even gave up his permanent position by the front door. But then Oona discovered Madonna – why couldn't she have discovered Val Doonican, their parents complained – and had to be stopped from trying to leave in wisps of black lace held on by ten crucifixes.

'It doesn't make any sense. You haven't been to Mass since you were eleven,' Dennis would argue with her doggedly.

'Religion is irrelevant, Dad,' she would say, flinging her eyes to heaven as if he were the most moronic man ever to pollute the planet.

The upside of all this was that he had acquired quite an eye for fashion over the years. He could put together a fetching ensemble for any occasion, and, out shopping, they couldn't keep him out of Zara. Happily, Nuala was already a shopaholic – they had met in the menswear section of Burton's department store forty-one years ago. On their wedding anniversary every year they drove a hundred miles to Ireland's largest designer discount outlet and spent a blissful twelve hours hunting out bargains.

'Do you think this suits me, Dennis?' she would say.

Dennis was a great help now that his teenage daughters had trained him, and he would declare authoritatively, 'No, but I think you should try it in the purple.'

And she would, and it would be perfect. He'd still come home with a horrible grey cardigan, though.

He looked tired today, Millie noted. Well, it had been a strain on him since Mum had gone into hospital. Millie knew there would be a bag of butterscotch on his lap, Mum's favourite, and the latest copy of *Hello!* magazine. They liked to see how the other half lived, and the fashion was out of this world. He would pull up his chair close to her so they could enjoy the pictures together. 'Posh Spice welcomes us into her beautiful new home, and denies plastic surgery,' he would diligently read aloud, before going on to admire the Beckhams' new couch. If it was a wedding issue – 'Lady So-And-So marries for the fifth time in a castle in Scotland' – then you could hardly get a word in edgeways for the two of them discussing the wedding dress.

'I've never liked satin,' he would declare authoritatively, while she would chip in with, 'Is that Nana Mouskouri in the background?'

'Give me two seconds to change,' Millie told Dennis now, and turned to race upstairs.

At least the trip to the hospital would take her mind off Andrew. She had a horrible, ominous feeling in her stomach that wouldn't go away.

She should probably ring him. Find out where he was; establish some kind of contact.

But then again, why wasn't he ringing her? He was the one who had broken upsetting news to a woman of advancing years, with potentially rising FSH levels and arms that ached to hold a baby. And he didn't even have the decency to have timed sexual intercourse with her before walking out.

She pulled off the slutty nightie and grimly threw it to the floor. She decided that she would not make the first move. As far as she was concerned, what had she done wrong, except want a baby?

Millie's mother had taken early retirement three years ago. She'd been a receptionist for the local vet. She'd always had a lovely, friendly manner and was totally unfazed by the kind of patient who usually ended up in the waiting room. 'Aren't you a handsome fella!' she would chirp to some big growling brute of a Rottweiler with a nail stuck in his paw, and within five minutes he would be rolling on his back and begging her to tickle his tummy. 'She keeps the place together,' the vet, Eamon Jenkins, would say every year when he gave Nuala a big box of Fox's biscuits at Christmas to say thanks.

The fecker, they called him now. The dirty rotten scut.

Three years ago he hired a new receptionist, Tracey, to come in on a Thursday afternoon when Nuala went on her half-day. Tracey was young, with dyed-blonde hair, and wore the kind of short skirts that could bring on cardiac arrest in men the age of Eamon Jenkins. At the same time Millie couldn't imagine that Eamon, who seemed to prefer cats to women, would be so shallow as to go chasing after Tracey. But within a month Nuala mysteriously arrived home on Friday evening with her P45. Tracey was never officially fingered as the cause, but they all knew.

'Let's take him to the cleaner's,' Oona had begged. 'It's unfair dismissal. Just because you're sixty-four and can't compete in the legs department.'

'Steady on,' Nuala had said. She was remarkably sanguine about the whole thing. 'To be honest, I'm just as glad. I was fed up of looking at hamsters and scooping up poo. We're going to go on a cruise around the world, aren't we, Dennis?'

'Are we?' said Dennis, looking startled.

But then again he had been retired for years, without any need for cruises to keep him amused. It didn't take a lot these days: the paper, *Hello!* magazine, maybe a trip to a shopping centre every now and again.

But Mum had other plans. Along with the cruise she was going to revamp the house now that she had the time. If she had to look at that green floral wallpaper for much longer she said she'd puke. And the garden needed an overhaul: Dennis's compost heap down by the wall looked like it was concealing a dead body. Oh, it was going to be all go in the Doran household from now on, and they'd scarcely have a minute to think.

And they probably *would* have gone on the cruise had Millie and Andrew not announced their engagement.

'I'll help with the organising,' Nuala had said, her cheeks pink with excitement. She liked Andrew, even if she had a peculiar mental block about his name and would occasionally call him Bert.

'Do I look like a fucking Bert?' Andrew would complain.

Nuala was a godsend. Watching her sort out invitations and flowers and bullying Oona into a huge mauve maid-of-honour dress, Millie thought she was obviously a woman at the top of her game. That randy old Eamon Jenkins had made a terrible mistake, they all declared.

And so it was all the more surprising when they'd found her fast asleep on a couch up on a landing in the hotel during the wedding speeches.

'It's all right,' Andrew had said. 'Mine wasn't that great anyway.'

She had been mortified. 'I'm sorry, I'm sorry,' she had kept saying.

'You were up half the night worrying about things,' Dennis had chided her. 'I think maybe it's time we went on that cruise.'

But they didn't. One thing after the other kept cropping up to stymie them. Dennis had a batch of cousins over from America who stayed for two weeks and ate all around them, leaving Nuala more exhausted than ever. Then Dennis had the flu. Nuala promptly caught it off him. It was a bad dose. It took her ages to get over it, and it left her more tired than ever.

'Do you want to go back to bed?' Dennis kept enquiring.

'For goodness' sake, leave me alone, I'm just over the flu,' she said irritably.

It hadn't improved her temper either. She could be quite short nowadays.

'I wonder does she need a course of iron?' Oona suggested.

They looked in at her in the living room. She was watching TV. She had taken to watching a lot of it while she was recuperating. If *Judge Judy* was on you wouldn't want to interrupt.

'Mention it to her,' Dennis said bravely. He even stood back in the hopes that Oona would go first.

In the end they decided between them it would be best if Millie led the questioning, seeing as she was the one who dealt with people all day long in that claims department, and thus was apparently trained in handling difficult situations. It was an argument they trotted out whenever anything unpleasant had to be done; over the years Millie had been pushed forward to tackle pesky double-glazing salesmen and any number of television licence inspectors, even before she had left school.

'Mum will listen to you,' Oona said encouragingly, before nipping in behind her for cover.

Millie waited until the credits on *Judge Judy* were rolling. There was just time before the repeat of *Coronation Street* begun.

'Mammy,' she begun tentatively.

Nuala looked up. 'I know exactly what you're going to say.'

Good old Mum. They all let out a sigh of relief. She was on the case already.

'I've already spoken to the doctor,' she said. 'He's recommended a course of vitamins, and also fish oil.'

'Fish oil?' Oona said, stepping out from behind Millie now that it was safe.

'And for Dennis too. It's very important in people our age. He thinks I might be low on Omega 3,' she said, and went off to make everybody a cup of tea.

Dennis was keen on the fish oil theory. Nuala had never liked fish, even fish fingers. Why, he couldn't remember the last time she'd even had a bit of whiting from the chipper. It was entirely possible that a deficiency could be doing terrible things to the two of them. He himself hadn't been feeling that great lately, now that he really thought about it.

Oona rolled her eyes.

But it seemed to do the trick. The two of them were happily popping pills and glugging down bottles of horrible-smelling fish oil to beat the band, and they looked better by the day.

'She's great,' Dennis assured Oona and Millie with relief whenever they enquired. 'Completely back to normal. And I'm better too,' he added, hoping that maybe somebody would ask.

Orla didn't. Brendan had just been made redundant and her mind was on other things. She'd barely seen the pair of them in a month.

Millie didn't ask either. She was lost in the world of TTC – shorthand for Trying to Conceive. Oh, what fun it was. It was difficult to concentrate on ageing parents when her attention was continually directed downwards. But she managed to phone every now and again – not during *Judge Judy* – and Dennis assured her that everything was fine.

This went on for ages, with things being apparently fine, and so it came as a bit of a shock to both Millie and Oona when Dennis had phoned them to say that Mum was in hospital.

Oona pulled up now at the drop-off area outside the main hospital doors. She turned to Millie and Dennis and enquired delicately, 'Does one of us want to go in first?'

Last week didn't Uncle Mick and Auntie Maeve and all the strapping cousins arrive up from the country to see Mum, totally unannounced, and carrying big pink helium balloons and several kilos of grapes, and they had all crowded in around her bed while she was asleep and had waited for her to wake up. Anybody would have got a fright, Dennis had thundered afterwards. Never mind a sick person. He would have to have words with them. Stern words.

It struck Millie as peculiar that they, her own family, were wondering whether they might have a similar effect on her as Uncle Mick and Auntie Maeve.

But then Dennis said very reasonably, 'It might be best if I go in first and check that she's awake, or not being seen by the doctor or something. Oona, you park the car. Millie, maybe you'd get her a bottle of something to drink in the hospital shop. She's gets thirsty in there with the heat.'

He squared his shoulders in a manner oddly like that of a mission commander. 'We'll all meet up in the ward in ten minutes.'

Andrew rang as Millie was leaving the hospital shop clutching a bottle of MiWadi orange.

Guiltily, she decided she would take the call, even though there were stern signs everywhere warning her that mobile use would cause havoc with vital pieces of hospital equipment. Mum wasn't on one, she thought, and was immediately appalled at herself.

To make up for it, she didn't even say hello, just blurted urgently into the phone, 'I can't stay on for long.'

'Oh,' said Andrew at the other end, sounding a bit nonplussed at this reception. What had he expected – that she would blow a kiss down the line?

'I just got home,' he said. 'Where are you?'

'At the hospital, visiting Mum.' When he didn't offer any more in-formation she asked, 'Where did you spend last night?'

'The Goodnight Inn.'

'I see,' she said, in a very cool voice. At least he hadn't said 'with Jessica/Sharon/Chantelle', or some other trollop he had picked up in a seedy club after going there in a rage and getting blind drunk.

The Goodnight Inn had paper-thin walls and a big dual carriageway running alongside upon which trucks thundered up and down twenty-four hours a day. It was also a favourite of hen and stag parties, and a night rarely ended without several rooms being trashed. It was doubtful he'd had a minute's sleep all night. Plus he'd left his inhaler at home last night – he suffered from a touch of asthma, and right now she felt it served him right – and could well have been choking for every breath. No wonder he sounded completely wrecked.

She felt better and better, but decided to be mature about the whole thing. 'I'll be home in an hour or so,' she told him, with a hint of forgiveness in her voice. 'And then we can talk.'

'Good,' he said. 'Because I think we need to.'

He wasn't sounding half as apologetic as he should. There was that distance again, that hint of impatience. But he was probably as tired as she, and stressed, as he usually was these days. And now there was Frankfurt to think about on top of it all, and the pressure of trying to conceive a baby.

They *did* need to talk. Badly.

A nurse passed her by in the corridor and she had to hide the phone by flicking her hair forward violently. The nurse looked a bit startled.

'I'll see you in a bit,' she hissed into the phone, and hung up before he had a chance to reply.

As she made her way up to the ward, she began to see things a bit more clearly. She might as well accept right now that he was going to take the job in Frankfurt; that he desperately wanted to, anyhow. She couldn't stop him, nor should she even try. So it was time to move on. Make plans. And one of the beauties of the female menstrual cycle, or at least Millie's, was that it was completely regular, and so lent itself wonderfully to the making of plans.

She began to feel positive. They could draw up a calendar and hang it prominently on the wall. They would mark it with oblique little signs (there was no sense in broadcasting to anybody who walked into her kitchen that she was ovulating that particular day) and work their schedules around it. If Andrew couldn't come home to Millie on Day 14, then she would go over to him.

It wasn't so bad when she put it like that. If they put their heads together they could do it. There was a bit of a spring in her step now. At least she felt in control. It might even be exciting. How many people got to fly to Frankfurt for a night of passion? She might even bring a different nightie on every visit. Keep him guessing. She felt relieved.

But only for about two seconds. She began to project into the future, always a dangerous thing to do. The whole getting-pregnant-at-a-distance thing might be a cinch, but what then?

Supposing he *did* take the job in Frankfurt? And she *did* get pregnant in Dublin?

She would be completely on her own Monday to Friday, getting bigger and bigger. The father of her child would be hundreds and hundreds of miles away up a mast (or whatever). He would miss all the trips to the doctors and the hospital. He wouldn't see the twelve-week scan, because they never did routine scans at weekends, only weekdays. He'd never hear the little heartbeat on the monitor at the doctor's office.

She was nearly in tears now at everything that he would be missing out on.

But they dried up pretty damn quickly when she fast-forwarded to the labour. The odds were five-to-two (again) that she would have the baby at the weekend. A fat lot of use Andrew would be to her in some office in Frankfurt. Who would hold her hand at the hospital when they pessimistically told her that she was only half a centimetre dilated, and to come back in a week? Who would even *drive* her?

This was very serious indeed.

If she thought further forward still — and she couldn't stop herself now — past the birth and all that, what then? Would she be a single mother for most of the week, alone in her house with only a baby for company? Supposing he stayed in Frankfurt for years and years? Would she end up pointing out a photo of him on the wall to her little son or daughter, and explaining gently, 'That man is Daddy. Do you remember him from that flying visit at Christmas?'

It would be a disaster.

Totally unworkable.

He would have to turn the job down. There were no two ways about it. At the same time, how could she tell him that? She couldn't. Well, she could. But she'd probably have to put up with him glowering at her from under his brows for the rest of his life because she had ruined his career and sent him crawling back to the bank.

Then the solution struck her. It was so easy and simple that she wondered why she hadn't thought of it before.

She would go with him.

They would relocate. Both of them, together.

She would give up her job. Get a new one in Frankfurt. Surely they were just as much in need of customer-care employees as Ireland. She was sure her qualifications and experience would transfer. The pay might even be better. Although probably not.

The more she thought about it, the more it began to make sense. They would get a big house in the suburbs. Or, more realistically, a little flat close to the city centre. But they would be together. A family.

She couldn't wait to tell him. It would be a great adventure.

Chapter Three

M um was sitting up in the bed in a pair of pyjamas that Dennis had bought for her on one of his shopping trips to Marks & Spencer. It was actually very difficult to find a suitable pair that didn't have any silly bears on the front, or slogans like 'Get It While It's Hot!' like the unfortunate ones the elderly lady in the bed next door was wearing.

'Hi, Mum,' Millie said. She bent to kiss her. In the harsh hospital atmosphere, Mum's cheek felt comfortingly soft and familiar.

'Hello, love,' said Nuala, delighted to see her.

'You look well, Mum.'

She did. Her hospital stay was nothing to do with exhaustion or serious illness, thank God, but rather an in-grown toenail that had gone septic and which they'd had to remove. Today she sat up against the pillows like a queen, glowing after three days of being looked after by an army of staff, while Dennis looked completely wrecked. She had even put on weight. The nurses said that they could hardly keep her in food, and she was wolfing down cereal and meat loaf and all the apple crumble they could throw her way.

Apparently she was the best sleeper on the ward too. Never stirred in the bed the whole night long, the nurses said, when some of them would be blazing a trail to the toilets and back every half-hour, or else snoring fit to bring the whole building down. Generally, one of them assured Millie, she was a model patient if only she didn't ring the bell so often.

Millie had been rather embarrassed. Mum had never been one for unduly disturbing anyone else. 'I'll have a word with her.'

'Ah, no, it's fine – she can't walk, that's what the bell is there for. Just maybe not so often.'

Dennis had been quite indignant. 'That one shouldn't be a nurse at all. I'm going to have words with her.'

But he didn't. It was only an idle threat, and he smiled cravenly at the very same nurse as they were leaving after their last visit.

'We don't want to upset them,' he had whispered to Millie. 'They might take it out on your mother.'

Nuala didn't look like the type who would have anything taken out on her. In fact she was reaching now for the bell again.

Millie, thinking of the nurse, moved quickly to stop her.

'What is it, Mum? There's no need to go bothering the nurses. I'm here, I can get whatever it is you want.'

'I doubt it,' said Nuala grimly.

Dennis emerged from the locker at this point, bumping his head on it. 'Damn,' he said. The entire contents of the locker were strewn on the floor at his knees. 'It's not in here.'

'I could have told you that,' Nuala said tartly. She looked around again in vain for a nurse. 'My purse has been stolen,' she told Millie in a low voice.

'What?'

'I think it might have been Alice. Her over there in the pink. She must have waited until I was gone to the bathroom and then come over and snatched it.'

Millie looked over at Alice. She was white-haired and round-cheeked, and wore a big white bandage on her leg. She didn't look much like a kleptomaniac.

'I'm sure she didn't, Mum.'

Millie looked back at Mum, sure she was having some kind of a joke.

But she seemed very serious. And Dennis was combing the contents of the locker like a forensic scientist, so it must be true.

'I'm telling you, I took it out to buy the newspaper from that lad who comes around, and I put it right back there on the top of the locker before I went to the bathroom.' She shot another dark look over at Alice. 'She only arrived yesterday. None of us know her well.'

Alice looked over at that point and smiled benignly at them all.

'Lovely day,' she called cheerfully.

'Hm!' said Millie back, nodding and smiling, hoping to God she couldn't hear the accusations being levelled at her.

It seemed outlandish. But at the same time these things happened. Valuables did get stolen and go missing in hospitals. Last year Millie's handbag had been stolen from her locker in the gym. She had been stunned, sure that none of the women she stripped off in front of on a weekly basis would stoop so low. But one of them clearly had.

'I'm going to report it to the nurses,' Nuala resolved.

Dennis had put all the stuff back in the locker. He shut the metal door on it quickly before it all fell back out. 'Why don't we check the bed? It might have slipped under the covers.'

'How could it be under the covers when I didn't leave it on the bed?' Mum's voice was rising querulously.

Dennis kept very cool and calm. You would think he was confronted with missing property scenarios on a regular basis. 'We're just going to check, that's all.'

'I'm telling you. You won't find it.'

She was upset now, and more upset when she was forced to get out of her nice warm bed.

'Mind my toe,' she told Millie, who was trying to help her.

She stood there, crumpled and stiff and cross – totally unlike herself – as Dennis quickly stripped down the blankets.

'Why don't we go for a bit of a walk now that you're up?' Millie suggested uncertainly. Hospitals could do odd things to people, she knew. Their world tended to get very insular. A change of scenery might be just the thing to snap Mum out of it. 'Mum?' she prompted.

But Nuala wasn't interested in a walk. 'The nurses told me when I arrived, you know. They said if you have anything valuable at all, send it home.'

'Yes, but I think they meant big diamond rings and things,' Millie said lightly. 'Not your purse.'

'But I don't have a diamond ring.'

'Yes, you do. Your engagement ring.'

Mum looked down at her left hand. 'Would you look at that! It's been robbed too.' She swung round to look accusingly at Alice again.

'No, Mum,' Millie hissed, feeling that things were getting completely out of control. She looked to Dennis for help. But he was wrestling with the mattress, and right now it was winning. 'You left it at home. In your jewellery box, remember? We said we wouldn't bring it into the hospital in case it got . . .' she managed to choke the word 'stolen' back just in time, '. . . lost.'

It would have been great had Dennis found the damned purse at that point, but of course he didn't. He patted the last bed cover back into place and scratched his head. 'It's a bit of a mystery, all right. Maybe it *has* been stolen.'

'*Dad*.' Millie was furious.

'What?'

They were drawing attention to themselves now. Other visitors were looking over, wondering at the commotion. Normally Mum would be mortified at causing a scene, but she didn't seem to care today.

And neither did Dennis. He looked at Millie as though she were the one who was causing all the fuss. 'It's a possibility, Millie. That's all. Now come on, Nuala. Let's get you off that sore foot and back into bed.'

He helped her back into bed and got her a drink of water. He plumped up her pillows for her and smoothed her covers. Finally she had a butterscotch. He popped one into his mouth too.

Millie was left standing there, watching the pair of them sucking with gusto, and wondering whether she had imagined the whole thing. Or whether the upset of the previous twenty-four hours had rattled her to such an extent that her reading of situations was completely off. She'd had hardly any sleep, after all. She was bound to be a bit on edge.

The purse wasn't mentioned again until Oona came into the ward, coat flapping and car keys jingling. She'd been gone so long that Millie guessed she'd had to parallel park.

'I was in the loo and I found this, you silly goose.'

She threw down Nuala's purse on the bed.

After all the previous dramatics, Nuala looked at it with an infuriating lack of interest now. 'Did you?' she said. 'I was sure I left it on the locker.'

'We found it, anyway, that's the main thing,' Dennis said with satisfaction.

He didn't look at Millie.

It was hard to believe that the entire visit so far had been taken up with the purse saga. And Millie had such exciting news too. She was desperate to tell Mum – tell them all – about her decision to move to Frankfurt with Andrew. Mum had visited Germany once on some kind of language exchange trip that time she did an evening course. They would have great chats.

'Sorry Andrew isn't here, Mum,' she said. 'Something came up.'

That might help lead her into it. There was no sense in mentioning about the row. Especially as it wasn't even relevant any more.

'Oh,' said Nuala.

She didn't ask what had come up.

'How's the toe?' Oona enquired cheerfully.

'They didn't dress it right,' said Nuala. It was obvious that this was the kind of conversation she really wanted to have. She lifted her foot onto the bed, the better to display their shoddy workmanship.

Oona bent over it, clucking. 'You're right, Mammy. That's a desperate, rubbish job. I'll go and tear strips off them, will I?'

'Oh, I don't know . . .' Nuala wasn't sure about going that far.

'When they dress it again tonight, tell them to be sure to do it properly,' Oona instructed her.

'I will,' said Nuala, all cheered up now.

Oona seemed to have the knack of dealing with Mum that morning. Millie felt put out, and more confused.

But maybe Oona was more self-sufficient than Millie, and didn't need still to go running to her parents with life's little ups and downs. Which weren't so little in Millie's case, in fairness. But then maybe Millie needed to grow up and stop looking for her parents to hold her hand. Her mother wasn't well, for heaven's sake, even if it was only a septic toe. She should ease up on her.

Anyhow, she hadn't even told Andrew yet about her decision. When they had decided on a date for the move she would make a special visit in to see Mum and tell her about it.

'Did you bring in *Hello!*?' Mum asked Dennis, knowing full well he had.

'I did,' Dennis confirmed happily. 'Will we read it?'

She didn't need asking twice.

Oona gave Millie a little look. 'Pass the butterscotch then. I need a sugar hit to sit through this shite.'

'Language,' Dennis said automatically.

And they all settled themselves around the bed as Dennis opened the magazine at the first page. He cleared his throat. '"Keira Knightley Befriends Orphaned Baby Elephants" . . .'

Andrew was asleep in the living room when Millie finally got home. He was sprawled on the couch in front of the telly, head at a painful angle and his mouth gaping wide open. Little exhausted snores filled the air.

Bless, thought Millie – the first nice feeling she'd had towards him in twenty-four hours.

He looked drained, she noted with some satisfaction. He had big dark circles under his eyes and was all beardy and unwashed-looking. There was a plate on the couch beside him bearing the remnants of what she guessed was a fried egg sandwich. Her heart melted a bit more. She sat down gingerly on the couch beside him. He gave a bit of a snort but licked his lips and settled down again. Good. He needed his sleep, she decided, positively tender now.

They just weren't cut out for all this fighting lark. Going around slamming doors and staying out all night might sound very dramatic but it was a pain in the bum in reality. Look at the two of them this morning! Completely wrecked by the whole thing. Not to mention having to fork out for The Goodnight Inn when there was a perfectly good bed at home.

They would laugh about it in the future. 'Here, do you remember that night you wouldn't have sex with me and stormed off to a hotel?' she would rag him indulgently. 'Me!' he would say. 'What about you in that nightdress that wouldn't cover a sparrow?' And then one of the kids (she was planning on two) would want something and they'd hurry off, the story forgotten.

She couldn't wait to see his face when she told him about her decision. He might even scoop her up like he had the day the'd got married, and twirl her around like in the movies – although she had been a good three-quarters of a stone lighter back then, of course.

Frankfurt might be a new start for them. The more she thought about it the more excited she became. And it wasn't just the whole baby thing, although she was convinced by now that a location change could be just the trick in getting that pink line. There were other benefits too – maybe a new job for her, new friends, a whole new city to explore.

They would be romantic again, she thought, gazing affectionately at his stubbly jaw. There would be no more sex-because-they-had-to. Andrew was right: it *had* become a chore, and they'd never keep it up the way they were going. Candlelit dinners, she decided. And walks through Frankfurt at night, hand in hand. And maybe she'd invest in a copy of *The Greatest Love Songs Ever*. What they would *not* do upon arrival in Frankfurt was immediately source the best Indian takeaway and install Sky Digital.

Of course they would come home regularly to see family and friends. She would want to see the girls in work. She didn't quite know how she was going to bear leaving them in the first place. And when they became parents (fingers crossed, please God, and a quick novena to Saint Thérèse) they would be back all the time so that their baby knew his or her roots.

It would be wonderful, she thought mistily now. Maybe Andrew's announcement last night was actually a blessing in disguise.

'Andrew?' she said softly. She couldn't wait to see his face.

He awoke with a wild snort. After a minute he managed to focus on her.

'What?' he said warily. 'Why are you looking at me like that for?'

Millie had thought she looked tender. 'Nothing.'

He hauled himself up on the couch, brushing a stray crumb of egg sandwich off his T-shirt. Then he rubbed his red, bloodshot eyes, sighed heavily, and croaked, 'Millie, I'm really sorry about last night.'

She hadn't been prepared for such an immediate apology. But now that it had come, she was delighted. 'Me too!' she said, caving in immediately, of course. 'I had a horrible night. I didn't sleep a wink! And I was really worried about you. I didn't know where you'd gone.'

She was going to give him a hug, even if he was a bit smelly, but he didn't seem in any hurry to cross the expanse of couch between them.

He was a bit aloof, actually, and aloof had never really been his thing. He looked like he was going off to a meeting, with his shoulders all bunched up around his ears.

'I needed to think,' he said. He even sounded a bit nervous, with his voice bobbing up an octave in the middle.

'So did I,' she assured him. 'I didn't just lie tragically in the bed waiting for you to come back, you know.'

He still didn't crack a smile. Instead his jaw worked a bit as though he were chewing something – more than likely the remnants of his breakfast.

'I have something to say,' she said, unable to contain herself any longer. If she were clever, of course, she would have held back on her announcement: made him grovel a bit first. But she had never been any good at game-playing and she was just too happy that they were back talking.

'So do I,' he said, cutting her off. He looked at his shoes, swallowed hard, and announced, 'I don't know if I'm ready for a baby right now, Millie.'

There was a startled silence. It was the kind of statement that she had only ever heard on soaps on the telly, uttered by tortured characters faced with a terrible decision. What was her cuddly Andrew, sitting on their battered old couch on a lovely sunny Saturday morning, doing uttering such a thing?

'Pardon?' she said, just to be sure.

He looked very, very uncomfortable. 'I'm sorry, Millie.'

To give her her due, she remained calm. Well, it was such a shock. She wasn't sure what it meant yet. She wasn't even sure that *he* knew what it meant. But someone had better clarify, quickly.

'It's not like you have to carry the baby, Andrew,' she explained carefully. 'Or breastfeed it. I don't know if anybody's explained it to you properly, but I'll be doing all that. Plus most of the childcare. Really, your bit is mostly in the beginning.'

He looked at her reproachfully. 'There's a bit more to having a baby than that, Millie.'

As if he would know. The only babies he ever laid eyes on were on the telly, all pink and smiling and chubby, and advertising bubble bath. It wasn't as though he'd ever held a real live one, or changed a nappy in his life.

'It's a big responsibility,' he lectured her.

This was all too weird and horrible. Surely in a minute he would reach over to tickle her tummy and go, 'Gotcha!' before wandering off to the fridge for an early beer.

But he remained where he was, at the far end of the couch, and very much the bearer of bad news.

'Are you saying you don't actually want a baby?' she said slowly. She had to be sure of what he meant.

He would laugh and say no, don't be silly, that she had picked him up all wrong. Wouldn't he?

'Not right now,' he said, with chilling precision.

She took a moment. She had to: her breath was caught in her chest.

'I see,' she said, even though she didn't at all. 'And when do you think you might want one? In six months' time maybe? A year? Or maybe when I'm slap-bang in the middle of the menopause? Maybe you'd feel good and ready then?'

Her voice had risen. Well, it was bound to. And he didn't even mind. Instead he just sat there stoically, accepting her wrath. Looking guilty as sin.

'Look,' he began. 'I know how much you want a baby right now.'

You don't, she wanted to yell. You haven't a fucking clue. You haven't wrestled with thermometers and mucus and how-to websites. You haven't once shaved your big hairy legs for me. You haven't stared at prams in the window of Mamas & Papas until you had a pain in your stomach with longing.

Nobody on this earth understood, except other women in the same position. The rest could only imagine.

But that sort of outburst wouldn't get her anywhere. She had to stay calm, salvage this thing. 'Yes,' she said. 'I *do* want a baby, Andrew. Very much. And correct me if I'm wrong, but I thought you wanted one too.'

Hadn't she asked him that very question at the beginning of their relationship? Hadn't they had a deal? A bargain?

'I know,' he said, looking completely miserable. 'And I do. But there's no sense in not being honest with you about how I feel.'

'Well, aren't you great,' she said.

He sighed. 'This isn't getting us anywhere.'

Anger was welling up in her. This time she didn't bother to hide it. 'So people get new jobs, Andrew. Big bloody deal! They get promoted, they get moved around to a different office, whatever. But it doesn't mean they have to go on some kind of soul-searching mission!'

But he just sat, rigid and lump-like. 'It's not just the job,' he said.

'What, is all the sex getting you down?' She was furious now.

'For God's sake, Millie, look at all the pressure we've been putting on ourselves the last couple of months! We used to have fun before, do you remember? We used to actually enjoy ourselves! But suddenly you've got tunnel vision. Everything's about having a baby. It's not about us any more. When was the last time we actually had a good laugh?'

She wouldn't give in to him, whether he had a point or not. 'I thought you were too busy at work to have a laugh.'

'Work is a challenge, Millie. All right, so it's stressful, it's long hours. But I'm doing something with my life. I'm getting on. And you know something? I'm not going to apologise to you or to anybody else because I didn't stay stuck in a dead-end job in the bank!'

He was looking at her as if she was the enemy.

'I'm glad you're enjoying the job,' she said, sitting on her hands in case she actually hit him. 'But, you know something, Andrew? We're married. We're husband and wife. Having babies is what people do. It's not something I dreamt up all by myself.'

He looked at her and shrugged. 'All right. So I guess it's me then. Fine. I don't mind, I'll take the blame.'

'I don't want you to take the blame . . .' She just wanted them to be OK. She wanted him to say this whole conversation was a horrible mistake, and that they were back on track.

'Look, last night was a row, Andrew. That's all.' She knew she sounded pacifying. She was past caring. 'We don't have to go off the deep end like this. We don't have to make any rash decisions.'

'It's not a rash decision,' he told her.

She felt cold dread then. He had obviously been thinking this way for weeks. Months even. But not saying anything. Letting her get her hopes up every month that they would conceive. Maybe he had been secretly praying that they wouldn't.

'I can come with you to Frankfurt,' she blurted.

'Millie . . .'

'I won't put any pressure on you, I promise. It won't affect your new job. And if I do get pregnant, you won't have to do a single thing. Honestly!'

'What, just share my gene pool?' he enquired coolly.

She stood. 'Instead you want me to wait until you feel ready. Which might be years. And then it'll probably be too late to have a baby at all.'

He sighed again. 'Don't be so dramatic, Millie. Maybe just until things settle down a bit more.'

'Until you're feeling just a little less selfish?' she enquired. 'Well, I'm not going to do that, Andrew.'

The worst thing was that he didn't say anything. Not a thing to dissuade her. Not a thing to stop her as she turned and left the house.

Chapter Four

B rendan was being very discreet. He bustled around the kitchen
making pots of tea and getting butter and jam for the scones that
he and the children had baked that morning – which, incidentally, were
beautifully light. For such a big man he moved around the kitchen
with the kind of grace that would put Delia Smith to shame. Drawers
and presses slid open and closed at speed as he assembled a delicious
spread and presented it all on matching plates and accompanied by a
napkin.

'Stop staring at Auntie Millie,' he scolded the kids.

'But she's crying,' Aoifa, the boldest, observed. She and Gary and
Chloe had gathered around Millie in a fascinated semicircle.

Millie tried to manage a watery smile for them but gave up halfway
through. The way she felt right now she would never be able to smile
again, even at small cute children. Especially at small cute children.

'Everybody cries sometimes,' Brendan assured them gravely.

'Even you, Daddy?' The children's fascination switched from Millie
to Brendan. Surely their father, who regularly shouted vile swear words
at Arsenal on the telly, and who could do twenty press-ups on one
hand, didn't *cry*. He wasn't a wuss, not like most of the Arsenal team.

Brendan handled it very well. 'Yes,' he said proudly.

According to Oona, he had taken up with a band of stay-at-home
dads on the Internet, and they discussed all kinds of things on their
forums, ranging from gender stereotyping to shifting stubborn stains.
There was a special section on dealing with difficult questions from
their kids. Non-avoidance was the key, apparently. Meet it head on.
Children were well able for the truth, and should be given as much
of it as possible (in an age-appropriate way, naturally).

But Brendan obviously wasn't quite there yet in that department
because he reclaimed a bit of his macho pride by clarifying quickly,

'Not all the time, obviously. Only when something really, really sad happens.'

The children spun around to Millie again expectantly.

'So what happened?' Aoifa enquired kindly. She had the makings of a psychiatrist in her already.

'Well,' stuttered Millie, and stopped. They were too young even to know about the birds and the bees, so how could she possibly explain that her husband had just more or less condemned her to a barren life? How could she condense a sorry tale of reproductive ageing, broken promises, and appalling selfishness into something short and child-friendly?

She couldn't. Also she was afraid that if she opened her mouth even a crack a stream of vitriol would pour out, frightening the life out of them, and she would be forever afterwards known as poor mad Auntie Millie who cried all the time.

Brendan came to her rescue. 'Go and watch the telly,' he told the kids.

'But we've already had our quota for the day,' Aoifa said.

'Have you?'

Apparently Brendan had been horrified when he realised exactly how much television Oona permitted them to watch, even though he had never noticed before, as she pointed out. The quality of the viewing upset him too; they were addicted to *The Simpsons*, and back episodes of *EastEnders*, which they found on some obscure channel, and young Gary wanted to be Phil Mitchell when he grew up. 'Aw'right, luv?' he would say to any female caller to the house, and give them a wink.

Under the new regime, television was now strictly limited to thirty minutes a day of quality viewing, usually a nature documentary, and he would teach them the names of some basic animals, like sheep and cows. 'Are you sure milk comes out of that?' Aoifa had asked, looking very concerned.

'TV, TV, TV,' the kids began to chant, exploiting his momentary memory loss.

He looked flustered now. He might be a new man, but he wasn't used to hosting crying women at the kitchen table. When Millie gave another little involuntary sob, he caved in. 'Go on then. Have some more.' But their joy quickly turned to pain when he said, 'I got a new *Art Attack* DVD from the library yesterday.'

'*Art Attack*?' Gary howled in outrage. 'I want *Power Rangers*!'

'No,' said Brendan very firmly.

Gary threw himself on the floor in despair just as Oona arrived in from the front room holding a bottle of gin.

'Have we any mixer for this?' she asked Brendan. Then she noticed

Gary under her feet. 'Ah, pet!' she said, scooping him up into her arms and covering him in kisses.

He looked up at her with his little wet eyes. 'Mammy, can I watch *Power Rangers?*'

'Of course you can, bubs,' she said indulgently.

'Yeah!' He accepted another kiss, and a tickle of his tummy, before twisting out of her arms and scampering off to the TV room. The other two were on his heels. They give the door an almighty slam after them.

Brendan looked a bit flushed. 'I just told them they couldn't have *Power Rangers.*'

'Half an hour is not going to hurt them.'

Brendan shot an embarrassed look at Millie. She tried to pretend that she hadn't noticed he had just been dissed by Oona, and went on snuffling into her hankie.

But Brendan obviously felt his pride was at stake, and so he said doggedly, 'That's not the point, is it?'

'What?' said Oona. She was rooting in the freezer for ice cubes for the gin. Already her hair was starting to curl up at the ends, despite the hairdresser's efforts.

'You can't override me like that. It dilutes my authority.'

Oona was opening presses now, obviously more concerned with diluting her drink. 'I didn't know you'd told them they couldn't watch it, Brendan. If you want, I'll go in and say they can't have it after all.'

'Oh, great!' huffed Brendan. 'So I get to look like the bad guy in all this!'

'Brendan, would you stop having a hissy fit? Millie is mortified.'

Actually, it had taken Millie's mind off her own tragedy for a moment. And it was gratifying to know that other people weren't half as happy and contented as you always imagined they were. Especially Oona and Brendan, leading such charmed lives now that she wore the pants. Not that you would ever want to say that to Brendan. He was very sensitive about comments like that. He hadn't taken it at all well at Christmas when Andrew had bought him an apron with a picture of a tanned naked torso on the front, wearing only a pair of sexy Y-fronts.

Oona had just made a similar trespass, it seemed.

'What a sexist thing to say!' he exploded.

'What?' She looked confused.

'Hissy fit! You'd never have said that if I was still working in the garage!'

'Brendan, if you were still working in the garage, the kids would be watching *Power Rangers* and you'd never have known.'

But Brendan was still shaking his head, looking totally appalled and disappointed. 'I'd have expected better from you, of all people,' he said.

'I wouldn't expect too much from me at all, Brendan,' Oona told him, with an edge to her voice. 'Oh, look, will we all just sit down and have a drink? Just like old times? You can even put the rugby on the telly in the corner. Millie won't mind, will you?'

But Brendan gave her a look of great superiority, and announced, 'You go ahead. I have to do the hoovering.' On his way to the door he paused by Millie and, in an offer reminiscent of the old Brendan, said, 'If there's anything I can do . . . go over and beat the shite out of him or anything . . .'

'Thanks, Brendan,' Millie said gratefully. 'I'll keep it in mind.'

'No problem.'

When he was gone Oona joined Millie at the table with two huge gin and tonics. 'You really have to watch your Ps and Qs around here,' she said with a sigh. 'It's all gone very politically correct.'

'He was right about the *Power Rangers*,' Millie felt she had to point out.

'Was he?' Oona didn't look too concerned. She pushed Millie's drink towards her encouragingly. 'Get that down you, and I just bet you'll feel like going home and having a good chat with Andrew.'

At the mention of his name Millie felt the tears rising again. 'We just *had* a good chat. That's why I'm here.'

'I know, but you'll both have calmed down.'

'But he wasn't angry,' Millie insisted. 'Neither was I. The whole thing was very civil.' That was the most worrying thing about it all. Nothing could be handily blamed on people losing their heads. 'I really think it's over,' she blurted.

'Ah, come on now, Millie.'

'I'm serious.'

'Why? Because he's a bit overwhelmed with the new job, and the idea of a baby on top of it scares the crap out of him?'

'You make it sound like he's normal.'

'No, but what I'm saying is this.' Before going on she cast a look over her shoulder to make sure Brendan hadn't come back in. 'In my experience, men can't multitask. Now I know I'm no domestic goddess, but give men two things to do simultaneously, and they go to pieces altogether. I think it comes from ancient times, when they just had to kill one wild boar between them, but we had to collect nuts, fruits, seeds, berries and firewood with three infants strapped to our backs.' She took a healthy slug of gin and said sagely, 'I'll just bet that's what's wrong with Andrew.'

'He didn't say anything about multitasking. Just about not being ready.'

Although what being 'ready' meant she couldn't fathom. It was more of that soap-speak. You would think having a baby involved massive amounts of serious mental preparation, much like swotting up for an exam. Did he intend to buy dozens of childcare manuals in the hopes of preparing himself? The task of being a father surely came naturally. No training required.

Not being *ready*. Hogwash! It just didn't suit him right now. But he hadn't the balls to say it.

Oona was still being Dr Phil – which was another programme Brendan had discovered that the children were addicted to. He had apparently gone mad. 'You two have been under loads of pressure recently,' she said solemnly. 'Maybe you need a holiday or something. A weekend away. Some quality time together.'

Millie couldn't see how two days in Galway or wherever were going to solve a damn thing. 'He wants me to make a choice, Oona. Him, or a baby.'

'Did he actually say that?'

'But that's what it boils down to. I'm thirty-nine – I can't afford to wait around for him to get his head together.'

Well, maybe she could, if technology and science were sufficiently advanced to enable her to have a baby in her forties. Or if luck was on her side.

But right now she didn't feel all that lucky.

She began to cry again. Oona took this as her cue to top up their drinks, even though Millie still hadn't touched hers.

'He wasted my time,' she said, her voice all cracked and heavy with grief. 'He wasted years of my life letting me think that he wanted the same thing. And he didn't. Or he doesn't any more. And he thinks it's perfectly fine to change his mind, just like that! What about me? Do I not even matter to him any more?'

'Of course you do,' Oona soothed.

'Not enough, obviously. Not if he's asking me to put off having a baby, when we're having trouble conceiving as it is.'

Oona was great when she put her mind to it. 'You are not having trouble. You've only been trying a couple of months. It took Brendan and me six months for Aoifa, and a whole year for Gary. So you're perfectly normal in that department.'

'But I'm still thirty-nine.'

Oona hesitated. 'Yes.'

'So it's not a great idea to put things on the long finger, is it?'

'Ah, Jesus, Millie. No matter what I say to that I'll be in deep trouble.'

'Just tell me. Because Andrew keeps saying that I have loads of time. And I don't, do I?'

Oona thought about it. 'No,' she said at last.

'Thank you.'

Although what she was thanking Oona for she didn't know. It didn't solve a thing. It just made her choices a bit starker.

Overhead there was a sudden and terrible wail, like the ceiling was shaking and would come in on top of them at any moment.

'Sorry,' said Oona. 'That's the new vacuum.'

In a few months of being house-husband Brendan had managed to break two vacuum cleaners. It had become a bit of a family joke – exactly what had he been doing to break two? He hadn't seen the funny side of it at all. 'Oh, that's right, patronise me,' he had said in a huff. 'Make silly jokes about men and housework. Be cheap.' He maintained that most modern vacuums were designed only for the most cursory, lazy clean, and were totally unable to cope with the kind of thorough job he liked to do.

To prove his point he had gone out and bought the biggest, badass cleaner he could find, the Dyson 'Cyclone', which could suck up anything within a twenty-yard radius. It wasn't even safe for the children to stand too near. The whole street would reverberate at least twice weekly with the ferocious noise of the thing. He would work it like it was one of the high-performance cars at the garage; feet planted wide apart, hips a-swagger, giving it full throttle. And his point was proven in the end: within two weeks of the new machine's arrival, Gary's asthma had improved beyond belief.

When the noise finally died down, and they could hear nothing but the gunfire and explosions from the *Power Rangers* DVD in the next room, Oona said, 'Look, do you love Andrew?'

'Right at this moment?' Millie enquired.

'Just try and forget about the row for a second.'

Millie did. She put aside the image of his evasive, hard expression this morning, and thought instead of the way his front teeth had an endearing overlap when he smiled (his father had spent the money for his braces on a horse at Aintree, he maintained). She thought about the way he could do an uncanny Chris Tarrant impersonation after four pints. She recalled the lovely solid feel of him in the bed beside her when she awoke at three a.m. She even smiled as she remembered the arguments they regularly had, not over politics or religion or the splitting of the atom, but rather over which series of *The West Wing* was the best.

He was never going to set the world on fire. But he had created a good few sparks in hers. She wouldn't have married him otherwise.

'Yes,' she said. Grudgingly. Reluctantly.

'Well, then,' said Oona.

'Well then, what?'

'Go home and try and work it out.' It was a bit irritating how Oona was now speaking to Millie so authoritatively, when she was the younger one, and not even a customer-care employee.

'There's no "working it out". He's given me an ultimatum.'

'No, you've just taken it that way.'

'Look what he's asking me to do, Oona – if that's not an ultimatum, I don't know what is!'

'At least weigh up your options.'

'I know my options. If I stay with him, I risk never having a baby!'

'If you leave him, you risk the same thing. I'm sorry if that sounds harsh.'

It did. Millie felt a bit peculiar. But at the same time it was true. It had taken her fifteen-odd years to find Andrew. Going by that, by the time she struck lucky again she could be well into her late middle age. And unless she had a miracle like the sixtysomething Italian woman, she could safely reconcile herself to a life without children at that point.

Oona said, 'Did I mention that Fiona and Finbarr Maguire are breaking up—'

'Shut up.'

'I'm just saying, with a good haircut—'

'Shut *up*.'

Millie finally reached for her gin and tonic. She needed it. She had a horrible sense of being backed into a corner. She couldn't believe that, after thirty-nine years, her life had been reduced to a big, fat compromise marriage with an immature husband hellbent on redis-covering his youth in a company full of teenagers.

'What am I supposed to do now?' she wailed. 'Trot after him to Frankfurt like an eejit, or else throw two fingers up at him and go all out to find a new man before I hit the menopause? If I'm not in it already?'

'Oh, I'm sure you're not. Have you had your FSH checked?' Oona enquired.

Jesus, Mary and Joseph, everyone was out to get her today. Even her own sister.

'It's six billion, and rising,' she snapped.

But Oona had a skin like a rhino and wasn't a bit offended. 'Do you want a baby?' she enquired.

Millie was incredulous. 'What do you mean, do I want a baby? What do you think I've been at for the last four months?'

'So you do?'

'Yes!'

'Then go to Frankfurt.'

'What?'

'It's your best bet. Wear him down. He'll give in eventually.'

'That's a very upstanding course of action.'

'I'm just being realistic here, Millie. You need to think about it.'

Millie did, right there and then. She pictured herself in a poky flat in Frankfurt, in an awful see-through nightie – black this time in the hopes of tempting him – and anxiously scrutinising his face when he came home for signs that he might be 'ready'. How would she even know? Would a little red light start flashing over his head or something? And then, the dreaded words: 'I just don't think I'm quite there yet, love. Maybe next month, eh? Now better pop into some clothes before you catch your death.'

Then, maybe in a year or two or three – who knew? – the magic day might finally come. He would lay down his briefcase sombrely and declare that he might possibly be in the right frame of mind, and could she please retire to the bedroom pronto while the mood was still on him?

And what then? Millie would be plunged into a desperate race to catch that last one good egg (the rest would probably be thoroughly rotten by then). Every month would be awash with stress and anxiety, and more fertility aids than you could shake a stick at. They might have to resort to medical intervention. Already she knew that the success rates for women nearing the end of their reproductive lives were not all that great. But she would do it, because she would be desperate. Because she had been left no choice.

The spectre was horrible.

Millie felt something happen inside her. A hardening of her heart. An implacability. Did she really want to put her whole life on hold for someone who was treating her so shabbily?

'No,' she said.

'Don't do anything rash now,' Oona pleaded. 'Or at least have another drink first.'

But Millie's mind was made up. 'I'm not going. However I walk out of this, baby or no baby, I'm going to have my self-esteem.'

Oona groaned. 'Millie, this is no time for self-esteem.'

'I'm not wasting any more of my time on him.' Millie was surprised at how definite she sounded. And how unemotional she felt.

'At least sleep on it,' Oona advised. 'I'll make up the spare bed.' She raised her head towards the ceiling. 'Brendan! Can you make up the spare bed?' Then she moved the depleting bottle of gin away from Millie. 'Maybe you've had enough.'

'But I've only had one drink. You sank all that.'

Oona gave Millie a very worried look. 'Are you sure about this? I mean, what about a baby, Millie?'

Millie pictured a baby in her head again, as she had so many times over the last few months. Only this time it didn't look anything like Andrew.

'I'm sure.'

The children woke her up the following morning by bouncing up and down on her legs.

'How are you feeling this morning?' Aoifa enquired briskly. You would never think she was only seven.

Millie didn't know. Tired. A bit numb. When she had eventually fallen asleep, it was only to dream that she actually *had* a baby. Rakes of them, in fact. They were in cots and buggies all over the house, and stacked three deep in the kitchen. All of them were roaring to be fed. In her dream Millie had vowed to breastfeed, and was running back and forth between them all, hitching her top up frantically.

Andrew wasn't in the dream. She didn't know how to interpret that. Possibly he was in Frankfurt, only popping home every nine months to impregnate her again.

'You're stopped crying,' Aoifa noted with satisfaction.

Millie was about to answer but little Chloe launched herself painfully onto Millie's knees. 'Be a horse!' she demanded, whipping Millie's legs with a cuddly toy.

For a moment Millie wondered whether her desire to have children was not a tiny bit misplaced. Maybe it was just the idea of them she liked. The reality was a bit difficult to bear, especially on a Sunday morning with a hangover to beat the band.

She and Oona had polished off the rest of the gin last night. Gin always made Oona cry. She'd started whimpering on her third drink and by the fourth she was in full flight.

'I'm sorry,' she'd sobbed. 'I know I don't have anything to be upset about, compared to you. In fact, I don't know why I'm crying at all, because I'm as happy as Larry. Since Brendan lost his job I've never had it so good. All the women in work are desperately jealous at the thought of me walking in home every evening to a hot dinner and the children all lined up at the door to greet me with their hair combed and their faces washed.'

'Really?' Millie was impressed.

'Well, just the once, back when he was in his perfectionist phase,' Oona admitted. 'Now he just makes sure they're in clean clothes.'

And at that very moment Brendan had popped his head in to enquire whether they wanted him to drive down to the shops for some more tonic before he went to bed. His ears were rosy red, no doubt from all the praise being heaped upon him in the kitchen.

'No, thanks,' Oona bawled afresh.

'Ah, poppet,' he said, all concern.

'I'm fine,' she assured him. 'You know me and gin.'

He clucked sympathetically, and said, 'You have a nice lie-in in the morning. I'll get up with the kids.'

That nearly killed her altogether. When he was gone, she'd collapsed on the table, howling, 'God, isn't he just brilliant?'

Now, Gary joined Chloe on Millie's knees. They creaked alarmingly under the weight.

'Careful there!' she croaked. She was feeling ancient this morning. She knew that when she looked in the mirror she would recoil with fright. There would be stray folds of flesh flapping all over the place, and probably a big line crisscrossing her face from a crease in the sheet, and which wouldn't fade until Tuesday.

When had she got so bloody old? Why couldn't she always remain twenty-three? And while she was on the subject, it would be handy if her FSH didn't keep going up too. Three or four was a good number for FSH apparently. Millie wasn't sure exactly how high hers was, but knowing her luck it hadn't seen three or four for a good long time.

'Uncle Andrew's at the door,' Aoifa announced.

The gin-tinged fog lifted from Millie's brain. She was suddenly wide awake. 'What?'

'He won't come in or anything. He just said he wanted to talk to you. Daddy said we were to come and get you.'

Millie's eyes flew to the window, even though the curtains were drawn.

He was outside. He wanted to talk to her. She forgot every cross and hurtful word that had been uttered last night and jackknifed up in the bed. 'Right,' she said to Gary and Chloe. 'Off.'

She packed them unceremoniously out the bedroom door. 'Tell Uncle Andrew that I'll be out in a minute, OK?' she instructed Aoifa. Lest there be any doubt, she urged, 'Tell him not to go away!'

There was no sense in getting her hopes up too much. He was hardly going to do a U-turn after everything he had said yesterday, was he? But all the same she fairly sprinted into the bathroom to try to do something with herself. The yucky pyjamas Oona had lent her couldn't be helped, but she patted down her hair with some water, and stole some of Oona's powder to take the unnatural shine off her nose.

She wondered should she apply some mascara too. But then she felt silly. Andrew was her husband. He had seen her in all of her states. He had witnessed the time she got a bee sting on her lip and her whole mouth had puffed up on one side, like a drunk who had got into a fight. He had consoled her that time she ate a whole box of Black Magic chocolates at one sitting and her face had broken out in a million zits.

Her early morning face would be no surprise at all to him, with the predicted big line down one cheek. He might even be moved by it. 'Heck, what have I been thinking!' he might say to himself. 'I love this woman! I want her babies — now!' Well, she could always hope, couldn't she?

There wasn't much she could do about her stale gin breath. It would be too low to use one of the children's Teletubbies toothbrushes, so she improvised by swishing a glob of minty toothpaste around her mouth instead. Why, oh why, had she overindulged last night? She never normally drank much at all. Not out of choice — there was nothing she liked better than a nice rosé, preferably a whole bottle of it — but alcohol wasn't exactly known for its fertility-enhancing properties, and so she had been forced to cut right back. For months now it had been sparkling water, Diet Coke or else a smoothie if she was having a real blowout.

'It's good practice for you,' Andrew had said (whilst slugging back a beer). 'You won't be able drink when we're pregnant anyway.'

Of course, back then it had been when 'we're pregnant'. At some point it had changed to 'you'. Now it seemed to be 'you, at some point in the dim and distant future whenever I decide that I'm ready.'

She had better go and find out.

There was the sound of gunfire and violent blasts as she descended the stairs. Having decided that Andrew was probably not armed, she tracked the noise down to the TV room.

Brendan poked his head out briefly. 'I let the kids watch *Power Rangers*,' he said bravely. 'I thought maybe you and Andrew might need the kitchen, even though he says he won't come in.'

Millie was very grateful. 'Thanks, Brendan.'

There was no point at all in asking where Oona was. Her snores could be heard all over the house. No doubt when she finally *did* get up Brendan would rustle her up a big greasy breakfast to mop up the gin.

It wasn't fair. Oona seemed to be holding all the spades in the Good Husband department. All right, so Brendan wasn't perfect, but he wasn't hanging around at the front door either, letting in all the cold air.

She took a deep breath as she descended the last step. She could feel her heart banging uncomfortably in her chest.

Andrew was waiting by the front door. Unlike Millie, he was dressed and washed and looking very presentable for a Sunday morning.

He looked up and saw her. He was very polite about the pyjamas by pretending not to notice them at all.

'Hi,' he said. His voice was as gloomy as it had been yesterday.

She tried not to read too much into it. He might have had a bad night on the asthma front. Sometimes it made him a bit hoarse. 'Hi,' she said back.

'I guessed you might be here.'

'Well, I didn't think we could afford two nights in The Goodnight Inn,' she said. Go on, she urged him – laugh. Crack a smile. Anything.

He didn't. He just kept looking like it was the end of the world. The last time she had seen him so miserable was when Ireland was knocked out of the Rugby World Cup.

'Why don't you come in?' she said, trying to lift the atmosphere. 'The kitchen is free. We could have a cup of coffee.' In the hopes of coaxing him, she added, 'Brendan made scones yesterday and everything.'

'That'd be nice, but I don't really have time,' he said gravely.

She gave a little laugh. It was a Sunday morning, for heaven's sake. 'Where are you running off to – Mass?'

No smile that time either. Suddenly she was sick of him. Here she was, making all the effort after a marital bust-up that had been instigated by him, and he couldn't even be bothered to make a little conversation?

'I'm not going to attack you, you know,' she told him tersely. 'The house is full of children. You're perfectly safe.'

'It's not that.' His shoes seemed to hold some fascination for him. 'I, um, have a flight at noon.'

She felt sick. 'To Frankfurt?'

Again, he addressed his shoes. 'Yes.'

'That was quick.' Her voice was colourless. She certainly hadn't expected this. Surely the ink wasn't dry on the blooming deal yet.

'They're anxious to get someone over there straight away to start things up.'

'Lucky they have you.' That came out a tad sarcastic. She wasn't a bit sorry. 'You, who has no commitments whatsoever.'

He felt that one all right. His chin rose an inch. 'They value me. They think I have a big future with them.'

'Bully for you.' She must stop this.

Now he was being the mature one. He put on his most grown-up face and informed her in a very responsible fashion, 'I just came round to let you know that I was going. And that I'll ring you during the week.'

You would think that he hadn't done a thing wrong. That last night was all her fault.

'Why?' she enquired.

'What?'

'Why would you ring me?'

'Well, to see how you are.' Mr Responsible again.

'You mean you actually care?'

He sighed – difficult Millie, no doubt he was thinking. Taking the gloss off his shiny new promotion. 'We have things to discuss.'

'No, we don't. You've obviously decided all by yourself that you're accepting the job.'

'Well, yes.' He managed to look slightly shame-faced. 'But we have other things to talk about.'

'Oh?' She waited. She was going to make him say it.

'The baby thing,' he said. You would think he was talking about the car, or a joint savings account.

'Have you changed your mind?' she enquired.

'Millie, let's not do this on the doorstep.'

She completely ignored that. 'Have you? Because unless you have, then we have absolutely nothing left to talk about.'

She could scarcely believe she was even saying such words. They were coming from somewhere deep inside her; some core of self-protection. A place where her dreams lay, still intact.

'I still stand by what I said last night.' He looked completely wretched. The dog.

'I see,' she said. It was a desperate effort to keep her voice from cracking. Or worse, to stop herself grabbing hold of his leg and begging him hoarsely to stay, that she would do anything to change his mind.

She was particularly proud of herself that she didn't do the latter. Instead she said, with a decent amount of dignity, 'I guess that's it then.'

There was a long, awful pause.

Then he said, 'I'd better go. My flight . . .'

'Yes,' she said. 'You don't want to miss that.'

And he gave her a jerky little nod and then he turned and walked back towards his car.

She stepped back from the door and closed it quietly on his retreating back.

There was a sound behind her. Gary had emerged from the TV room. He had obviously been dispatched by Brendan to see how things were going.

'Aw'right, luv?' he asked anxiously.

Her voice was a bit shaky, but she told him, 'Yes. I believe I am.'

Chapter Five

The initial euphoria lasted for several days. She had actually done it. She had refused to accept a shoddy compromise. She had run a rat out of town, even though he had been going anyway.

'You go, girl!' she mentally yelled that whole week, whilst giving the air a good punch.

She was amazed at her own nerve. For all her gin-filled bravado with Oona, she had been sure that, upon seeing Andrew's face, she would buckle under the desire to have a baby and end up scurrying pathetically after him to Frankfurt.

But she hadn't. She had stood strong.

Now that she had the telly to herself in the evenings she didn't have to watch any pesky sport. Instead she tuned into MTV, where girl bands galore roamed about aggressively, singing songs that seemed to be aimed specifically at her: 'Hey, SISTER, don't you take no stuff from no MISTER,' and she would jive around in her pyjamas, occasionally shouting, 'Yeah!' She had never really understood all that rap stuff before, but she did now. It spoke to her very soul. Those teenage girls in their hot pants and bra tops (and really far too much make-up) singing about male oppression and female empowerment and, yes, damned *choice* was where Millie was at now.

She was no man's tool. She was no man's fool!

(She had made that one up by herself and was quite proud of it. If there had been an address at the end of the programme she would have sent it in.)

After a couple of days of loading up on rap, she began going around with a rather hostile stare, which frightened innocent men on the bus and in the shops. They tended to draw away from her, clutching their briefcases to their chests protectively. She developed the urge to spit on the pavement, or start chewing tobacco or something. And

God help any man who made the unfortunate mistake of calling her 'love'.

By Wednesday she felt so empowered that she started to put his things away. And she didn't even cry. No, she just put her new Alanis Morissette CD on at high volume and got right down to it, no sentiment allowed. She noted that he had only taken enough for a short stay in Frankfurt and so no doubt he'd run out of underpants by the end of the week and have to come back and collect the rest of his stuff. If he had the nerve. Well, he'd find it in the attic, in big black bin liners, and none too carefully folded either. And wasn't it great that she had all that space in the bathroom to herself, now that she had chucked all his horrible blunt razors and ancient hairbrush into the bin?

For a second she felt horribly emotional as she looked at her toothbrush sitting by its lonely self on the suddenly empty expanse of the bathroom shelf. It was touch and go whether she'd burst into tears. But she wouldn't give in to him. She would *not*. She choked the tears down furiously, looked hard into the mirror over the sink and announced, 'I love myself unconditionally.'

Normally she wasn't a self-help fan. She had never bought any of those books on how to win friends and influence people, although maybe she should have. But she had never had to come through anything like this before. In the last week she had somehow become a Survivor. A trooper. She was the kind of woman who regularly appeared on the Oprah Winfrey show – minus the velour tracksuit and blue eyeshadow, of course – under the banner of Women Who Kicked That Man Right Outta Their Hair.

She wasn't alone in thinking she was great. Oona thought she was brilliant altogether.

'I'm really proud of you,' she'd said, once she had finally got up, late that Sunday afternoon. But then of course she had to go and spoil it all by adding, 'Just so long as you're sure.'

The litmus test was the girls in work. Most of them had shared the same office for fifteen years. The most intimate of personal details were routinely swapped over the photocopier and, between them all, there was scarcely a life experience that hadn't cropped up yet. Usually two or three times. Marital breakdowns, teenage pregnancies, fights with the in-laws, adultery, drink, drugs, you name it, and the girls would have advice to offer, or an opinion to give. You could tell them anything – in fact there was no sense in trying to keep it from them – and it was like having a whole team of agony aunts in one room, although Dorothy usually didn't get involved. If you were going to have a bad day, there was no better place to have it than in the claims department of ALP Insurance Limited (terms and conditions apply).

Millie didn't say anything on Monday morning, because that was the most chaotic time in the office. Not in terms of actual workload, of course, but in the amount of news that had to be caught up on from the weekend.

'Did you confront him?'

'He says it isn't his.'

'Well, if it's not his, then whose is it?'

'He says he's never seen it before in his life. That maybe someone planted it.'

'Planted it!'

'I know.' There would be much grim shaking of heads. 'I told him to think about it. That we'd talk again in twenty-four hours.'

Meanwhile the phones would ring and ring incessantly with a string of policy holders trying to make claims. The girls didn't ignore them deliberately or anything like that. It was just that all the calls in the claims department seemed to go the same, rather depressing, way.

'So you do have a house alarm but you didn't actually have it switched *on* at the time of the burglary?' they would say down the phone, voices carrying an ominous hint. Then, after much tutting and long, gloomy pauses, they would say, 'I'm afraid I'll have to refer you to Paragraph 3 in Clause A of Section 14 in the terms and conditions, which quite clearly states that such an omission on your part renders this policy completely null and void.' When they hung up, of course, they would turn around, wringing their hands. 'God, girls, I feel just awful. There's no doubt about it, we're all going to burn in the pit of hell for this.'

And everybody would rally around, because they too had been filled with such moments of self-hatred. 'It's not your fault,' they would murmur. 'They make us do this. And at the end of the day we all have to earn a living.' Tissues would be passed around, and information about exorbitant bills for school books or young Adam's sports gear shared. After a while somebody – usually Deirdre – would cautiously offer, 'The guy should have had his alarm on, anyway.' Looks would be exchanged. 'Well, of course he should! What person goes out in this day and age without putting their alarm on?' Righteous indignation would steal over the office. 'It's practically an invitation to thieves and robbers! And then he comes ringing us up, like it's all our fault that he didn't bother his barney to secure his own home!' They would only stop short of constructing a voodoo doll of the claimant out of Diet Coke cans, and stabbing it with Bic pens. Shortly after somebody – usually Deirdre – would offer to go to the Spar for doughnuts and all would be right with the world again.

Millie waited until Thursday morning to announce her drama, when all the news from the weekend had finally been exhausted. You could have heard a pin drop at the coffee station. Well, if it hadn't been for all the ringing phones in the background.

Jaz clamped a hand over her mouth. 'You kicked him *out*?'

'Well, he was leaving anyway,' Millie felt she had to clarify.

'Girls!' Jaz cried urgently to anybody who might actually be engaged in work. 'Gather round. It's serious.'

And it was. They all knew that she had been trying for a baby. For months now they had been offering all kinds of advice, usually based on how they themselves had got pregnant.

'Don't do it too often,' Yvonne had advised. She was the matriarch of the office by virtue of age and the fact that she brought in home-made cookies on people's birthdays. 'Every second day is sufficient.'

'Make sure you're doing it often enough,' Jaz had said bluntly. 'Handcuff him to the bed if you have to. And have you tried a pillow under your hips?'

Millie had. It hadn't worked, except to exacerbate her gastric reflux.

'I've no advice to give you,' Deirdre had said. 'But I just wanted to say good luck.' She really was the sweetest.

So they all understood how big this thing was for Millie. The phones were immediately put to recorded message, although this was a firing offence, and everybody pulled their swivel chairs around to hear all the gory details.

'Tell us everything,' Yvonne advised.

Millie rather savoured the attention. They wouldn't let her leave out a single thing, not even his flight number. They paid particular atten-tion to her final announcement that she didn't think they had anything else to discuss. They made her repeat it twice, and the way she had closed the door on him, and then Yvonne clasped a hand on her arm and squeezed it hard.

'You poor child. You poor child,' she kept saying.

But that was the girls for you. They took everything very person-ally. In some ways they were better than a family, and Millie suddenly felt like crying.

'The creep,' said Jaz grimly. 'And I always liked him too.'

She looked outraged, as she did at least fifteen times a day. Nobody did indignation better than Jaz. She was the bane of management's existence, always complaining bitterly about the brevity and infrequency of tea breaks, or drawing their attention to some obscure clause in her employment contract that said she could have one day a year off for the purposes of 'religious devotion'. Of course, once she got the day off, they all looked for it, and they packed up a big picnic with white wine and went to the zoo. Jaz wasn't a bit sorry. 'We're entitled, girls. Never forget that.'

Millie was grateful for their show of support this morning. But at the same time she felt she had to ask, 'Do you think I did the right thing?'

'Girl!' Jaz cried. 'You did the *only* thing!'

Yvonne was in agreement. 'He didn't exactly leave you with a lot of choice, did he? It was a hard call, Millie, and one that I certainly wouldn't like to have to make. But I don't think there's a single one of us here who wouldn't have done the same. Am I right, girls?'

They all nodded furiously, even Dorothy in the corner.

'I don't know how he can live with himself,' Jaz said. She was practically quivering in outrage. 'What's after happening to him at all? At the staff barbecue last year he was oohing and aahing over all the kids there, you'd think he was dying for one himself.'

It was very tempting to join in Jaz's outrage. 'It's that new job,' Millie said, giving in to it. 'It's like he's a different person.'

They were all ears as she catalogued his long hours and new haircut, and the slick new suits in two sizes smaller than usual.

Jaz was clicking her tongue. 'When they start to drop the pounds you know you're in trouble,' she said. 'They're getting themselves ready, you see. To go back on the market. Oh, they're gougers, the lot of them.'

Actually, Andrew's weight loss had more to do with stress and missed meals than any great plan to get himself into shape, but why mention that? Or indeed her own near-obsession with reproductive gadgetry. In the current scenario Andrew was being painted thoroughly black whilst she was the innocent victim, and it was all enormously satisfying.

'How are you feeling anyway?' Deirdre asked gently. She always waited until everybody else had exhausted themselves. At least she'd be guaranteed of getting a word in edgeways.

'I'm not too bad,' Millie told her gratefully.

'If you want some company any evening, let me know. Of if you need to talk, just pick up the phone. Day or night.'

'I wish I were you,' Jaz said with a heavy sigh.

'Oh, stop,' Deirdre cried, embarrassed.

'I do,' Jaz insisted. 'You're so lovely and kind and sweet, and I'm so mean and dark and evil.' Then she cheered up. 'Does this mean you're single again, Millie?'

Millie hadn't really thought about that. Well, she had, but she hadn't gone so far as to recategorise herself. It was quite a big jump from 'married' to 'single' and she wasn't sure whether she was ready for it yet.

In her head she was still half of a whole. And while the last few days on her own had been exhilarating, it hadn't sunk in yet that it was a permanent state.

'I don't know,' she said, suddenly starting to blub. Within seconds her bravado lay in tatters as tears poured down her cheeks uncontrollably. 'Sorry,' she croaked.

'Oh God!' Jaz cried. 'I'm a desperate eejit, I'm really am.'

'There, there,' said Yvonne, throwing a comforting arm around her. Deirdre pressed a wad of tissues into her hand.

Their kindness made her cry harder. She felt like there was a dead weight of grief on her chest, choking off her breath. She couldn't even speak. She just sat there in her swivel chair, howling like a baby.

'You're just upset,' Yvonne said consolingly. 'You've had a terrible week. And to think you kept it to yourself for the past three days without saying a word to anybody!'

They all clucked, and shook their heads gently, admonishing her with kind glances for not immediately turning herself in to their tender care.

'Here, do you remember that time me and Gerry had that fight?' Jaz asked nobody in particular. They all wondered which particular fight she was referring to, as there had been many. 'I thought he was after leaving me. I must have cried buckets that day.'

Actually, she usually issued more threats and curses than actual tears, but it was very nice of her to draw attention away from Millie, and she was grateful.

She felt better now. The tears must have been building in her for days, only she was trying so hard to be bolshy and strong that she had refused to let them out.

'You know, this could be a wake-up call for him,' Yvonne mused. 'I've seen it happen before. You wouldn't believe how many men are out there who have no idea what they have until they lose it.'

Yvonne always spoke as though she led a life full of strife and hardship, populated by losers and dimwits, and that she went to bed every night with the worries of the world on her shoulders. As far as anybody knew, she lived in a nice semi-detached in Templogue, had two lovely kids, and her husband seemed like a very nice man. 'Nobody knows what goes on behind the scenes' was another of her favourite sayings, so perhaps there were all kinds of unspeakable horrors lurking in the shadows of her life that the girls knew nothing about, although they knew every other detail of her life, including the pattern on the new dinner plates she had bought from Habitat.

Either way, Millie was glad to have her. Yvonne could be relied upon not to fly off the handle.

Besides, Millie liked what she was saying.

'He might be in Frankfurt at this very moment, repenting hard, and wondering how to get you back.'

'Do you think?' Millie said eagerly.

Because maybe, in the back of her mind, she *had* been waiting for him to repent. Even while MTV had blared feminist songs, she had kept the living-room door open just in case she might not hear the phone ringing in the hall. If he loved her at all, and wanted to work things out, he'd get on the phone any day, wouldn't he? She was still his wife. At some point wasn't he bound to get in touch?

He probably wasn't ringing because she had told him not to. She had said – impulsively – that they had nothing left to talk about. Oh, she hated it when she said something she regretted five minutes later.

Thankfully Yvonne was there to lift her hopes.

'A bit of time away won't do him any harm in the world,' she pronounced now.

'So he might come around yet?' Millie coaxed, even while she felt like she was betraying every one of her rap sisters. Not to mention herself.

'I can't say for certain, Millie. But he's hardly going to throw away a good marriage to a lovely woman like you.'

Even though he apparently just had. But nobody wanted to dwell on that.

And just to make sure that nobody did, Jaz said, 'Surely to God, girls, it's time for chocolate doughnuts.'

Yvonne made an executive decision. 'I think we can have an early coffee break this morning.' She squeezed Millie's arm again. 'In light of the circumstances.'

And Millie felt cosseted and comforted, and safe amongst these friends who would do anything for her, including let her have the only chocolate doughnut the Spar turned out to have left.

Chapter Six

Her security blanket was rudely ripped from her that evening by the arrival of Andrew's sister, Barbara, on the doorstep unannounced.

'Hello, Millie!' she said with a big smile. But it was fake. Barbara had always been hopeless at putting on a front, which Millie had always found rather endearing.

She didn't particularly tonight. This was Andrew's sister, after all. They shared the same, unreliable, genes. She even had Andrew's nose, short and wide and ending in a little knob. The very sight of it made Millie sick.

Barbara tried to cover the awkward silence by prattling on. 'Not interrupting your dinner or anything, I hope?'

'No,' Millie said, hoping there wasn't a big telltale ring of pasta sauce around her mouth. She had been pleasantly wading through a massive plate of the stuff when the doorbell rang. In the freezer was a tub of Ben & Jerry's ice cream for later on. With cookie bits in it.

There was no doubt about it, good, old-fashioned comfort eating had finally kicked in. She was no stranger to it, unfortunately, even though she'd vowed it wouldn't happen this time. She would not give Andrew the kind of power to turn her into a twelve-stone blimp overnight. But even though she began each day thinking that way, and made several stern resolutions to eat only things that were green, by teatime she had generally consumed the better part of four thousand calories.

Naturally it was entirely his fault.

But her appetite had gone now. There was only one good reason Barbara was here: he had sent her.

Not that she was going to admit it. 'I was just in the area and I thought I'd pop by,' she said.

Millie looked past her to where her new boyfriend was sitting in his car, engine gunning impatiently, at the gate. It obviously was going to be a very short visit.

'That's very nice of you,' she told Barbara. Then, out of pure badness, 'Why don't you come in for a cup of tea?'

'Oh! Um, no thanks.' She threw a nervous look over her shoulder. 'Louis doesn't drink tea.'

Louis looked like he only drank cider, preferably from a two-litre flagon. He was Barbara's Bad Boy, and many an evening over at theirs, Millie and Andrew had sniggered behind their hands at his black leather trousers, which he'd obviously found on the snug fit rack. 'Drop your fork on the floor,' Andrew would beg Millie. 'I want to see what happens when he bends down.' (Millie had thought this hilarious at the time but now, of course, she realised that Andrew was just being childish and immature. Which was his true nature.) Barbara, whilst infatuated with Louis, seemed at a loss what to do with him half the time. She looked perpetually worried that he would grow bored, or throw a tantrum, or something. He took her to biker rallies and car shows and strange pubs, and she did her best by buying a denim jacket and trying not to offend him. He in turn treated her like she was constructed of china, and wrote her love poetry ('God, I'd love to read it,' Andrew had said, wiping tears of mirth from his eyes. He really was a jerk, Millie decided now, choosing not to remember that she had wanted to read it too.)

Anyway, whatever it was they saw in each other, they had been going strong for a year. He had moved in his two duffel bags and massive sound system two weekends ago and they had rarely been seen in daylight hours since.

'So! How have you been?' Barbara was wilting with embarrassment at the situation. Despite herself Millie felt sorry for her, being sent over by that pig of a brother of hers. He hadn't even coached her in a good excuse, like she wanted to borrow a cup of flour or something.

'I've been fine,' Millie said. She was mortified too, especially as she was wearing pyjama bottoms and a horrible old sweatshirt. She had hoped to have the night to herself, so that she could stuff her face in comfort and then spend the rest of the evening bitterly regretting it.

'That's good,' said Barbara desperately.

Louis revved his engine loudly behind them again, making her jump violently. The fright seemed to propel her to the point, which was a relief for both of their sakes. 'Andrew asked me to come over.'

Millie wanted to curl up her lip in utter contempt at the mere mention of his name. Yet she also wanted to burst into tears.

In the end she managed to do neither. 'Did he?'

'Look, I know there's been some . . . stuff between you two.' Barbara's big blue eyes were wide with sympathy. And why not? She was a nice woman. She and Millie had always got along. Naturally she would have sympathy.

But sympathy was a dangerous thing. If Millie gave in to it at all, she would find herself at the kitchen table with Barbara, throwing back a bottle of cheap red wine and bawling about how her heart was broken and how she'd never recover. Next thing the wedding photos would be hauled out. And probably the used pregnancy tests. It was a horrible spectacle. Especially when most of what she said would find its way back to Andrew, in a truncated yet damning form. 'Poor old Millie,' he would say on the phone to Barbara. 'Who would have thought she'd take it so badly?' Rule number one of relationship break-ups: families stick together. Your sister-in-law is never, ever, your best friend in these things.

'Yes,' said Millie. Coolly. Distantly.

'He didn't tell me the gory details or anything,' Barbara was quick to assure her.

Naturally. Especially as he himself wouldn't come out of it smelling too rosy. But no doubt he had painted Millie as some baby-crazed pre-menopausal loo-la, who had ruined their marriage by her single-minded obsession. 'It was all she could talk about in the end,' he would say, his voice cracking with emotion. 'I just couldn't take it any more.' Oh, she would like to give him a good slap. Two slaps.

'I see,' she said, wondering whether or not to enlighten Barbara as to her brother's true nature.

But that might spoil things. Andrew had obviously dispatched Barbara for a reason. Millie felt that treacherous hope rise in her again. Perhaps this was his way of reaching out to her (although the telephone would have been handier). But he might not have wanted to speak to her directly. He might have sent Barbara in to gauge her mood first.

It was possible. After all, he still loved her. Or, at least, he had never said he didn't.

And she still loved him. Or she could again in time. At a push. Helped along by her raging hormones.

All right, so it wasn't perfect. But what in this life was? Every single thing worth having involved compromise in some shape or form.

'I just want to say that I'm really sorry the way things have worked out,' Barbara said, obviously choosing her words carefully.

Millie found that she wasn't keen on them. They were a bit too final for her liking. And why was Barbara looking at the ground in that kind of evasive, embarrassed fashion?

'He asked me to come round and collect his things,' she announced, rather miserably.

Millie felt sick, even though a part of her had expected this. But not from Barbara. And did she mean *all* of his things? Was he actually gone for good? Had he sent his sister over casually to announce to his wife that, yep, it really was over? It was too much to take in.

'Just, if it's a good time,' Barbara said, seeing her face. 'If it's not I can come back on Saturday.'

Millie said the only thing she could to cover her shock and to salvage her pride. 'I'm busy Saturday.' Even though she wasn't.

'OK,' said Barbara.

'I'm going to an art gallery.' She wasn't sure where that came from. It was hardly the kind of place she and Andrew had frequented. But it sounded grown-up and sophisticated, and she went with it. 'With some friends.'

'That's great, Millie.' Barbara was looking at her kindly now, no doubt thinking what a good old chump Millie was to get out and about so quickly and have a life again. She would be able to report back to Andrew that, contrary to expectation, Millie wasn't keening in a corner with a bottle of Blue Nun, fondling Andrew's used shirts and heading straight for rehab.

'Male friends,' said Millie loudly. 'All of them.' She managed to stop herself before she came across as even more pathetic. She took a breath. 'Why don't you come in?'

'Thanks.'

Barbara turned round to the car and gestured at Louis. Probably some kind of coded message – that she was going in, and that if she wasn't out in ten minutes he'd better come to break the door down.

Louis gave a stiff little nod at Millie. No doubt Andrew had warned him not to get out of the car, that Millie would be bound to jump on him and try to have sex with him, so desperate was she to have a baby.

'Hello!' Millie said, giving him a devil-may-care wave. But then she let her hand drop. She'd probably never lay eyes on him again. She didn't have to be nice.

'Come on then!' she growled at Barbara. She'd probably never see her again either.

'Oh! Sorry,' said Barbara, tripping over herself in her haste.

'They're in the attic,' Millie said, turning to go into the kitchen.

Poor Barbara stood in the hallway, completely confused now. 'What are?'

'His clothes. They're in bin liners. You'll have to search through them.

Some of the stuff is from last year when he was much, much fatter. In fact, you can tell him from me that he was probably clinically obese only I was too polite to say it. Oh, and mind your head on the wasps' nest up there.'

Barbara's mouth was hanging limply open now. 'You have a wasps' nest?'

'Probably,' said Millie. Well, there was some kind of suspicious-looking growth on the rafters, and she had definitely encountered a wasp at the top of the stairs when she had been up packing his stuff up. There was no harm in warning Barbara.

'Here's a torch,' she said, throwing one over. She added kindly, 'The light up there is broken.'

Barbara nearly broke her neck trying to catch the torch. Then she threw a look of trepidation towards the stairs.

'I'd go with you, only my dinner is getting cold,' Millie said apologetically.

Barbara eventually went off. Andrew's stuff was only just inside the trap door; she would have no problem finding it. And it was marked too, in big red marker on the outside. Millie was just being a bitch; shooting the messenger because her big fat fraud of a husband couldn't be bothered to show up in person.

She sat down at the table. She didn't touch her dinner. She put her head in her hands and she cried as quietly as she could.

Barbara was sensitive, because she didn't come back into the kitchen. In fact, Millie never even heard her come back down the stairs, or the front door closing or anything. She only knew she was gone at all by the sound of the car revving outside, and the wail of the exhaust as it drove away.

There had been a story recently in a Sunday newspaper about an over-weight woman who had discovered on a routine visit to her doctor that she was seven months' pregnant. All right, so it had been in the *News of the World* or something, but bizarre none the less. 'Imagine my surprise!' she had said in the interview. And she hadn't even had the decency to look all that surprised. It probably happened to her all the time, Andrew had said. She had probably had her other kids that way too – she just popped down to the GP to pick up some cream for that stubborn wart only to discover that number three or number four was on the way in a matter of weeks. 'You're kidding!' the paper had quoted her as chortling.

Millie had been unaccountably cross about it. How thick could you be? she had fumed to the girls in work. Or, indeed, how overweight?

How could that woman have failed to notice that there was an actual whole other person growing inside her? Did she not think that her roll of fat was suspiciously rounded, not to mention that it seemed to be giving her a good kick every now and again?

It was maddening.

These women didn't just live in the pages of trashy Sunday newspapers, more was the pity. They infiltrated Millie's Trying to Conceive forums too, where they would pop up periodically to taunt everybody else who was desperately trying to get pregnant. 'I haven't had a period in three months. Is it possible that I might be pregnant? My boyfriend and I never have unprotected sex – oh, except for that one time about three months ago. Worried, from Sligo.'

Millie had found herself shouting at the computer, 'Go and take a pregnancy test, you stupid cow.' Somebody else had obviously advised her to do the same, because she was back a week later to sicken them all further by announcing breathlessly, 'The doctor says I'm four months along. And it's twins! You must all think I'm a complete klutz!'

Actually, Millie thought she was totally irresponsible. If she didn't know she was pregnant then she probably wouldn't have been taking her folic acid. Or eating right. And no doubt throwing back bottles of beer with her big lump of a boyfriend. Those twins would have a better start in life by being reared by a couple of wolves in an inhospitable forest than with a woman who couldn't be bothered to take a pregnancy test on their behalf.

Steady on, Andrew had murmured at that point (from the pages of a report). But it just seemed so unfair. How come it was so easy to get pregnant when you weren't even trying, but impossible when you actually were? Millie seemed to have spent most of her twenties desperately avoiding pregnancy, and most of her thirties desperately trying to achieve the state.

Ah yes, the irony. It was hilarious.

And to think she had put such energy into her efforts at birth control! It had been a constant source of worry back then. All those suspicions about Jacuzzis and toilet seats. The frights over burst condoms. Not that they had routinely burst or anything; there hadn't exactly been an epidemic. But she'd had her scares and didn't really trust them after that.

Oona had tried out the 'revolutionary' female ones, stirring up great interest amongst everybody, but had ended up using them as bin liners instead.

The birth control pill, the 'rhythm method', the cap, abstinence, even prayer – Millie and her friends had tried them all. Most of them even used a combination, just to be on the safe side. But still someone would periodically wind up in the pub, freshly pregnant and sobbing into a pint of Guinness, 'I don't even know his surname. To be honest I'm not even sure of his first name. I think it's Paul. Or Tommy. Oh, I am never, *ever* having a one-night stand again.' As if she'd have the time, what with being a single mother with a tiny baby.

Back then they had all thought that having a baby would ruin their entire lives. A *baby*? They weren't even that keen on the look of them. A lot of the newborns could be mistaken for little old men. And there were terrible stories going around about them needing constant nappy changes and demanding to be fed every four hours. Imagine! Who would get up to them when they woke in the middle of the night, the girls had wondered very seriously – a nanny? Certainly *they* couldn't, not with a job to go to in the morning and a serious social life to keep up, involving trips to the pub at least four times a week. Maybe they could bring the baby to the pub in its car seat, they mused, and put it on the bar.

No, babies were for other women – dare they say it – ancient women, who had reached some kind of career plateau and had married some boring guy they'd met in the office, more for something to do than anything else, and the only excitement left to them was to reproduce.

Millie wasn't going there in a hurry. She had her whole twenties ahead of her. More to the point, she and her friends were the generation whose mothers had been forced by law out of the civil service the day they got married, and never let their daughters forget it. 'Get out there and invent something, in the name of God,' they would plead. 'I didn't give up my career in the telephone exchange/secretarial pool/asbestos factory just for you to meet some lovely fellow and waste yourselves on having babies.'

And anyway, Millie and her friends didn't *know* any men who wanted to have babies. A lot of them were only babies themselves, falling around Temple Bar with thirteen pints in them, and still hoping to get laid. Or else the guys from the advertising agency across the road, with their sharp suits and slick haircuts, who would take you off for a posh dinner on a Friday night before walking hand in hand with you around St Stephen's Green. But mention babies to them and they'd chew their own arm off to get away.

If it was babies you wanted then you would have to seek out men of a 'certain age', as in over thirty-five, which meant going to dinner dances, and staid pubs in the suburbs, or possibly even tagging along with Dad to the golf club annual 'do'. 'God, can you imagine!' the girls would squeal in horror at the very thought, and knock back another cocktail in some trendy bar in town. There was plenty of time for all that in the future.

Back then nobody had warned Millie that she might not have a choice. That Andrew, her husband, would decide the whole thing for her just like that.

She felt powerless. Helpless. And angry. They'd made *vows*, for heaven's sake. In a church in Terenure, to the lusty strains of Mariah Carey, and witnessed by a hundred of their family and friends. Looking into his harmless blue eyes that day, she would never have guessed that he would turn round and deny her her life's dream, and all for what? Fucking broadband.

Her anger grew. Who did he think he was, anyway? The great giver of life? The guy had some kind of God complex, she decided viciously. He thought he could swan around the place, graciously bestowing or cruelly denying the gift of a baby as though it were his divine right. Castration was too good for him. Possibly death was too good for him.

Thanks to him, she was lying awake at four a.m. hoping wildly that she was one of those women who was actually pregnant but just didn't know it yet. Well, if it had happened to that obese woman, then why not Millie? Her stomach was certainly padded enough. And her last period had been very light. It might not have been a period at all, but what was called 'implantation bleeding' on the Internet. A trip to the GP on a totally unrelated matter might be all it would take to verify it. 'You're kidding!' Millie could chortle (before rushing out to ring *News of the World*). And then it wouldn't matter about Andrew. His bit would already be done. She wouldn't even let him see their child when it was born. She wouldn't even let him know that she was pregnant, she thought maliciously. It would serve him right.

But of course it wasn't true. She wasn't pregnant. There was nothing growing around her middle except a spare tyre. Her longed-for baby hadn't been conceived yet.

And, after Barbara's visit this evening, might never be.

She began to cry again. And there was no one to comfort her. The bed she had shared with Andrew for the past two years felt cold and empty, and way too big for one person. She had better get used to it.

She had told Oona that she still loved him. Was this even true? How was it possible to love and miss somebody who had let you down so badly?

She pictured his familiar, friendly face, but felt only fury and despair. It was as if all the love they'd had between them was cancelled out by the events of the last week. Everything was coloured by his decision to deny her a baby. How could she ever be happy with such a man again?

She couldn't. And she knew then that it really was over. There would be no more hoping that he would ring. Reconciliation was out of the question, unless he changed his mind.

And it was obvious that he wasn't going to.

She lay very still in the bed for a minute. It began to sink in. Her marriage was officially over. After a little more than two years.

And without a single thing to show for it, except a house (which had been hers to begin with) and a wedding photo album.

No joint 'assets'.

No baby.

And that was what was upsetting her the most. She curled up into a little ball in the bed, her arms wrapped fiercely around her middle. She felt physically empty, like there was a big void inside her that would never be filled, except by a baby. How was it possible to be so bereft for something you'd never had to begin with?

She thought about the future. It would be just her now. And it wasn't Andrew that she was missing, but rather a little shadow at her feet; a small hand tugging at her trouser leg; the call of 'Mummeee!' The school runs, the trips to the doctor and the dentist, the birthdays, the Christmases with Santa coming to visit.

Ah, Jesus. The tears were flowing so hard now that she was nearly choking herself. She pulled herself up in the bed and blew her nose hard. Self-pity wasn't going to get her far tonight. Or any night.

At least she had her dignity left, she tried to console herself. And her Alanis Morissette CDs. And her family and her wonderful friends. He hadn't taken those away too.

But it seemed a very high price to pay, all the same. Too high.

Chapter Seven

'I have so much love to give,' she told Oona two days later.

Oona looked a bit startled. She peeled off her rubber gloves. She was wearing one of Aoifa's Barbie scarves in her frizzy hair. Vera Duckworth wasn't in it.

'That's nice,' she said. 'Pass us the vacuum there.'

Brendan had reluctantly lent them his Dyson Cyclone. He had only parted with it on the condition that they treated it right. 'Don't lay it on its side, it doesn't like that. And there's a special fitting if you want to get in between the banisters on the stairs.' They had no intention of doing that, but they took the fitting anyway. 'And don't leave it on while you go off to fill the kettle for a cup of tea.' This was directed at Oona rather accusingly. He then loaded it into Oona's car boot, folding it in so carefully that she enquired whether they were dating.

He had wanted to come over himself, of course. There was no one more qualified than he to give a house a good spring clean. But Oona had turned down his offer firmly; she and Millie were perfectly capable of cleaning their own mother's house in preparation for her discharge from hospital tomorrow. She would enjoy knowing that they had been on their hands and knees, hard at work. 'Thank God everything I taught you hasn't been wasted,' she liked to say. 'Exactly what else did she ever teach us,' Oona had enquired in a low voice to Millie, 'except how to shop for Ireland?'

Anyway, two males in the one house would be guaranteed to cause some friction. Brendan could be rather free with his advice on domestic matters, which didn't go down all that well with Dennis. He was forever passing on recipes he had discovered on the inside of soup can labels, or giving him little tips on how best to marinade meat. Dennis, whose domestic skills were basic but in his opinion adequate, wasn't keen on being talked down to by his son-in-law.

'Oh, you can dish it out, but you can't take it,' Oona said to Dennis, delighting in the situation.

'I liked it better when he talked about cars,' Dennis grumbled. 'I enjoy a good chat about tow bars and alloy wheels. But how long you should defrost a chicken for . . . ?'

'How long?' Oona wondered immediately, not having a clue.

'Is he ever going to go back to work?' Dennis enquired.

Oona gave him a scathing look. It was one she had perfected over many years, to the point where it involved every single muscle in her face, and some in her neck too. It was a fearsome sight to behold and had caused many another man to wilt.

It didn't knock a bother out of Dennis. 'What?' he said.

'Dad,' she said very slowly as though she were speaking to a cretin, 'I am shocked at you. Actually, no, I'm not shocked at all. After that remark you made about women wrestlers last year nothing would surprise me. What Brendan does *is* work! In many ways it's more important than what I do in an office all day long. Those kids are our future! They are tomorrow's citizens! If we don't invest in them now, what hope have they of turning out to be responsible, decent members of society?'

'So he's not going back to work then?' Dennis said doggedly.

Oona had to put him into the kitchen at that point and instruct him to make tea for her and Millie.

'I'll slip a little something into yours,' he told Millie quietly. She had broken the news of Andrew's departure to him earlier. 'And you know, if you don't feel up to cleaning, that's perfectly fine. Mum won't mind at all.'

He squeezed her hand, which was a big gesture for him. He wasn't a touchy-feely person. He couldn't even watch other people at it. When they were kids, and gathered around *Dallas* on the telly on a Saturday night, Oona and Millie used to wait in great excitement for Cliff Barnes to make the inevitable pass at Sue Ellen or April or whoever else was handy. As the wet sounds of kissing filled the living room Dennis would squirm and sigh and cross his legs repeatedly, until eventually he would say, 'Anybody for a cup of tea?' and bolt to the kitchen without waiting for a reply. Millie and Oona would have wet faces with the fun of it all.

'He's quite romantic really,' Nuala would chastise them.

'Stop, Mum, or I'm going to be sick,' Oona had begged. How could anybody be romantic in a horrible cardigan and a great lop of hair combed over the top of his head to conceal the bald patch, they had whispered late at night when they should have been asleep. And Mum was as bad, in that flowery pinafore thing she wore over her own clothes to 'protect' them. It made her look like a sack of potatoes tied in the middle. They obviously hadn't had sex since she herself was conceived, Oona decided, and even then no doubt they'd had to grit their teeth.

Dennis was being very nice to Millie today, even though he hadn't really grasped the significance of Andrew's departure to Germany.

'He'll come back,' he assured her now. 'Once things are up and running in the new office.'

'He won't. And anyway, I don't want him to.' She was surprised at how cold and definite her voice was especially when she had cried into her pillow again until four o'clock this morning. Four a.m. was starting to become a significant time for her. It seemed that she was destined to cry every night until that time, then when it arrived she fell asleep immediately, and with great relief. She wondered what would happen when the clocks went back. Would she get even less sleep?

'I'm just saying. People have rows.' He added bravely, 'Your mother and I had them.'

Yes, little tiffs over who had left the carton of milk out of the fridge overnight. They had never been the type to shout at each other, 'You ruined my life, you sod!' Or, 'I wish I'd married Susan Carroll instead of you!' They'd had far too much in common, such as shopping centres and television and sucky sweets, for any of that kind of lark.

But Mille could see what he was trying to do. With Mum in hospital, he obviously felt there was some kind of maternal void to be filled. The thought of having a go at this himself obviously filled him with doom, judging by the look on his face, but he wasn't going to let that put him off. Millie was in need, and he wouldn't shirk his duties.

'Andrew will be home soon too,' he said. It was plain he was plumping for the optimistic note. Otherwise she might cry, and that would frighten the life out of him altogether. 'You'll see. It was just a row,' he said kindly.

'I don't think so, Dad.'

'Are you sure?' he said hopefully.

'Quite sure.'

'Oh.' His brow crinkled. It was obviously on to Plan B. If only he had a Plan B. 'Men and women are different,' he began eventually.

In the background Oona snickered, and he faltered.

'Sometimes men need a little time to come around,' he said, lowering his voice so that Oona wouldn't hear.

'That's no excuse, Dad.'

Dennis looked unhappy. 'I suppose not,' he said eventually.

She could see he wanted to say more, but wasn't sure enough of himself to do so. If only Mum were home, you could nearly see him thinking. She would be great to deal with all this stuff.

Neither of them mentioned Millie's desire for a baby. Millie was glad. She didn't think it was a conversation she could have with her father, no matter how maternal he tried to be. He liked children, and was quite good with Oona's, but she didn't think she could explain to him about primeval longings and insane urges to procreate, at least without him going very red.

Thankfully Oona was there to offload on instead. She hadn't gone red since about the age of six.

'Look,' she said, when Dennis was safely ensconced in the kitchen making tea, 'do you want me to fix you up with Finbarr Maguire?'

'What?'

'You just said you had all this love to give.'

'I don't mean that kind of love.'

Oona didn't get it. 'From what I hear, Finbarr's separation is pretty nasty. He could do with a bit of loving. Not to mention you.'

Oona had brought her over a big bunch of flowers that morning. And a voucher for a weekend in a health spa. 'I'll go with you,' she had promised. 'We'll get loads of treatments done and get drunk every night and come home looking gorgeous.'

But Millie was cross with her now. 'How could you possibly think I want to get into bed with Finbarr Maguire when Andrew is only gone a bare week?'

'I suppose you won't want to rush into anything,' Oona conceded. 'You'd probably want to give it a couple of months. Heal a bit.' She must have been watching *Dr Phil* again with the kids while Brendan was out. It was probably where Aoifa got her psychiatrist tendencies.

Millie tried to ease the conversation away from men. 'I'm talking about maternal love, Oona.'

Oona turned off the vacuum. This was serious.

'Sometimes I feel like I'm bursting inside. That I have so much to give a baby. And I'd be a really good mum, Oona. I don't want to sound like I have a big head or anything, or that I have rakes of experience of them, but I just know. Does that make sense?'

'You'd probably do a much better job than me,' Oona agreed.

'No, I wouldn't, your kids adore you even if you can't cook to save your life. Brendan does everything for them but the minute they hear you coming in the door their faces light up, and they forget completely that you burnt holes in their favourite T-shirts.'

Oona looked misty-eyed at the memory. 'The little pets.'

'I look at you with your kids, and I think if I don't ever have a child there's nothing much left for me.'

'Millie.' Oona looked alarmed.

Millie was impatient. 'I don't mean I'm going to top myself or anything.' She liked telly and Ben & Jerry's ice cream far too much for that. 'But I won't feel . . . complete or something.'

Oona sat down on the bottom step of the stairs. 'Lots of people have very good lives without children, Millie. Some people *choose* not to have them because they want to do other things with their time. You can't say that your life won't be worthwhile without children.'

Millie could see what she was thinking; that there was little point in punishing herself like this when Andrew was gone and she didn't have a choice in the matter. That she'd be better off looking at ways of having a good, childfree life.

'But I didn't choose not to have children,' she said stubbornly.

'I know.'

'I mean, I didn't do anything wrong. He was the one who walked out of the marriage, not me. So why should I have to go without children?'

Oona looked at her. 'Eh, because you don't have the necessary sperm, for the want of a better way of putting it?'

'Exactly,' said Millie.

Oona reached out with the vacuum head and pushed the kitchen door closed on Dennis. 'We don't want him to have a heart attack,' she said. She took a breath. 'Millie, I think you're very upset. I would be too.'

'But it hasn't happened to you.'

'I'm just saying; it's a natural reaction to try and do something. To take action. But trust me – right now, you need to just let it all sink in. Because you're not thinking straight at the moment.'

'But it's not fair,' Millie insisted.

'I know. Life sucks sometimes, Millie. Life is crap sometimes.'

'And that's it? That's your great theory?'

'He doesn't want kids. You can't make him.'

'I don't care about him any more. I don't even want to talk about him. This is about me. I have choices too, you know.'

Oona looked confused. 'You can't have a baby on your own, Millie.'

Millie was reckless now. She had started this conversation more to vent her frustration than anything else. She hadn't really been trying to float any ideas of single motherhood. The notion was, frankly, preposterous.

Or maybe it was just that she had never given it any thought before now. She had hardly had occasion to.

Yet she demanded, 'Why not?'

Oona was round-eyed. 'Why *not*?'

'Women do!' Millie said. 'It's possible.'

'How?'

'I could go and . . . shag somebody I met in a bar!' On Day 14, naturally. And without using any protection, naturally. It could be tricky.

Oona was coming over all protective now. 'Millie, you're off your rocker. You're deranged with grief and desperate to do something – anything. But having sex with some drunken eejit that you meet in a seedy bar is not the way. Now stop it before I have to slap you. I have my hand nicely warmed up from the kids' backsides earlier.'

Millie deflated. She felt completely depressed again, and slightly foolish. Imagine suggesting having sex with some total stranger just to try to get pregnant! It was ludicrous. Oona was right. The past week had been a rollercoaster and she was in no position to go chasing after quick fixes.

'Let's go to the health spa,' Oona coaxed. 'We'll have a load of treatments and bottles of chardonnay. Was I telling you my neighbour had a seaweed wrap there and lost half a stone? I'm hoping they can do something about my arse.' She reached around and tried to hike it back up an inch or two, moaning, 'God, Millie, how did we get to be so ancient?'

She wasn't thinking, course. It wasn't a jibe specifically aimed at Millie's ovaries or anything. But even so, Millie felt even more depressed. She could almost feel her FSH levels rising within her like malicious sap. It would take more than a seaweed wrap to bring them down.

'Tea's up!' Dennis announced, pushing the door open with a tea tray. His cheeks were a little flushed. Millie wondered whether he had overheard some of the conversation about sperm. But it could just be the general heat. He'd had the boiler on full throttle since yesterday in anticipation of Nuala's arrival home. It was so humid that the green wallpaper was wilting on the walls, but would he turn it down? 'She'll be used to hospital temperatures,' he had fussed.

'No fig rolls?' Oona said, looking at the tray in disappointment. 'You hardly expect us to do all this cleaning for nothing.'

Dennis informed her, 'I had to get bandages for your mother's foot and buy a little footstool so that she can prop it up in the evenings. I didn't have time to get fig rolls for you.'

He handed over Millie's cup of tea. The 'little something' he had slipped in it turned out to be two spoons of sugar.

'Get that down you. You'll feel much better.'

'Thanks, Dad.' Millie tried to choke down the oversweet concoction. Still, it might give her a lift. She felt she could do with it. Once she had finished cleaning her parents' house, her whole weekend stretched in front of her full of nothingness. Oona had said for her to come over and stay at hers. But what would that achieve? It would only make it harder to come home to an empty house.

She had tried to go shopping that morning. Just to get out there and be around people. But, walking through the shopping centre, she had felt marked — as if everybody could see what had happened to her in the last week. Then, perversely, she had been upset when the cashier in the bookshop had been short with her — could he not *see* that Millie was traumatised? Was tragedy not stamped all over her face?

After half an hour of trying to be normal and failing miserably, Millie had gone home. She'd cried for a good hour and then hit the kitchen presses.

Bloated and red-eyed, she had finally flopped back in her chair and thought, this is it. From now it was just her and all the food she could carry home from the supermarket.

Fig rolls, she thought now. Now that they had been mentioned she had a sudden and intense craving for them. She would buy three packs on the way home and eat them whilst slowly tearing up her life plan and setting fire to it.

She was jerked from this pleasant line of thought by Dennis announcing, 'I'm thinking of getting Mum an electric chair.'

'Dad, euthanasia is only legal in the Netherlands,' Oona told him sternly. 'And even then they use drugs, not electric chairs.'

Dennis glared. 'I'm not talking about that kind of electric chair.' He plucked a brochure off the telephone table. 'This came this morning.'

The brochure was glossy and expensive and in cheery bright colours. On the front was a photo depicting a smiling elderly woman being seamlessly borne up a set of stairs in a comfy padded chair. When you opened it there were more elderly people, all at various stages of elevation, and all looking as happy as sandboys. One of them even had a newspaper on her lap, no doubt to pass the journey.

'She'll be on crutches for a while. I thought it would help.'

'Dad, knowing her she'll throw out the crutches after a day, and you'll be left with this giant electric chair taking up the entire stairs. And she'll probably trip over it, and end up back in hospital with a broken leg.'

Dennis winced. 'That's not even funny.'

'Neither is this. She doesn't need it, Dad. She's fine.'

Actually, she wasn't that fine at all, in Millie's opinion. But now was not the time to bring it up. Dennis was already wound up enough about her being in hospital. It wouldn't do to go suggesting that there might be something else wrong with her as well, that an electric chair wouldn't fix.

He was fussing again. 'Let's get on with the cleaning then, will we?'

You would think he was doing some of it himself.

'I haven't even finished my tea,' Oona grumbled. She reached over to put the mug down on the telephone table. But she had never been known for her grace and elegance, and the mug missed the telephone table by a mile, sending hot tea cascading with a steaming hiss onto the 1.2 litre engine of the Dyson Cyclone.

The nurse who was usually on Mum's ward had gone on maternity leave.

'What, just this minute?' Millie joked. Her smile was plastered on, and she was bitterly regretting her airy offer yesterday to pick Mum up from the hospital.

'No, yesterday,' the new nurse told her earnestly. 'You probably didn't notice she was pregnant. She was tiny. She was wearing size ten jeans up to a month ago.'

'Really?' said Millie, trying to look as disinterested as possible. Honest to God, was the whole bloody world pregnant? In the car park she had bumped into a pregnant woman, and had had to practically squeeze past another in the corridor outside. No doubt she would meet several more before the day was out. That was the way it worked, wasn't it? It was like that time she had reversed into a parking meter and driven off in a panic. Within days she was seeing policemen everywhere, even behind the cold counter at the supermarket.

'She didn't even know she was pregnant until she was four months along,' the nurse prattled on.

Millie was going to advise her that the *News of the World* might be interested, but stopped short. It wasn't the nurse's fault, or the pregnant woman in the corridor outside. The whole world wasn't having babies just to spite Millie. It was simply a fact of life, and something that she would have to endure.

And she didn't want to become bitter about it, like some of them on her Internet forums. 'If I see another pregnant woman this week I'm going to hurl my bloody guts up,' one of them had railed only yesterday. Millie didn't want to be like that. Well, not yet anyway. Give her a year or two and she could well be up there with the best of them, starting some kind of anti-pregnancy club.

'Is my mother ready to go?' she enquired, determined to get off the subject altogether.

The nurse became efficient. She began to go through some files. 'What's her name?'

'Nuala Doran.'

The nurse's face changed. 'Oh.'

'In Ward Two—'

'I know what ward she's in.'

Mum must have been ringing the damned bell again.

'I'll have her out of here as soon as possible,' Millie said guiltily.

She had parked near the hospital doors so it should be a fairly quick getaway. Dennis, meanwhile, was at home cooking a 'light lunch', which seemed to involve about twelve different dishes. He had been in a lather of sweat when she'd dropped by to pick up a bag for Mum's things. Oona hadn't been seen since yesterday, when she'd gone home to break the news of the Dyson's demise to Brendan.

But she would drop by later, she promised, to check on Mum. Or maybe tomorrow. She didn't seem to have found anything strange about Mum's behaviour during the hospital visits, and Millie hadn't mentioned it to her.

'I don't think she'll be going home today,' the nurse was saying. She gave a little sigh.

'No, she is,' Millie assured her. 'She just has to be seen by a doctor first, and get discharged.'

'The doctor has already seen her. The infection hasn't cleared. And, by the way, you might want to explain to her that it's nothing to do with the way the dressing is actually applied.'

'Um, right.' Millie was more embarrassed. 'When do you think she'll be out?'

The nurse again consulted the notes. 'It'll be another day or two. But you can be sure that we'll be discharging her at the very first opportunity.'

'Yes. Thank you.'

'Why don't you go on down to her?' the nurse suggested. 'She was looking for a drink of water five minutes ago, maybe you could give her one.'

She didn't want one now – she was flat out on the bed, fast asleep. The copy of *Hello!* magazine was open on her lap. She had been looking at the pictures of some footballer's wedding. The bride's dress was a fright.

Millie pulled up a chair quietly and sat down. She thought how peaceful Nuala looked in sleep. Happy and carefree and almost young. Millie wondered whether people simply changed as they got older. Did they just slow down, become a little wearier, a little grumpier than usual? There didn't have to be some big explanation for it. The purse thing was probably just a case of growing old.

It was a shame, though. Mum had never been a cross or odd person – the opposite, in fact. She was always laughing and having a joke. She was a Sunday's Child, as she had pointed out to Millie and Oona from when they were very young.

'The child that is born on the Sabbath Day is bonny and blithe, and good and gay,' she would instruct them.

'I want to be a Monday's Child,' Oona had begged. 'The one that's good-looking.'

Even back then her hair had been unmanageable and her cheeks plump and round. But, as she liked to say in retaliation, the childhood photos of Marilyn Monroe were nothing to write home about either.

'You can't choose,' Millie had told her. She wanted to be a Monday's Child too, but was worried that Mum would say that she was a Wednesday's Child, full of woe. Who the hell wanted to go through life with a face that would stop a clock? The only thing worse would be Friday's Child, loving and giving. She would probably end up in a convent or on the missions or something.

Nuala had smiled tenderly at Millie. 'You're a Thursday's Child. The one with far to go.'

Millie hadn't been too sure about that either. Would it involve a job with very long commuting hours? Or perhaps it meant she would live to a very old age. She might become Ireland's oldest woman. Which was hardly her life's dream, if she were being honest about it.

'It means you'll have a very interesting path ahead of you,' Nuala had said, which didn't really enlighten her. 'Maybe not without its difficulties.' Millie must have looked alarmed because she was quick to assure her, 'But you'll get there in the end.'

But get where exactly? That was the question.

Nuala had then turned to Oona, who was licking the palms of her hands and ruthlessly patting down her frizzy hair, no doubt still hoping to claim the crown of Monday's Child.

'You're Saturday's Child,' Nuala had told her. 'You'll work hard for a living.'

Oona must have had some terrible premonition of how true this would turn out to be, because she immediately tried to get out of it. 'I'll take Wednesday,' she begged. 'Or Friday. I'll even swap with Millie.'

Further proof that Thursday was an inauspicious day.

'Hard work never hurt anybody,' Dennis had intoned from behind his newspaper. He was a great man for clichés all his life. There was really nothing he liked better than a good cliché, the hoarier the better.

Oona had rolled her eyes so far back that they nearly got stuck. Clichés had that effect on her. 'Are you sure you're right, Mum?' she'd said. 'You might have been in so much pain that you got the days wrong.'

'I had an epidural, and I'm positive,' Nuala had assured her.

But Millie wondered now whether Nuala *had* got it wrong – in her case anyway. Because if Thursday's Child had far to go, then surely Millie had barely got off the starting blocks yet.

She sat in her hard plastic chair beside Mum's bed and did a mental review of her life to date. It didn't take very long. About ten seconds, in fact. There were no great academic or career highs or lows, nor were there likely to be, unless she retrained as a paramedic or something. Advancement through the ranks of APL Insurance, while possible, would hardly bring her to the attention of the world.

She hadn't travelled much. She had no hobbies or interests out of the ordinary (could watching telly be classed as a hobby?). She wasn't planning on running for the local council. All in all she was a perennial low-achiever, one of life's amblers who wasn't going to enter the *Guinness Book of Records* on any score whatsoever.

Maybe 'far to go' referred to Andrew, and his escape to Frankfurt. That may well be where the 'difficulties' Mum had warned of kicked in. But Millie's understanding was that these difficulties were a mere hiccup, and would give way to greater things. Why then was she going home alone to a weekend of misery and fattening food?

Mum *must* have made a mistake. Because there wasn't a thing about Millie's life to date that suggested she might be capable of higher things.

Still, maybe it was all to happen yet. She consoled herself with that thought. She might wake up in the morning and go on a diet and actually stick to it. And, as every woman who had ever gone on a diet knew, her whole life would magically be transformed once she was fifteen pounds lighter. It was cellulite that kept you down, not your own apathy or fear.

Or, better still, Andrew might pick up the phone and tell her he'd made a terrible mistake. Well, why not? Interesting and wonderful things *did* happen to people for no reason whatsoever.

And if anybody deserved something nice to happen, Millie did. She may not quite have lived up to the expectations of a Thursday's Child (which were a bit steep in her opinion), but she had done her bit. She was a customer-care employee, for goodness' sake – didn't that count for something? It even had the word 'care' in the title. It *had* to make her more worthy than, say, a property developer or one of those people who tried to lend elderly people money on the strength of their homes. None of them set out at twenty-five minutes past five on a Friday evening to find a family a seven-seater car to replace the one that had just broken down, and get it to them in rush-hour traffic (nor did Millie, if she could help it).

She was nice, dammit. She was a decent human being who paid her taxes, and watered her neighbours' gardens when they were away. She was a loyal friend – the girls in work would vouch for that. Mum would put in a good word too, if she weren't snoring her head off. All in all there wasn't a thing wrong with Millie, apart from being a size twelve around the waist and a size fourteen around the bottom and, well, she could live with that, thank you very much. And she wasn't looking for a bloody medal or anything, but was it too much to expect that somebody up there with a bit of clout might decide, 'She's all right, that Millie one. Let's give her a break for once in her shite, un-interesting, low-achieving life'?

'Hello, love.' Mum was awake. Her head was at an awkward angle and she didn't look all that pleased to find Millie there. But even though the poor woman was barely awake, today Millie was taking it personally.

Because today she felt like a nobody. A failure. A Thursday's Child who really should have been born on a Wednesday (which was full of woe).

'Andrew's gone,' she blurted to her mother. 'He's left me.'

She didn't know why she said it. It was hardly the news to greet her poor sick mother with. But at least *something* had happened. Her entire life hadn't been a blank page to date.

Dennis had not told Nuala, that much was clear from her face. Millie didn't know why. But he had been strangely reluctant when she'd asked him if he were going to. 'Maybe we should let her get out of hospital first,' he had said, a tad overcautious about what was, at the end of the day, an ingrown toenail.

The news was out now anyway. As it should be. Nuala was Millie's mother. She wanted her to know.

'Our marriage is over,' she added, just for dramatic effect.

Nuala seemed momentarily floored. Well, during hospital visits people tended to confine themselves to vague enquiries about what she'd had for tea. And there was Millie, offloading her marital misery without so much as a 'How's your toe today?' Naturally, it would take her a moment to adjust to the seriousness of the conversation.

But then she was fine. She couldn't move much in the bed because her foot was propped up awkwardly on a pillow, but she reached out a hand to Millie at once.

'Oh, love,' she said. She looked very upset.

It was enough to set Millie off crying again.

The woman from the next bed was staring at her.

She didn't care. She opened her mouth and words poured out: the trying for the baby, which Mum knew anyway; Andrew's transformation in the new job; his change of heart and his swift exit to Germany. Mum tutted and clicked her tongue sympathetically and shook her head at all the appropriate moments.

'So it's all over,' Millie ended up brokenly. It was a relief, actually, to get it all out. 'And I don't know what I'm going to do now, Mum. I thought I had it all sorted, you see. And now the whole thing is ruined.'

'Now, don't be talking like that,' Nuala scolded magnificently.

Millie relaxed. Now Mum was going to kick into action. Forget septic toes and childish battles with the nurses over bell-ringing – this was the real Nuala, with common sense pronouncements such as an apple a day kept the doctor away, and bread crusts made hair curly (if only Oona hadn't eaten so many of them). Nuala would take this thing with Andrew by the throat and make sense of it to Millie. She would come up with a plan of action, which would involve either sleeping on things, or else not letting the grass grow under her feet, or indeed any other number of comforting, if scientifically unproven, remedies. To Millie's ears they would be like chicken soup.

She waited with great anticipation. It was marvellous to be able to offload the whole stinking mess on Mum and let her take charge.

Mum wasn't saying too much at the moment, though. Maybe she was formulating some course of action that would be staggering in its audacity, and breathtaking in its wisdom.

Then: 'I told them ages ago that I wanted a glass of water.'

'Sorry?' said Millie.

'The nurses. I rang the bell and everything. I don't think it's working. I'll try it again.'

And she yanked the bell four or five times for good measure.

She pulled a little face at Millie and said, 'That new nurse who took over, she's not a patch on the old one. She left to have a baby, did you know that?'

Millie was astounded at her insensitivity. To have mentioned babies to someone in Millie's terrible position was, well, preposterous. And this was her mother, of all people.

She felt like she had been slapped. She sat there, looking at her mother as though she were a stranger.

'Would you mind pouring me one, love? The heat in here is killing me.'

Right now Millie wished it would. But she rose and went to the locker and got her mother water. Nuala drank gratefully.

'That's better.' Then she said, 'Now, about Andrew . . .'

At least she had remembered they'd been having a conversation about him.

But Millie didn't want to talk about it any more. She couldn't.

'It's fine,' she said.

'It's not,' Nuala insisted.

She saw now that Millie was upset. And that she herself may have been the cause of it.

'Millie . . .'

There was something about Nuala that took Millie's anger away: a look of anxiety, of confusion.

'It's fine, Mum,' she said.

'Is it?' She was watching Millie keenly.

'Come on. Let's have a look at *OK!* magazine.'

She had bought it just to give the two fingers to *Hello!*

Nuala was delighted. She sat up in bed a bit better and pushed back her hair.

Millie wondered fleetingly whether Nuala had deliberately switched off. Who wanted to be stuck listening to someone whingeing on about her bad lot? Especially when Nuala had had such high hopes that Millie would have far to go. What a let-down: instead, Millie was moaning by her bed, all washed up at the age of thirty-nine.

Millie was glad now that the conversation had been cut short. Nuala might have ended up cross at the waste of it all. Millie herself was cross at how she had let things get into such a state. And there was no sense at all in waiting for someone – Andrew, or God, or the insurance industry – to come and make it all better. More plainly put, if she had far to go, then she had better get off her behind fairly pronto.

She was thirty-nine, and the clock was ticking.

'Now listen carefully,' she warned Nuala as she opened the magazine. 'Because I'm not reading anything twice, OK?'

Chapter Eight

'I'm going to have a baby on my own,' Millie announced in work that Monday morning.

It hit the office like a thunderbolt. Everybody froze in position. Yvonne, who was in the middle of dealing with an early claim, said, 'I'll have to call you back.' She hurriedly added, 'Oh, and I hope your neck is better,' before hanging up and turning to stare at Millie.

Even Dorothy over in the corner looked up. Hardly anything startled her. She hadn't even left her desk that time Jaz went around shouting 'Fire! Fire!' as a protest when the company didn't fix one of the fire extinguishers fast enough.

'What?' Jaz snapped. She had no sense of humour that morning, as she had already officially declared. It was to do with the B&Q chain of stores, and a remark her husband, Gerry, had (allegedly innocently) made over the weekend, along the lines of her turning into an animal the minute she came within spitting distance of one. A rabid animal, were his precise words, even though, of course, he tried to take them back after she explained succinctly that it was her on her hands and knees all summer long in the wilderness of their back garden, not him. That the last time he'd 'helped' he had killed all the rose bushes. And who the hell did he think mowed the lawn twice a week? Santa Claus? So if he had an issue with her buying a stone ornamental fountain in the shape of a giant lily pad topped by a smiling cherub, or indeed a plastic model of Sylvester Stallone, then she'd like to hear it.

The girls had listened to this merry tale without too much alarm. Not a Monday morning went by without Jaz arriving in with some story of a marital bust-up over the weekend.

But Millie's news – well, that was news indeed.

She repeated now, 'I'm going to have a baby on my own.'

Her voice was quiet and determined, even though her heart was thumping in her chest dementedly. She couldn't believe she was saying it out loud. It wasn't even a proper decision yet: more a possibility, or else a wildly unfeasible notion. But ever since that conversation with Oona, she hadn't been able to get it out of her head. She was at the 'why not?' stage. She might well get to the 'definitely not, what a crazy idea' stage, but right now the possibility was before her, filling her with excitement, and an equal measure of fear.

But she was sure of one thing: the only way it was going to happen was if she made it happen.

'Oh. My. God.' Jaz had a hand clamped over her mouth. She was a great one for the dramatics.

'Or at least I'm thinking about it,' Millie quickly clarified. She didn't want anybody rushing out to organise a baby shower just yet.

Not that there was any danger of that. They were all looking at her like she had grown a couple of extra heads. Even Dorothy was still looking, when normally she would have gone back to work at least two minutes ago.

'A *baby*,' Jaz breathed. It was like she had never seen one in her life before. 'Oh my God,' she said again.

The rest of them were saying nothing at all. They just stared. Behind them, phones flashed furiously, and were completely ignored.

'You all think it's a terrible idea, don't you?' Millie blurted out. Immediately she felt mortified for even bringing it up. Why, oh why, had she opened her big mouth? She hadn't even worked the thing through in her own head yet. And now she had invited judgement before she was ready for it.

But she had wanted support. Someone to bounce the idea off. And the girls had seemed perfect. Yvonne and Jaz and Deirdre, and even Dorothy – the gang of Agony Aunts that had seen it all, and would support you no matter what. Or so she had thought.

'No, no, we don't think it's a terrible idea at all,' Yvonne insisted. She paused, her brow wrinkled. 'I don't know what I think of it, actually,' she admitted. 'It's just such a *surprise*, that's all.'

'I know,' Millie admitted.

'Especially after everything that's happened.'

The dust hadn't even settled; that's what she was thinking. Andrew had barely touched down in Frankfurt, and there she was, making all kinds of wild, possibly insane, plans.

Millie said, 'It's not exactly how I planned to have a baby. I know it's not ideal. But it's probably the only option left open to me.'

There she was again, in defensive mode; acting like she was doing something wrong when she hadn't even done it yet.

The girls were looking at each other now. Little glances darted back and forth. Stuck for words, the lot of them. Wondering what in the blazes to say to this latest instalment in the Millie/Andrew saga.

Jaz was the first one to break rank. 'Well, I don't know about anybody else, but I think it's great,' she declared. 'A new baby in the office! I think I was the last, was I, girls? With Jack? And that was back in 2004 – years ago! All I can say to you straight away is to buy a good support bra. That was one of the mistakes I made, as you can see. And don't start eating for two, because you'll spend the next five years trying to shift it. As you can see. But there's a very good diet book called *Getting Back into Shape After Being Pulled Out of It*. It didn't work for me but you might have better luck. I'll look it out for you when I get home, but if it's in the spare room you might have to wait, seeing as himself has been banished there. I don't want to get his hopes up by walking in.'

'I'm not actually pregnant yet,' Millie cautioned before Jaz got too carried away. But she was fiercely glad that somebody bar her was getting excited about it. She wasn't alone in thinking that the birth of a baby, however it was conceived, was something to be joyful about.

The rest of them were starting to warm up a bit too, now that the initial shock had worn off.

'All I can say is good luck to you,' Yvonne declared. This was the official seal of approval. 'It won't be easy, there's no sense in telling you that. But with the right support system, and a bit of organisation on your part, then why not?'

Jaz's sense of righteous indignant was stirring now. 'At least you have the choice. You can come out and say that you want to have a baby on your own. Look what it was like for women in this country forty years ago! Having to drive to the border with Northern Ireland to get the bloody birth-control pill. Single mothers being vilified and made to give up their babies. I'll tell you, between the Church and the State, we were nothing short of crucified!' She paused. 'Oh, shut up, Jaz.'

Deirdre asked tentatively, 'How would you go about it?'

'What?'

'Getting pregnant.'

There was a silence. Nobody had had the courage to ask this until now. It wasn't like Millie could hope for an immaculate conception, so everybody knew she would have to procure the necessaries elsewhere.

'Don't be giving Dorothy a heart attack,' Jaz warned Deirdre.

'Don't,' Dorothy agreed, who had very sharp hearing. 'I'm due to retire in two years' time and I have a villa in France.' The only thing she said to Millie was, 'In my opinion, babies need a mother *and* a father.'

She went back to work, leaving Millie wilting again. Dorothy could be counted as a no, then.

Jaz brushed it off. 'Don't worry about her. She just has to get used to the idea.' She pulled her chair in close. 'Now,' she said gleefully. 'Let's get down to brass tacks.'

There was nothing the girls enjoyed better than technicalities. When Rita on the floor below had been having her IVF last year, they had been well up on the lingo of 'stimming' and 'hatching' and would moan and fan themselves when Rita recounted how she had to give herself injections in her tummy. Sometimes *every day*.

'Well,' Millie said, not having quite addressed the question herself, 'I would need some, um, help.'

The whole area was rife with euphemisms. Even the most cursory research on the Internet was choked with non-offensive terms and coy ways of couching things. You could hardly find the word 'semen' at all, even though it was the very thing everybody was looking for – gallons of the stuff.

'From a man?' Deirdre prompted.

'Did your mam never explain the facts of life to you?' Jaz enquired kindly.

Deirdre was indignant. 'There are various ways of doing it, you know. There's the donor route, or else she could find someone she knows.'

Yvonne, no doubt protecting the general tone of the office, interjected with, 'Oh, we don't want to get bogged down in the minutiae. I'm sure there are ways and means.'

Jaz wasn't about to put such an important question off. 'Deirdre's right. You could ask someone you know.'

Millie hadn't even thought that far. She couldn't imagine having such a conversation with the few single men that she knew – 'Oh, before I forget, there was something I wanted to ask you . . .' Presumably married men were a no-no in this situation.

'How about Keith over in Accounts?' Jaz suggested. 'He looks like he might be up for anything.'

'Not to be a father,' Yvonne said firmly. 'He's only nineteen.'

'Frank, then.' This was greeted with several loud groans. 'What? He's mature. Single. And I happen to know that he has several nieces that he dotes upon.'

'He's got a beard,' Deirdre said.

'What's that got to do with it? She won't have to kiss him or anything – will you, Millie? I presume it'll be a turkey baster job – unless you're going the *au naturel* route?'

Deirdre couldn't help herself; she burst into a fit of nervous giggles, no doubt at the thought of Millie hopping astride a bearded, naked Frank.

Yvonne brought the conversation to a swift close. 'This is a serious subject, girls. It's not something to have a laugh over in the office.' That quietened them down. She looked at Millie. '*You* know how complicated the whole thing is.'

Actually, she hadn't a clue. She had just pictured a beautiful baby at the end of it all. And if she had thought about the father at all, she had imagined some benign, altruistic soul with a degree and nondescript blondish hair, who saw going to the sperm bank as something akin to taking his granny to the dentist on his day off.

Certainly, she never pictured Keith from Accounts. And as for beardy Frank? The very thought of having a friendly sex session with him for the purposes of getting pregnant made her want to giggle like Deirdre. And then puke. But so did the idea of retiring with a turkey baster to her bedroom while Frank did the necessaries in the bathroom opposite, a copy of *Hustler* in his hand. It was the stuff of low-grade comedy movies.

Yvonne was right. It *was* a very serious subject. And one she had given no proper consideration to yet. It was far too easy to get swept along in the excitement of the idea. Who wouldn't rather pick a colour scheme for a proposed nursery in the spare room (yellow, she had already decided, which could do for a boy or a girl) than a man to be the father?

She hadn't even had the Donor-v-Generous Male Friend debate yet. She didn't really want to either. Oh, couldn't they just hash it out between themselves?

There wasn't even anybody to discuss it with. Not properly anyway, the way you could with a husband, or significant other. But she had better get used to making decisions on her own. She would be choosing to be a single parent, after all. There would be nobody else to bounce ideas off, nobody to turn to at three a.m. when junior spiked a temperature of a hundred and three. 'And, oh my God, he's jaundiced!' No sane voice to tell her, 'Don't be ridiculous, it's just the reflection off the nursery walls. Why we couldn't have painted them plain old white . . .'

Millie was suddenly petrified. The whole thing was mad. Crazy! Maybe she was the one with the temperature. She wasn't even that great at changing light bulbs by herself – how could she cope on her own with a child who, if Oona's stories were anything to go by, would be mostly hungry, windy, sick or repeatedly filling his nappy?

'I suppose you'd have to give up your job too,' Jaz mused aloud.

'What?' Millie said weakly.

'Well, who'd look after the baby?'

Indeed. Certainly not the sperm donor, or Keith from Accounts.

'It's something else you need to think about,' Yvonne advised her needlessly.

Millie already had, but it was just another hazy vision, involving her working from home while the baby played happily at her feet with a box of office supplies – not about how she was going to reroute customer calls from the office to her own home. Somehow she had imagined that Tommy from Maintenance could swap over a few wires or something if she gave him a bottle of wine at Christmas.

But it was daft, now that she really thought about it. The baby would get hungry. Or, worse, staple itself to the floor. Tommy might electrocute himself. The company could tell her, justifiably, that her job was not suited to working from home.

It was insane. The whole thing.

'I was just wondering—' Deirdre began.

'I don't know!' Millie snapped. 'I haven't thought about it yet, whatever it is!' She took a breath. 'Sorry. It's just all very . . . new to me.'

Money – she bet Deirdre had been going to bring that up. If she were looking at giving up her job, it would become an issue. And babies were expensive – about a hundred thousand to get each one to the age of eighteen, Oona had worked out. She would have to go on welfare, although she doubted it stretched to anything like that. Or do a whip-round of her friends, or even rustle up the odd cake sale. She would become 'Millie, who never had a cent, God love her. Or that poor child.'

Deirdre wasn't put off at all by Millie's little outburst, worse luck. 'I was just going to say that I wonder if it might help to talk to Lisa from downstairs. She's bringing up two on her own.'

Lisa looked perpetually harassed and exhausted. She was always late for something or other, and could usually be spotted either sprinting to or from her car, hair flying wildly, because she hadn't had a chance to get it cut since Christmas two years ago. Often she had food down her top too.

Millie suddenly wondered if she could take a half-day. She felt she needed to go home and have a lie down, with a damp facecloth on her forehead or something. And wait for reason to return.

What was wrong with her life as it was anyway? Nothing! Except for all the crap in it recently, of course, but she would get over that eventually, with the help of MTV and a few bottles of wine. The main thing here was not to lose sight of all the good things she had

– her health, her house, family, friends, and all the Ben & Jerry's she could eat.

More importantly, she had a full night's sleep every night, and she didn't have to worry perpetually that she was going to be late for Tiddlywinks crèche, only to be greeted by a fractious child demanding to know who his father was, that Alex and Ben had one each, and Oisin had two.

Rash decisions were one of the great evils of this world, she decided. Along with Andrew, of course.

'Anyway,' she said loudly, to draw the entire conversation to a close, 'it was only an idea. That's all. I'm probably not even going to go through with it.'

That night she counted her blessings. The process involved putting on the trashiest TV programme she could find, which turned out to be an extreme reality show about trying to turn short, obese people into top models. Andrew would never have stood for it. 'It's rubbish,' he would be moaning. 'They're never going to make her fit into that dress unless they slice lumps off her.' Then he would pale. 'My God, they *are.*' He could never stomach blood and guts on the telly, not even in medical dramas, and would be rolling about on the couch hiding behind his hands, and begging her to switch it over.

Thankfully she didn't have to put up with him any more – another blessing – and so she could watch what she wanted. Better still, she could do so whilst eating a large bar of Galaxy (hm, it really was smooth as silk, just like the advertisement). And drinking a glass of red wine. Blessing galore! And she could have a second glass if she wanted. Why not? She was her own woman: independent, intelligent, young(ish), who could, and was, spending her evening the way she damned well pleased. There was a lot to be said for that.

And even if nothing else brilliant ever happened to her in her whole life, she was still better off than a whole lot of people in the world. And she should be grateful for that, right? Look at all the people who had no proper homes, or enough food, or even clean water to drink. It seemed churlish to be complaining in comparison. She was downright lucky when you weighed it up like that. Just because her life plan, which had happened to include a baby, hadn't quite worked out was no reason not to appreciate all the things she had.

Her life was good. Her life was fine.

But it rang a bit hollow. And kept ringing hollow all the way through the makeover programme. It was a particularly good episode too, with three stylists ominously gathered around their unfortunate victim, who had been caught on camera with her hand in a family-sized bag of salt and vinegar crisps. 'You have to help yourself, Stacy. We can only do so much.'

Any other person would have told them to stuff it. But not Stacy. She blubbed through most of the programme, whilst being ridiculed and bullied and followed into the toilet by the camera – 'We hope you haven't got any food stashed in there, Stacy!' But even through the tears and humiliation, you could see her steely determination to get what she wanted, which presumably was to be a top model. She didn't care that her wobbly behind was on view for the whole world to see. She just kept her eyes on the prize.

Millie had started out snickering at her, but now she felt strangely inadequate in comparison. Old Stacy had guts and determination. She wasn't going to sit back in the comfort zone and count her blessings.

Oh God, someone save me, thought Millie – now I'm seeing reality show contestants as role models.

The phone rang. It was Andrew.

'Millie?' he prompted, when she didn't immediately say anything.

Well, she was shocked. When she had wanted someone to save her, she hadn't meant him.

'Hi,' she said cautiously. She was glad he couldn't see her, sprawled across the couch in trackie bottoms surrounded by wrappers and a wine bottle.

'I just wanted to see how you are,' he said.

His voice reminded her of that time he'd had to wear a tuxedo to a wedding once and his dress shirt was too tight around his windpipe, and it came out all squeaky and an octave higher than usual. He must be terrified she was going to attack him.

'I'm surprised Barbara didn't tell you.' You coward, the inference was.

He cleared his throat nervously. 'I sent Barbara around because I didn't think you'd be ready to speak to me last week.'

Plus, of course, he'd needed socks. Millie wondered wildly how Barbara had got them to him. Had she chartered a cargo plane to fly all his stuff to Frankfurt? Had he flown back in the meantime? Where had he stayed – with Barbara and her nutter boyfriend? Had he been in the same country over the weekend and she hadn't known it? She might have run into him at Tesco and been caught completely unawares.

'I'm actually trying to watch the television,' she said. She wasn't. Her heart was racing. She felt that stupid hope rise in her again. Maybe Yvonne was right. A couple of weeks in Frankfurt might have been enough to bring him to his senses. Certainly, counting her meagre blessings was helping bring Millie to hers.

Then he said, 'Look, Millie, I know we've split up and everything.'

It was like someone had let all the air out of her. She shrank back against the sofa, wanting to keen in misery.

Well, at least she knew now where she stood. Apparently they had officially 'split up'. It really was over. He wasn't going to mention about her coming to Frankfurt, and biding her time until he might be ready for a baby. He wasn't going to because in his mind it wasn't even the remotest possibility.

He was waiting. Probably in case she would contradict him.

'Yes,' she said.

So while she had been keeping half an ear out for the phone, he had moved on entirely. In his head, they were finished. In her head, she had probably thought so too, but had reasonably assumed there might be some further discussion between them before they came to that mutual conclusion.

Foolish, foolish her. She was as delusional as Stacy, who really thought she was going to be up there with Kate Moss.

'I was hoping we could still stay friends,' he said more confidently, now that that nasty business was out of the way.

He couldn't even be bothered to think of something original to say. Just trot out the usual old stuff, he had probably figured. That way he couldn't go too wrong.

'I doubt it,' she told him nastily.

'Oh.' He was a bit surprised at that. There he was, ringing her up out of the goodness of his heart, and she wasn't going to play ball. 'She refused to end it amicably,' he would now be able to tell everybody, with a martyred sigh.

She was starting to get very angry. 'Why on earth would I want to stay friends with you?' she demanded.

'Millie . . .' The nervous bob was back in his voice.

'Why would you think I'd even want to *speak* to you again?'

He got down to the real reason he was ringing. 'We have things to sort out. Paperwork. The house.'

That did it. The one sanctuary left to her. 'The house is mine. It was mine before I ever had the bad luck to clap eyes on you, and if you try and get one red cent out of it, I swear to God I will fly over there and walk into your new office and tell everybody exactly what you've done.'

She surprised herself with that. And him. No doubt he was thinking of his new German colleagues, average age twenty-one-and-a-half, and how totally uncool it would be if his ex-wife were to come barging in from Ireland waving ovulation predictor sticks around in a rage.

'Look, I just want to tie things up, that's all,' he mumbled.

She just bet he did. All nice and neatly, and then he could move on with his new life without a backwards glance, leaving her to cope as best she could with the pain of childlessness.

'You don't even have the decency to wait until the marriage has gone cold,' she said, disgust colouring her voice. 'Don't go ringing me up again about this, do you hear me?'

Now he could tell everybody how bitter and unreasonable she had turned out to be. That he had tried to phone her up to see how she was, but only got dog's abuse back.

'Right,' he said.

He didn't apologise, or wish her well, or express any regret at all at how things had turned out.

'Did you ever love me?' she blurted out. Then she was mortified. But, actually, she wanted to know. Because if he had, the same way as she had loved him, then this wouldn't be happening.

'Millie . . .' he said reluctantly.

He refused to say yes, of course. Just a simple admission. A recognition that their marriage hadn't entirely been a sham.

But he wouldn't give it to her. No doubt he was afraid it would compromise him. Or add to the unpleasantness of the phone call or something.

He had no backbone. He was, she saw, a person without any real character at all. It was only now she was seeing it.

'Never mind,' she said, wanting to wash her hands of him as quickly as possible. 'Oh, and Andrew?'

'Yes?' he said.

'You would have made a lousy father anyway.'

And she hung up on him.

Chapter Nine

There was a private clinic in Ireland that advertised a sperm dona-
tion programme on their website.

'I'm just making a very initial enquiry,' Millie mumbled into the
phone. She was in the storeroom at work on her lunch break. She felt
like a fugitive.

The girl on the other end of the phone was lovely and chatty. She
wasn't a bit fazed by the word 'sperm' and repeated it at least ten times,
which Millie found rather reassuring.

'All of our donor sperm comes from Holland,' she informed Millie
confidently. Millie wondered why Holland was such a hotspot for donors.
Did they have particularly virile men over there? Or a well-developed
social conscience?

The girl went on, 'All donors go through a rigorous screening process
for any infectious diseases. The sperm is then quarantined for six months,
the donors retested, and only then is it released for use.'

Millie had a vision of numerous test tubes exploding in a laborat-
ory somewhere on the day of release.

She must stop these unseemly thoughts. What was *wrong* with her?

'What would I know about the donor?' she asked.

All she needed now was for Tommy, the maintenance guy, to walk
in looking for a light bulb or something.

'Oh, very little,' the girl assured her, as though this were an asset.
And Millie supposed that maybe it was. The way she felt today, she
wanted to go it completely alone. At least that way she only had
herself to rely on. She, for one, would not let any child down. No
backbone deficiency when it came to *her*. 'Eye colour, height, educa-
tion. That's about it. And the donor himself is assured of anonymity
by law.'

'I see.'

There was no going back then. No little crack left open for father to find child, or vice versa.

It was an enormous decision to make on behalf of somebody else.

'If you wanted to go ahead and have a second child by the same donor, then in our programme you can reserve some sperm for the future.'

Millie's stomach rose nervously. 'Let's just take one thing at a time, will we?'

'Of course. Anyway, we'll go through everything in detail when you come in.'

'In?' said Millie, rather stupidly, as though there were an option to get inseminated over the phone.

'We could see you Tuesday week for a chat.'

She made it sound very inviting, as though Millie would be going for a pleasant coffee morning amongst friends. Millie was tempted. Plus, the photos on the website showed a lovely, bright waiting room with several couples relaxing on leather sofas or even surfing the Net at computer stations while they waited for the medical gurus to do whatever was necessary. Another photo showed a smiling doctor in a white coat, holding a chart upon which he seemed to be completing a large, elaborate tick. Another success story, surely. There appeared to be no sign at all of the sperm donors, but of course they were all in Holland, probably drinking coffee too, and surfing the Net in another waiting room.

Millie wanted to be a part of it. She wanted some doctor to do the necessaries, before triumphantly marking her chart with a large tick.

Still her nerve wavered. 'I'd have to think about it a bit more first,' she demurred.

But not for too long. She would be forty in eight months' time.

'Sure,' the girl said. 'And have a chat with your husband.'

Millie was a bit taken aback by that. 'My husband?'

She had a brief image of his face, somewhere in Frankfurt, upon learning that she had been phoning up fertility clinics.

'We have a counselling service available for participants in all our programmes.' The girl sounded tactful. 'Many men can find this particular programme difficult. If he'd like us to send him some initial information . . .'

Oh, she was tempted; a lovely, fat brown envelope full of leaflets on sperm landing on his office desk at coffee break.

Still, in this business that was just called time wasting.

'My husband has no problem whatsoever with it,' Millie assured the girl. 'In fact, he's told me I can do whatever I want.'

It was true in a way.

'We'd still need to see you as a couple,' the girl insisted.

The conversation was feeling a little less friendly now. Was Millie just encountering roadblock number one?

'Why?'

'It's normal procedure to treat patients as a couple. For instance, we would want to do a sperm analysis on him. We would do a count, and test for mobility and motility.'

Millie was now wishing that she would stop saying the word sperm.

'Oh, his mobility is very poor,' she assured the girl at the clinic. 'And his motility even worse. Zilch, I think, at the last test.' She had no idea what motility meant. But it felt rather good to put him down so thoroughly behind his back. 'The doctors said he was one of the worst cases they'd ever seen,' she added spitefully. 'A total no-hoper.'

The girl was a bit taken aback at that. 'We'd still need to assess him again. It mightn't be as bad as you think. And levels can fluctuate up and down.'

Millie knew it was time to stop pussyfooting around things. 'Look,' she said. 'I'd be seeing you as a single person.'

Immediately the whole tone changed.

'You don't have a husband?' She sounded hurt, like Millie had lied to her.

'I do, unfortunately, but we've broken up through no fault of mine. And now I want a baby on my own.'

There was another uncomfortable silence.

'I'm very sorry, but we don't treat singletons.'

Millie felt herself flushing. What was she, diseased?

'Can I ask why?'

The girl sounded unhappy. 'We can only treat couples. If it was up to me . . .'

'Why can't it be up to you?' Millie tried for a little joke. There must be a way around this. These were people who had developed cutting-edge technology, yet they were getting all biblical when it came to who was going to benefit from it.

'I'm very sorry,' the girl said again.

Millie had never been militant – well, with Jaz around there had never been any need – but right now she felt there was something important to be said, and she was going to say it.

'In other words you operate a policy of discrimination?'

The girl, no doubt used to this kind of attack, had gone into official mode. 'I understand you're disappointed. But we can only treat couples.'

Millie came out from under the pile of coats she had been cowering behind. There would be no hiding from any of this.

'Well, then,' she said loudly, 'I guess you won't be treating me.'

There was no doubt about it: looking for a sperm donor on your own seemed to be a highly questionable thing to do.

The next clinic she rang gave her the same response as above, only the girl was less chatty.

Millie lost her patience with the third clinic. 'Look, do you treat singles?' she asked straight out.

That flustered them. No doubt they were expecting the usual embarrassed, mumbled enquiry, from people who had already lived through numerous monthly disappointments; people who were upset and vulnerable, and who didn't know what was wrong with them, except that something was.

Anyway, the answer to Millie's question was, again, no.

'Is it for pious reasons?' she asked. 'You know, that you disagree with the morals of it or something?'

'I'm just the receptionist,' the woman on the other end said in fright.

'All right, but do you think you could ask the boss and get back to me? I'm just interested to know why.'

Then the woman lowered her voice abruptly. 'Look,' she hissed, 'we don't broadcast this. But we do treat lesbians.'

So Millie had found company: lesbians, who no doubt had to put up with the same crap on the phone as she did.

'Do I have to pretend to be one?' she enquired.

'I'm saying that we have an unofficial policy, so to speak. Not everybody has to be in a heterosexual couple.' The woman was practically whispering now.

Millie whispered too. 'Do we get a separate entrance around the back?'

'No, no,' the receptionist assured her earnestly. 'If you want, I'll ask the doctor. I'm sure we'd be able to help you.'

Millie wondered whether all her consultations would be held in furtive whispers. Would they make her sign a confidentiality clause so as not to incriminate them? She supposed she should be grateful they were prepared to treat her at all.

But she found that she wasn't. She felt she was being judged. She was angry. Was this going to be her baby's first introduction to the world? Embarrassed whispers and back-door policies? Because, officially, single women could not avail themselves of donor sperm in Ireland.

'Thanks anyway,' she said. 'But don't bother.'

But if Millie thought the clinics were judgemental, then she wasn't prepared for the heated debate that raged on the Internet on the whole subject when she ventured onto it that night.

'In the name of all that's right and holy, would you not get down on your knees and pray to the Lord for the right man to come along?' one person implored a single woman who had naïvely confessed online that she was going down the donor sperm route. 'Put your trust in Him who is great and He will send a nice man to look after you and any baby you might have together. I'll light a candle for you tonight.' Hopefully she had set fire to herself.

'You selfish scut,' another objector bellowed. 'Thinking only of yourself and not some poor, confused child who will grow up wondering forever who her daddy is, and all you'll be able to tell her is that he's some penniless lout who jacked off over a dirty magazine to earn fifty quid. Shame on you.'

And, indeed, after reading several more pages of recriminations Millie felt so ashamed that she slunk behind the couch for a while, head down, and cheeks boiling with mortification for even thinking up such a scheme. She was bad. No, she was *evil*.

Reason prevailed around half seven, which handily coincided with dinnertime. She sat at the kitchen table, grimly forking in a salad – unconsciously she had started eating healthily again in preparation for a pregnancy – and got very cross. Bloody cows. The ones who said the nastiest things were usually the ones who had three or four children at home, making them, in Millie's opinion, the least qualified people to comment on anybody else's struggle to have a baby.

'I love myself unconditionally,' she said defiantly a couple of times, and refused to reach for the Ben & Jerry's tub.

Dennis rang just as she was washing up and innocently enquired how she was.

'I'm thinking of committing a crime,' she told him darkly.

'What?' His hearing wasn't what it used to be and he was obviously wondering now whether it was letting him down.

'Never mind.' She could never confide in Dennis about donor sperm. It would send him into a total spin. He would go red, then white, before fumbling furiously in his cardigan pockets as though looking for something. A change of subject, perhaps.

But supposing she *did* go through with it? He and Mum would have to know. She couldn't pretend that she had accidentally got pregnant. Even they knew that there was nothing lurking on toilet seats or in Jacuzzis any more.

They'd have a hard job explaining a new baby to their cronies in their road – especially as Dad had only got up the courage at the weekend to tell them that Millie had broken up with Andrew. Would he show them photos of Millie's baby, like he had with all of Oona's? 'The chin is our side of the family,' he might tell them haltingly, embarrassingly, 'and the, um, ginger hair is obviously from the other side.'

Millie wanted to hide behind the couch again. Who would have thought the whole thing was so complicated? She just wanted a baby, that was all. Why did it have to come with so much baggage?

Married people had it so easy. No moral dilemmas. No trouncing from vigilantes on the Internet. Millie began to deeply resent them.

'I'm worried about your mother,' Dennis announced now.

'Why?' She had been fine when Millie had phoned earlier. In fact, she hadn't wanted to talk to Millie at all, because her soaps were on and she wanted to get a good seat in the television room. That Alice one was always trying to block everybody's view, with her big fluffy white hair. It was like an enormous cotton bud, Nuala had declared, and if she wasn't careful someone might sneak up on her in her sleep and cut it all off. Then, as though perplexed by her own churlishness, she had asked Millie, 'Did I really say that?'

Millie wondered whether Dennis was finally going to admit that he too had noticed how oddly she was behaving recently.

Not a hope.

'The longer she stays in there, the more chance there is that she'll pick up one of those hospital superbugs,' he said fussily.

'What?'

'MRSA or one of those. It gets in through wounds and infections. And with that toe of hers . . .'

'Dad, I think you should go to the pub.'

'What?'

'Look, Mum is being looked after really well. She couldn't be in a better place. And now that they're keeping her till the weekend, why don't you take the extra few days to relax? Play a round of golf.'

'I haven't played golf in years.' He made it sound like an offence.

'So take it up again. Oona and I were only saying the other day that you need more time for yourself.'

Actually, they'd been saying that between him and Mum, they were being driven up the walls. In fact, Oona had turned around to her own kids and said, 'The minute I hit seventy put me in a home, even if there's not a thing wrong with me. Don't give it another thought. There's a nice place at the foot of the Wicklow Hills called Sleepy Hollow or something – I might even put myself down on the waiting list now. The only thing I'd ask is that you call by on my birthday and Christmas with a couple of bottles of wine. Better make it a case.'

'We will, Mammy,' they had promised.

'You little sweethearts,' Oona had said, hugging them tightly.

'I suppose I could ring up Bernard,' Dennis reluctantly conceded now. 'I think he's still a member of the golf club.'

'There you go! And your golf clubs are under the stairs – I saw them the other day when we were cleaning. The fresh air would do you the world of good.'

She felt like she was humouring him. But somebody had to. It must be pretty tough being with Mum all day every day, especially if she got out of bed on the wrong side. And then him dancing attendance on her, when there wasn't a thing wrong with her (allegedly). There was more chance of him keeling over. Mum would probably step over him to get to her copy of *Hello!*.

'You'll ring Bernard?'

'I'll ring Bernard,' he said, sounding bullied. 'And don't you go committing any crimes.'

He was delighted with his little quip, and rang off in good humour, saying he was going to dust off his golf clubs.

Millie was nearly sorry he was gone. Now it was just her and sperm donors. Or the lack thereof. She decided if the Irish clinics wouldn't do the job for her, or at least not without making her feel she was doing something wrong, then she would go to the English ones. She went online again. They were much more liberal over there, weren't they?

Whether they were or weren't didn't matter at the end of the day, because they had hardly any sperm donors. It was nothing to do with the morals of it all, but rather a new law that removed anonymity. Apparently not too many men were keen on coming out from behind their magazines to be identified by their offspring or, maybe more saliently, being stiffed for school fees or medical bills further down the line. Even fewer of them wanted some hitherto unknown child, but with the family nose, turning up on the doorstep some Sunday afternoon unannounced to interrupt a peaceful family lunch.

'There's only one sperm donor in the whole of Scotland,' someone else moaned on the Internet. Millie didn't know whether it was true or not but it sounded fairly bleak. 'What are we going to do at all?'

Give up. That's what Millie felt like doing. It was hard enough to grapple with the ethics involved, but when it became physically impossible to get the procedure done, then what choice had she got?

The private fertility clinics in England had a waiting list of up to three years. Some of them didn't even *have* a waiting list, because there was no point – they had no sperm.

At the end of three years on a waiting list, Millie would be forty-two. What chance was there then? By that stage she'd have to go for a donor egg along with the sperm, because her own would probably be beyond redemption. Try explaining baby photos after *that* one.

Then, just as she was about to turn off the computer for the night and go to bed, she happened to stumble across the solution to all her problems.

It was simple.

She would go abroad.

Chapter Ten

B rendan was a big hit at the local mother and toddlers' group. One of the first things he did was to request, politely, that the word 'parent' be substituted for 'mother', and they all hastily agreed, throwing up their hands in horror at their own sexism.

'You're the first father we've ever had,' Nancy said apologetically.

Brendan assured her that he didn't frighten easily, and when he turned up to the Parish Centre that first Thursday morning in tight jeans and with a cute child in tow they didn't know what had hit them.

'Lovely flapjacks, Nancy,' he said appreciatively. 'You must give me the recipe.'

At first nobody was sure what to say. Some of them didn't even want him there, if the truth be told. Now they couldn't gossip about Emily O'Driscoll's appalling new haircut, not with a man in their midst. Others had never met a house-husband before, except for that fellow at school who wore green corduroy trousers and smelled like a wet dog. Wusses, that's what their own husbands called the kind of men who left their womenfolk to bring home the bacon. Not that Brendan looked like a wuss; not with those bulging biceps that were brushing accidentally against Nancy, who was looking a bit red in the face.

Finally, as everybody was wondering what to say, didn't Brendan himself break the ice by spilling his coffee down his front and blurting, 'Fuck' in front of all the mothers and children. Old habits died hard.

He was immediately appalled. Half the mothers broke out into nervous giggles.

'That was unforgivable,' he said. 'I'll leave now, this very minute.'

'No, no!' they all chorused. They assured him that language lapses happened to them at the best of times. Meanwhile, Nancy dabbed at his chest with a napkin.

'I've had a horrible morning with the kids,' he confessed to them all.

He didn't need to say another word; finally, a man who understood the stresses and strains of looking after children single-handed! It wasn't just women, in their unpaid, unappreciated, dogsbody jobs that went by the fancy title of 'Stay-at-Home Mum'. Who wouldn't shout obscenities after the mornings most of them routinely had, trying to stuff one or other of the kids into a school uniform while the rest of them pelted cereal at each other over the kitchen table? And with a husband conveniently at his desk in the city since half past seven that morning, oblivious. The very same husband who had the gall to call men like Brendan a wuss!

A fresh cup of coffee was poured for Brendan and he was welcomed into the circle as one of their own.

The male perspective was a great addition, they were declaring piously to each other in the Parish Centre kitchen within weeks — particularly for the children, who barely saw their own fathers for five minutes a week. And Brendan was marvellous with them. Look at him out there now, playing football with them on the front lawn! And they did look. Sometimes if it was warm he took his jumper off.

He was extremely useful about the place, too. He did all sorts of odd jobs that the mothers could probably do themselves, if only they could be bothered. Instead they stood at the foot of the ladder as Brendan climbed up to the high ceiling in the centre to replace the light bulb that had been gone for weeks. 'Well done, Brendan!' they would call, and he would glow with pleasure. Then Nancy's car wouldn't start one day, and she was all set to ring the AA but Brendan wouldn't hear of it, and he got under the bonnet himself and fixed it in no time at all. He replaced the rusty lock on the back gate and he was the only one young Carl, fractious and bold, would listen to when things got out of hand at the sandbox.

'Don't make me put you over my knee, young man,' he would threaten. He would assure the mums that he didn't mean it at all, of course, but it did the trick and Carl would slink off, chastened.

The numbers in the playgroup began to go up a bit, it was noted. Women who hadn't been coming for weeks began to turn up. 'Look at Terri,' Nancy said in disgust. 'Wearing make-up!' Nancy was wearing some too.

They went on a nature walk one Thursday, and into town to a museum on the bus another morning. The kids loved it. And they had started a rota where people took it in turns to bake something to have at coffee time. It had turned into a bit of a friendly competition.

Brendan had brought in his delicious gingerbread two weeks ago, and it was agreed that it was the winner so far.

'Who said men can't cook?' he would rag them all, and they would chuckle and pull their chairs a bit closer.

'We're going on a picnic next Thursday,' he announced at home that evening. He was making big long lists of things to take. 'Nancy's asked if I can pop over to pick up her gazebo in case it rains.'

'I'm sure she has,' Oona said. She informed Millie, 'She fancies Brendan.'

'Naturally,' said Brendan with a bit of a swagger. 'They all do. Did I tell you I looked under Terri's car bonnet this week?'

'You should start charging,' said Oona. 'Be a nice little sideline for you.'

'I think they're all dying to meet you,' said Brendan. He winked at Millie. 'Nancy was asking me only this week what you were like. Maybe you should pop down, see the competition.'

'Ugh. No thanks,' said Oona. She had never been able to stand mother and toddler groups even when she'd been at home full time. There had been far too much talk about breastfeeding for her liking, and they had all looked shocked that time she suggested they put the children into the supermarket crèche for an hour and go for a boozy lunch.

'I'll have to tell them I'm separated so,' Brendan informed her. 'That'll be sure to get them excited.'

Oona lifted a cynical eyebrow. 'Stop it now before I get jealous.'

Brendan looked at her. The jokiness was suddenly gone. 'No danger of that, is there?'

And he left the room. Millie looked after him. It had all been so nice and civil too, with cosy chats over tea and slabs of Brendan's gingerbread – it really was delicious. Oona moaned in between slices that she had put on five pounds since Brendan had given up work. In comparison, Millie's stomach was churning so much that she could barely choke down a couple of bites.

'Don't mind him,' Oona said by way of explanation. 'Gary was up twice during the night with earache. Brendan wouldn't let me take my turn. And now today he's wrecked, and grumpy, and frankly, Nancy is welcome to him.' Then she looked at Millie and said, 'So what's wrong with *you*?'

'Me?' Millie jumped guiltily.

As usual nothing escaped Oona. 'You've done something, haven't you?'

'Done something!' Millie managed to scoff. 'Like what?'

'I don't know. But you've been squirming around in your chair the whole afternoon. You weren't even listening properly while I was telling you what that shop assistant told me about my colouring, and how I should never, ever wear purple.'

Oona had had more enforced time off, thanks to Brendan, and had ended up in the make-up department of Brown Thomas having a makeover. She had come home wearing so many cosmetics that the children hadn't recognised her. 'Mammy, what happened to your eyes?' Aoifa had asked fearfully. Not to talk of all the money she'd spent buying the actual products – all this free time was starting to take a terrible toll on the family finances.

'I *was* listening. And nothing's up with me,' Millie insisted, even while her face turned incriminatingly red under Oona's penetrating stare.

'Has Andrew been in touch or something?' she demanded.

'He certainly has not.' For good measure Millie added, 'Thank God.'

Oona lifted an eyebrow. 'You've changed your tune.'

'I have not. I never sang any tune, except that I wanted a baby, and that if he didn't then it was over. Which it is.'

'At least you don't look too upset about it today.'

'Have I not been upset enough?' Millie demanded. 'Have I not cried and screamed and got drunk and comfort-ate my way into size sixteen pants? What do you want me to do, start bawling all over again at your kitchen table?'

Oona cast a look into the living room. The children were peacefully playing with an educational jigsaw that Brendan had bought. Actually, they were trying to stuff the pieces through the cracks in the floorboards, but they were doing it quietly.

'Better not,' she said. She looked at Millie with genuine concern. 'You know, it's great to hear you talking like that, Millie. Bouncing back. I was worried about you there for a while. The way you were going on about the whole baby thing that day at Mum and Dad's, it was like you were a bit obsessed.' Then she reached over to squeeze Millie's hand, which was rather alarming. She usually only did that when she'd had too much gin. 'Look, I know the last few weeks have been hard on you. And then wanting a child so much . . . giving that up is not going to be easy. But I think you're coping really, really well.'

'Yes,' said Millie primly. 'Thank you.'

If only Oona knew. In Millie's back pocket lay a printout of an email she had received yesterday afternoon from Instituto Familia Alicante, or IFA.

It felt like stolen property: warmth emanated from it in waves, burning her backside through the material of her jeans.

She hadn't meant to go emailing them. She had just gone on to their website to have a look at the clinic, after it was recommended by another woman on a forum in Millie's same position. Millie was fully sure that it would be some poky place set down a dark alley, probably in a red-light district, and that clients would have to knock three times before being furtively ushered in.

It was a pleasant surprise to find that it was a rather regal-looking period building sitting on the main thoroughfare, with lovely hanging baskets in the front, and a bright red door that was half open. A simple plaque on the wall unapologetically announced its name and the nature of its business. It looked, well, normal.

So did the pictures of the staff. And none of them was wagging a judgemental finger, she was glad to see. There was no 'Married People Only' sign over the door. The doctors and nurses and embryologists smiled kindly out at her from the web pages, wearing coats that were reassuringly white. Even better, when she clicked to see what services they offered, she found that they had donor sperm by the bucketful. Or at least there was no shortage of it. The clinic emphasised that it specialised in treating patients from overseas.

Which would be Millie. But still she was reluctant to ring them up. Her bad experiences with the Irish clinics were putting her off. She was worried too that the person on the other end would speak Spanish – naturally – and Millie would have to explain her business in pidgin English. She knew some Spanish from school, but only things like, 'I would like to buy some juicy apples, please.' She had never been taught how to ask for donor sperm.

It was easier to email. And it was comfortingly anonymous. Anonymity was becoming a defining feature of this whole business, she was rapidly realising. So she typed a few stilted lines explaining her status; single, hopefully still fertile, and seeking donor IUI. Presumably they would know what she meant.

She herself had been completely baffled by the various abbreviations even up to yesterday; on the Internet forums women were undergoing a variety of procedures from IVF to ICSI to FET (which was something-egg-transfer. Flaming?). There was other jargon too – if the women weren't 'stimming' they were 'down-regging' and giving out yards about their insensitive, moronic DH while they were at it. Millie was sure DH was a particular fertility doctor – a Dr Hardy, perhaps – but surely they couldn't all have the same doctor. And why didn't they just ditch him if he was that bad? Then she found a list of abbreviations and discovered that DH was Dear Husband. She got the hang of it quickly after that. It wasn't that hard really. All the procedures were just a means to the same end: a baby.

Still, just in case the Spanish clinic didn't know what IUI was, or something got lost in translation and she ended up getting some other procedure done that she hadn't planned on at all, Millie wrote down 'donor intrauterine insemination' in full, even though it sounded a bit too bovine for her liking.

She sent the email off and let out her breath. They would probably send her a brochure in a few weeks or something.

The 'ping' of the computer half an hour later announcing that she had email nearly made her jump out of her skin.

It was them. She looked at the email in the inbox for an age before she plucked up the nerve to open it up.

She needn't have worried. The IUI was no problem, they typed back, using the abbreviation. Her single status was no problem. Her own fertility might be lower due to her age, but they thought there wouldn't be a problem. The waiting list was very short, so no problem there.

Everything was no problem. They – or rather a woman reassuringly called Maria – said 'no problem' about four times. To Millie's ears they were the sweetest two words she had heard in a long time.

Hardly able to believe her boldness, she emailed back again. What was the procedure for getting treatment done?

Another ping, only ten minutes later this time, scarcely knocked a bother out of her. Already she felt in a cosy relationship with Maria. She would probably find out that they had gone to school together or something.

If she wanted to go ahead, Maria wrote, she would have to fly over to the clinic twice. Once for the initial consultation and once for the actual treatment. Maria, in the meantime, would email her some information about the clinic, its treatments, and the doctors she would be working with. It was the first mention Millie had ever heard of working 'with' doctors – usually she went into consulting rooms expecting to be talked down to, and she was rarely disappointed. Maria also promised to send her a list of accommodation and the clinic's costs for treatment. The clinic also provided a translator, if necessary, although they all spoke English (Millie felt ashamed at her own lack of Spanish) and there was a guide who could pick Millie up at the airport and ferry her to her hotel and then the clinic if she so chose.

It all sounded so *easy*. Millie could hardly believe it. Why would she bother with the Irish clinics at all? Especially as it was thirty-two degrees in the Algarve today, and the sun was shining . . .

No problem, thought Millie mistily, imagining herself relaxing in the heat whilst possibly being pregnant at the same time.

Not that she would find out while she was still in the Algarve or anything. By the time she was due to take a pregnancy test she would be back on home soil.

The thought brought her up short. Pregnancy tests? The *Algarve*? Sitting at Oona's kitchen table now, in rain-soaked Ireland, and with Oona looking at her grumpily, she felt her excitement die out with a damp fizz. No problem? Fuck that.

She couldn't even bring herself to tell her own *sister*. It was all right running the idea past the girls in work, but confiding in Oona was something else entirely. What if Oona seriously disagreed with it? What if she went and told Mum and Dad, and the three of them threw up their hands in horror? They might even be so appalled that they might try to talk her out of it, or else refuse to have anything to do with it. Millie might be strong enough to go through this by herself, but she didn't know if she could bear her family's disapproval.

It might look easy, going to Spain. And logically it was. But it didn't really change the fundamentals, Millie realised.

Oona hadn't said anything in ages, she noted. It was most unlike her. She was definitely off form.

'And what's wrong with *you*?' Millie asked keenly. the sisterly perception thing could cut both ways.

'Apart from the fact that I'm painted like a monkey?' Oona enquired.

The make-up had already started to slide down her face. She wasn't the kind of person who could hold onto hairdos, make-up or clean clothes for any length of time. The mascara was pooling under her eyes and would no doubt give the children another fright unless she went and wiped it off.

'I know,' she suddenly said brightly. 'Will we go out?'

Millie was very surprised. 'Out?'

'Yes.'

'Where?'

'On the town. And don't look at me like that. It's Saturday night, for God's sake. You're single.'

'Thank you for reminding me.'

'Someone has to,' Oona said bluntly. 'There's no sense in burying yourself in my kitchen on a Saturday night.' She fluffed out her already frizzy hair. 'Besides, I'll never look this good again.' She caught sight of her reflection in the glass-fronted press by the cooker, and amended it to, 'Well, goodish anyway.'

Millie didn't want to go out on the town. She wanted to go home and reread her emails. She wanted to lie on the sofa and dream.

'But I thought Brendan had got a movie out and you were having a quiet night in,' she reminded Oona.

It was quite a romantic movie too, Millie had noted – *Sleepless in Seattle*. Millie bet that Brendan already had plans for tonight, and they didn't involve babysitting while Oona went out and got drunk.

She suddenly felt tearful: sitting in with movies and bottles of wine had been what she and Andrew had done best. They hadn't always been romantic – 'Don't make me watch that shite,' Andrew had begged that time she had produced *Bridget Jones* – but the two of them would snuggle up on the sofa together, her legs thrown across his lap, and he would circle the inside of her ankle with his thumb.

Tears rose unbidden. She would love to be going home to that tonight. The thoughts of rereading her clinic emails, with no one to share them with, suddenly seemed lonely and desperate.

Across from her Oona gave a tiny sigh. 'Oh,' she said. 'I'd forgotten.' She went to get up. 'I'd better go and take this muck off my face so.'

'Leave it on, you look lovely,' Millie urged. 'Give Brendan a treat.'

There was a funny look on Oona's face. After the little spat between them earlier, perhaps Millie had said the wrong thing.

Oona just said, 'Hm.'

There was a bit of an awkward pause. But maybe Millie just imagined it. She already felt incriminated by the email in her pocket, and the fact that she was keeping it from Oona.

Still, there was no need to go discussing things with her family just now, she decided. She felt herself relax. After all, she hadn't actually done anything yet.

Chapter Eleven

Mum had been home for a fortnight. The good news was that her toe had recovered well, although she would have to mind it for a while. The bad news was that she had got very used to being waited on hand and foot in the hospital, and seemed to expect the same level of service at home.

'Can somebody make me a cup of tea?' she shouted from her lair in front of the television.

Dennis hopped to it pronto. She liked it in a cup and saucer now, like they used to serve in the hospital, and with a biscuit on the side: a bourbon cream, maybe, or a nice ginger nut.

'She's flipping institutionalised,' Oona complained. Mum had been very put out when Oona had called over with the children on Tuesday outside the usual hospital visiting times. And hadn't brought grapes. 'All she needs is a bell and she's away.'

But why would she need a bell when the hospital had provided her with a sturdy metal crutch, which she had taken to banging on the floor when Dennis was a bit slow? It came in particularly handy upstairs, when she could give the ceiling a good clatter, propelling him towards the landing at break-neck speed.

But he didn't seem to mind at all. In fact he saw it as his duty. He had come over all protective since her hospital 'ordeal' (her word), and wouldn't let anybody pitch in to help at all.

'But that's why we're here,' Oona said. 'To help. You hardly think it's because we actually want to see either of you.'

Dennis was too puffed to manage a retort. He had already been up and down the stairs about fifteen times, getting Nuala's bed socks and her magazines and popping a hot-water bottle into her side of the bed. He looked strangely exhilarated by his efforts too, which was just plain weird.

111

'You girls can go,' he kept insisting. 'I can manage your mother just fine.'

'She's had a toe job, Dad, not brain surgery,' Oona pointed out baldly.

'I heard that,' Nuala chipped in from the living room. 'And I need some more milk whenever anybody's got a minute, or are you all too busy standing about talking about me?'

When she spoke like that, it was like there was nothing in the world wrong with her. Which there wasn't, Millie kept reminding herself. Or at least nothing that anybody else had noticed. There was Oona off to get more milk, sighing and grumbling aloud, 'You're an awful old woman, do you know that?' And Nuala had cackled, just like normal.

Yet yesterday Millie had got a smell: a sour, rancid smell in the living room when she had bent over to collect Mum's empty tea cups. It dawned on her that it was coming from Mum: Mum, the shopaholic, the great lover of fashion, who would never leave the house without a dab of perfume on.

'This probably sounds very silly, but has Mum had a wash recently?' she had asked Dennis, half-joking.

Dennis had been warming some soup on the stove. He didn't turn to look at her. 'Not in a few days. We haven't had time, what with the foot and everything. I'll run a bath for her this evening.'

A few days? The smell Millie had got was from someone who hadn't washed in a lot longer than that. Maybe not since the hospital.

'I'll stay and help,' she offered.

'Oh, there's no need.'

'I know, but I'd like to.'

'That bathroom is too small for us all. Thanks anyway, but we're probably better on our own.'

He must have got her into the bath last night, because there was no smell off her today. Millie stuck her nose right down close to have a good sniff when she went in to take her empty cup. Nuala was quite offended.

'What? What?' she had said.

'Nothing.'

'Here, is there any word of Andrew?'

She was still trying to make up for her gaff that day at the hospital. Millie could tell that she still wasn't sure of the exact nature of the offence, but was aware that she had definitely offended.

Millie supposed she should appreciate her efforts.

'No.'

'I don't like to think of you in that house all on your own,' Nuala fretted. That was her biggest worry; she didn't like it that Millie was obviously heartbroken, of course, but the immediate concern was that some thug would get wind of the fact that Andrew was in Frankfurt (how, was anybody's guess) and break into the house in the dead of night. 'Set the alarm before you go to bed, won't you?'

'I will.'

Nuala took some comfort from this assurance. She squeezed Millie's hand. 'There's somebody else out there for you, you know.'

'Ah Jesus, Mam.'

'I know, I know. It's probably a bit too soon to be thinking that way. But you just wait and see.'

Maybe she was right. And it wasn't as though Millie had an awful lot else to do except sit around and wait.

'Look, here's *Head to Toe* on the telly now,' Nuala announced, pleased. 'It'll take your mind off things.' *Head to Toe* was her favourite fashion programme. The presenters were always so nicely turned out.

But Millie wasn't in the mood for a discussion on this season's colour – which seemed to be brown once again – and she retreated to the kitchen.

Dennis was there, quizzing Orla. 'Do you know a recipe for fish pie?'

Oona just laughed.

Millie was suspicious. 'Why?'

'She had fish pie in the hospital and she wants it again. I just thought I'd make it for her.'

Fish pie contained Omega 3. Rakes of it. And Mum didn't like fish. It was unlikely she'd suddenly developed a taste for the hospital version.

But Dennis just gazed harmlessly back.

'Why don't you go off for a round of golf with Bernard?' she said suddenly.

Get him out of the house, she decided. That way she and Oona could have a good snoop around and see what was really going on. Because something was. There he was, cooking fish pies, yet failing to notice that his own wife smelt like a rotten old trout herself.

Dennis wasn't budging. 'I'm in the middle of getting dinner.'

'I'll get dinner.'

'I'll drink wine and supervise her,' Oona chipped in.

'It'll be ready just as you get back,' Millie promised him.

But Dennis had a final trick up his sleeve, 'I've given it up. Golf.'

'What? But you've only just taken it up again.'

'I know. But I told Bernard I wouldn't be down any more now that your mother's home from hospital.'

All the more reason he should keep it up.

'We're here to help, Dad. Oona and I. We could easily come and sit with her any night while you're down at the club.'

'Oh, I don't think so,' he said, as though they were bound to make a balls up of things the minute his back was turned.

'She won't thank you, you know,' Oona said. 'If you go on like this, you'll only burn yourself out. And then someone will have to look after *you*. It might even be me, God help us both.'

He wasn't listening. He fussed and fidgeted and implied they were in his way, until eventually the lack of welcome drove them both towards the front door.

'I'd better be going anyway,' Oona said with a sigh. 'Brendan's going over to have a look at Nancy's gazebo, and I think I'm required to stand at the door looking jealous.'

Millie wondered whether Nancy really *was* making a play for Brendan. Could she be the reason that the sun had stopped shining on Brendan and Oona's idyllic domestic arrangements?

There was another possibility: Oona might be pregnant again. She always got moody, or rather moodier than usual, when she was expecting.

'I don't even need to do a test,' she had said grimly on her last pregnancy. 'I'm like a bitch from hell. I just *know*.' Her boobs usually popped out like two air bags as well within days of conception.

Millie desperately tried to remember now what Oona's boobs had been like before she'd put on her coat at the front door. Had they been bigger than usual? The way she had been sitting at the table had made it hard to see. Not that Millie had been actively looking or anything.

Supposing she *was* pregnant? Millie turned the possibility over in her head and felt a wave of jealousy so strong that she was shocked.

Oona, pregnant. Again. With number four. And Millie resolutely not pregnant. And never likely to be at this rate. The clinic email had been put away in a drawer sometime during the week, due to lack of nerve.

She might as well be honest about things, at least to herself – she would be gutted by such news. No, sickened. Appalled. Green with envy.

All very unattractive qualities in anybody, and especially in a sister who was expected to be supportive, and who had genuinely rejoiced in her last three turns at becoming an auntie.

But it was different back then. Millie had had a husband. And expectations of becoming a mother herself. She'd had no idea then that she would be forever destined to stand on the sidelines.

She didn't even think she could pretend to be happy about it. It would be too much effort. She would probably stop going around to the house to avoid the sight of Oona blossoming – or, rather, ballooning, which was what she usually did.

And there Millie would be, flat as a boy (well, apart from that the little mound of fat from all that ice cream).

Oona would be tactful, of course. She would do her absolute best to spare Millie's feelings. She and Brendan would be killed playing the whole thing down, and would have the children warned on pain of death not to go talking about the new baby in front of Auntie Millie. Oona would try to pretend she wasn't having one at all, and that its arrival was an entirely unexpected event.

And then Millie would be faced with a newborn. Her sister's newborn. She would, no doubt, hold the baby, feed it, cuddle it, wishing with every fibre of her being that it was hers.

She couldn't bear it. She really couldn't. If Oona announced she was pregnant Millie would move. To France or something. Or India, even further away. She would seek out a sleepy village full of old people, where there were no babies at all.

But that was just running away, wasn't it? Even if Oona wasn't pregnant, somebody else would be sooner or later. Someone in work – Jaz had been looking a bit broody again – or one of the neighbours, or the girl behind the counter in the Spar. There was no getting away from pregnant women, even in India.

So she might as well just face it. Babies were everywhere. She couldn't blame her own childlessness on other people; especially when she had choices. She didn't *have* to be childless. Didn't she have an email at home that offered her a way to have a baby too?

Maybe it was time put up or shut up.

And at that, the fog of indecision and procrastination that had defined her life for weeks seemed to lift. All right, so the Instituto Familia Alicante wasn't an ideal solution. She'd far rather have gone down the traditional route. But she had done her homework. She knew the pros and cons. She had thought it through as best she could, and any decision was an informed one, even if it would never be a perfect one.

'See you, Mum!' she shouted, following Oona out the front door.

'Oh, yes, see you, love,' said Nuala, barely turning around from the television.

But Millie didn't care; she felt energised and uplifted and excited. She went home that evening and before she could agonise about it any more she emailed Maria at the clinic and made an appointment.

Chapter Twelve

'I need you to measure my FSH,' she told Dr Mooney down at the surgery the following Friday morning.

'Your FSH?' Dr Mooney said, looked rather too startled for someone who had only recently been preaching to her about the evils of raised FSH. Well, now was his chance.

'Yes,' Millie confirmed nicely. 'My follicle stimulating hormone.'

He looked disapproving now. He wasn't too keen when patients flouted their knowledge in front of him. 'Leave the diagnosis to me,' was his favourite saying in the world. As far as he was concerned, the Internet was the source of all evil – singularly responsible for sending people into his surgery in a panic that they had a brain tumour, when often it was because they were wearing shirts that were a neck size too small. Oh, the stories he could tell about bird flu panic and mothers refusing to give their children the MMR vaccine all because of some scare story they had read about on the Internet. Also, he had found himself put on the spot several times recently by computer-literate patients who asked probing medical questions about things they knew nothing about, and nor did he.

'You said it was an indication of my ovarian reserve,' Millie reminded him. 'I have no idea what shape my eggs are in and I thought I would, you know, just get it checked out.' She smiled harmlessly.

But he wasn't falling for it. 'Is there any particular reason why you're worried?'

Now she was going to be forced into all the white lies. She gave a little sigh. She had never been great at lying. She hoped her face didn't start going its usual puce.

'My husband and I have been trying for a baby,' she told him. At least that was true, if a little out of date.

He frowned for a bit, then his face cleared. 'Ah, yes! Andrew, isn't it?'

117

'Yes,' said Millie, beaming like a happy wife.

'How's his asthma?' Dr Mooney enquired chattily.

'Much better,' Millie assured him, even as she hoped he was choking for his last breath in some dusty office in Frankfurt. 'So . . . the FSH test?'

But instead of whipping out a syringe, Dr Mooney was opening up her file on his computer. Millie sighed. This wasn't going to be the short appointment she had hoped for.

'How long have you been trying now?'

'Three months,' she said, without thinking.

'Oh, that's nothing,' Dr Mooney said. He lectured, 'It takes the average healthy couple six months to conceive. Really, the best thing to do is to try and relax about it, and I just bet you'll be back here in another three months, pregnant.'

Well, hopefully, but not in the way he thought. But first she had to get the damned FSH test done.

'Actually, it's been more like five months,' she told him. It was nearly the truth. There had been the three months of active 'trying' with Andrew, then on the fourth month he had stormed out on Day 14 (*why* couldn't he have waited just one more day?). And he had already been gone nearly a month.

'I see,' said Dr Mooney. He pondered for a moment before enquiring, 'And you're sure you're having sexual intercourse at the right time of the month?'

'Positive,' said Millie.

Next thing he would be asking if they knew what bits went where.

He didn't. 'Normally, I don't do any tests until a couple have been trying a year,' he informed her.

A year! Millie nearly choked. Why did everything have to be so difficult in this conceiving game? That they would make you have fruit-less sex for a year before they'd give you a few miserable blood tests?

She had to remind herself that she wouldn't be having fruitless sex for a year. She'd be having no sex at all. She didn't know which was worse.

But Dr Mooney was reading laboriously through her file. 'However,' he said, 'given that I see that you're thirty-nine . . .'

'Yes,' Millie said humbly. Bloody ageism. It was everywhere.

He was all business now. 'The first thing is to check whether you're ovulating at all. What day of your cycle are you on?'

'Day 3,' said Millie.

'That's very handy,' he said, delighted. 'Day 3 is when we can test for FSH.'

Which was exactly what Millie had planned. She had done her Internet research, after all. But there was no sense in annoying him by flaunting this. She rolled up her sleeve hastily and thrust her bare arm at him before he changed his mind.

'We'll do progesterone on cycle Day 21,' he informed her.

'Great,' said Millie. She couldn't believe her luck – that had been the next test on her list. Rashly she enquired, 'Is there any chance I can get infectious diseases done here too?'

He was startled again. 'What kind of infectious diseases?' he enquired, syringe poised over her arm warily lest he might catch something.

'Never mind,' she told him sunnily. She would go to a clinic in town. They wouldn't ask any questions. They would just take her money, test her and give her the required results.

Thank God she'd had the laparoscopy done last year. Imagine asking Dr Mooney for one of those. He would be most surprised. And it wasn't like he could perform it on his little examining table over by the wall. It was a hospital procedure, requiring a referral to a consultant, and no doubt joining the back of a big long queue.

It would also have required an explanation. A medical reason. They didn't bore a hole in you and have a detailed look inside your uterus just because you told your GP on a Friday morning that you quite fancied one.

The clinic had requested that she have the investigation. Maria had cheerily emailed her a list of tests that had to be performed before they would consider her a candidate for treatment. Along with the FSH and the progesterone, they wanted her blood group, her rhesus factor, infectious diseases tests for HIV and hepatitis, and the laparoscopy. They weren't going to put everybody to the trouble and expense of treating her with donor sperm in Spain if it turned out that her tubes weren't even open.

Thankfully, Millie already knew that her tubes were as clean as a whistle (she had never thought in her life that she would be glad for such a thing). Not that her tubes had been worrying her when she'd had the laparoscopy done last year. Instead it was unexplained bleeding that had sent her to Dr Mooney, even before she and Andrew had been trying to get pregnant. Dr Mooney had hummed and hawed and declared that it was outside his area of expertise, which was a fairly big concession on his part. He couldn't resist hazarding a guess that it was endometriosis, though, before referring her to a gynaecologist. The gynaecologist who had performed the laparoscopy had a 'good look round', he assured her. He'd even checked her tubes while he was at it, even though nobody had asked him to do so. It turned out that she didn't have endometriosis at all – Dr Mooney had sniffed defensively at that – and, as a bonus, her tubes were perfect. The bleeding was an infection and a course of antibodies cleared the whole thing up in a week.

The clinic had been happy with this.

And Millie was spared the thorny explanation to Dr Mooney that she was going to avail of donor sperm in a foreign country in the hopes of having a baby on her own.

'Now,' said Dr Mooney, popping the blood sample into a plastic sack, blessedly ignorant and benign. 'We should have the results of these in a couple of days. But I wouldn't worry too much.'

Millie felt slightly guilty in the face of his kindness. Lying to her GP wasn't something she was particularly proud of.

But he just wouldn't understand. Much less support or encourage her. He had once given out to her when she'd admitted that her alcohol intake was probably skirting the upper recommended limit. She'd probably have scandalised him altogether if she'd told him that she and Andrew sometimes consumed the entire weekly limit in one sitting. But that was before they'd been trying for a baby, naturally.

She couldn't imagine his face if she told him the truth. The shock might be too much for him. He might have to call for Tanya, his secretary, for assistance – probably in booting Millie out.

She knew that she couldn't go on like this – not telling people, and lying to her medical providers. And she didn't intend to. But the people that she *would* confide in would be chosen precisely because they would be supportive and non-judgemental. The rest, she decided, would be told only on a need-to-know basis.

And right now Dr Mooney didn't need to know.

'Thank you,' she said. 'I'll make an appointment to come back for the progesterone test.'

'In the meantime, keep trying,' he instructed her cheerily.

'I will,' Millie assured him.

For the next couple of weeks, Millie found it hard to keep her mind on her work. Not only was her own private life the centre of attention, but she was competing, as ever, with the others. Currently, Jaz was on a diet. The whole office knew about it, and was suffering along with her. Instead of heading off to the Spar at lunchtime for her usual tuna and sweetcorn baguette with a pack of cheese and onion crisps on the side, she now brought in a salad from home in a Tupperware container. It looked limp and watery and very small.

'Jesus, girls, it's not worth losing three pounds over,' she declared, looking into it woefully.

But lose three pounds she must. She and her husband Gerry were having a weigh-in on Sunday morning. He had gone on a diet too, because one evening they had both flopped down onto the couch simultaneously and one of the legs gave way – the leg under Jaz, to add insult to injury. Even though she was only a sylph compared to Gerry. He had a big round belly on him over a skinny little bottom – the unhealthiest kind of weight, Jaz had told him. She carried most of hers on her hips and thighs, as he had pointed out in retaliation.

'We'll go on a diet together,' he had declared. 'We can support each other.'

But within a week there were all kinds of dirty tricks going on, such as Jaz's low-fat yoghurts being stolen from the fridge, and the weighing scales being tampered with in the bathroom. Gerry declared he hadn't touched either the yoghurts or the scales, and blamed the children. Then he announced that he had already dropped two pounds in four days. Before Jaz's stunned eyes he had donned a tracksuit and runners and set off for work. He was, he threw at her over his shoulder, going to jog to the office.

'He's only doing it to spite me,' she complained to the girls. 'He knows I can't jog to work, seeing as it's flipping twenty-two miles from home. He just wants to win on Sunday, and then eat a big fry-up.'

Apparently the winner of the weekly weigh-in got to eat a full Irish breakfast, while the other presumably had humble pie.

'Do you two have to fight over everything?' Yvonne said, looking pained.

'Of course,' said Jaz. 'Then we have fantastic make-up sex.' She thought about this. 'Actually, we don't. We just fight.'

She had lost only one pound in the whole week. And she had been so good and everything! She hadn't even cracked when the sandwich lady came around with all those little chocolate muffins, even though her stomach was rumbling so loudly that she could hardly hear the claimants on the phone. Which was a blessing really.

Yvonne wondered whether her lack of weight loss could be anything to do with the rice cakes she had been bringing in to try to fill the gap.

'They only have thirty-seven calories each,' Jaz argued. 'They're practically air.'

'Yes, but how many did you eat yesterday?'

'I don't know. A few.'

Yvonne went and looked in Jaz's desk drawer. She took out all the empty wrappers, and she worked out that Jaz had consumed nearly twelve hundred calories' worth of rice cakes during the day.

'You could have had a Big Mac and fries for that,' she said.

'Stop,' Jaz cried in anguish. Then she took a few deep, motivating breaths. 'Right, girls. Throw away the rice cakes. I have two days to lose three pounds and beat him on Sunday morning.'

Deirdre looked worried on Jaz's behalf. 'Do you think that's safe? It'll be like a crash diet. You'll only lose water.'

'Water is good,' Jaz cackled. 'Anyway,' she said, 'I've spiked his Lean Cuisine lunch with an ounce of butter.'

'You wagon,' said Yvonne, delighted.

Even Dorothy in the corner snickered.

By the time Millie walked in from the doctor's at eleven o'clock with the result of her progesterone test Jaz had already gobbled all the salad and was nearly on the floor with the hunger. 'Give me some good news,' she implored Millie. 'Your progesterone is fabulous.'

The girls knew she'd been back to Dr Mooney, and why. She had debated not telling them about her momentous decision to go ahead and be a single mum. But they already knew that she was thinking about it. Also, between the tests and the visits to the doctor and the two trips to Spain, she would have to take loads of time off work, and there were only so many weddings and funerals one could invent. Fingers crossed, there might even be antenatal appointments coming up. It seemed silly *not* to tell them.

Anyway, she needed the support. Nobody knew but them. If she didn't have someone to confide in, she would burst. All right, so they mightn't all be totally mad about the idea of donor sperm – Dorothy had been rather distant this past week – but they were her oldest friends, and they were behind her. Some of them, like Jaz, were over the moon about the whole thing.

'Oh. My. God,' she had breathed when Millie told her she was flying out for her first appointment in thirteen days' time. 'You're really going for it?'

'Yes,' Millie had said, sounding surer than she felt.

'Well,' Jaz had declared, 'I'm delighted for you.' And she had drawn Millie into the biggest, warmest hug, and Millie was so overcome by her generosity that she had burst into tears. Again.

'Sorry,' she had said. 'I don't know why I'm crying. It's very exciting, really.'

They hadn't minded her tears at all. They were probably getting used to them by now. Yvonne just got her a tissue, while Jaz had efficiently asked, 'Have you booked a flight? Accommodation? Is your passport in date?'

'I don't know.' Millie had bawled afresh. That was all she needed:

her bloody passport to be out of date. 'I haven't done anything except book the appointment.'

'Don't worry,' Deirdre had said kindly. 'We'll sort everything out.'

Millie was glad. She needed Deirdre and Yvonne and Jaz. Because there was nobody else, and there never would be if she went through with this.

'Are you all right?' Jaz had asked, concerned when Millie's tears didn't dry up as quickly as they should have.

'Fine. It's just such a big decision, that's all.'

'Well, of course!' Yvonne had said. 'Girls, someone put on the kettle for a cup of tea for Millie here.'

There had been tea and tears all week. It had been the strangest time of Millie's life. She had thought that by finally making a decision she would be calmer about the whole thing. More settled or something. Instead she had been an emotional wreck. She was always bursting into tears: she cried at the sight of a buggy in the street, and a hospital drama on the television, and in front of the man who made her sandwich at the deli counter in the Spar yesterday.

'Did I put too much mayonnaise on it?' he had asked, worried.

'No, no, it's perfect,' she had wept.

When she wasn't crying her eyes out she was careering along on pure adrenalin. She was going to Spain! To have a baby! In the sun! Well, not in the sun, obviously. She would have the baby in a maternity hospital here in Ireland. But still – a *baby*! With arms and legs and a head and a little mouth that would one day shout, 'Mama!'

At that point her hands would start shaking like that time she'd had three double espressos, and she would have to go and lie down for a bit and wait for it to pass, at which point she would usually start crying again.

Thirteen whole days to go. She'd never get through them. Every minute seemed to last a blooming hour. And wasn't thirteen an unlucky number anyway? She'd been relieved when she got the first day over with, and then there were only twelve days left to go. Then eleven.

And work helped a bit. Listening to people complaining about their whiplash took her mind off things for whole minutes at a time. Although maybe not entirely, because she often had to ask people to repeat things because her mind would have drifted off to a consulting room in Spain where she wondered whether they would enquire why she was having a baby on her own. Would they want to know about Andrew? Would they even care?

And the girls were just great. Millie didn't know what she'd have done without them. They were being very delicate about the whole thing and had managed to avoid asking for all the juicy details, even though they were obviously dying to. To amuse themselves they had spent the week coming up with baby names, even though Millie told them that, according to the clinic's statistics, there was only a fifteen per cent chance of her coming home pregnant. That didn't stop them, though.

'Patrick!' Jaz would shout out. 'Something Irish.'

Yvonne would contradict her. 'Why not something Spanish, seeing as the dad will probably be from there?' And she had winked at Millie. 'How about Jesus?'

'*Jesus?*' Jaz screeched. 'You don't want to saddle a child with that.'

'It's a popular Spanish name,' Yvonne preached. She liked to go into the Irish Film Centre and see arty foreign films with her husband on a Sunday afternoon. 'Or Angel.'

'No, no, no,' said Jaz. 'You don't want the poor kid to get the stuffing beaten out of him in the playground.'

'Anyway,' said Deirdre, now that there was finally a gap in the conversation, 'it could be a girl.'

For some reason that seemed to strike a chord with everybody. Nobody bothered thinking of boys' names any more. Millie's baby was going to be a girl, naturally, and all they had to do now was come up with a name for her.

'Emma?'

'Or how about Daisy?'

'I knew a girl called Daisy once and I couldn't stand her,' Jaz said flatly. 'I quite like Susan.'

Over in the corner Dorothy said, 'I have a Spanish friend called Bonita.'

They all looked at each other.

'Bonita,' said Jaz slowly. 'Do you know something? I like it.'

'I love it,' said Yvonne. 'So different.'

'Yet not unpronounceable,' Jaz added hastily. 'Again, I'll just mention the playground.'

'It's perfect,' said Deirdre simply.

Millie's baby was now Bonita whether she liked it or not. And she did like it. But deciding on a name seemed so far in the future that she couldn't really get her head around it. She had so many mountains to climb first, not least of which was getting pregnant. She certainly wasn't going to get involved in baby-naming competitions in the office.

'Let's take one step at a time,' she'd said. 'I mightn't even get pregnant. There's only a fifteen per cent chance.'

'Oh, pooey,' said Jaz, waving a hand dismissively. 'Think positive. You'll be one of the fifteen per cent.'

Millie didn't want to get her hopes up too high. The success rates were low. The clinic had advised her that if she chose to go down the IVF route her chances would double. But Millie didn't want to do IVF. Not now. It was too much to think about going through on her own. Donor IUI was as much as she felt she could handle at this point. Maybe in the future, if this didn't work.

And it mightn't. She had to keep remembering that.

If only the girls would. She had scarcely got her coat off from the visit to Dr Mooney when Jaz announced, 'We've been very busy while you were gone.'

'What, working?' said Millie innocently.

'Don't be ridiculous,' Jaz scoffed. 'We've been finding you somewhere to stay in Spain. Well, technically Yvonne and I didn't – we put young, sweet, innocent Deirdre on the job, didn't we, Dee? None of the supervisors would suspect her of surfing the web during office hours. Not with a face like that.'

Deirdre beamed proudly. Her angelic smile and general air of goodness had got them out of many a scrape over the years. You would never think to look at her that she had drank seven Bacardis and Coke at the office party last Christmas before getting up on a table and belting out 'Private Dancer'. Jaz had never let her forget it.

'We figured that maybe you hadn't had a chance to do anything about it yourself,' she said to Millie.

Millie hadn't. Maria from the clinic had emailed her a list of accommodation that clients usually used. She hadn't got around to looking any of them up, never mind booking them.

'Anything will do,' she said.

'Show her what you've got, Deirdre,' Jaz instructed.

They all gathered around Deirdre's computer as she brought up the first of a series of brochures she'd downloaded from the Internet. 'I thought you might prefer self-catering to a hotel,' she said efficiently. 'That way you can do your own thing without having to explain yourself to people.'

Millie couldn't imagine that anybody would be remotely interested in her date with donor sperm, but at the same time she didn't think she would want to be around lots of people, say like in a hotel, especially raucous holidaymakers with nothing on their minds except getting a good tan.

It wasn't a holiday for Millie. It was a very serious business, and a very emotional one. She might want to cry all the time, or shake like a leaf, and she'd rather do it in the privacy of her own self-catering apartment.

'Yes,' she said, 'that's probably best.'

'This,' Deirdre announced, 'is the Alta Vista Apartments.'

The brochure opened on a picture of a startlingly blue pool surrounded by inviting multicoloured parasols and lots of tanned, thin folk lying on towels. Built around the pool were blocks of low-rise, tasteful apartments with balmy balconies and a separate entrance to each one up quaint little steps.

'Girls, wouldn't you do anything to be there right this minute?' Yvonne breathed. They'd holidayed in West Cork last year. It had rained.

'It's got a double bedroom, air-conditioning, and is a two-minute walk to the beach,' Deirdre detailed.

'And it's got loads of nice restaurants nearby,' Jaz pointed out. Her stomach rumbled miserably.

'It's lovely inside too.' Deirdre brought up the interior of the apartment on screen – clean and bright, and with a cosy table and chairs on the balcony.

But Millie wasn't interested in the restaurants or drinks on the balcony. There was only thing on her mind. 'How far is it from the clinic?'

'A ten-minute taxi ride away.'

Contrary to what some people seemed to believe about foreign fertility clinics in countries like Spain, they weren't usually set on sandy beaches and with cocktail bars to the side. Millie's clinic was in the nearby town, in the business district, and from the list of accommodation Maria had sent on, it seemed that most people attending it stayed in the holiday apartments and hotels nearby, and travelled in.

'It's got Sky TV,' Yvonne said, as if that clinched the deal.

'Plus, it's really cheap for a week,' Deirdre concluded.

'I don't want it for a week, I just want it for a couple of days.' Her appointment with the clinic was scheduled for the Tuesday. She had intended to fly in on the Monday and leave on the Wednesday.

'They only rent it by the week,' Deirdre told her. 'I can look up some hotels for you again, but it'll probably cost you as much, if not more.'

Millie didn't want to haggle over money. It felt unseemly. She wasn't looking for a holiday on the cheap; she was going on the most important trip of her life, to try to have a baby.

But of course it was going to cost. Fertility treatment was expensive. And the clinic weren't shy about charging. Millie had swallowed hard when Maria had emailed through a list of their costs. The first instalment was due the day she went to the clinic, and the rest before the actual treatment. There was no option to pay in instalments, and no refund if it didn't work.

But it would be worth it, Millie told herself. What was mere money when it came to having a baby?

'Book it,' she told Deirdre, recklessly wielding her and Andrew's joint credit card.

'Are you sure? I have more brochures here,' Deirdre said.

'No, that one looks fine.'

She just wanted it done now. She needed to book a flight too before it got too late.

Then Jaz said, 'Why don't you stay for the week?'

'What?'

'The apartment is booked anyway, you might as well.'

'It's not a holiday, Jaz,' Millie said rather sharply.

Jaz was undeterred. 'Look, we all know that going abroad is not an ideal solution, Millie. But it doesn't mean you have to beat yourself up about it. You don't have to hide away indoors wearing a hair shirt the entire time you're over there, being absolutely miserable.'

But that was the thing: Millie's own continued ambivalence. Somehow it seemed wrong to be catching some sun and reading a bonkbuster when she was still conducting an internal battle with the rights and wrongs of the whole thing. And now Jaz was suggesting she slurp a few piña coladas on top of it?

But Jaz wasn't suggesting that at all. 'You could just relax for the week. Take some time to think about it all, away from work and home and everything. It would do you the world of good.'

Put like that, it sounded rather sensible. Perhaps that was just what Millie needed: time. And she would have all the information from the clinic to process too. Instead of turning her into a fertility tourist perhaps a week in a nice, quiet apartment might be a very necessary part of this whole experience.

'I suppose,' she conceded.

'Plus, you haven't had a holiday in a year,' Jaz said persuasively. 'You and Andrew were supposed to go to Italy, remember?'

That had been just before they'd been trying to get pregnant. He had an aunt in Florence and they were due to visit with her in the spring. But it turned out that it would be right in the middle of Millie's fertile period and the idea of having furtive sex every night in her spare bedroom was off-putting, to say the least. 'She's deaf as a post, she won't hear a thing,' Andrew had argued. But Millie had been prim about it (it had been only their first month trying). 'I don't want a child conceived like that,' she had said. 'It might have all kinds of issues later on.'

When she thought of that now . . . She hadn't even known what the word 'issues' meant back then.

So they had decided to wait until she got pregnant first. Which of course she didn't. And then Andrew got the job. The aunt was still ringing up Millie, wanting to know when she was coming over. Andrew hadn't even bothered telling her that he and Millie had split up.

'Don't think of it as a holiday at all. Think of it as a period of reflection,' Jaz said cajolingly. 'And you can't help it if the sun is shining outside . . .'

Millie laughed. 'You're incorrigible, Jaz.'

'I've been called worse,' Jaz said cheerfully.

Chapter Thirteen

Oona was cheesed off about the whole thing. 'I thought we were going on a spa weekend,' she grumbled.

'Sorry,' said Millie, feeling dreadful. 'Spain just kind of . . . came up.' Now she felt deceitful too. Also, given that they were in the swimwear section of a department store, she felt hideously fat. All in all, it wasn't one of her finer mornings.

Oona was suspicious. 'How do you mean, "came up"?'

Millie crossed her fingers behind her back. 'Personnel rang. They said I absolutely had to take some holidays, or else forfeit them altogether. So I just booked something on the spur of the moment.'

'But *Spain*?' Oona wondered. Her suspicion was only deepening. 'I'd understand if you went to a *city*. Lots of things to do and see. But a sun holiday with nothing on offer but a beach? Which you won't even lie on, because you come out in blotches.'

'Not always,' Millie said defensively, although she usually did. She'd have to wear long-sleeved tops and big shorts if she was going to survive at all. There would be no question of lounging about in a bikini . . . She was hunting that morning for the biggest swimsuit she could find, and it wasn't just to cover her skin, either.

Oona harrumphed under her breath. She was feeling particularly fractious. There was an irritated little crease between her eyes, and her hair was escaping in all directions from its bun at the back. And she had shouted, 'Oh, bugger off and leave me alone,' at the children, when normally she never uttered a cross word to them, no matter what they did.

Millie tried to sneak a look at her boobs – *were* they bigger than usual? But it was hard to see properly with the coat she was wearing. Possibly they *were* slightly larger. Please God, no.

But it was also possible that God didn't listen to self-serving, mean-spirited prayers, and would repay Millie for her lack of Christianity by blessing Oona with twins.

Oona saw her looking. 'Have I spilled cereal down me?' she said, scrabbling half-heartedly at her chest. Anything was possible.

'No, no,' said Millie hastily. 'Look, Spain was a last-minute deal, that's all. After the whole thing with Andrew, maybe I felt I deserved a little break.'

She could feel heat rising incriminatingly up her neck again. Damn. Surely lying should get easier the more you did it.

To divert attention she grabbed a hanger and said, 'Maybe I should try something on.'

Her choice unfortunately was a psychedelic pink one-piece swimsuit with a fake buckle around the waist. She would look like a reject from *Dynasty*.

Oona brushed her aside with professional ease. 'Here, let me.'

She was a woman used to shopping. She had the family genes, after all, and had inherited Nuala's gift of getting through a clothes rack roughly every thirty seconds. The one job Brendan had left to her when he had taken over as house-husband was the weekly family supermarket shop. Nobody could hold a candle to Oona as she charged efficiently up and down aisles, dragging two trolleys in her wake. And she always looked so happy too.

'Oona will go with you, she'd love it,' he had immediately said that morning when Millie had innocently let slip that she was off to do a spot of shopping. 'That's if she ever gets up.' He had given a little laugh and looked at the ceiling. 'She was in bed at nine o'clock last night, and she's still not up. I hope she's not coming down with something.'

Millie's heart had sunk: another indication that Oona might be pregnant. She tended to turn sloth-like very early on in every pregnancy, and would only emerge from slumber towards the end to graze every few hours, and wash when the mood took her.

'Stay out as long as you want,' Brendan had urged them, when she had finally surfaced. 'I'm taking the kids to a Let's Make Music class.'

The kids had shrieked in protest. Gary had thrown himself on the floor and made retching noises.

'You'll love it,' Brendan had assured them. 'They teach you how to make your own instruments out of bamboo sticks.'

If she were being honest, Millie hadn't wanted company at all. She had only intended to buy a bottle of sunscreen, a swimsuit and maybe a T-shirt or two. After all, she wasn't technically going on her holidays, and had no intention of stocking up on fancy flip-flops or beach reads. But now that Oona was with her, she could hardly get out of it;

Oona, who was in a bad mood, sleepier than usual, and with boobs that were like missiles, now that Millie got a good look at them. They were pointing in her direction too, taunting her.

'You'll need a sarong for the beach,' Oona declared authoritatively. 'And what are you going to wear out at night?'

'Out at night?' Millie repeated stupidly.

'You're hardly going to stay in the apartment every night and cook.'

That was exactly what Millie had intended to do; a nice bowl of pasta balanced on her knee in front of Sky News.

'I'm not comfortable eating out on my own, especially if I'm all dressed up. People might think I'm strange.'

'Well, you are,' Oona said kindly. 'You say you booked this holiday because you wanted a break. Yet you don't plan on going out, you've only chosen one swimsuit, and you're not going to go on the beach because you come out in blotches. What exactly *are* you planning on doing?'

Visiting the clinic on Tuesday, and no doubt spending the rest of the week replaying the appointment in her head. They would probably give her literature too, lots of it. She would have to read it all. She would need time to think, to plan, to worry, and ultimately to decide whether to return the following month for the treatment or not.

'Things,' she said stoutly. Her chin rose up a fraction. She didn't have to explain herself to Oona. Who was *two years* younger, never let it be forgotten. 'It's my holiday and this is the way I want to do it.'

She must have sounded convincing because Oona just shrugged and said, 'I suppose. And you deserve one, after everything. It's just a shame about the spa weekend, that's all. I was looking forward to it.'

And she gave such a deep, tired sigh, an *exhausted* sigh, that Millie couldn't contain herself any longer.

'Are you pregnant again?' she blurted out.

Oona looked at her, astonished. 'Me? Pregnant?'

Then she burst out laughing. It was a funny kind of a laugh: a bit off key or something.

'So you're not?'

'No.'

Millie didn't know how she felt. Relieved, certainly. And a bit small and mean for feeling that way. But it certainly was one less cross to bear.

'Although I'm sure Brendan would like another one,' Oona said rather dismissively. 'He could show off his perfect parenting skills to Nancy and the rest of them. As for me, I'm done in that department, thank you very much.'

She sounded very definite about it. 'Why are you asking anyway?'

'Oh, no reason,' Millie said swiftly. 'You just seem a bit moodier, that's all.'

'Yes, well,' Oona conceded.

'And your boobs are bigger.'

'Have you seen my backside?' she complained. 'Brendan served up boeuf bourguignon last night, accompanied by a bottle of Chateau Leoville-Barton, with steamed pudding to follow. Even the kids ate it.'

'Lucky you,' said Millie. She'd had lentil curry (high in zinc) followed by yoghurt and wheatgerm (high in Vitamin E). These were tips from an eating-for-optimum-fertility website. If she weren't going to Spain next week she would never let another grain of wheatgerm pass her lips.

'Lucky everybody, really,' Oona said hastily, lest she sounded ungrateful. 'Gary has grown another inch in the last month. We're wondering now whether he was malnourished all this time.'

She plucked out another hanger and held it up for inspection. 'Here, we should have brought Mum,' she said. 'She'd put together a beach wardrobe for you in no time. It'd be the highlight of her week.'

Millie decided it was time to speak out. 'Have you noticed anything a bit odd about her lately?'

'Mum?'

'Yes.'

'She was always a bit odd, if you ask me.'

'Seriously.'

Oona looked at her as though she were stirring up trouble for nothing. 'What do you mean, Millie?'

Millie felt foolish. She didn't want to say anything about the body odour. It felt disloyal or something. And it had an explanation, according to Dennis. He had explanations for quite a lot, it seemed.

'Nothing I can really put my finger on,' she said limply.

'You mean the bad temper? The way she cuts you off mid-sentence even though you could be telling her that you needed a heart trans-plant?'

So Oona *had* noticed. Millie felt tremendously relieved. 'Yes.'

'I thought it was just me,' said Oona.

Millie's relief was swiftly replaced by worry. 'What do you think it is?'

'I don't know. Maybe nothing. Maybe it's just a part of getting old.'

'But Dad's not like that.'

'Dad? He's ten times more cracked than she is.'

But that was just normalising things again. And Millie knew it wasn't normal: not for Mum anyway.

'Will we say something?' Millie said.

'Yes,' said Oona decisively. 'We'll mention it to Dad.'

What good would that do? Dennis hadn't apparently noticed a darned thing. He thought it was perfectly natural to go around accusing other hospital patients of thieving and skulduggery.

Oona saw her reluctance. 'We can't go barging in there, Millie, frightening the life out of her. Anyway, she probably just needs a trip to the GP.'

'I suppose,' said Millie. She felt better and better. Oona was right. There was no sense in blowing things out of proportion. Along with the Omega 3, Mum could well be deficient in a whole host of other things that could be put right with a simple trip to the surgery, or even a lentil curry.

She felt even better when Oona said, 'Anyway, Auntie June is coming up next week. That's just what Mum needs to cheer her up.'

Auntie June was Mum's sister and she came up from Wexford once a year to visit for a week. She ran a dog kennel, which had always tied in nicely with Mum's job in the vet's, and the two of them would spend many happy hours swapping tales of recalcitrant animals, and their owners, who were usually worse. Cups and cups of tea would be made, and Mum would bake her special carrot cake, and they would hoot with laughter in the kitchen till all hours.

Dennis tended to make himself scarce the week of Auntie June's visit. She had no interest whatsoever in television or shopping, for starters. Instead she liked visiting art galleries, and going for long, blustery walks up hills, the steeper the better. He would suddenly find all kinds of urgent things that needed to be done, such as car services and trips to the accountant. 'They like to be on their own anyhow, to catch up,' he had said to Millie.

Auntie June hadn't seen Mum at all since she'd got her toe done, so her visit was even more eagerly anticipated than usual. Dad had been preparing Millie's old room – the spare room now – all week, and he looked even more wrecked than usual.

Maybe Auntie June was just the tonic that Mum needed.

By this time Millie had a trolley full of stuff, all picked out by Oona. It included a rather risqué red top that showed plenty of cleavage.

Oona looked at the sexy top, in sudden doubt. 'Are you sure you'll be all right in Spain on your own?'

Millie laughed. 'Of course I will.'

'I'm serious, Millie.'

'What do you think could possibly happen to me in a family resort?'

But Oona was coming over all bossy and worldly-wise. 'These resorts might look very friendly in the brochure, but some of them are a lot different when you get there.' Her voice hit a new, gloomy low. 'Especially at night.'

'Only a minute ago you were picking out tarty clothes for me to wear out to bars and restaurants.'

'I've changed my mind.' She dumped the red top down hastily and cast a concerned look over the rest of the pile.

'Oona, I'm not a child.'

'No, but you're not exactly Miss Experienced, are you? Look at all the losers you've managed to attract in the past.'

The shop assistants heard that, of course, and immediately inspected Millie from head to toe in detail, as though taking a lesson in What Not To Do.

'I am not going to Spain to find a man,' Millie hissed. She had never been more certain of anything in her life.

'That's what you think. They might have other ideas. And, let's face it, you've always been too nice for your own good.'

'Yes, well, I've changed,' Millie said darkly. 'Andrew has beaten all the niceness out of me. He's turned me into a man-hater. Those Spanish men had better be afraid of *me*.'

But that just seemed to alarm Oona more. 'I'm not happy about this,' she kept saying.

'You don't have to be. It's nothing to do with you.' Just to spite her, Millie grabbed back the red top and slapped it down defiantly on the counter in front of the superior shop assistants.

Then Oona suddenly said in a bright, false voice, 'I've had a great idea.'

'What?'

'I could come with you.'

'What?' Millie hadn't expected this. She didn't *want* this.

As if sensing this, Oona clutched her arm hard. 'Please. I could really do with a week away.' Just for good measure she turned her head so that Millie could properly appreciate the dark circles under her eyes. Although why she had dark circles was anybody's guess, when she was pampered and cosseted and waited on hand and foot by that living saint of a husband of hers. 'Come on, Millie. Let me come with you. We'll have great fun.'

Brendan said it was a brilliant idea. Oona could do with the break – again, from what, nobody was sure – and Millie wouldn't have to go on holiday on her own.

'But I was quite looking forward to going on my own,' she protested.

Why couldn't she just put her foot down and say no? Because she was too nice, that was why. Andrew hadn't beaten it out of her at all. Another black mark against him.

And besides, she couldn't think of a good enough reason for insisting that she go on her own. What could she say, without mentioning the clinic?

'It's OK,' said Oona hastily, obviously seeing some of this on Millie's face. 'I won't interfere or anything. We'll give each other plenty of space and all that.' And she gamely offered to sleep on one of the pull-out beds in the living room and leave the big double bedroom to Millie.

'You won't even know I'm there,' she reassured her.

There was no answer to that. Millie was stuck with her. Which wasn't the end of the world, she supposed. It wasn't going to interfere with her plans. When her clinic appointment arose she would declare that she needed some of the aforementioned space and go off. She would tell Oona that she had been shopping, or had gone for a scenic walk.

More lies. Where would it end? Millie's nose had begun to feel a bit tingly lately and she was sure that it had looked larger in the mirror that morning.

'Don't you two go picking up any fellas now,' Brendan said, wagging a finger at them mock sternly.

'You either,' Oona said gamely back. 'Or women, for that matter.'

'Oh, I'll probably just hang out with Nancy and the gang,' Brendan said carelessly.

'I've got my eye on her,' Oona reminded him.

And it was all very friendly and cheery, and Millie tried not to notice the tension in the air.

Then Brendan said, 'I'm just thinking – you should bring Dennis with you too.'

Orla and Millie burst out laughing.

'Good one,' said Oona.

'I wasn't joking,' he said.

'What? Dad? To *Spain*?'

She and Millie exchanged looks. They were together on this one. And skilled too. Over the years they had successfully conspired to keep him from accompanying them to parties, debutante balls and on first dates with unsuitable-looking boys.

'I don't think so,' said Millie.

'Auntie June is up next week,' Brendan pointed out.

'So?' said Oona.

'Mum and her would be delighted to be rid of him for the week. So why not?'

Millie could think of at least a dozen reasons, not least of which was his habit of wearing big black socks under his sandals. He also didn't like 'foreign food'. That included pizza and pasta. And salad. Plus, he was fond of telling everybody that he didn't sleep well in any bed except his own, so it was unlikely he would manage too well on the second pull-out bed – especially if Oona was in the same room. There would be war.

And Millie didn't want to end up lying to him too. Oona might be bought off easily enough with explanations of walks and trips to the shops, but what about Dad? Knowing his love of shopping, he would insist on coming with her.

'Because,' Oona told Brendan bluntly, 'this is supposed to be a holiday. Not an endurance test.'

For some reason Brendan was in a very sanctimonious mood that morning. 'You two are killed saying how that man needs a break, what with your mother after being in hospital. And yet here you are, off on holiday, and you wouldn't take him with you . . .' He let his voice trail off in disappointment.

'Stop it now, Brendan,' Oona said dangerously.

'I am a carer,' he said proudly. 'And so has your father been, for the last few weeks. I never thought I'd have anything in common with him, but anyhow. And I don't think he'll mind me saying on his behalf that it's a tough, thankless job and that respite from it is necessary.'

'God, play the violins,' Oona cried in disgust. 'You went out for pints last night. I don't know what you're complaining about.'

'I'm not complaining. I'm merely stating that this is an excellent opportunity to treat your father to a nice holiday. And besides, he and Auntie June don't like each other, even though everybody pretends that they do.'

But Oona wasn't taking all this lying down. The carer thing had obviously got under her skin, even though she had held down a job *and* been the primary carer for years, yet nobody was banging on about that, were they?

'You've been on that forum again, haven't you?' she said to Brendan viciously. 'With those other stay-at-home dads. They're always putting ideas in your head!'

Apparently the American dads were the worst. Very militant altogether. They were always taking offence at something, and calling for respect. They wrote blogs with names like 'Stay-at-Home and Proud of It!' Other dads would post in with concerns like, 'How do you convince other moms at the playground that you're not a pervert?'

Furious debate would usually follow. Then someone would post a recipe for cupcakes and spoil the whole thing.

'We support each other,' Brendan said, unapologetic. He eyed them both sternly. 'I just hope you two are going to do the right thing here regarding your dad.'

'Oh, shut up,' Oona howled. Doing the right thing had never come easily to her. 'He won't want to, anyhow.'

'He has no excuse, what with Auntie June coming up next week,' Brendan lectured.

Oona gave a last desperate look at Millie. 'You could say no. After all, it's your holiday.' That hadn't bothered Oona too much when she'd decided to jump on the bandwagon herself.

'We *should* invite him,' Millie said with a martyred sigh.

It would take her mind off things, she decided valiantly. And Dad *did* deserve a break. She would still go to her clinic exactly as planned, and everybody would get what they wanted.

At the back of her mind was the knowledge that at some point she would have to tell Dad anyway. And Oona, and Mum. Much as she would like, she couldn't keep what she was going to do a secret for ever. Would it be so awful if they discovered on holiday what she was up to?

Oona was still glaring at Brendan. 'I hope you're happy with yourself. Now we'll have no fun at all with Dad tagging along. We'll spend the whole holiday looking for restaurants that serve cabbage and potatoes, and trying to find seats in the shade.'

For some reason Brendan looked pleased.

Chapter Fourteen

'Millie, hurry up! The taxi's going to be here in a minute!'

It had been decided that Millie, Oona and Dennis would travel to the airport via taxi. Oona had offered to drive, but tensions were already high enough between her and Dennis, without throwing a fraught car journey into the mix. They had already fallen out over luggage, passports, socks-under-sandals – 'You're not going to disgrace us' – and which of them snored the loudest. Mammy, the kids had all yelled.

Millie was exhausted just listening to the pair of them. Her act of self-sacrifice in letting them tag along was coming back to haunt her. But at the same time it provided an excellent distraction. It stopped her thinking about things too much. She was afraid that if she had too much time to mull over her actions she would chicken out altogether.

Instead she buried herself in the practicalities. And there were many. Yesterday she had done a big supermarket shop with Mum to keep her and Auntie June going while they were away. Despite having years of retail therapy under her belt, Mum couldn't find the frozen peas anywhere, and it took her twenty minutes to eventually locate them – right under her nose, as it turned out.

'Thick,' she had raged. 'That's what I am. Pure thick and stupid.'

'Yes, and you passed it on to me, damn you,' Millie had said.

She had been trying to keep things light even as she notched up this new worry. Could it be that Mum needed glasses too?

The GP had found nothing wrong. Dennis had taken her down to the surgery during the week, even though he professed his hurt and astonishment at Oona and Millie ganging up on their own mother like that.

'We're not, we just want to be sure that she's OK,' Millie had said.

'I live with her. Do you not think I'd have noticed if there was something wrong?'

Apparently not. But he went off with her anyway, arm around her as though to protect her from her evil daughters.

He'd returned with her triumphantly an hour later.

'She's fine. He couldn't find a thing wrong with her. He said she was in great shape for a woman her age.'

'He did,' Nuala had confirmed. 'He said my memory and reflexes were excellent. Maybe I'm a little low on iron but apart from that I'm fine.'

'I'm going to the shops for liver and bacon this second,' Dennis vowed. He was delighted. This was better than the Omega 3.

'Oh, lovely,' said Nuala.

It struck Millie afterwards Nuala hadn't queried at all why they thought she should go to the doctor. There had been no outrage from *her*, no protestations that she was fine. She had looked more surprised than relieved when there was nothing found.

But the pea incident in the supermarket had left Nuala unusually anxious and upset. 'They were under my nose. The peas. How could I not have seen them?'

Millie had wanted to tell her that the same thing happened to her sometimes too. But Nuala didn't need appeasement. She got enough of that at home.

And so Millie had said, 'What do you think it is, Mum? Do you think there's something wrong?'

Nuala had just shaken her head. 'I don't know, I don't know.'

'Maybe you could see the doctor again.'

'He's says I'm fine. That I've had the flu, and an operation, and that I'm cracking on a bit.'

'I'll go with you this time. We'll talk to him together.'

Nuala was backtracking now. The peas were safely in the trolley. *Judge Judy* was on in half an hour. 'Maybe when you get back from Spain,' she said.

By the time they got home she was in great form, and the lapse wasn't mentioned again. Millie was too busy getting ready for Spain to worry any more about it.

Or, indeed, anything else.

Only at night, lying there sleeplessly looking up at the ceiling, did she truly allow herself to think about what she was planning to do. Even then she could only manage bite-sized chunks of reality, such as, what if the baby was sallow-skinned? In other words, Spanish-looking? It was highly probable, even though Maria said they had a supply of blond-haired, blue-eyed donors for their Northern European clients. But there was always the possibility that a recessive gene would pop up and Millie would produce a baby that looked absolutely nothing like her and very much like Julio Iglesias. Which was fine – she liked Julio Iglesias. But it raised many interesting scenarios, not least what she would say to kind-meaning but nosy old ladies at the supermarket check-out, who wouldn't think twice about saying, 'The daddy's not Irish I'd say, is he?' And poor little Bonita, when she was old enough to understand such nonsense – what would she think? That she was an oddity in a land full of pasty, white-faced nosy Irish folk? That she didn't truly belong?

At that point Millie would screw her eyes tightly shut and practically will herself to sleep. The following morning there would be some other urgent thing to sort out before she travelled, and the previous night's anxiety would be conveniently forgotten.

But there was no avoiding it now: the day had finally arrived. They were flying out at noon. They had all decided to meet at Dennis's house and travel on from there.

Except that Dennis didn't want to go. He hadn't wanted to go from the very start. 'Spain?' he had kept saying, as though it were Outer Mongolia. 'Why on earth would I want to go to Spain?'

'For a holiday,' Oona had nearly shouted. 'For a break, you daft man.'

'But what about your mother?' And he'd turned to look at her as though she might self-combust at any moment.

They'd explained it to him as plainly as they could that, first, Mum had been given the all-clear by the doctor, and secondly, that Auntie June was coming for the week.

'So there's no need for you at all,' Oona had said helpfully. Then she had given his arm a squeeze. 'Come on. You might even enjoy yourself.'

But he had been tetchy and unhappy all week. He'd hung around the house, and Nuala, like a bad smell. As of yesterday morning he still hadn't packed, and he'd gone checking his passport in the hope that it was out of date.

It was Nuala who'd finally lost her cool. 'Oh, just go,' she'd said. 'You're driving me up the walls.'

Well. She hadn't said that when she'd been roaring for her mid-morning cup of tea. But it had been enough to send Dennis off the deep end, and he'd climbed the stairs stiffly to pack his selection of black socks as though the whole world was out to get him.

And now Auntie June was here, in his house. She was the kind of woman you heard before you saw.

'Dennis! Do you know where Nuala's wellies are? I can't find a thing in this press out here.'

141

Apparently she had coaxed Mum into a walk at the nearby park, although it was far too flat and small for Auntie June's liking. Dennis hadn't been keen on the idea at all. Mum's toe wasn't up to anything too strenuous yet, he felt.

He mentioned this now, foolishly.

'Nonsense,' Auntie June declared merrily. 'We always find with our dogs that a good run around the paddock does wonders for them, especially if they're recuperating.'

She looked remarkably like a well-fed Labrador herself, with a mane of puffy blond hair and plump haunches. In fact it was Dennis's opinion that she had been around animals for too long, and had acquired a certain directness that he found unappealing. She thought nothing of picking up a cardigan and having a good sniff of it before deciding that it was clean enough to wear again.

Mum seemed to be enjoying her stay, though. They'd had a great old natter in the kitchen last night till all hours, leaving Dennis to cool his heels on his own in front of the telly. They'd even forgotten to bring him in a glass of wine, although he knew full well that Auntie June had opened the bottle she'd brought up with her. He had wondered if it was on purpose.

'Nonsense. She has a heart of gold,' Nuala had declared. Oh, she was feisty now that she had her sister up, Dennis had said afterwards to Millie.

Today Nuala was all bundled in a big cardigan and a pair of thick socks in preparation for her walk. She looked very cheerful about it too, and failed completely to notice Dennis's look of abject misery as he hung around by the door.

'You'll send us a postcard, won't you?' she urged Millie and Oona, jolly.

'We'll be home before it arrives,' Dennis said gloomily.

They all looked at him sharply, even though he was right.

Then the back door burst open and Brendan traipsed in from the garden with the kids. He had been showing them Dennis's wilting plants in the hope of distracting them. It hadn't worked. The minute they saw Oona, standing there in her new red sundress and with a pair of sunglasses perched atop her head optimistically, they rushed at her and wound themselves around her legs pathetically.

'Don't go, Mammy,' Gary pleaded. 'Don't leave us.'

'We could come too,' Aoifa suggested desperately. 'We'd be very quiet.'

Chloe just sucked her thumb, even though she hadn't done so in a year. She had wet the bed last night too.

'Daddy's going to be here. He'll look after you,' Oona said brightly.

The three kids turned in unison to look at Brendan as though he were a convicted child beater.

To his credit, he smiled. He put on what Oona called his Barney voice and told them, 'We're going to do so many fun things while Mum is away!'

That brought Gary out in fresh tears. 'Don't leave us with him,' he implored Oona.

Chloe went and hid behind Oona's dress, peeping out at Brendan suspiciously.

Brendan lost his temper. 'Oh, for heaven's sake,' he snapped. 'Who got your breakfast this morning? Who cleaned your faces and wiped your snotty little noses? How about a little gratitude around here?'

He glared at them. They cowered. The on-line dads would have been disappointed at this lack of restraint on his part but he looked like he didn't care.

'It's always the same,' he said to Oona accusingly. 'Is it because you breastfed them or something, is that it? Maybe I should grow a big pair of knockers! That might make them like me more!'

The kids were alarmed now. 'Mammy . . .' Gary whimpered.

Oona gave Brendan a very stern look. Then she reached down and scooped all three children up in her arms (Brendan had never quite worked out how she managed it) and cuddled them close.

'Ah, come on now, pets,' she said to them cheerily. 'What's all this fuss about?'

And she kissed them and whispered in their ears about bringing them back presents – 'but only if you're very, very good' – and how she would ring them every night, and how they were to look after Daddy while she was gone.

'Do we have to?' Gary asked, pained.

'Yes,' Oona said firmly. 'You're the man of the house while I'm away.'

Gary quite fancied this. He gave her a wink and said, 'Aw'right, luv.'

Brendan just looked on rather sullenly through all this. Oona studiously avoided looking at him.

It was a relief when Millie's mobile phone rang, and everybody could pretend that none of that nastiness had just taken place.

It was Dr Mooney from the surgery.

'I have to take this,' she said.

'All right, but be quick,' Oona urged. 'There's the taxi now.'

Millie's FSH level had turned out to be surprisingly low, and with her progesterone excellent too, Dr Mooney had said, not bothering to hide his surprise, 'You're actually in very good reproductive shape for a woman your age.' Why was he ringing her now then?

'You said you were definitely having intercourse at the right time?' he opened after the requisite greetings.

'Oh, yes,' said Millie. 'Lots of it. Every day usually.'

He was a bit taken aback by this. 'Every day seems a bit excessive.'

'Just during my fertile time,' she assured him.

'What I mean is that if Andrew's sperm count is a bit on the low side of normal, then intercourse every day might not leave enough time to replenish stocks, if you know what I mean.'

Millie was wondering how she had ended up discussing Andrew's sperm count over the phone, when he had been gone weeks and weeks.

'We'll try and cut down,' she promised Dr Mooney. She wanted to get rid of him. The taxi would start honking in another few moments.

'I wouldn't worry too much,' Dr Mooney said. 'We'll find out when the results come back.'

'What results?'

'I'm going to order a sperm analysis for him.'

'What?'

'We don't just test the woman, you know. It's equally likely to be a male factor. Which is why we always do a sperm analysis of the husband at the same time.'

Millie tried a laugh. 'Honestly. He's never been short in that department. The opposite, in fact.'

Dr Mooney wasn't having any of it. 'We'll get it done just in case.'

'Right,' said Millie weakly. 'I'll tell him what you said, and get him to make an appointment.'

Dr Mooney would forget all about it. His memory wasn't what it used to be.

But he was on the ball today. 'No need,' he told her cheerily. 'Tanya's already phoned him on his mobile to get him to come in.'

Chapter Fifteen

Millie first noticed them on the plane over. They had been drinking, and a bit too friendly with the air hostesses. Then they had got on to the bus that had collected most of the passengers from the flight. They had jostled past Millie on their way to the back of the bus like a bunch of over-excited schoolboys – and some of them were nudging forty, judging by their big bellies and receding hairlines. Hopefully they would be dropped at another resort on the way.

They weren't. They'd followed Millie, Oona and Dennis off the bus and into the Alta Vista Apartments. Now, like Millie, they had obviously decided not to bother unpacking but to catch the last of the afternoon sun, and were grouped around the pool. More beer had materialised. They were laughing very loudly, and jumping in and out of the deep end. One of them had procured a beach ball from somewhere and they were throwing it back and forth amid a running commentary.

'And he shoots . . . and he scores!'

Honestly, thought Millie primly. She was lying on a sun lounger at the other end of the pool, with Factor 35 on, and her spanking new, rather voluminous, white shorts. Oona and Dennis were up in the apartment trying to work the kettle – Dennis declared that if he didn't get a cup of tea soon he would faint.

'Can we not just give him a double gin and tonic and knock him out?' she had murmured hopefully to Millie.

Millie, meanwhile, had taken one of three new beach reads she'd packed and had retired to the pool. Jaz had bought them for her. 'One is about a woman who enjoys threesomes. It'll take your mind off things,' she had said reassuringly. Yvonne had presented her with a bag of boiled sweets for the plane journey, and Deirdre, a rather nice straw hat for the beach.

145

Dorothy, rather worryingly, had given her a religious medal. Somehow Millie didn't think it was to stop the plane from falling out of the skies.

The book wasn't that gripping. Not that Millie was reading it or anything. Really she was thinking about Andrew. Every time she did she came over in waves of hot and cold, and her toes curled up in horror.

She could just imagine the call from Dr Mooney's office to his mobile in Frankfurt. Dr Mooney's secretary, Tanya, could be alarmingly cheerful.

'Oh, hello there! I was just wondering if you could pop into the surgery and give me a little sample?'

There had undoubtedly followed some confusion on his part. 'A sample of what?'

Tanya had probably thought he was being defensive. No man ever wanted to believe it was his fault, she had been known to say. She had most likely called up Millie's file at that point: 'Well, Millie's already been in to have all her bits and pieces checked. Let me see, progesterone, FSH . . . oh, that's not too bad at all for someone her age. So now we just need to check out your little swimmers!'

Andrew might have started to twig at this point. 'Are you talking about fertility tests?'

'You can do a sample at home if you're more comfortable and bring it in,' Tanya might have said encouragingly.

At that point, Millie imagined, Andrew would have demanded to speak to Dr Mooney.

Millie had been delighted to leave the country. In fact, she couldn't skip it fast enough. She had been the first on the plane with her seatbelt on, leaving the whole mess behind.

It was only when she landed that she realised that her mobile phone still worked in Spain. Perfectly. The minute she turned it back on after landing she expected it to beep angrily at her, announcing that she had a voice message from him.

He would be furious. Livid. He would demand to know what she was up to. Was it some kind of scheme she had cooked up with Tanya to try to guilt-trip him into wanting a baby? Or else had she gone completely loopy?

But there had been no message. Possibly he was holding out to berate her in person. Or else he was up a mast and unable to get to his phone.

But now, hours later, there was still no phone call. Not even a vicious text message. It looked less and less likely that he would contact her at all.

Maybe he wasn't angry. He might even be treating the whole thing with some minor amusement – good old Millie, so obsessed with having a baby that she was after an immaculate conception. Or else he might think that she was so unable to come to terms with the break-up that she was living in some makey-uppy land where their marriage was fine, and that he was just away on an extended business trip. He might even have advised Dr Mooney, caringly, that Millie might be more in need of a short course of Valium rather than having her FSH checked.

'You could be right,' Dr Mooney might have concurred sympathetically.

Crossly Millie turned off her phone altogether. To hell with Andrew. She had a plan. And it didn't involve him, thank you very much. Why should she care what he thought?

Because they had been married. They had supposedly loved each other. They had been planning a family together. He had only been gone a matter of weeks.

And he didn't care. He didn't give a hoot about her any more. He wasn't even curious as to why she was pursuing fertility tests after he'd gone. Wasn't it funny how some people could move on so quickly?

But then look at her. Lying on a sun lounger by a pool in Spain, about to have fertility treatment as a single woman. She wasn't exactly a slouch herself in the moving-on department.

For a minute she wished he *would* ring. She would tell him disparagingly, 'I don't want *your* sperm. I'm abroad right now, and I'm going to have a baby via a very nice Spanish donor, thank you. It's going to be a girl, and I'm going to call her Bonita and she'll be all mine. She'll be nothing whatsoever to do with you.'

He might very well fall off his mast with shock.

Millie herself was still half in shock that she was actually here. Ever since the plane had touched down she'd had a slight sense of unreality. While Oona and Dad had been craning their necks to look out the bus windows and pointing out unnecessary things – 'Oh, look at all the palm trees, Millie!' – she had been suspended in a delicious kind of apprehension. After all the planning and angst and sleepless nights, it had finally come together. She was in Spain, even if most of her family had tagged along. The clinic was only a couple of miles up the road. In three days' time she would walk through their doors, and sign up to become a donor sperm recipient, so long as her nerves held out.

And actually, her nerves weren't too bad. She had expected to be much worse. She had thought that the nearer she'd got to the appointment date, the more she would want to chicken out.

But she felt surprisingly calm. The sun helped. It put a nice rosy glow on things. Also, she was rapidly getting sucked into the holiday atmosphere that pervaded the whole place. Reality had been suspended and the usual rules didn't apply.

Why *shouldn't* she have donor sperm if she wanted? Why *shouldn't* she have a child on her own, even if that child had no hope whatsoever of knowing her father? Millie would love her enough for two people. She didn't need a father, not when she had Millie. They would have such fun together, the two of them.

On that pleasant note, she was about to drift off.

'Watch out!' somebody called in warning.

It was too late. The beach ball, soaking wet, landed violently in Millie's lap. The pages of her new book on threesomes were covered in chlorinated water. So were her nice new white shorts.

'For feck's sake,' she spluttered, struggling to sit up.

Then a pair of tanned, rather nicely formed legs arrived up at the side of her sun lounger. Looking upwards she found that they belonged to a man with dark brown eyes and floppy brown hair. He was wearing shorts and a T-shirt, which was wet down the front.

'Sorry,' he said.

She didn't remember seeing him earlier. He was definitely one of the more presentable members of the group, most of whom were now looking over from the other side of the pool with drunken amusement, no doubt delighted that they had disturbed her afternoon siesta.

One of them gave a wolf whistle. Millie stiffened. Honestly!

'Sorry about that,' the man said. It was unclear whether he meant the beach ball or the whistler.

'I'm all wet now,' she pointed out unnecessarily.

'You might as well join us in the pool so,' he said lightly.

Millie blinked. Was he seriously suggesting she hook up with him and his infantile friends? No doubt they would try and undo her bikini top, had she been wearing one.

'I don't think so,' she said.

He looked over at them too. 'They're not normally that bad,' he told her apologetically. 'It's just that they don't get out on their own often.'

She didn't know whether he was joking or not. He looked serious enough. Could they be on some kind of day-release scheme? Probably not all the way from Ireland.

'A good thing too,' she said. That was a bit less frosty. She might as well be civil if she had to face them at the pool every day.

But his next words weren't encouraging. 'We're here on a stag week.'

Oh God. A whole week of them getting plastered around the pool and tying each other to poles naked. How was she going to psyche herself up for her clinic visit with that lot around? They would upset her karma. Worse, they might even upset her hormones – and after Dr Mooney telling her she'd got them just right and everything.

'Jamie over there, he's getting married next month.' He pointed to a man in the pool who was at that moment balanced precariously on another man's shoulders. They were swaying from side to side and singing a Beyonce song. They looked like a pair of mating hippos.

'What a catch,' Millie couldn't help muttering.

'He's a late developer,' the man assured her. 'But we have high hopes for him.'

He had a twinkle in his eye. Which was lovely had Millie been in the mood for it. But she wasn't. She wanted to retreat to her own pleasant little world again of fertility clinics, and getting pregnant. She wanted to write a birth plan in her head, even if that were definitely jumping the gun. And this man was taking up her time.

Plus, out of the corner of her eye she could see Dennis approaching, swatting flies away with a copy of *Crossword Weekly*. There would be no chance at all now of fantasising about anything, not with him asking her whether she knew what the main ingredient of guacamole was, and how many letters were in it.

She handed the beach ball back briskly to the man and lifted her novel. Hopefully he would get the hint.

He didn't. He lingered, tucking the ball under his arm and rocking a bit on his feet. Nice feet too, she noted despite herself. Andrew had had horrible feet – big wide spades of things, with hairy toes and scaly bits in between that he routinely neglected.

Millie was suddenly aware of her own feet and legs, stretched out on the sun lounger on full view. He was looking at them too. She was cursing herself that she hadn't lashed on a bit of fake tan.

Then she caught herself up short: what was she *thinking*? About how attractive she might appear to this stranger? She was in Spain on a deadly serious mission, not to pick up some cheap guy who was obviously on the pull for the week with his friends.

Who were still looking over from the other side of the pool with great interest, and big smirks on their red, inebriated faces. Jamie might be on his stag week, but Millie would bet the rest of them were married, probably with a couple of kids at home. No doubt they hoped to have a bit of 'fun' in Spain without anybody finding out.

Oh yes, Millie had their number all right. She was quite proud of her cynicism. She supposed she had Andrew to thank for that. He had taught her only too well about men's fickleness, and indeed fecklessness:

men who ran a mile from responsibility and duty; silly, immature men like this one standing in front of her. She couldn't see a wedding ring on his finger, but she bet it was in his pocket. That's if he'd ever had the necessary gumption to get married at all.

She must have been glaring quite ferociously at him because he brought the beach ball a little bit closer to his chest protectively.

'Will I see you at the bar later?' he ventured. Foolishly.

'The *bar*?' she enquired in her haughtiest voice.

'Yes,' he said. He pointed to the front of the complex, and said reasonably, 'It's that building over there where I believe they serve alcoholic drinks.'

She bet they did. The more the merrier. No doubt he was hoping to tank her up on a couple of cocktails and notch up his first holiday conquest.

She fixed him with another ferocious stare. He seemed quite taken aback now. He probably thought an apparently single woman like herself would be easy game.

'I don't drink,' she informed him magnificently, even though it was a big fat lie. 'Or smoke, or do illicit drugs, or one-night-stands. Better luck elsewhere.'

She lifted her book again and retreated behind it, even though the page was soaked and she couldn't read a thing.

But her words obviously had the desired effect because when she looked up again he was gone.

'Pass the sunscreen,' Dennis said gamely.

At some point between leaving the house and touching down in Spain he had got over his snit. Or, more likely, he was out to prove to everybody, Mum and Auntie June included, just how much he could enjoy himself now that he had been liberated from his pesky domestic situation. For the past hour he had been sighing blissfully and declaring heartily, if a little falsely, 'This is the life!'

Oona kept looking at him askance. 'Are you feeling all right, Dad?'

'You know, I can't remember the last time I had a proper holiday,' he told them. 'We never really *go* anywhere, your mother and I.' He wrinkled his nose. 'It's always shopping centres, and retail parks, and to be honest there's only so much of that you can take.'

And with that he shook out his ratty old bath-towel across a sun lounger and settled down between Millie and Oona. He had already dispensed with his socks, his sandals, and was busily undoing the buttons on his floral patterned shirt.

'Steady on, Dad,' Oona said in fright.

But he tossed his shirt aside in a cavalier fashion to reveal a pale, hairless chest. It had been concealed under a grey cardigan for so long that you could nearly see the pattern of it on his skin.

'I don't see why I shouldn't come home with a bit of a tan,' he declared in an alarmingly hearty tone. He handed the sunscreen to Oona. 'Here, do my back, will you?'

She grimaced at Millie. This was one of the disadvantages of having left Mum at home. It was her job to do this kind of dirty work; for years now she had been doing his back, his boils, his verrucas and the big patch of dry skin on his thigh that you'd need a strong stomach to approach (and then only at an angle).

Of course, they were all wondering how she and Auntie June were getting on at home, but nobody could mention it. Dennis certainly wasn't going to, even though Nuala had extolled him to ring as soon as they got there.

'Just to let us know that you've arrived safely.'

He hadn't phoned.

'She might think we've crashed,' Millie had said.

'Wouldn't she see it on the news?' Dennis had said darkly.

And of course he had Sky here, which they didn't have at home. He was particularly delighted about that. 'I'm set up for the week now,' he had said. 'No more *Hello!* magazine or *Judge Judy*. I tell you, it'll be a relief.'

There had been one brief, tense moment earlier when he remembered that he had neglected to tell Auntie June that Mum didn't like raisins in her Alpen any more. Dennis usually picked them out one by one, but whether to go ringing up to alert anyone to that fact?

It was then that the true extent of his hurt became apparent. 'She can pick them out herself,' he had announced. Then, in a very carefree voice, 'Who's coming for a swim!'

'Imagine if he's like this for the week?' Oona muttered to Millie now.

But thankfully all his enforced good cheer seemed to have worn him out, because he settled down sleepily on his lounger. Great. They might get an hour of peace.

But he had one last parting shot. 'I hear there's a casino up the road. I thought we might check it out later on.'

On that note he closed his eyes and promptly seemed to fall asleep.

'That's just talk,' Oona told Millie. 'At least I hope so.' The sight of him snoozing set her off yawning too. 'God, I'm wrecked. Although Brendan made me have a lie-in and everything this morning, even though he's the one left behind to look after the kids.'

151

'He's very good to you.' Normally Millie didn't interfere with other people's relationships, but honestly, it was sod's law that she had ended up with no husband at all, while Oona had bagged a man who just kept on getting better and better.

'I know, I know.' Oona sounded more grumpy than appreciative.

Still, you never knew what went on behind closed doors, Millie acknowledged (although it could include group sex, ouiji boards and wife beatings, according to Jaz, during her more inventive moments).

'Can I ask you something about Andrew?' Oona said suddenly.

Millie started unpleasantly. His name was beginning to have that effect on her. 'If you really, really must.'

'I know you two were probably having lots of sex.'

'Sorry?'

This was certainly unexpected.

Oona added hurriedly, 'I mean, if you were trying get pregnant.'

'Well, yes,' Millie conceded reluctantly. She had no wish to cast her mind back to those fumblings under the sheets with Andrew. Her lunch was beginning to come back up, for starters. 'We aimed for every second day.'

Oona's eyes nearly popped out of her head. 'You had sex every second *day*?'

Millie began to feel like a bit of a freak. 'Not all the time,' she amended. 'Just in the middle of the cycle. It was all based on my chart, you see, and my temperatures, and having timed sex.'

'Timed sex!' Oona screeched. 'What, like, you used a stopwatch?'

Millie smiled too. It did sound a bit ridiculous. But there was no denying that both her and Andrew had wanted the deed over and done with as quickly as possible. A duty shag.

'It wasn't much fun,' she confessed.

'It doesn't sound like it,' Oona said. For some reason she looked greatly cheered up. 'Here, do you remember in the early days, when you'd tear the clothes off each other and spend the afternoon in bed?'

Millie did. 'Or the back garden.'

'The back garden!' Oona hooted again. 'Oh, yes.'

Dennis stirred between them. They tempered their giggles.

'You couldn't have sex in our back garden now,' she said wistfully. 'Not with all those vegetables Brendan has sown in his mission to get the children to eat organic. You could end up impaled.'

'The living room floor then,' Millie suggested.

'Yes, well,' said Oona. She looked away. 'Brendan could give it a quick once-over with the Dyson once we're done.' The humour had

152

gone. She sounded a bit fed up. Millie wondered what had started the conversation. Before she could ask, Christian passed by.

'*Hola,*' he said.

'*Hola,*' Millie and Oona rabbited back in their appalling Spanish.

Christian was the bloke who had greeted them at reception. He had flashed them a big white smile before picking up their suitcases. He had slung them up on his shoulders one by one as though they weighed only a feather and set off up the steps in front of them, leaving them to follow his denim-clad bottom.

'Great,' Oona had whispered to Millie. 'Something to look at.'

She had only been joking, of course. At least, Millie hoped. You couldn't really lust after Christian – he wasn't a man, only a boy. It wasn't right or decent. Even just thinking about him in those terms made Millie feel all grubby and ancient.

Oona didn't seem to share her reservations. She watched openly as he strutted past with several black refuse sacks and chucked them into a wheelie bin at the other side of the pool. His sleeveless T-shirt, economical to start with, rode up each time he slung a bag in. He had lovely skin too, brown and smooth and extremely touchable.

'I wonder what age he is?' Oona murmured.

'I'm not getting into this conversation.'

But Oona gave Millie a sideways look. 'I was thinking about you.'

'Oh, *really.*'

'After everything that's happened, a nice holiday romance is exactly what you need.'

Millie would never fit in a holiday romance as well as fertility treatment, but she didn't tell Oona that.

'Not with a toy boy,' she said firmly. 'Or with anybody.'

'He's not that young. Twenty, I'd say. Or maybe twenty-one.'

'And you'd know, would you?'

'I would,' Oona confirmed. 'I have an eye for these things. Oh, he's coming back now.' She urged Millie, 'Sit up a bit. And would you not roll up those white shorts? They're a bit middle-aged.'

Oona herself was resplendent in a red bikini. Her boobs were huge in it, but otherwise she wasn't too saggy at all for a woman who'd had three children, as she'd said herself.

'There's nothing wrong with me,' Millie retorted. She didn't care what Christian thought of her.

In any event it didn't matter because he scarcely looked at her. He came right up beside Oona and loomed over her. His shoulders were so broad that he blocked out the entire sun and Oona had to take off her sunglasses and squint up at him.

'Yes?' she said.

'I hear your kettle is not working properly,' he said.

'Sorry?'

Christian jerked at thumb at Dennis, who was snoring gently, his mouth wide open. 'Your father. He stopped at reception and complained.'

Oona looked at Dennis as though she would like to kill him. 'Oh! No, the kettle's fine. It took a bit longer to boil than we expected, that's all.'

Christian digested this information. 'You have super-quick kettles in Ireland, then?'

Oooh. Sarcasm, definitely. And he was looking Oona up and down now in a manner that could only be described as brazen. Millie felt quite left out. *I* was propositioned earlier on, she wanted to point out peevishly.

But that would spoil the cosy little back-and-forth that Oona and Christian had going on between them.

'We have good kettles, yes,' Oona confirmed to him snootily, even though she would barely recognise a kettle if it came up and introduced itself.

'Maybe I should examine it,' Christian said. At this stage he was looking at her bottom.

'The kettle?' said Oona, just to clarify.

'Yes. In your apartment.'

'If you want.' She shrugged carelessly. This had the effect of setting her boobs off. Christian had to look away. He seemed in pain.

Millie had a sudden vision of Brendan back in Ireland, probably on his hands and knees on the kitchen floor assembling a matchstick ship, or something else thoroughly educational.

'Let's go then,' Oona said.

She rose and put on her sarong. Then she set off across the concrete, Christian following like a puppy dog behind.

Chapter Sixteen

Millie had never set foot in Spain before now. Embarrassingly, she hadn't even been all that sure of its precise location until Dennis had spread out a big map on the kitchen table at home to work out the route from the airport to the resort, even though the bus was picking them up and dropping them to the door.

'They'll probably take that autoroute there,' he had said with great excitement.

Millie just knew that Spain was down there somewhere in Southern Europe. And that it was a warm place. And if she really plundered her store of clichés, she knew that Spanish people liked bullfighting and big plates of paella and the women sometimes wore flouncy flamenco dresses like that doll she'd had when she was about six and that Oona had chewed the head off.

It was appalling, actually, how little she knew. Not a blinking thing. Nor was she likely to learn much, cosseted in the Alta Vista Apartments where the staff spoke better English than she did, and where most restaurants served a full Irish breakfast. Apart for the sun, you'd hardly know you were in Spain at all.

Yet the whole purpose of her trip was to try to get pregnant with a child who would, genetically at the very least, be half-Spanish.

Little Bonita.

Born in Ireland but with one foot in Spain.

She might have Millie's nose but it was just as likely that she would have a crop of luxurious brown hair and dark eyes and crave paella all the time.

Her child's Spanish heritage was something Millie had never really thought about before. Now she wondered how she could *not* have thought about it. Had she been going to try to ignore it? Pretend that he or she was one hundred per cent Irish, and that the Spanish bit didn't

155

really count? What would she say when Bonita asked about her country of birth? Lie? Or, worse: 'Sorry, pet, I haven't a bull's notion about Spain, I just went there because it was handy and they had loads of anonymous sperm donors. But look, here's a map belonging to your granddad. He'll be able to show you all the major autoroutes.'

Now it seemed like a terrible oversight, Millie's non-relationship with Spain. Her lack of any kind of connection.

But she had no connection to Poland either, or Bulgaria, or any of the other European countries that were a magnet for women seeking fertility treatment. Spain had just been easier.

Easier. Imagine telling little Bonita that. Millie would die of shame.

It wouldn't be so bad if there were a traceable father. Someone waiting in the wings until her child was eighteen. Bonita could look him out in her search for her Spanish roots. He might even be willing to take her in hand. Millie could picture Bonita flying out to spend some time with her father in the homeland. They would explore Spain together. Bonita would tell him about the terrible Irish food her mother had cooked all these years, when really she had been dying for tapas. He would teach her Spanish customs and traditions and maybe even his mother, Bonita's grandmother (Millie fondly pictured a benign, wizened old lady in a rocking chair), would teach her a few basic flamenco steps. And then, having fully come to terms with her Spanish side, Bonita would come back home to Millie, naturally. (Or else she might decide she was more Spanish than Irish, and resolve to move to Barcelona for ever, of course. But that was for another day.)

Unfortunately there would be no traceable father. Donor anonymity meant just that. No grandmother either, or aunts or uncles. There would be no one but Millie to nurture and cherish Bonita's heritage. God help her.

I am a bad mother, Millie thought miserably. And she wasn't even one yet. But the further she got towards her goal, the more she realised the implications.

'Don't over-think it,' Jaz had cautioned her. 'So long as you love her, she'll be fine.'

Millie had thought that too. Well, it was handy, wasn't it? But now that she was here, on Spanish soil, she wasn't so convinced. Love was all very well, but there were some things you couldn't ignore either.

On Monday morning Millie managed to shake off Oona and Dad after breakfast and came down to the reception area where it was cool and dark and there were some comfortable chairs. Thankfully there was no sign of Christian. She didn't bother with her racy book about threesomes, or the English language newspapers, but instead industriously spread out the two Spanish phrase books. She started with the most essential phrases, as outlined by one of the books: 'I'm hungry', 'I'm thirsty', 'Can you tell me the way to the pub?'

The other book wasn't much more advanced. One of the first phrases in it was how to ask for more beer. Both books were obviously aimed at tourists, and probably Irish tourists at that. But they would do until she got into town later to buy a proper book. She might even try to see if she could find a Linguaphone course. The language was the key, she had decided. It would be the first step in her new relationship with Spain, and her daughter's. She had no idea how many years it took to become proficient in Spanish. But she would stick with it. She had to. It would, she now realised, be completely wrong to bring a child into the world without giving proper recognition to that child's genetic heritage. She and Bonita would take on Spain together.

'*Hola*,' said somebody beside her.

It was him again. The man from the pool. Taking the mickey, of course, because he had overheard her muttering to herself.

Millie consulted her phrasebook. Then she looked at him and said, '*Dejeme solo, por favour.*'

Her accent was rubbish and he looked stumped.

'It means, leave me alone,' she explained.

She had been joking, kind of, but he looked a bit pissed off.

'Yes, I'm getting that message,' he confirmed politely. 'But I'm actually looking for Christian. Not you.'

That stung. She tried to be nice now. For some reason he was the kind of person you didn't really want to be rude to, even though he was some jackass from an Irish stag party.

'I haven't seen him,' she said helpfully.

'Right.' He looked gloomy. 'Our kettle is broken.'

Two dodgy kettles. That must constitute an epidemic.

And he looked very much in need of a hot cup of coffee. The eyes were hanging out of his head and he had that greenish appearance that comes with a lot of drink. His mates, she bet, were laid out on their beds, unable to move. They had been partying non-stop all weekend. Millie had occasionally seen them loafing about by the pool while she had passed through. And they had staggered into the bar last night while she and Orla and Dad had been having a sedate drink. She had felt the man from the pool looking at her but she had turned primly back to her glass of white wine. They had only been warming up when she had left twenty minutes later.

'Good night last night?' she couldn't resist asking.

'Not bad,' he said, manfully swallowing a beery burp.

Then he grinned at her. His whole face transformed. He had lovely, even teeth and his eyes crinkled up at the sides. 'Actually,' he admitted, 'I think I'm going to die at any moment.'

She found herself grinning back.

'There's no chance you're a nurse or anything?' he said hopefully.

'No. But if you *do* happen to fall down and crack your head on that hard tile floor, you can ring me up and try to claim on your insurance.'

He looked wary. 'Are you one of those . . . claims people?'

He made it sound like she was on a par with a serial killer.

'Yes,' she said gently. 'Didn't I say *try* to claim?'

He laughed. It was a lovely sound. 'You should meet Sandra, Jamie's fiancée. She works in the loans section of the bank. You couldn't get a thing out of her either.'

Millie couldn't believe how friendly they were being after such a bad start.

Not that it meant anything, of course. But it was amazing how a little light-hearted banter could lift your whole morning.

Naturally it didn't last long.

'Do you mind me asking what you're doing here?' he asked suddenly.

'Sorry?'

'In Spain.'

Millie shrugged harmlessly. 'I'm on holiday.'

'So you say. But it's quite obvious that you're not enjoying yourself.'

She shifted defensively. Why did he think she wasn't enjoying herself? She could be having a whale of a time for all he knew!

'What, because I don't go and get out of my head every night?'

And jump into bed with him.

He looked a bit impatient at that. 'It's a beautiful morning outside and you're sitting in the dark learning Spanish like you were back at school.'

Millie closed her phrase books quickly. Possibly she should have chosen somewhere more private to do her crash course. 'I happen to think it's important to know some of the language when you visit a different country,' she said in a very superior voice.

'Really?' he said, one eyebrow arching sceptically.

'Yes. And contrary to what you think, I'm having a perfectly nice holiday, thank you very much.'

'You left the bar at nine o'clock last night.'

He had noticed. A tiny part of her was gratified.

'I'm not here to drink,' she said.

'So what *are* you here to do? Learn obscure Spanish phrases and avoid getting a tan at all costs?'

158

Whether this was a reference to her sensible white shorts she wasn't sure. But it was enough to heat her cheeks and goad her on.

She'd had no intention of actually telling him the truth. Imagine! But maybe she wanted to shock him: to wipe that superior look off his face. Maybe the strain of keeping things from Oona and Dad was getting to her and making her reckless. Or else it was just the fact that she would in all likelihood never set eyes on this guy again, and it didn't matter anyhow.

Whatever the spur was, she found herself announcing, 'If you must know, I'm here for an appointment with a fertility clinic. I'm hoping to have a baby via donor sperm.'

Talk about a conversation killer. He didn't quite blanch, but he looked as if he wished he had never started the conversation in the first place. She fully expected him to make some fumbled excuse and gallop off back upstairs. It would make a good story for the others, when they finally woke up. 'Here, remember that strange woman by the pool? The one in the gigantic shorts who we said was probably frigid? Well, guess what, lads!'

But he didn't go anywhere. He just blinked a bit through his hangover, and scratched his head.

'You're single?' he clarified eventually.

Millie's chin rose. She might as well carry on with the truth. 'Yes. Well, I am now. My husband didn't want children.'

He went a bit greener at this – first fertility issues, and now a broken marriage. And he had only come down to try to get his kettle fixed.

And still he didn't say anything. He just kept looking at her with those sleepy brown eyes. Wouldn't you think he'd offer an opinion at least? Everybody else had one, whether you wanted it or not.

'I suppose you think it's a bad idea,' she challenged him.

He considered this for a long moment.

'Actually,' he said regretfully, 'I think it's a terrible idea.'

Oh. Well, now she knew. Nobody could accuse him of sitting on the fence, that was for sure. She gathered up her books rather quickly. She shouldn't have told him. Stupid thing to have done. And all for what? To score a few points off him? A stranger whom she would never see again. Really stupid, she berated herself,

'Luckily, it doesn't matter what you think,' she said.

'No,' he agreed.

'I'm thirty-nine and I have to get a move on.'

'Absolutely.'

She seemed to be on some kind of self-destructive trip this morning, because she just couldn't shut up. 'It's all right for you men. You can have a baby whenever you want. We're the ones with this horrible timetable hanging over us. We're the ones checking our flipping FSH.' She glared at him.

'And FSH is . . . ?' he said.

'Follicle stimulating hormone. It's the worst one of all.'

'It sounds pretty nasty all right,' he said sympathetically. 'Personally I've only ever had a jab for the German measles.'

Suddenly she found herself smiling again. He was too. Why did they keep doing that, smiling at each other?

'Sorry,' he said. 'That was facetious. Especially in the light of your . . . issues.'

'I prefer to think of it as my journey.'

'Yes. Put that way, it sounds better.'

Millie was all set to be insulted again but then decided that she wasn't. So he didn't agree with her having a baby on her own. At least he'd had the gumption to say it right out. Not like Andrew, who hadn't wanted babies for ages but couldn't pluck up the courage to say it until the last minute.

The man gave a last look around for Christian, decided that he was a no-show, and pushed away from the reception desk.

'Right, well, good luck with things,' he said to Millie.

That was nice too. Even though he thought it was a terrible idea.

'Thank you,' she said. 'Oh. And you're the only one who knows, OK? I haven't told my sister or my dad yet.'

She was immediately sorry she'd said that too. Now he would presume that she was embarrassed and ashamed at what she was doing, and secretive along with it. Talk about handing ammunition to someone on a plate.

But he just said, 'My lips are sealed.'

That made her look automatically at his lips. She blushed and looked away quickly.

'I hope you enjoy your week,' she said rather formally.

'If I last it,' he said bravely. 'I have a few miles on the clock too, you know. The rest of them call me Daddy.'

He couldn't be much above his late-thirties. If even that. Maybe he had a few lines around his eyes but Millie could forgive that. They added character.

Was she blushing again? Yes. Damn.

'By the way,' he said, 'I'm Simon Burke.'

'I'm Millie Doran,' she said.

'It's nice to meet you, Millie.'

★   ★   ★

Nuala and Auntie June had been out for dinner the previous night.

'Dinner?' said Dennis, nonplussed.

He and Mum didn't really go out to dinner. Why get ripped off by those cordon blue places, he maintained, when there was a perfectly good lasagne in the freezer at home? A few frozen chips alongside, and a tin of peas, and it was a meal fit for a king.

Oona regularly accused him of being totally unsophisticated, but he just took that as a compliment.

'We went to a fish restaurant in town,' Auntie June elaborated. 'She loved it.'

Dennis was obviously torn between the obvious Omega 3 benefits of this excursion, and his chagrin that Nuala was completely fine without him. Living it up, in fact.

And she didn't even have the decency to tell him about the fish restaurant in person. He was unsure where she was, and Auntie June wasn't saying. He couldn't very well go asking, because that would spoil the big show he was putting on of having such a good time that he had scarcely given them a thought.

'We're just going down to the pool now,' he told Auntie June in a breezy voice. 'It's about twenty-seven degrees. Just perfect.'

It was far too hot for him only he wouldn't admit it. And he had got burnt too. Oona wasn't that exact with the sun cream, and there were big angry red streaks across his back from his couple of days by the pool. Luckily he couldn't see them.

'We might even be going to a restaurant ourselves later on,' he added for good measure.

Millie would bet it would be a fish restaurant.

'Good for you,' Auntie June said cheerily. She had the kind of voice that carried. She had phoned Oona's mobile phone, which Dennis now had pressed up to his ear, but Millie and Oona could still hear her side of the conversation quite clearly.

'Don't worry about Nuala anyway,' she said, adding insult to injury. 'She's just fine. That toe is nearly healed as good as new.'

'Good, good,' said Dennis, airily.

'Oh, just ask to speak to her, Dad,' Millie butted in. 'You know you want to.' Honestly. Talk about being childish.

Dennis shushed her. He listened intently to the phone.

'Sorry, what was that, June?'

Auntie June's voice came echoing briskly over the phone. 'I said, I hope you don't mind me pointing it out, but there's a bit of a whiff off her.'

Nobody else would have brought it up. But after a lifetime of living amongst dogs, Auntie June was completely unfazed by things like odours. In fact she quite enjoyed them. No doubt she was looking forward to running a bubble bath later on and giving Nuala a good scrub.

Dennis's face didn't change. But Millie knew he was fully aware of her and Oona behind him, listening to every word. Especially her.

His voice was very calm when he spoke again. 'Are you sure it's not those hydrangeas? They can get up quite a stink this time of the year.'

Oona looked at Millie. Millie could see she was wondering what the heck was going on. '*Hydrangeas?*' she whispered to Millie.

Indeed. Auntie June was having none of it either. 'Dennis, I know the smell of hydrangeas. This was not that smell. When was the last time she had a good wash?'

Dennis wasn't getting into it. Not with Auntie June, in any case. His colour was high and his mouth thin. 'I wonder if I could speak to her?'

'She's not here. She went for a walk on her own. I told you I'd get her out and about,' Auntie June said with satisfaction.

Dennis got off the phone quickly after that. He didn't look at Millie. But he knew that he couldn't get away with it this time again.

'She's not that keen on baths these days for some reason,' he told them, looking rather embarrassed.

'What?' said Oona. 'Tell her to have a shower then.'

'She's not that keen on showers either,' he said stiffly.

Oona looked at Millie. This was certainly unexpected.

'I'm sure it'll work itself out,' Dennis said, putting an end to the conversation.

He sat there quietly for a while, looking a bit bruised and lost, and Millie felt sorry for him, even though a part of her wanted to strangle him.

Even Oona eased up on him. 'You know, maybe you should stay here for the afternoon. Let that sunburn go down.'

Millie thought it wasn't a bad idea. 'You could watch Sky News. That nice Adam Boulton might be on.'

'You just don't want an old goat like me trailing after you for the afternoon,' he said flatly. 'I wouldn't blame you.'

'Nonsense!' Oona cried valiantly, even though it was true. She cunningly deflected the heat from herself. 'It's Millie who doesn't want *us* tagging along.'

In other words, her absence that morning had been noted.

'Don't be ridiculous,' said Millie piously. 'Of course I want to spend the afternoon with my lovely family.'

Big fat lies. What she had really planned to do was callously ditch Oona and Dad again and go to see the clinic. Her appointment wasn't until tomorrow morning but she had planned on a little recce first. She just wanted to stand outside and look at the building, that was all: the pile of bricks and mortar that housed her deepest hopes and dreams. Not to mention many test tubes of frozen, anonymous, Spanish sperm.

But there was no chance of that now. Maybe it was just as well. Dad really did look in need of some TLC.

She linked her arm with his. 'Come on. Let's go out.'

'Where?'

'We'll find somewhere.'

'*Hola.*' Christian, having been missing for the most of the morning, suddenly materialised as Oona and Millie passed through reception.

Millie guessed that he had spent a good deal of that time doing his hair, which was so tousled and windswept that it couldn't possibly be natural.

He seemed to have chosen his wardrobe with great care too. He wore a tight white vest that was made of the thinnest of material – you could actually see his nipples through it, though Millie tried not to look – his jeans were the spray-on kind, and she wouldn't have been at all surprised had there been a pair of socks or two stuffed down the front. Or maybe not.

'Oh! Ah, um, hi,' said Oona, her voice oddly high.

But naturally she was bound to be unsettled by such relentless attention on her breasts. Christian was staring at them again. His fingers were flexing in a manner that suggested that he would like to spring over the reception desk at them.

It would have helped had she worn something a little less clingy. A touch less Lyrca, a dash less colour. But the bright yellow top she had chosen only served to make them the centrepiece of the entire room.

Had she worn it on purpose? Surely not. She certainly hadn't gone to any trouble with the rest of herself. Her nose was shiny and freckled from the sun, and her hair was like a giant, sun-streaked halo around her head.

But she looked healthy, and kind of earthy. Maybe that was what appealed to Christian. He might be fed up of all those gorgeous, skinny, dusky Spanish girls, and quite fancied a plump, big-breasted mature Irish woman. Maybe there was hope for them all yet.

'Did your kettle boil OK this morning?' he enquired in a most leading manner.

He had spent over an hour on the kettle that first evening. Dennis had eventually awoken and trotted up to see what was keeping them, and had found Christian lounging on the balcony, stripped down to his vest and sipping one of Dennis's beers. Oona had said that it was the least she could offer him after he had fixed the kettle. Which wasn't actually broken in the first place, Millie wanted to point out.

'Yes, thank you,' Oona murmured. 'It was piping hot.'

This set Christian off twitching again. A pink tongue darted out to wet his lips and his neck was going all red.

Millie cast a warning look at Oona. She really should know better than to wind up a young, innocent (or maybe not so innocent) lad like him in such a manner. Even if it was just for fun. Could she not see the effect her breasts alone were having on him? After this encounter he would probably disappear to his bedroom for the afternoon, wherever it was, and engage in pursuits that Millie didn't even want to think about.

But Oona was rather pink in the cheeks herself. Still, it was a very long time since anybody had flirted with her. She was probably in shock. They would laugh about it later.

Dennis arrived in reception then. They'd left him upstairs faffing about with mosquito cream. If he was being forced out on some scenic walk it was only a matter of time before he'd get bitten, he'd declared. He really was down in the dumps.

'There you are,' he said ungraciously to Christian. He still hadn't forgiven him for drinking his beer. 'My daughters and I are going out for the afternoon,' he announced. He seemed to be under some misapprehension that this was a grand five-star hotel where the owners (a) personally knew everybody who was staying there and (b) cared about them. 'Would you be able to recommend some places for us to visit?' He only stopped short of saying, 'My good man.'

Christian blinked. He was more used to requests to summon ambulances for holidaymakers who had drunk too much and fallen off their balconies.

He lifted one shoulder in a disinterested shrug. 'I can give you some leaflets.'

Dennis was used to disrespect. He was used to young men not meeting his eye. What he was not used to, in recent years at least, was hot young Mediterranean men blatantly ogling his younger daughter's assets, as Christian was doing now. Openly! Brazenly! Dennis hadn't seen the like of it in twenty years, not since that time he had found Oona under a bush with a college student, and he had been doing more than ogling.

Dennis was the wrong man to mess with that afternoon. He'd taken on Auntie June and he'd take on this fellow too.

And so he drew himself to his full height of five foot nine inches, moved in front of Oona protectively and squared up to Christian at the reception desk. All he was missing was his grey cardi.

'We don't want any leaflets to do with old churches,' he told him threateningly. 'Or museums, if we can help it.'

Christian eyed him back dangerously. He had obviously had some experience of dealing with the belligerent fathers of attractive daughters he was intent on bedding. He wasn't cowed by this one. He produced a sheaf of leaflets from under the desk.

'Art houses?' he retaliated, squaring his shoulders too.

'No,' Denis spat.

'Animal sanctuaries?'

'You must be joking.'

Oona and Millie held their breaths. Dennis so far had the upper hand. And he knew it too.

Christian was forced to play his trump card. He drew out a leaflet from the bottom of the pack. 'Shopping centres?'

Dennis hesitated. He was tempted. 'What kind of shops are we talking here?' he said gruffly.

'All the big design houses,' Christian told him seductively.

That did it. 'We'll take it,' Dennis conceded. He never liked giving an advantage to these young whippersnappers, but at the same time there was nothing he liked better than a good browse in the thirty-per-cent-off aisle. Besides, no doubt he was thinking, what possible harm could come to Oona, now that she was in her late thirties, married and a mother of three? And her with a lovely house-husband back home who could whip up the lightest soufflé in Ireland and who worshipped the very ground she walked upon?

'Don't tell Auntie June,' he told Oona and Millie. Then, snatching the leaflet from Christian's hand, he led the way out into the sun. 'Come on, girls,' he said, as though they were four again.

Christian waited until Dennis was gone before saying slyly to Oona's bottom, '*Adiós, Bella.*'

She jumped a foot in the air.

Chapter Seventeen

They had a great time shopping. They spent the whole sunny afternoon inside a neon-lit, air-conditioned shopping mall, going up and down escalators and accumulating an array of expensive-looking bags.

'Should we not be lying on a beach or something?' Oona had briefly worried. 'Or going to visit a historic landmark that we can take photos of and show them around when we get home?'

Dennis soon put paid to that by announcing excitedly, 'They're selling Gabor shoes at forty per cent off down in the basement. We'd better go quick.'

The whole thing had greatly cheered him up. The beauty of it was that you wouldn't see every Tom, Dick and Harry marching around in the same gear at home. Everything they bought would be unique. They'd be like something out of *Hello!* magazine themselves. Then he went and spoilt it all by buying two new grey cardigans that were identical to the wardrobe full of grey ones that he already had at home.

But mostly he had bought stuff for Nuala. He picked out skirts and blouses and a lovely new winter coat in a deep purple. He knew at a glance the correct waist size, or the right trouser leg length.

'She'd look nice in this, wouldn't she?'

'She would, Dad.' Millie hesitated. She didn't want to spoil the afternoon but at the same time there were things she wanted to know. 'About the bath thing, Dad . . .'

He said straightaway, and in a rather rehearsed fashion, 'She has quirks, Millie. That's all I can call them. I wouldn't worry too much about them if I were you.'

'This is not about me, Dad.'

'Look, I know you're concerned. But she's fine. I'm looking after her. She's perfectly all right.'

They weren't the answers Millie wanted but she wasn't going to get any more; he had noticed a whole rail of discount handbags and had gone galloping off. He only stopped when Oona pointed out that he'd never get it all into his suitcase on the way back, and he'd end up paying an excess charge at the airport. And what if he got searched at security and they found all those women's clothes?

'I think we'll have to go out tonight and show some of this off,' Oona declared happily. She had been in high good humour all afternoon, which wasn't like her at all. And her cheeks looked rather flushed. Millie was putting it down to the sun.

She felt rather flushed herself. But she knew the reason why: Simon.

She kept thinking of his eyes. They had been so nice and open and friendly, too – up to the point where she had told him of her intention to become a single mum via donor sperm. There had been a definite change in them then. They hadn't exactly grown frosty but they had looked at her in a different way. As though she had disappointed him or something.

And he didn't even know her! Or the first thing about her!

What was his problem, anyway? Couldn't he bear the thought of sisters doing it for themselves? Perhaps he was peeved that he had loads of sperm going spare, and she hadn't taken him up on the offer of even a drink, never mind anything else.

She decided she didn't like him any more. Not that she had liked him to begin with. Well, she had, a little bit. But if he was going to come over all judgemental just because she was availing of donor IUI, then frankly, to hell with him.

'You haven't bought anything at all,' Oona suddenly said accusingly, as though this were a mortal sin.

'I didn't see anything I liked,' Millie said evasively.

How could she think about shopping when she had such an important day ahead of her tomorrow? She would be meeting with doctors who held her future in their latex-covered hands. She would be poring over the files of anonymous Spanish men whose son or daughter she might one day give birth to. How could Gabor shoes compare, even if they were forty per cent off?

Andrew rang just as Oona had persuaded Millie to trying on a pair of knee-high boots that she suspected made her look like a farmer.

She nearly dropped the phone in surprise and, if she were to admit it, fright. Here it came: the bollocking about Tanya from Dr Mooney's surgery ringing up looking for a sperm sample.

'It's me,' he announced tersely.

The assumption was that she would know exactly who 'me' was.

That, naturally, she had been thinking of him twenty-four hours a day since he had gone.

She should have said, 'Who?' of course. Just to show him.

Instead she rather cravenly said, 'Oh, hello!'

Like she was pleased to hear from him or something.

Oona had copped what was going on. She took Dennis's arm and began to lead him firmly in the direction of the shop's coffee bar. She gave Millie a look that was half encouraging and half sympathetic, and then abandoned her completely in favour of a double latte.

Millie decided she would seize the initiative. 'Look,' she told Andrew rather loudly, 'I'm sorry about Tanya. It was all a big mix-up.'

She would just leave it at that. Blame it on a clerical error or something. He might think there was some other fellow at the surgery with a name like his, and a wife he couldn't impregnate.

'Tanya?' he said. Then, 'Oh, that. I didn't know what she was on about.'

That was all he said. There was no interrogation. No fury. No curiosity at all, really. You would think he dealt with misplaced requests for sperm samples every day of the week.

He really didn't care. That much was becoming ever clearer.

'Right. Well, that's sorted then,' Millie said, rather limply.

So what was he ringing her up for? She felt a treacherous ray of hope spring up in her. Even though she hated his very guts.

But if she hated him so much then why did the sound of his voice make her feel like crying? It was the stress of everything, she decided. She wouldn't be here in Spain at all if it weren't for him.

His next words sent her heart into freefall. 'I got a statement from the bank today.' He sounded like he had been bottling it up for about three hours.

'Did you?' She had got one last week, but hadn't bothered opening it. He must have phoned up the bank and got them to redirect his post.

'From our joint savings account,' he said, emphasising the word 'joint'.

'Oh.'

His voice went up a notch. 'There's a whole load of money gone from it. Thousands of euro, Millie.' Then, in the manner Agatha Christie, he said accusingly, 'And I haven't touched it. So it must be you!'

Well, of course it was her. How else was she to pay for the clinic fees, and the flights and the accommodation? Given that she was the type of person who spent everything that she earned, usually on nothing tangible, her own current account wasn't able to bear the strain.

And so she had dipped into the joint savings account. The rainy day account for when the roof fell in, or one of them got seriously ill ('Oh stop!' Millie had cried when Andrew had said this), or when they wanted to upgrade from their little semidetached to a big mansion in the countryside with an indoor pool and a couple of horses galloping around the paddock ('I notice you're not saying stop now,' Andrew had ragged her).

Saving money hadn't come naturally to either of them, so the balance had been hard-earned. Andrew had reluctantly cancelled several monthly laddish magazine subscriptions. In turn Millie had declared that they were spending far too much in the local Italian restaurant and that from now on, she would cook at home – a decision they both came to regret very quickly. But they persisted, and between them they had managed to salt away a good few thousand in the special savings account.

All right, so she should have asked. She could have lied that she was changing her car or something. But at least half the money was hers, wasn't it? To be spent in whatever way she wanted.

And in some ways it was poetic justice. He had refused her a baby, and so it was only right and proper that their joint savings account pay for fertility treatment for her. Put like that, she didn't feel a bit bad about it.

'That's right,' she said. She wasn't going to deny it, especially as the bank probably had rakes of CCTV footage of her standing at the tellers' desk, requesting the cheque.

She wasn't prepared for the severity of Andrew's reaction.

'That's called stealing,' he thundered down the phone. 'Do you realise that? Just because I was gone, you thought you could help yourself?'

'For God's sake, Andrew. It's only a few thousand. I'll put it back.' Talk about an overreaction.

'Bloody right you will.' There was something in his voice that she had never heard before: a bullying tone. A hint of a threat. 'Every cent of it. I might have known you'd pull something like this behind my back.'

Millie was half incredulous. Was he really ringing her up to scream down the phone about a petty sum of money? Their marriage breakdown hadn't exercised him as much.

'Half of it's mine,' she argued, trying not to betray her upset. 'You can take your half if you want.'

'I've informed the bank,' he told her, in the coldest voice possible. 'They're freezing the account as we speak. You won't be able to touch another cent without my signature.'

Money. Was that what their lovely, friendly marriage of two years had boiled down to? A few lousy euro in a joint savings account.

He was a stranger now. There was nothing left of the old Andrew.

Just some hostile, emotionless man who didn't even want to know what she'd used the money for. She might have needed an operation, for heaven's sake! Or a prosthetic limb, or something. Wouldn't you think he'd have at least been curious?

But Andrew's interest in her life seemed over. Now he just wanted his share of what was left.

Millie was fiercely glad she'd withdrawn the entire clinic fees that day. He could freeze the account, but he'd already paid for her treatment.

'Oh, go and stuff it!' she shouted childishly, and hung up.

Simon was sitting at the bar that evening when she walked in.

Millie noticed him immediately. He was the only one of his group not wearing a large green leprechaun hat and carrying a four-pint tankard of beer. Two of them were already sliding off their seats, including the groom-to-be, Jamie.

What a crowd of idiots, she thought viciously.

She ignored them and elbowed her way to the bar. She needed a drink. A big one. Or else a stiff one. Would it be too rude to ask for a big stiff one?

Christian was behind the bar.

'Do you do everything around here?' she asked.

'Yes,' he said sulkily. 'And the pay is shitty. But at least I get to meet nice women.' He didn't mean Millie. Both of them knew that. But he might at least have pretended. He might have had the decency to bolster her ego, left in shreds by a horrible call from her nasty husband.

Instead he looked past her to the door and enquired, 'Where's your sister tonight?'

Upstairs snoring her head off in a belated siesta in front of Sky News, that was where, and probably dribbling.

It was time to burst Christian's bubble, and in the mood Millie was in, she was just the person to do it. 'Look, Christian, you seem like a nice person, and you're very, um, sexy.'

'Yes,' he agreed proudly.

'But I should point out at this stage that my sister is married. With three children.' This didn't seem to be having the desired effect on him. He gave her a look as though so say, 'And your point is . . . ?'

She would have to lay it on a bit thicker. 'The youngest of whom is still in nappies and has recently started to suck her thumb again, and who is at this moment probably bawling her eyes out for her mammy.'

In a further effort to diffuse his lust, she said, 'She also has a husband called Brendan. He's massive – about six foot five. And handy with his fists. He's capable of anything once he gets a couple of pints in him.'

She let this hang in the air ominously for a bit.

Christian brooded silently for ages. Either he was contemplating a crying baby or else a vicious husband flying into a jealous rage and possibly doing him damage.

Then he looked up and announced, 'This Brendan, he's not much of a husband.'

Either he was very brave or very stupid. Or else completely undone by lust. Were Oona's knockers really that great?

'You mightn't want to say that to his face,' Millie advised him.

But Christian looked rather righteous. 'He has neglected his wife.'

'What?'

'He's not paying her the attention she deserves.'

Millie felt on safer ground now. 'Listen, you've totally got the wrong end of the stick. He's a house-husband. He does everything for her. She doesn't lift a finger from one week to the next. He even volunteered to look after the three kids while she went off on holiday! There isn't a man on this earth who could do more for his wife than Brendan.'

Christian waved a hand dismissively. 'I mean sexually,' he pronounced. 'Anyone can see that. She's a woman who has lain untouched for many months.'

Millie had a vision of Oona splayed out upstairs, her big feet up on the sofa. It was most uncomfortable to speculate about who had been touching her, and how much. She was her sister, for heaven's sake. There were some places you just didn't go.

At the same time she felt she should defend her, or else Brendan – she wasn't sure which. 'I'm sure their sex life is perfectly . . . adequate.'

'I can tell.' Christian looked rather smug. You would think he had a degree in spotting sexually deprived female holidaymakers. Undoubtedly he had consoled more than a few in his time.

Well, he wouldn't be consoling Oona – even if she *had* been questioning Millie closely about the intensity of her own love life only the day before yesterday.

Millie wondered now whether there were indeed cobwebs in her sister's marital bed. And if so, what or who had caused them?

Nancy popped into her head. Nancy, with her big bouncy bob and her drop scones. Was it possible that Brendan was inspecting more than her gazebo?

'It's a waste,' Christian declared. 'A woman like that!'

'Yes, that may be, but it's not really anything to do with us,' Millie told him firmly. In other words, hands off.

But Christian didn't look like he was put off at all. Worryingly, he looked like she had just laid down a challenge.

'Can you get me a cocktail?' Millie begged.

She was exhausted with her sister's problems. It was time to move on to her own, which were legion and never-ending it seemed. She was desperately upset about the phone call from Andrew, even though she tried not to be. It just all seemed so petty and small. He had fought harder for his share of the spoils than he ever had for her. There was something about the whole thing that was shocking.

'Something very strong,' she added.

'Coming right up,' Christian promised her, and went off in the direction of a vodka bottle.

But she couldn't even enjoy her pity-party in peace. Out of the corner of her eye she could see Jamie, the drunken groom-to-be, wobbling towards her. Please God he was only on his way to the toilets to vomit or something.

He wasn't. He came right up to her and, after missing twice, leaned a big, beefy, sunburnt arm on the bar beside her. He gave her a stupid smile, and said, 'Hello.'

Millie recoiled from the stench of beer.

'Sorry,' he apologised. 'We're on a bit of a session.'

'No kidding.'

'I'm Jamie.'

'Yes, I know. And you're marrying Sandra, who works in the loans section of the bank and who would probably tears strips off you if she knew you were drinking so much.' She wagged a finger at him sternly.

Jamie looked briefly troubled. 'You're right. She'd murder me.' But then his face cleared. 'But she knows Simon is with us. He never lets us do anything too mad. The lads wanted to go to a lap-dancing club last night, but Simon said no.' He added hurriedly, 'Don't tell Sandra that.'

He looked across reverently at Simon. Millie did too. Simon was studiously ignoring her gaze. But his neck was so red that it looked like it had been slapped. And there was something about the set of his shoulders that told her that Jamie was in for it later on.

'He's a lovely guy,' Jamie told Millie earnestly.

'Good for him.'

'Now, normally I don't try and matchmake for him . . .'

'Thank God.'

'It's just that I know he likes you, and here we all are on holiday . . .'

'And you thought maybe I'd be up for a quick holiday fling?'

Jamie blinked hopefully. 'Are you?'

'No!' She glared at him. 'Besides, I thought you were getting married to Sandra?'

He looked wretched again. 'You're right, you're right. Old habits die hard and all that. I wouldn't have had a quick fling anyway.'

'I wasn't offering,' she reminded him.

Jamie got back to the task at hand. 'You and Simon have a lot in common. He doesn't do quick flings either.'

Simon was coming across as an all-round saintly guy. Didn't drink too much, didn't sleep around, ran a mile from half-naked women winding themselves around poles. Got uptight and moral over things that were none of his business, including her fertility treatment.

'He sounds like a bit of a bore,' she said clearly.

Jamie was offended now. 'He certainly is not! No, he can let his hair down along with the best of them. He once went on a bender with me for five days, we ended up in Wales. He's great craic when he gets going. He's just not an eejit, that's all.'

Unlike the rest of them.

'Glad to hear it.'

Millie just wanted to be left in peace now. She had a headache, courtesy of Andrew.

But Jamie was hanging on unsteadily to the bar, talking up his mate Simon. Like she cared. 'He'd kill me for saying this, but he can be a bit slow to make a move sometimes. Go over and chat her up, we said to him. Buy her a drink. She's a lovely-looking bird. I mean, woman. But he wouldn't. I think it was maybe because you knocked him back the other afternoon.' He looked at her rather reproachfully.

Millie wanted to tell him that Simon's sudden lack of interest in her was not so much her refusal to join him for a drink but rather his problem with her intention to have a baby on her own.

'I just don't think we have much in common,' she told him firmly.

Jamie played what he obviously thought was his trump card. 'He's the last one of us to get married. He'd never admit it, but he's dying to settle down. He's just never met the right woman.'

Millie could feel Simon's eyes on her now. He was staring at her from across the room. But he wasn't getting up to come over.

She didn't look back. Instead she consulted her watch. It was nearly nine o'clock. She decided she would take her drink up to the apartment with her. She wanted to get a good night's sleep before her appointment in the clinic in the morning. She wanted to go to sleep and block out the telephone conversation with Andrew.

'I hope he finds her,' she told Jamie kindly, as Christian brought over a lethal-looking cocktail with an umbrella sticking out of the top. 'But it's not me.'

Chapter Eighteen

The clinic had a cappuccino maker.

'Have a biscuit too,' Maria said to Millie encouragingly. 'And there're magazines there while you wait.'

Maria was as lovely in person as she'd sounded in her emails. She was warm and welcoming, and ushered Millie into a comfy waiting room.

'Are you nervous?' she asked kindly.

'A bit.' It came out as a squeak. The truth was that Millie had a lump in her throat the size of a fist.

'Don't worry,' said Maria. 'He's nearly done. You won't have long to wait.'

Millie was in no hurry to see Dr Costa. She was suffering from a severe case of last-minute nerves. They had kicked in last night when she'd got back to the apartment. She couldn't even drink her cocktail. Oona had finally woken up on the couch, and kindly drunk it for her. She had enjoyed it so much that she had gone off down to the bar to get another one.

'Back in a minute,' she had promised.

'Do you want to watch Sky News?' Dennis had asked – as though there were anything else on.

'No, thanks, Dad. I'm going to have an early night.'

He had looked at her keenly. 'Everything all right?'

She was surprised he'd noticed there might be something up with her. The euphoria of the shopping trip had worn off hours ago and he'd sunk back into gloom. He wasn't even bothering with the pretence of enjoying himself any more. Oona was fit to hit him over the head with a crude object and dump him in the pool.

It was on the tip of Millie's tongue to spit it all out. But she didn't want to add to his bad mood by telling him that he may well

175

become a granddaddy again should her dalliances with donor sperm work.

Plus, she didn't have the courage. Plain and simple. Somehow she knew that the fact that she hadn't told her family yet didn't bode well for her future as a single mother with Bonita.

'I just need a good night's sleep,' she mumbled pathetically.

But she couldn't sleep, of course. She tossed and turned and fretted about tomorrow, and wondered what in the blazes had led her to this place. Andrew, of course. It was all his fault. He had forced her down this road.

She indulged in several violent fantasies of him being killed or maimed horribly in an industrial accident, or indeed any accident at all. She must have drifted off on his screaming, agonised face, because when she looked at the clock again it was two a.m. Someone was creeping unsteadily around the apartment. Dad? Or a foolhardy burglar after their passports? She was about to search around for a handy poker when the noise stopped, only to be followed swiftly by a loud snoring. Oona! Who'd had several more cocktails, judging by the racket from her. Had Christian made them for her?

Millie had eventually got up very quietly at six. She was too excited to stay in bed, and too scared. She had no idea what lay in store for her at the clinic. She hadn't even known what to wear. She didn't have anything formal, and it seemed inappropriate to show up in a T-shirt and shorts. In the end, she decided on a printed wraparound skirt and a smart white T-shirt.

Another thought struck her now as she sat in the waiting room – something she hadn't thought about before.

'I won't have to . . . take my clothes off or anything, will I?' she blurted to Maria. She would if they asked, of course. It was just that she wasn't prepared.

Thankfully Maria didn't burst into uncontrollable laughter at the naïve question. Or look horrified. At this point she had probably heard it all.

'Not today,' she said reassuringly. 'This is just the initial consultation.' She added, 'But you will have to for the actual treatment.'

'Yes, of course,' said Millie quickly, lest Maria think she was a total hick.

Maria didn't. In fact she came over all protective. 'It's all right,' she said. 'You're not expected to know these things. Most of our patients never in their wildest dreams thought they'd end up in a clinic like this. They thought they'd have kids the normal way, like everybody else – get married, throw out the condoms, aim roughly for Day 14, and hey presto. But it doesn't work out that way a lot of the time.'

'No,' Millie agreed, relaxing. Wasn't Maria marvellous!

'And sometimes the only problem is the lack of a man. We get a lot of singles like yourself – ladies who never met the right man, or ladies who *did* meet the right man but he didn't stick around.'

'That was me,' Millie said, suddenly wanting to blub.

'You poor thing,' said Maria sympathetically. She didn't pry into the exact circumstances. 'But, you know, you've come to the right place. We treat hundreds of women here every year. Not all of them have gone home with babies, but a good few have.' She jerked her head reverentially towards a closed white door at the end of the corridor. 'If anybody can get you pregnant, it's Dr Costa.'

Millie looked too, having an incongruous mental image of some big stud emerging to give her an oily smile, and shout, 'Next!'

She was glad Maria couldn't see inside her head. She would be appalled.

Anyhow, there was no sign of Dr Costa. The couple that had gone in before Millie were taking a long time. Millie had tried not to stare at them in the waiting room earlier. They in turn had barely nodded at her.

Well, it was a difficult one. What was there to say? 'Are you here for a baby too? So are we!'

The things they had in common were too painful and too intimate to get into a casual conversation about.

So they had all read their magazines and politely ignored each other, until the white door at the end of the corridor had mysteriously swung open and Maria had directed them in to the unseen Dr Costa.

Millie hadn't caught a glimpse of him then either. Maybe he didn't exist at all. Maybe the whole clinic was all a moneymaking scam and there was just a big hole in the floor behind that white door that you fell through, having first been robbed of your traveller's cheques.

She must stop this. The clinic was a highly reputable fertility clinic. Besides, just one look at Maria's earnest, compassionate face said that she wasn't in this lark for the money. This was a vocation for her.

Millie tried to relax but it was impossible. Her palms were sweaty and her stomach felt like it was in a vice. She picked up a copy of a magazine to try to take her mind off things. It was in English too – another of Maria's little touches.

Mum would have enjoyed the magazine. It had loads of pictures of weddings and surgically enhanced celebrities. At the thought of her Millie felt a fierce pang of longing. Mum would have come with her, had she known. No matter what her opinion of what Millie was doing, she wouldn't have let her sit here all by herself in this clinic, without somebody even to hold her hand.

'Millie?' said Maria.

Millie looked up. Maria was gesturing towards the corridor. The white door at the end of the corridor had swung mysteriously open. Where the couple before her had gone was anybody's guess.

'You're next.'

Dr Costa wasn't oily at all. He had a face that crinkled when he smiled, and soft fuzzy white hair and a big dimple in his chin. He was, Millie decided, a dote.

He also had several photos on display of himself and his five children, so he was obviously doing something right.

There was no trap door in his office either, only big comfy cream leather chairs and a desk that was reassuringly devoid of unwashed coffee cups and two inches of dust.

Her file was open in the middle of it.

Dr Costa looked up from it now, and spoke in the kind of steady, confident voice that immediately instilled trust. It was a voice that said anything was possible.

'Intrauterine insemination with donor sperm is very straightforward. It's simply the injection of prepared sperm through a soft catheter into the uterine cavity on the appropriate day of the cycle.'

That didn't sound too bad at all. She already knew what it would entail from her own research, of course. But it was still reassuring to hear it directly from Dr Costa; that there wasn't some horrible, hidden procedure involving clamps and stirrups and gallons of tears, probably her own.

The way he was putting it, it was no worse than getting a smear done. And, actually, at Millie's last smear Dr Mooney had been unable to locate her cervix – 'It's in there somewhere, I just have to find it,' he had puffed – so IUI actually sounded a lot less painful, not to mention embarrassing.

'You might experience some mild cramping during the procedure but that should resolve itself quickly,' Dr Costa told her. 'We ask you to lie down for fifteen minutes afterwards, but then you can leave the clinic and carry on as normal.'

Carry on as normal? Millie already knew that she would probably wrap herself in cotton wool for several days and lie in a horizontal position with a pillow under her hips. Meals would be taken through straws. She wasn't going to go through all of this only to have everything fall out the minute she stood up.

'That all sounds great,' she said, her nerves rapidly disappearing.

Dr Costa cautioned, 'There is a small risk of infection – maybe one per cent – and you'll have to inform us if you get any chills, temperate rises, that kind of thing.'

One per cent? thought Millie. Phooey! A tiny risk compared to the possibility of taking a real live baby home.

Her confidence grew. This was going to be OK. This was going to be fine.

'Now,' he said, 'we need to talk about timing.'

Nothing he said could have put Millie more at her ease. Timing was her forte, her *raison d'être* for months on end (as Andrew would testify). She could set her watch by her own cycle.

'Day 14,' she said confidently.

'Sorry?'

'That's the day I ovulate. I can show you if you want.' She had brought along her temperature charts for each menstrual cycle. She had drawn a little picture of an egg in a nest on each day that she had ovulated. Andrew had hooted when he had seen it. But she had known that some day it would come in useful.

Disappointingly, Dr Costa seemed happy enough to take her word for it. 'We can go by that if you really want,' he said, 'but usually we prescribe stimulants.'

He meant ovulation stimulants. Millie had read stories about them on the Internet, and their side effects. For every woman who took them successfully, there seemed to be another who complained of fierce headaches, horribly throbbing ovaries, night sweats that soaked the bed, and psychotic exchanges with their husbands. Sometimes all at the same time.

On balance, Millie would rather trust her thermometer.

'Why?' she enquired.

Dr Costa was very reasonable about it. 'We don't want to schedule a treatment, and bring you all the way out here to Spain, only for us to the miss the right day, or for you not to ovulate at all. With the stimulants, we can control it.'

'I suppose,' Millie conceded. She wondered should she mention her excellent FSH. It might have a bearing on things. On the other hand she didn't want to sound like she was boasting.

It could be worse, she decided. Other fertility treatments demanded much more serious drugs. She was probably getting off lightly with a few ovulation stimulants.

Dr Costa was firing off a prescription on his pad. 'You start taking one a day from the third day of your treatment cycle. Then, from Day 10 onwards, you'll use ovulation predictor kits. Do you know what they are?'

'I do,' Millie grimly assured him. She and ovulation predictor kits were old friends. Many of them still lived in her underwear drawer.

'When you get a positive result, we'll do the insemination within twenty-four hours. You'd probably want to fly out a day or two beforehand,' he told her.

'That shouldn't be a problem,' she said.

She waited for him to go on. But that was it. The whole thing explained in five minutes. It couldn't have been simpler.

'Have you any questions?'

She had a million. She'd rehearsed them over and over during the night, and in the taxi ride on the way out.

Naturally, she couldn't remember a single one of them now.

'If you think of anything, you can always email us,' Dr Costa said kindly. He was obviously used to stage fright.

'Thank you,' said Millie. She felt drained. She would go for a coffee somewhere, or a walk, and digest the information. She would write it all down before she forgot it.

But the appointment wasn't over. 'Adriana will go through the donor selection process now, and take you through the legalities.'

Millie had no idea who Adriana was. The woman who knew the legalities, obviously, and who had a handle on the sperm donors.

'Do I have to choose?' she asked, with some trepidation. She had a vision of a large freezer being thrown open for her inspection, and being confronted with dozens and dozens of test tubes. How would one look more suitable than the other? Would some of them send out vibes in her direction, along the lines of 'Pick me! Pick me!'? The father of her child would be somewhere in there, below freezing point, and she had no idea in the world how to choose who that man would be.

And she didn't want to, she realised. She didn't want the responsibility. It was terrifying. What if she got it wrong? She might pass up a brain surgeon in favour of a petty thief, all because of luck or fate, or because one test tube looked fuller than the other – not that that was any indication of anything.

Thankfully nobody was going to throw open their supplies of sperm for her perusal.

'It's a bit more technical than that,' Dr Costa assured her. 'We match as closely as possible based on blood group and then phenotype. That is, we take into account appearance.'

They would choose a donor who looked roughly like Millie, then. To be brutally honest about it, not many Spanish men did.

Dr Costa wasn't going to shirk this issue. 'While we strive for fair-looking donors for our Northern European clients, we cannot guarantee anything,' he told her.

She'd better not hold out for a blue-eyed blond child then. Not that she was.

'Anyhow, Adriana will go through all this with you in a minute.' He flipped to the back of her file. 'All you have to do now is sign the consent form.'

He passed over a form. It was the aforementioned consent form. It actually had 'Consent Form' written on the top of it in English, just so there wouldn't be any confusion.

Millie felt ice cold again. It was all very well sitting across the desk from cuddly Dr Costa, discussing the finer points of IUI, and having a little lively discussion about ovulation stimulation drugs. It was another thing entirely actually to authorise him to inject her with the sperm of an anonymous stranger.

Dr Costa hadn't noticed her fright. He was chatting away. 'It's up to you when you decide to start the treatment. But in your case I wouldn't leave it too long.'

Her age, he meant. He was kind enough not to bring it up baldly. Millie had a sudden urge to hop up onto the couch in the corner and demand to be impregnated immediately.

'Maybe in the next cycle or two,' Dr Costa said encouragingly. 'You'll only have to be here for a couple of days. Hopefully the next time we'll hear from you will be with news of a positive pregnancy test.'

He probably said that to everybody. Give them a bit of gee-up before sending them off into the world, even though he had already explained very clearly to Millie that the success rates of IUI were poor, compared to IVF. Only about fifteen per cent, which she already knew.

But all she heard now were the magic words 'positive pregnancy test'. That faint pink line, which had thus far in her life eluded her. The pink line that she had thought she had no possibility of ever seeing after Andrew had walked out the door.

She picked up the pen and signed.

Chapter Nineteen

S he got another taxi back to the holiday complex. But her head was too full to go straight up to the apartment, even though Oona had left two messages on her mobile phone wondering where she was.

'We're by the pool,' she had said in her last message. 'It's your turn to put suntan lotion on Dad's back.'

That was enough to send Millie across the road in search of the public beach. It was still a bit early for most people, and only a few dedicated sunbathers were out and about. A lone swimmer was ploughing up and down in the water efficiently, throwing up white splashes.

Millie picked a quiet area by the rocks. She kicked off her shoes and sat down. The tide was out, and the clean white sand was warm under her bare feet. It was an idyllic spot. And she maybe, possibly, had a fifteen per-cent chance of having a baby.

It was really happening. She had signed on the dotted line. She had filled out a phenotype form (Eyes – blue. Hair – brown, but roots a little grey if you looked closely. Height – five foot five. She had lied by an inch about that, because she didn't want them to match her with someone just as short, and Bonita would have an uphill battle in clothes shops all her life).

In a week or so Adriana would send her a reference number for her sperm donor. That was all she would know about him, apart from his phenotype. No educational qualifications, no details of profession.

'But most of them are students,' Adriana had reassured her, lest Millie think they were all illiterate losers.

That had knocked her back a bit. A student? He would probably be barely over the age of twenty-one. She wouldn't sleep with a twenty-one-year-old in real life (she should be so lucky) but now might end up having a baby by one? It was a difficult concept to get her head round. Plus, it cast a whole new light on what she had intended to tell Bonita about her father – that he was most likely some altruistic soul who had reared his own family and had gone done the donor route out of a selfless desire to bring happiness to someone else. In reality he would be some guy barely out of his teens who had done it for the money, which he had probably promptly drunk in the nearest bar, if he was anything like an Irish student.

She might have to rethink her story.

'Our donors may be young, but they're very healthy,' Adriana pointed out.

And that was the point. Youth was best in the fertility game, everybody knew that. The younger the donor, the better the chance of success. Millie might prefer a nice, mature forty-something but the chances were that half his sperm would already be banjaxed. No, far better to go with a fit, healthy, young lad whom she would never clap eyes on in real life anyway.

The clinic knew what they were doing. She was sure of that. And they had been so nice and friendly, and nobody had once looked at her like she was some very sad woman, if not entirely misguided, to be attempting to have a baby on her own. The opposite, in fact. They had assured her that they would do everything in their power to help her.

Nobody in Ireland had done half as much for her. In fact they had done their level best to turn her away.

'See you next month!' Maria had called optimistically as Millie was leaving.

'Yes,' said Millie, all gung-ho then, of course, having just signed the consent form. 'I'll be in touch!'

She was still walking on air a bit. Sitting there on the beach, with a prescription for fertility drugs in her pocket, Millie felt for the first time that it was all within her grasp. Within a few short weeks she would be back in Spain, raring to go.

And you never knew – she might actually be one of that lucky fifteen per cent.

'You can always have another go if it doesn't work first time,' Maria had said reassuringly. 'A lot of people take two or three treatments, or even more.'

Dr Costa had murmured something about moving on to IVF at that point, but Millie wasn't going to think about that this morning. Right now she felt more positive than she had in a long time. If it wasn't too early, she'd start popping those pills right now, and to hell with the nasty side effects. Bring it on! Well, maybe not the psychotic episodes.

The swimmer was emerging from the sea.

Millie lazily watched.

It was a man. He rose from the waves like Daniel Craig – all sinewy and wet and practically naked. Water cascaded down his bare chest, and he glistened under the sun.

He was gorgeous.

It was Simon.

Millie squinted. Surely not. She grabbed her sunglasses and jammed them on. Possibly it was a trick of the sun. But no. It definitely was Simon.

He was wearing a pair of tiny swimming trunks, and he was very tanned. A mean little part of her wondered whether it was fake. How could anyone get so brown in so few days, even if all they did was get pissed by the pool? But a man like him surely wouldn't lower himself to use fake tan, so it was probably real.

She looked past him to see whether any of his mates were floundering about in the shallows, unnoticed by her yet. Usually they travelled in a pack.

But there was no sign of them this morning. Just Simon, giving himself a bit of a shake by the water's edge. Then he slicked back his hair, looked up the beach, and spotted her.

He waved.

She half-heartedly waved back. She wasn't sure she wanted to get into a conversation with him right now – not when she was feeling so positive about single motherhood. He might rain on her parade.

But he was coming towards her. She wasn't sure where to look. She didn't want to keep staring at him, in case he thought she fancied him or something. Which she did, of course.

'Hi,' he said, with a big easy smile.

'Simon,' she said. 'I didn't recognise you with your clothes off.'

It was best to keep things jokey, she decided.

He duly laughed. Again, she thought what a nice sound it was.

'I don't think I've ever seen *you* with your clothes off yet,' he said back.

It was a joke too, but of course she went bright purple. And he didn't mean *naked*, just in a swimsuit. At least she was pretty sure that's what he meant.

'As you know I'm not here to sunbathe,' she said lightly.

'That's true,' he agreed.

Thankfully, it was left at that.

'Mind if join you?'

She shrugged. 'It's a free beach.'

He flopped down on to the sand beside her. His wet leg was only inches from hers. She felt all itchy and jumpy. In fact she thought about sex. It just popped into her head, unannounced. Sex with Simon.

She was horrified. What was she *thinking*? She was a woman fresh from an appointment at a fertility clinic. She was sure Dr Costa hadn't meant for her to go straight out and start eyeing up virtual strangers. She should have done that *before* she consulted him, he would say. It would have saved her a lot of time and money.

She switched her gaze sternly towards the sea. That was better. No more lewd thoughts about his legs, or any other part of him. She had simply been too long without sex, that was all. Anyway, didn't men think about sex every twenty minutes or something? She hadn't thought about it in over six weeks, so she was entitled to one little slip, surely.

'Look,' he said, 'I'm sorry about last night.'

'What?'

'Jamie coming up to you like that in the bar.'

'Oh.' She gave him a sideways look. 'I know a lot more about you now than I did before.'

Now it was his turn to go a bit red. She enjoyed it.

'What did he say?' he asked, looking pained. 'Because I'll deny everything.'

She laughed. She was doing a lot of laughing, along with the episodes of idiotic smiling. Oh, what the hell – just because she was going to have IUI didn't mean she had to turn into a nun. 'Only that you're the last one of the gang to get married. That you're dying to settle down but you just haven't met the right woman yet,' she said teasingly.

He went really red now. It was kind of cute, on a man his age. He was, she realised, a bit nervous in front of her.

'I'll kill him,' he swore. 'I'll kill him with my bare hands, and I don't care what Sandra says.'

'I'd imagine it'd be a happy release for her.'

'Ah, he's not that bad really. He just goes a bit wild whenever he gets out from under her thumb.'

'I didn't hear you denying it, though. That you want to settle down.'

But he just shrugged and looked her straight in the face. 'I'm not denying it.'

'You must be an aberration so. Most men try to avoid marriage for as long as possible. Even when they *do* settle down, a lot of them find that it doesn't really suit them.'

Oops. That came out a bit bitter. She tried to give a bit of a laugh, just to show she was joking, but that came out even more bitter. She tried a third time. Now she sounded deranged, and she screeched to a halt abruptly.

'Are we talking about your husband here?' Simon enquired rather gently.

She was going to deny it. It was none of his business anyway. His eyes were so sincere and, well, *brown*, that she admitted, 'Yes. He was a bit of a louse.'

'He sounds like it.'

She was gratified that he was rooting for her.

'Actually he was a total shit.' Well, she didn't owe him any loyalty. And Simon looked so interested and compassionate. She didn't feel that she had to put any sugar-coating on it. 'He didn't mind the being married bit so much. It was the thought of having children that sent him running up a pole in Frankfurt.'

He was a bit puzzled by that.

'It doesn't matter,' she said. There was no sense in explaining Andrew's career, especially when she didn't know what she talking about herself.

Simon enquired, 'When you say he didn't want kids, do you mean he didn't actually like children *per se*? Because I suppose they can be quite noisy and messy. And sticky.'

'Well, of course they're sticky, they're children!'

'I know,' he said hastily. 'Personally I like children. I have five nieces and nephews and I'm always taking them to the cinema and McDonald's, and buying them toy guns and other unsuitable things. They tell me that I'm their favourite uncle, but I suspect that's just for commercial reasons.'

She bet he was a great uncle. He was probably the type who got down on the floor and played horsy and cops and robbers. He would never arrive for a visit without a bagful of multicoloured sweets that were full of E numbers and additives, but that tasted great.

He said, quite openly, 'I'd quite like my own one day.'

Millie didn't think she had ever heard a man say anything like that. Well, not any men that she had met, anyway. But Simon didn't seem to be afraid of subjects like children, or fertility treatment, and nasty relationship break-ups. He was most unusual, if not downright odd.

'Why are you looking at me so suspiciously?' he enquired now.

'No reason,' she said hastily.

'Is there something wrong with a man wanting children?'

'No, no.'

'Once I meet the right woman, of course – or at least one I can persuade. I don't have the same options as yourself when it comes to going it alone.'

She blinked. 'That was a bit unnecessary.'

Just when they were getting on so well too. But he didn't seem a bit sorry for having said it.

'But it's true. I mean, you seem to have ready access to donor sperm – if you can pay for it, of course, which a lot of people can't. I doubt I'd find a woman to not only give me her eggs, but carry the child to term as well, before handing it over. But then again, maybe that depends too on how much money you're willing to pay.'

Millie picked up her handbag and began to brush sand off her skirt.

'You're going?' He seemed very surprised. Did he really think that she was going to sit there while he pontificated about what he obviously viewed as her buying power in the fertility market?

'I am,' she said.

'I wouldn't have put you down as someone afraid of a little friendly debate.'

'I have no problem with debate. But for some reason I'm not in the mood for it this morning.'

'I can imagine,' he said. 'How did it go at the clinic anyway?'

She stopped in her tracks. Was he flipping psychic as well?

'How did you know I was at the clinic?'

'You have a prescription sticking out of your pocket,' he said apologetically.

'Oh!' She jammed it back in. Great. So now he knew she was going to be on stimulation drugs next month. Right now he knew more about her proposed fertility treatment than anybody else in the world. A man she barely knew! And didn't like very much again.

'Sounds nasty,' he commiserated. 'Those drugs.'

'They are perfectly standard drugs for this type of treatment,' she said frostily. She wouldn't mention anything about the side effects. No doubt he'd have an opinion on that too.

'Did you get your sperm donor sorted?'

'Not yet. But in the next week or two?'

'So you'll be all set then?'

'I think so, yes.'

He nodded. 'Good, good.' Really he meant, 'Bad, bad.' She didn't know why he didn't just set up a stake right here on the beach, tie her to it, and set her on fire.

She stood and hopped about putting her sandals on. He watched. She felt clumsy and unsteady under his scrutiny, and at one point nearly keeled over into his lap.

'Do you want to have dinner tonight?' he asked.

'What?' she snapped, sure that he was having some kind of sick joke.

'Dinner,' he repeated reasonably. 'My liver can't take any more drinking sessions with the lads. There's a lovely little restaurant around the corner that Christian has recommended. I think his granny owns it. They have the whole place sewn up around here.'

She kept looking at him suspiciously; sure that he had an agenda. Which was probably needling her about her clinic visit for his own entertainment.

But he looked back at her perfectly harmlessly. Sincerely, even. She wasn't sure how to handle it. One minute he was perfectly lovely and sensitive and cute, and the next he was trouncing her over the head with unpleasant theories about the fertility game.

'I should probably spend the evening with my father and sister,' she said, fudging the issue.

He shrugged. 'OK. If that's what you want.'

He wasn't going to throw himself upon her feet and beg and plead. And the last thing she wanted to do was look at Sky News with Dennis, while Oona nipped downstairs for cocktails.

'Why?' she said at last. 'Why would you want to have dinner with me?'

'Because I like you.' He said this as though it were completely obvious, and that maybe she was a bit thick.

'Oh. Um, right!'

He was far too straightforward for someone whose recent experience of men largely involved lies, deception, cowardliness and cheap flights to Frankfurt.

'I like you too,' she said back bravely.

For some reason this made him smile. Millie felt about five.

But he said, 'Thank you. I'll pick you up about eight.'

Brendan could hardly be heard on the phone for the roar of the new Dyson in the background.

'I've just been giving the place a quick once-over,' he shouted. 'The girls are coming around for tea.'

'The girls?' Millie enquired.

'Nancy and the rest. They have a rota going and today it's my turn.'

Millie had an unlikely vision of Brendan holding court at the kitchen table, surrounded by yummy mummies and cucumber sandwiches.

'Hold on till I just turn this thing off,' he said.

The noise of the vacuum thankfully died away.

'That's better,' he said. 'Where's Oona?'

Good question. Dennis said he had dropped off to sleep by the pool and when he woke up she was gone. She hadn't even taken her mobile phone, which had just rung a second ago with Brendan on the line.

Millie shouldn't have answered it, of course. But she had thought that maybe it was urgent: that there was something wrong with one of the kids.

'On the beach, I think,' she said evasively.

She felt like she was covering up. But surely Oona wasn't *up* to anything. Just because she had been drinking cocktails into the small hours last night in a bar on her own (allegedly) and had now gone mysteriously missing was no reason to be suspicious of her.

'I just wanted to ask her if she saw the muffin tin,' Brendan said.

'Pardon?'

'I know, it's just that she was using it to pot plants in the last time I saw it. And now I can't find it anywhere and I wanted to run up a batch of chocolate chip muffins for the girls.'

At least he kept saying, 'the girls' as in plural. It wasn't just Nancy. Millie wondered exactly how many other mums were coming over. If he was cooking up batches of muffins there must be more than just one or two. Hopefully a whole gang of them, with dozens of squealing kids in tow. It would be difficult to flirt with Nancy in the midst of all that.

Listen to her – riddled with suspicion!

It was all Christian's fault. He had poisoned her mind by insinuating that Oona was neglected and untouched. She and Brendan could be having rampant sex at every opportunity, for all anybody knew. It was just pure coincidence that Oona had been asking Millie about the frequency of her own sex life.

'So, are you missing her?' she found herself asking Brendan leadingly.

'Oh, we're managing,' he said back airily.

Not the response of a man itching to get his hands on his wife.

'To be honest, we're too busy,' he grumbled. 'You wouldn't believe the number of visitors we're after having. And I had five phone calls from friends wondering how we're "coping" on our own.'

'I suppose people are just trying to help out.'

'But why would I want help? Is it just because I'm a man? I cope all year round on my own, but the minute Oona takes off they're ringing me up and dropping around stews and pints of milk!' he said indignantly. '"You needn't bother," I said to one of them yesterday – it's not as though Oona ever managed a square meal in her life. And there was never a drop of milk in the house when she was in charge either.'

Millie wondered whether he had been on his website again. No doubt his sorry story had provoked a heated debate amongst the other Stay-at-Home-Pops (or SAHPs, as they called themselves for convenience. Not to be confused with SAPS).

There was one final outrage. 'My auntie Dervla tried to take the kids yesterday afternoon. She said that maybe I wanted to go to the pub for a few pints. In the middle of the afternoon! If I was a woman I'd be up for child neglect.' He really was cross now, and Millie could see his point. 'Thankfully, Gary jumped out from behind the sofa and shot her with his toy gun.'

Millie could hear Gary in the background now. Initially she had thought it was the Dyson on low throttle, but it was actually him whinging and complaining, and it was getting louder.

'I want to speak to Mammy,' he was saying.

'It's not Mammy, it's Auntie Millie,' Brendan explained.

Millie tried not to take offence as Gary greeted this news with sounds of disgust. 'Mammy! Mammy!' he began keening desperately.

'Now stop it,' Brendan said firmly. 'She'll be back on Saturday.'

'Saturday?' This plunged Gary into fresh depths of grief.

'Get off my leg, Gary. This instant.' Brendan sounded testy and irritated. Millie guessed that this had been going on all week.

'Sorry, Millie.' He sounded embarrassed.

Gary's cries had obviously alerted the other two, because there was the sound of feet clattering across the floor, and more whinging. Millie could hear Chloe crying and crying in the background like a little lost soul.

'For God's sake!' Brendan exploded.

Then he must have jammed his hand over the receiver because it all went very quiet for ages.

When he eventually came back on, there was silence in the background. He sounded defensive. 'Sorry about that. They were absolutely fine all morning. We did finger painting and everything, and went for a lovely long hike in the fresh air. They were as happy as Larry. I don't know why they have to start up that racket the minute I get on the phone.'

'Oh, it's often the way,' Millie said soothingly. Then, just in case he had done something terrible to the children that would account for the sudden creepy quiet in the house, she enquired, 'Um, are they OK?'

'They're fine. I put on *Star Wars – Attack of the Clones* for them. And yes, I know it's full of guns and violence and probably sex, but they won't watch *Bob the Builder*, OK?'

'I wouldn't either,' she assured him. Best not to inflame him further.

'Look, there's no need to tell Oona about it, OK?'

'*Star Wars?*'

'No, no – she lets them watch far worse. I meant about the crying. I don't want to spoil her holiday.'

Not much chance of that. At that moment Millie looked out the window and saw Oona stroll in by the side of the pool. Christian was with her. They were laughing their heads off.

'Will I get her to give you a ring later?' Millie asked.

But Brendan said, 'Better not. Nancy's invited us over for dinner tonight. We probably won't be back till late. Tell her I'll give her a buzz in the morning.'

Chapter Twenty

'You've got a *date*?' said Oona.

She couldn't have looked more surprised had a pig jetted past in mid-air. It was a bit annoying, actually.

'Yes,' said Millie, offended.

Was it really so unbelievable that she might attract a man? Any man? In a cheapish resort in Spain where they were thick on the ground, and you'd want to be carrying the plague not to catch the fancy of at least one of them? And even that wouldn't put some of them off.

'Sorry,' said Oona hastily. 'It's that you were so sure that it was the last thing you wanted.'

Well, yes. She had come to Spain for donor IUI. Not that she had thought about *that* in the last two hours. Oh no. Thoughts of single motherhood had been merrily abandoned in favour of rambling reminiscences of Simon's semi-naked body. And decisions over what she should wear tonight.

Was she shallow? Lightweight? Did she even *deserve* to become a mum if her head was turned by the first man who asked her out for dinner?

She had made a decision to go it alone, yet she couldn't even stick to it for five minutes. What a wimp.

'Good for you,' Oona was saying. 'A little romance is *exactly* what you need.'

She should know. From the blush on her cheeks it looked as though she had grabbed a bit of it herself that afternoon.

So far she had offered no information as to her whereabouts. But Millie was biding her time.

'So who's the lucky guy?' Oona said. She was in remarkably good humour.

Millie told her.

Her enthusiasm took a dive. 'One of the stag group?' she screeched. 'The ones who are pissed all the time, and hurling each other into the pool?'

'Yes,' Millie was forced to admit.

'Please say it's not the one with the beer belly and the snake tattoo.' She had just described Jamie.

'It's Simon. He's got brown eyes, and brown hair.' He was coming across worryingly brown. 'He's quite good-looking,' she said, trying to glam him up a bit.

But Oona was shaking her head blankly and saying, 'Nope. Can't place him at all.'

Why would she, when she had been making eyes at Christian? It was a wonder she still recognised Millie and Dennis. She'd barely looked at them since Saturday.

'What were you doing with Christian this afternoon?' Millie blurted.

She couldn't keep it in any longer. Ever since she'd put the phone down on Brendan, she had been having disturbing visions of Oona and Christian rolling about behind the reception desk, Oona's breasts everywhere. These alternated with even more disturbing visions of Brendan and Nancy, getting it on in the gazebo, with plates of scones dotted about just in case they got hungry.

The poor children, thought Millie. Little Gary and Aoifa and the baby. And Nancy had a couple of kids too. As for Christian, well, you couldn't be certain.

Millie felt she was watching a car crash in slow motion, but was powerless to do anything to stop it. In some ways she felt responsible. If they weren't in Spain at her instigation, then none of this would be happening.

'He took me to a market stall owned by a friend of his who makes the most fabulous toys,' announced Oona, bold as you like. She had obviously decided that attack was the best form of defence. 'I wanted to get something to bring back to the kids. And look at what I got!'

She dug into a shopping bag and held up three piñatas, miniature size, in different colours.

'They're full of sweets, and the only way to get them out is to bash them to bits violently with a stick,' she said. 'Brendan's going to go mad.'

This wasn't about piñatas, and both of them knew it.

'That was very kind of Christian. To take time out of his day like that,' Millie said, injecting as much insinuation into her voice as possible. 'Especially when he seems to be so busy.'

'Wasn't it?' Oona said, avoiding Millie's eye. 'I told him just to point me in the right direction, but he insisted on coming with me.'

Oh, she might sound very innocent, but Millie always knew when she was hiding something.

She decided to put the screws on; see if she cracked. 'I've just been on the phone to Brendan.'

But Oona just said, brazen as you like, 'Oh? How is he?'

'He's having Nancy and "the girls" over for tea. He's baking chocolate chip muffins as we speak. And then –' she paused dramatically – 'he's going to Nancy's house for dinner.'

That was her *pièce de résistance*. No woman should ever invite another woman's husband over for dinner while his wife was away. It was just plain dirty tricks.

Oona would know that. She would fly into a rage and ring Brendan and threaten all kinds of terrible things upon him unless he cancelled forthwith.

She just laughed. 'God help him. I heard she was a terrible cook.'

Well, if that wasn't the kettle calling the pot black.

'He seemed to be quite looking forward to it.'

'I suppose he has to have something to do,' Oona said. And that was it. No burst of jealousy. No furtive looks over her shoulder in the direction of reception. Millie deflated. Her amateur sleuthing was getting her nowhere. Or else Oona was a particularly good liar.

Which, actually, she was. Otherwise they'd never have managed to get past Dennis standing guard at the front door during their youth.

'We're just going to help with the meals-on-wheels for the elderly,' Oona would tell him brazenly on a Saturday night, even though she and Millie were wearing six-inch heels and hardly any clothes.

'Do you think I came down in the last shower?' Dennis would spit, the buttons on his grey cardi rattling ominously.

'All right, sorry, that was a fib.' Oona would look shame-faced. 'Really, we're going on a door-to-door collection for a poor home-less boy that was found by the side of Mulligan's pub in only his underpants.'

There would be another terrible, tense moment as Dennis would look down on the tops of their quivering, hair-sprayed heads. He would take a deep breath, the better to denounce Oona's lies and deceit further.

This would go on for ages, with Oona's lies getting more and more outlandish, to include undercover police work and UFOs. And the breeze from the open front door would be slowly turning their little bare legs blue. Even Dennis, who normally thoroughly enjoyed catching Oona out, would be getting fed up.

And then, miraculously, the music from *The Late Late Show* would filter out from the living room, saving them all. *The Late Late Show* was second only to *Coronation Street* in importance in the house. If Dennis and Nuala missed it then they would have nothing to talk about with the neighbours for the whole week. It was social suicide.

'Tell me the one about the poor homeless boy again,' Dennis would say hurriedly.

Oona would look up cautiously. 'He needs money to go to school.' Even though school was free. 'Millie is going to sing on people's doorsteps.' Millie couldn't sing. 'And I'm going to tap dance.' Another filthy lie. 'We hope to raise at least fifty pounds for the poor little fella.'

That was good enough for Dennis. 'Good girls,' he would say with relief. 'Here's a tenner to start the collection.'

And off they would go to Mulligan's pub to spend the tenner on large bottles of Ritz, and flirt with boys who were not homeless but who would, no doubt, be down to their underpants later on.

Oona obviously remembered those days too, because she lectured Millie now.

'Be careful tonight.'

'I beg your pardon?'

'You know exactly what I mean.'

'Don't do anything you wouldn't do?' Millie said loftily. Piñatas, her eye.

'Or at least wear a condom,' Oona advised.

Oona didn't appreciate the irony of that. But why would she? She had no idea of Millie's true purpose in Spain.

Millie felt guilty again. She had never thought of herself as a particularly good liar – nowhere near Orla's standard. But she must have got better somewhere along the way. Look at all the porkers she had told in the last month! She had lied to everybody – parents, sister, friends, doctors. She was practically pathological.

Simon knew the truth.

Not that he agreed with her or anything.

But it was nice that somebody knew, apart from the girls in the office.

Millie suddenly felt a horrible burst of nostalgia for Jaz and Deirdre and Yvonne. And even Dorothy, with her gruff ways and put-downs.

They would want to know all about the clinic and Dr Costa, and what he had told her. Actually, knowing them, they'd be more interested in Simon, and what he looked like, and did he have a nice body?

Yes.

He had a lovely body.

There she went again! Veering off the subject of babies and on to mere men. It was worrying.

She must remember why she was in Spain. Dinner with Simon was all very well, but it didn't change a thing.

There was trouble back at the ranch.

And things had been going so well too. Auntie June and Mum had gone out again the previous night, to the cinema this time, and had spent a lazy day gardening and gossiping, just like old times.

Then, shortly after tea, Auntie June had made an innocent mistake. Well, it wasn't as if anybody had warned her. At half past seven she'd picked up the remote control and switched the channel to her favourite programme, *Beware of the Dog*. Which was on at the exact same time as *Coronation Street*.

Nuala didn't say anything. Not a word. Even though she'd had every opportunity. She'd just sat there stiffly in her chair as Auntie June had shouted animatedly at the television, 'Oooh, look! She just took a lump out of his leg! Bad dog!'

When the programme was over, Nuala had risen and gone to bed, just like that, and was refusing to get up.

'She's been in bed eighteen hours now, and frankly, the room needs airing,' Auntie June reported now.

'What?' said Dennis. It was obvious that this was outside the bounds of his own experience.

And Millie and Oona's too. They looked at each other, wide-eyed. Mum, in bed for eighteen hours? This put the frozen peas in the shade.

Auntie Millie seemed to be waiting for Dennis to tell her that the whole thing was a big joke; that somehow he and Mum had cooked up the stunt between them and that she had been secretly filmed, and that any minute they would all shout 'Candid Camera!' down the phone at her from Spain.

She was out of luck.

'Does she do this often?' she enquired now, her amazement clear.

She wasn't going to get a straight answer from Dennis. Millie watched as he slipped smoothly into automatic damage limitation mode.

'*Coronation Street* is one of her favourite programmes,' he said reasonably. 'She hasn't missed an episode in ten years. Naturally she's a bit upset.'

He was impressive. He sounded so plausible that he nearly had Millie going for a minute. But then she had to remind herself of the ridiculous facts: Mum, in bed, for eighteen hours, because somebody had got to the remote control first.

It wasn't normal at all.

Auntie June seemed to agree. Her splutters floated from the phone. 'For God's sake, Dennis. It's a soap. It's not like she actually missed anything. Those blooming stories are all the same.'

'You didn't actually say that to her, did you?' Dennis said, closing his eyes in pain.

'Of course I did. I tried to talk some sense into her. I said, 'Nuala, I don't know what's got into you today, but I'd be obliged if you didn't take it out on me.'

So there had been a bit of a barney. Millie could just picture the scene; all Auntie June had been missing was the little whip she used to keep particularly troublesome dogs in line.

Perhaps Mum had made a reasonable choice after all.

Now that she had got things off her chest, Auntie June was prepared to be conciliatory. 'I'd put it down to her having been in hospital,' she advised Dennis. 'A few weeks in there can make even the most reasonable person a bit self-centred.' She even managed a bit of a laugh. 'She'll be mortified later. Oh, I won't let her forget this.'

'Yes,' Dennis agreed, even though his lips were white. 'I wonder if you could take the phone up to her? I'd like to have a word.'

But he wasn't running the show any more, as he was about to find out.

'Oh, I don't think we should indulge her, Dennis, do you?'

'Sorry?'

'She'll come down when she's hungry.'

Dennis went a bit still. 'You mean you haven't taken her up any food?'

Auntie June was incredulous now. It was obvious that she thought Dennis had Nuala ruined. 'She knows where the kitchen is. You hardly expect me to go taking trays up?'

Of course he did. That's would he'd have done. But he was hundreds of miles away in Spain and Auntie June was in his house, and there was absolutely nothing he could do except curl and uncurl his left hand helplessly. Actually, he looked like he was itching to give her a good slap.

'Maybe you'd tell her I called,' he said thinly.

'Of course I will.' Then, sunny again, she assured him, 'She'll be fine by this evening. You're on your holidays. I don't want you worrying about a thing.'

And she rang off, leaving them all with the disturbing vision of Nuala in a darkened room upstairs under the duvet, possibly with a copy of *Hello!* magazine and that little night-light from Oona's old room.

Actually, it didn't sound too bad at all. Quite cosy, in fact.

'Do you think she's all right?' Oona ventured. It was plain from her face that she thought Mum was bonkers.

Dennis looked pale. Millie didn't want to alarm him any further. 'Yes,' she said firmly. 'What possible harm could come to her in her own bed?'

They pondered on this for a bit.

'Not much,' Dennis eventually conceded. 'But still . . .'

Indeed. It was downright odd and peculiar.

And somehow there was the unspoken feeling that Auntie June was the worst person in the world to deal with it.

Chapter Twenty-One

Surprisingly, Simon was a big hit with Dennis. He arrived promptly at eight o'clock to collect Millie and wore a nice shirt and spoke to Dennis respectfully about football and the weather.

'I hear it's going to be twenty-eight degrees tomorrow.'

'No!' said Dennis, who loved nothing better than a good discussion about how blessed hot it was in Spain. It made a change from complaining about the rain back home. And it was great that something was taking his mind off the telephone conversation with Auntie June.

'If I were you, I'd stay indoors tomorrow,' Simon advised.

He caught Millie's eye. She raised an eyebrow cynically, letting him know that she knew full well that he was sucking up to her father

He piously ignored that and artfully brought the conversation around to the apartment's TV channels. 'You only have Sky News? We have BBC and everything in our apartment.'

'BBC?' said Dennis enviously. He was fed up to the back teeth of twenty-four-hour rolling news.

'You just have to know how to tune it in. Do you want me to have a go?'

Dennis would have signed over his house to him at that point. 'If you could . . .' he said happily.

The two of them went off into the living room chummily. Dennis could be heard offering him a beer. Things were indeed rosy in the garden.

Oona joined Millie now, clutching a gin and tonic. Well, as she said herself, if she were stuck at home with Dennis for the evening while Millie had a hot date then she needed all the help she could get. She looked in appreciatively at Simon in the living room. 'You didn't say he was gorgeous,' she said gleefully.

'I suppose he's OK,' said Millie. For some reason she didn't want to give Simon too much credit.

Or maybe it was just her nerves. She hadn't been on a date in years. They probably weren't even called dates any more. There was probably some new sophisticated in-word that she hadn't heard of yet. It was only last year that Deirdre in work explained to her what 'friends-with-benefits' meant. Millie, with her advanced years, had been shocked.

Suddenly she felt every one of those years now. She was too old for this lark. She felt ancient and dull, standing there all dressed up in what she had thought was a nice summer dress, but was probably hopelessly fuddy-duddy. She hadn't even put on much make-up for fear of looking a drag queen at her age.

What was she doing, going off to dinner with a man she barely knew, a man from a stag party, for heaven's sake? Even if he was reasonably handsome and proficient at dealing with Dennis?

The whole evening stretched before her, full of awkward small talk and cheap red wine. They would swap carefully edited snippets of their lives and make sure to laugh at the other's jokes. No doubt at the end of it all he would make the obligatory lunge at her outside the apartment, and she would give him the obligatory knee in the groin, and they would both wake up with hangovers in the morning and wonder what the hell that had all been about.

She didn't think she had the energy. Not fresh from a marriage breakdown. She felt raw and cynical and hurt, and right now she didn't think she would ever be able to truly trust a man again.

Wasn't that partly why she had come to Spain? She was washing her hands of the whole thing. She no longer wanted a man in her life, not even for basic reproductive reasons. She had made a decision to go it alone.

She wondered if she could feign a headache. He would be annoyed, but could always hook back up with his stag party. And she could stay home and memorise Dr Costa's prescription.

And in a way it would be more honest to pull out now. She wasn't sure what Simon hoped to get out of this 'date', but if her heart wasn't in it then she should at least let him know.

At that moment Simon looked over his shoulder at her from the living room and winked.

Actually winked!

It was totally unexpected and rather intimate – well, just plain *dirty*.

Millie felt heat rising in her. Lust, actually. Low-down, barefaced, good old naked lust.

Well, it had been a while.

And she did like him a bit. Quite a lot, actually.

She would, she decided magnanimously, go on the date after all. She didn't want to let him down. Not when he had dressed up so smartly and everything for her. And the table had probably been booked. And what about Christian's granny, who owned the restaurant? She was probably relying on revenue from people like Millie and Simon. In fact, if Millie *didn't* go on the date, it could have a serious impact on the local economy.

Simon had lovely shoulders, she noted now. Broad and strong. The kind made for falling asleep on, or having a good cry on, or just for leaning on.

Oh, hang it, she *wanted* to go out with him.

But just for tonight. And it would be separate from everything else in her life, including her decision to have a baby on her own.

Oona threw back the last of her gin and tonic and was watching her rather jealously. 'You're very lucky, Millie.'

Millie had to think about that one. 'You mean because I'm separated, childless, and looking forty in the face?'

'You have possibilities. You're going on a date, for heaven's sake. A proper date, full of what-ifs and maybes, and things bubbling under the surface.'

Millie didn't know if things would go *that* far.

'I'd rather have stayed married,' she said frankly. But would she really? For the sake of having babies, yes. But for Andrew? No. She was quite definite on that.

Oona was pitched into deeper gloom. 'There are very few what-ifs left when you're with a man who's wearing an apron.'

Please God she wasn't going to pick that moment to reveal the extent of her marital woes. Millie might be cancelling her date after all, just as she had decided that she wanted to go on it.

'Maybe *you* should go on a date,' she suggested brightly, hoping she didn't sound like she was going for the quick fix. 'You and Brendan. Get a babysitter. Go somewhere romantic. Just the two of you.'

'Do you think I haven't tried that?' Oona said. 'We went to that flipping five-star hotel for our anniversary in May, do you remember? With the award-winning restaurant, and the romantic woodland walks, and our own en-suite Jacuzzi. We were both in bed asleep by ten o'clock.'

This was going from bad to worse. Millie sneaked a look in at Simon and Dad. It seemed they had discovered a whole plethora of American channels too, and there was great excitement. All Dad needed was one shopping channel and his holiday was made.

Meanwhile Oona was looking rather distraught.

'You're bound to be tired,' Millie tried to console her. 'What with you working, and him looking after the kids . . . you're probably just wrecked.'

But it just sounded like an excuse. Oona knew it too.

'Are you going to suggest a course of fish oil?' she enquired.

'Have you and Brendan sat down and talked about it?'

'No. But it's not for the want of trying on his part.'

Millie didn't quite understand that. 'Maybe you should – I don't know – tell him how you feel.'

Oona gave a little laugh. 'How I *feel*? I don't think that's a very good idea.'

'Oona . . .'

Oona looked in at Dad and Simon. They were finishing up. 'Look, it doesn't matter.'

Clearly it did matter. And had for some time now.

'We'll talk later,' Millie promised. 'When I get back.'

But Oona looked like she regretted having said anything. 'Don't rush back on my account. Not when you have a date with a gorgeous man.'

Simon heard that, of course. But he was obviously too well brought up to show it, and when he rejoined them it was with a poker face (which didn't fool Millie for one second).

'You look lovely,' he told her.

Even though she knew it was probably just a formality, she immediately felt more attractive.

'Thank you.'

He looked from Millie to Oona and said, 'I hope I'm not interrupting anything.'

'Not at all,' Oona assured him. 'We were just talking about sex.'

He thought she was joking. He dutifully laughed.

When they finally managed to extricate themselves from their apartment, Millie felt she had to apologise for her family.

'They're quite normal when you get to know them.'

'They seemed perfectly normal to me,' he said, nicely. 'Do I have to face your mother yet?'

Millie thought of Mum upstairs in her bed, fuming with Auntie June, and refusing to come out. And probably plotting revenge.

'She's not here,' she said. 'She, um, stayed at home.'

But somehow he seemed like the kind of man you could confide in about Mum's peculiarities. He wouldn't find it amusing, or say she was imagining it, or feed her the same old tired line about how it was probably all down to age.

She had a feeling he would listen, and empathise. And offer his big broad shoulder to cry on, if she wanted.

He was, she decided, a responsible human being. She hadn't come across too many of those in her history of failed relationships.

'That's the nicest way you've looked at me since we've met,' he informed her, looking rather pleased with himself.

Millie immediately schooled her face into a sterner expression. 'I didn't mean to,' she said.

They were doing that grinning thing again. God, she must get a grip.

'Are you hungry?' he said.

'Starving,' she admitted enthusiastically. Belatedly she realised this probably wasn't the best admission on a first date. She should probably pick at a lettuce leaf or two in the hopes of impressing him with her tiny appetite.

But he just said, 'Good. I booked the table for nine. I thought that way we could go and have a drink first.'

There were many small, dark, intimate bars scattered around. Millie's heart gave a little jump at the thought of being pressed up against Simon in some cosy snug, flaming sambucas in hand. Although maybe not. She had never been good around fire. A nice glass of white wine, maybe.

'That sounds lovely.' She hoped she didn't sound too enthusiastic. But who would have thought that she'd be enjoying herself so much? With a man she had started out disliking.

Then, as usual, he went and spoilt a perfectly nice moment by saying, 'Are you allowed to drink? On those drugs?'

The way he said it you would think she was always sneaking into some grimy alleyway, sleeve rolled up, to shoot up with extra-strong ovulatory drugs.

'I just thought I'd mention it,' he said hastily. 'I don't mean to spoil things.'

But he just had.

'Thank you for your concern,' she informed him frostily. 'But I haven't actually started them yet. And even if I had, I'm sure a glass or two of wine wouldn't do any harm. I don't think mixing the two causes women to swell up and burst or anything.'

He looked like he wished he'd kept his mouth shut now. 'Sorry.'

'But if at any time I feel myself in danger around the nether regions I'll be sure to let you know.'

The little rosy glow had gone, now that her fertility treatment had entered the discussion. That tended to happen, she noticed. In which case the subject was probably better avoided altogether.

He was standing there in his lovely stripy shirt looking rather miserable.

She was miserable too.

'Could I make a suggestion?' she said after a bit.

His head snapped up eagerly. 'That we don't talk about your fertility treatment?'

'Yes.'

'I think that's an excellent idea.'

'At least that way we won't start throwing plates at each other in Christian's granny's restaurant.'

'I'm not a violent person,' he assured her.

'But still. Let's avoid the subject.'

'Agreed.'

And they smiled at each other again like two people who had just plunged their thumbs into the hole in the dam, stemming the flow for the moment but knowing that eventually it would explode in their faces.

But at least it wouldn't be tonight.

Simon was a very good listener. After they had ordered their meal he cocked his head to one side and fixed Millie with those lovely brown eyes and invited her to tell him all about herself.

Foolish man.

'Well,' she began, rather flattered.

He didn't realise that she was freshly single, and reeling from an empty house where there was nobody to talk to all day long. Not a soul with whom to have the most mundane of conversations, such as, 'Did you remember to put the bin out?' She didn't even have a cat to off-load on. They must have been building up inside her like a pressure cooker, all those hours of discussions and exchanges that were never had, because the minute she got any kind of invitation at all, she opened her mouth and she was off.

She told him about her job, her family, and Jaz's diet in work. She described to him in detail her school days, her lack of pension, her tendency to comfort-eat. With no shame or hint of embarrassment at all – where was it when you needed it? – she lay bare her history of failed relationships, and her marriage break-up to Andrew. She barely stopped short of describing her dreams to him.

At one point, feeling warm and fuzzy, she remembered thinking, I feel like I've known him for years. But she'd had two glasses of wine at that point.

He would have to take some of the blame too. Every now and again

he would encourage her with a, 'Really?' or, 'Tell me that bit again.'
Like he was actually interested. And that would set her off
again, detailing some other obscure area of her life that hadn't got a
good airing in years.

But she realised now that he had said nothing at all in about fifteen
minutes. He was probably catatonic.

'Sorry,' she said, grinding to a swift halt. 'I'm going on a bit.'

'I have that kind of face,' he assured her.

She was mortified. 'I'm finished now.'

'You couldn't be.'

Was he being sarcastic? He didn't look it. But she didn't know him
well enough to tell.

'No, I am, really.'

'But you were in the middle of telling me about the phone call
from Andrew about the money.'

Yes, stupidly. As though a man on a first date wanted to be titillated
with that sorry story. Millie was beyond mortification now. What kind
of a woman spoke for hours about her ex on a first date?

A bore, that's what.

Or someone who hadn't got over him yet.

She was probably guilty of both tonight.

At any second Simon would discreetly call for the bill and try to
make a swift getaway – probably back to his friends who were having
some *real* fun. She couldn't blame him. She really *was* out of practice
at the dating game.

'It's still very fresh, isn't it?' he said quietly.

She looked up quickly. She hadn't expected sympathy, much less
understanding. But he didn't seem in any great hurry to get off the
subject. In fact, he looked like he was settling in for the night; his
elbows were planted squarely on the table, and he had just refilled their
wine glasses.

'Yes,' she said. 'Sorry.'

'You don't have to be,' he said.

'I didn't mean to go on about him like that.'

'I'm glad you did.' He shot her a little smile. 'But maybe we should
change the subject now, what do you think?'

'Definitely,' she said with relief.

There was a little lull after Andrew's departure from the table. Millie,
so comfortable up to now – too blooming comfortable – was suddenly
rather aware of the romantic atmosphere that surrounded them.
Christian's granny favoured deep reds and dim lights and candles, and
there was some kind of smoochy music playing in the background.

All the other diners seemed to be on first dates too, judging by the amount of hand-holding and smouldering looks going on.

It was all heavy-duty stuff. Millie wouldn't have been surprised if there were rooms being let out upstairs on an hourly rate for diners who were too overcome to make it home.

Simon seemed quite relaxed, though. He was content to watch her over the candle on their table. In the meagre light his brown eyes reminded Millie of a Labrador's – big and warm and rather devoted.

She cleared her throat and said rather briskly, 'So! I feel you know everything about me and I know nothing about you.'

'There's very little to know,' he assured her. 'Hardly anything, in fact.'

'I'm sure that's not true.' At least, she hoped it wasn't.

'Well,' he said, 'I was born in Dublin, I have two sisters, five nieces and nephews, my parents are alive and well, and I like walking.' He thought for a minute, brow scrunched up. 'No, I think that's about it.'

She laughed. 'Such a colourful life.'

'I know,' he agreed.

'And what do you work at?' Then, in case she might have touched a nerve, and he was in fact an unemployed bum, she said delicately, 'That's, of course, if you *do* work.'

'Sometimes,' he assured her. 'I'm in computers.'

Oh God. Not another one of them.

'Have I said something wrong?'

'No, no,' she said. Oh, she might as well tell him. 'My husband works in computers. Well, broadband to be precise.'

'I know nothing about broadband,' he told her to her relief. 'Not a single thing. I work in a completely different area.'

How different could it really be? But thankfully Millie knew next to nothing about computers and she happily bought this explanation.

'Let's move on to something else, will we?' she said hastily.

'How about we talk about my love life?' he suggested.

She hadn't been about to suggest exactly that. But now that he had brought it up . . .

'I suppose you know all about mine.'

'Yes,' he agreed. 'Mine isn't half as interesting. I'm forty-one, single, never been married.'

'OK.'

'Do you not want to ask why?'

'No,' she said, even though she was dying to. Oona always maintained that men who reached the age of forty without getting married were usually odd.

Simon had obviously heard this too. 'You're not worried at all that there might be something wrong with me?'

Millie demanded, 'Well, is there?'

He thought that was funny. She was delighted. She was far too eager tonight, some cynical part of her noted.

'Apart from the fact that I snore after a few pints, I think I'm pretty OK,' he said.

'Good thing you sleep on your own,' she said impulsively.

Oh God. Another *faux pax*. Supposing he didn't? Supposing he had several 'friends-with-benefits'? Supposing he slept with his dog for company?

Worse again, what if he thought she was angling to join him there?

But he just agreed, 'Good thing.'

So he *did* sleep on his own. She was curiously relieved. Another box to be ticked off, along with the boxes for a good listener, sense of humour, able to handle potential in-laws, and lovely brown eyes.

You would think she was sizing him up as boyfriend material. Partner material.

Madness. Because that wasn't what she wanted, right? She was going to become a single mum, with the emphasis on 'single'. There was no room in her life, not to mention no need, for a new man right now.

'It's getting late,' she said.

'What's wrong?' he said.

'There's nothing wrong. I just mentioned that it's getting late.'

'You're getting all frosty on me again. And I haven't even mentioned donor sperm.'

'You just did.'

'But only to illustrate a point. Not to debate the rights and wrongs of it. I think you already know my opinion on that.'

'Yes, I do, thank you. There's no need to go repeating it.'

'Correct me if I'm wrong but I think I've only said it once.'

'Once was enough.'

'If you don't mind me saying so, you're going to have a tough time if you can't accept that people might disagree with your decision. Because a lot of them will.'

'I know that. And who said I can't accept it?'

'You set a condition that we weren't to talk about it tonight.'

'And you agreed.'

'Only out of politeness.'

'I didn't realise you were so *polite*.'

'It's the way I was brought up,' he said proudly. 'You can thank my mother.'

Millie wanted to be cross but couldn't.

'Will we go back to not talking about it?' she said. 'My fertility treatment.'

He looked pained. 'Do you think we can?'

'I don't see why not.'

'Well, because it's such a big thing?' he suggested tentatively.

'It's only a big thing if we make it a big thing,' she promised him. 'Do you think?'

He wanted to be persuaded, Millie could see that.

'Absolutely. Besides, it's none of your business.'

'You're right,' he said humbly.

'So let's not spoil the evening. We've been having such a nice time too.' Then, remembering that she had hogged most of it with meandering tales about herself, she added hastily, 'Well, I was anyway.'

'I was too,' he said.

She searched his face for any hint of derision or pain, but he looked fairly genuine.

And she felt all light and happy and good about herself. Having felt pretty damn crappy for the last six months, it was a strange and uplifting feeling.

'Let's go for a walk,' she suggested impulsively.

'Where?'

'On the beach. Let's feel the sand under our feet and feel the wind in our hair.' Wow, she thought – she was even being poetic.

'You're on,' he said.

Simon had had a long-term girlfriend called Jodi, who was American and, from the occasional giveaway look on his face, had broken his heart. The witch.

'I suppose we were together about seven years.'

Seven years! Longer than most of Millie's relationships combined.

'We met when she was over in college, studying as a mature student. She was supposed to go back home but moved in with me and got a job in Ireland instead. I just presumed she was going to stay for good.'

This fine tale was recounted by the water's edge. It was beautiful night, even if the wind Millie had hoped for hadn't materialised. But the sea provided a beautiful backdrop, and also a focal point for any tortured looks that Simon might want to throw at it.

He didn't seem much given to tortured looks, though. He spoke very matter-of-factly about Jodi and without any self-pity at all, even though Millie felt he was entitled to.

'Then one day she upped and left. Said that she wasn't happy, that she was going home. I was stunned. I had thought things were going great.'

'Ah,' said Millie sagely. It was a trap many people fell into, including herself. Whilst she had been grappling with lubricant and the like, Andrew had been busily distancing himself from his marriage.

'I had been going to ask her to marry me and everything,' Simon admitted. 'Our eighth anniversary was coming up the following month. Instead I ended up driving her to the airport.'

'You should have let her get the blinking bus,' Millie said stoutly. 'What a . . . toad!'

'Actually, she wasn't,' he said very reasonably.

Millie immediately felt childish and small in the face of such maturity.

'She was very nice, and at one point we loved each other a lot. We just ended up not wanting the same things, that was all.'

The same as Millie and Andrew, then. No need to say it out loud. But the look they gave each other, of empathy, of sympathy, sent little waves of warmth up and down Millie's spine.

'I didn't go out with anyone for ages after that,' Simon confessed. 'Then nobody I met seemed right. Maybe I was too picky or something. But it just never seemed to click. And then the next time I look, all my friends are getting married, or else having kids. And here I am still, forty-one and on my tod.'

'Me too,' Millie said. 'Although I'm not forty-one,' she added hastily. 'I'm a good bit off that yet.' She hoped that wasn't bending the truth too much. Still, eighteen months was a fair old stretch, wasn't it?

They both cast rather moody looks out at the sea, and pondered being on their tod.

'It's not so bad,' Millie offered bravely. She felt she should talk it up a bit, otherwise they would both feel like pathetic losers. 'You get the bed to yourself, and the remote control, and there's a certain satisfaction in being completely independent.'

'That's fine if it's what you want. If it's not, then it sucks,' Simon said baldly.

He clearly didn't want to be on his own. And wasn't shy about admitting it, either. Again, his forthrightness struck her. Men didn't often come out and say such things. Women did every day of the week, of course – dozens of them, mostly those approaching forty and getting desperate. Women like herself, watching their childbearing years go down the drain, and being forced into corners and perhaps into making desperate decisions.

'Jamie says I should get a dog,' he said. 'A big sloppy one with lots of hair and wet eyes. He says after a month or two I won't be able to tell the difference.'

Yes, that would be Jamie all right.

Simon seemed to be waiting for her opinion on the matter. He had turned around to face her fully. The moon was casting a rather flattering light on him, and giving him the kind of cheekbones she was sure he didn't have in broad daylight.

What was she going to say? Buck up? Or that he would be fine; that unlike her he had loads of miles on the clock yet?

'I'm sure you'll meet someone eventually,' she ended up saying rather limply.

That was diplomatic enough, wasn't it? Also, she didn't want him to think that she was putting herself forward for the job.

He didn't say anything. Maybe he was disappointed in her wishy-washy response.

'And I suppose you always have the dog as a back-up plan,' she said, trying to lighten the mood.

But he didn't smile. 'I'd really like to kiss you,' he confessed, 'but I'm worried that I'll only upset you. You know, what with it being so soon after your marriage breakdown.'

Millie didn't know what to say. She felt shy and nervous and hot in equal measures. And flattered. Not to mention terrified. What the hell was she supposed to say to that – 'Yes, please'?

Did she even *want* to kiss him?

Oh, who was she kidding? Ever since he'd given her that dirty wink he'd had her on the starting blocks all night.

His mistook her silence for a lack of enthusiasm.

'Normally, I don't come out and say it as baldly as that,' he said hastily. 'I *can* be more sophisticated, just so you know that.'

'So I'm an exceptional circumstance?' she said.

'Yes,' he said simply.

Millie had never been the recipient of a scorching look before. Mild passion, yes; and Andrew used to give her the odd lustful look after two pints of Strongbow. But nobody had really bestowed upon her the kind of look that said that if they didn't get up close to her *now*, this minute, then the rest of their lives wouldn't be worth living.

Simon was giving her one of those looks. It sent shivers through her. It made her feel like she was possibly one of the most attractive women in the world. Scratch that – *the* most attractive.

'It's been long enough,' she said. 'Since my marriage breakdown, I mean.'

The boldness of her. And her with a prescription back at the apartment for enough ovulatory drugs to populate a small country. Which she fully intended using, it should be stated. Wasn't possessing such an item completely incompatible with kissing men she hardly knew on a beautiful Spanish beach bathed in the light of the moon?

She decided she would think about that in the morning.

'I was hoping as much,' he admitted.

And so, to the backdrop of the sea, and with waves gently lapping at their feet, and with the moon beaming down upon them benignly, Simon took her in his arms. It couldn't have been more romantic. He was just the right height, too. Millie got to bend back obligingly, and feel very waiflike and delicate.

As their lips touched, there wasn't a thought in her head of babies or motherhood or clinics.

Shallow, but true.

He was a great kisser. And having kissed a good many frogs over the years, Millie felt she was a reasonable judge of these things. Simon was experienced, but not overly; or if he was he hid it well. He also smelt lovely, and tasted even better. It all felt so perfect that it went on and on, with neither giving any indication of wanting it to stop.

But eventually the tide starting coming in and Simon got his shoes wet.

'Damn,' he said.

With lots of shy smiles they extricated themselves, because otherwise God knows where it might lead – probably with them ending up being washed out to sea.

'It's a good thing my apartment is full of smelly men,' Simon said lightly, revealing exactly where he hoped it might lead. He looked a bit heavy-lidded and hot, which was gratifying.

'And mine is full of my family,' Millie said back.

But they were only pretending, really. Nothing else was going to happen, for a whole variety of reasons. They didn't know each other well enough, for starters. Her marriage break-up was only a matter of weeks ago. And it was only a first date; neither of them was the kind of person who hopped into bed with someone minutes after kissing them for the first time.

And she was starting fertility treatment.

It sat between them like a stone, even though they were both madly ignoring it.

'Are you sure I haven't rushed you into anything?' Simon looked concerned, lest her mind was still on Andrew.

Which wasn't very likely, after that wonderful kiss. No, Millie's mind was on only one man at that moment.

'Let's never mention his name again,' she said cheerily.

'And I'll never mention Jodi's name again.'

They were talking like they would be seeing each other again. Like they had some kind of future.

It was slightly ridiculous, given that they were on a beach in Spain, having just snogged in the best tradition of a holiday romance. And holiday romances tended to last just about as long as it took for the plane to touch down again in wet, foggy Dublin.

But it didn't feel like that. When he took her hand it felt solid and warm and right, and they walked up the beach towards their apartments in a comfortable silence.

Chapter Twenty-Two

The first person Millie saw upon entering the Alta Vista Apartments' bar was Oona. She was plonked brazenly on a stool by the bar, legs crossed, and with one foot swinging back and forth seductively.

Christian sat snugly beside her, in one of his tightest T-shirts, and with his head bent at a very intimate angle to hers.

Millie couldn't believe her eyes. But right before them Christian reached across to put an arm around Oona's shoulders and give her a little squeeze.

'Have we got a situation here?' Simon enquired of Millie carefully.

Of course, he didn't know about Christian and his fixation with Oona going untouched − a situation he had cunningly managed to rectify tonight. Millie quickly checked out his other hand, and was relieved to find it was safely resting on the counter and not squeezing some other part of her sister's anatomy.

'That man,' she said grimly, 'is a scut.'

'He must be only about nineteen,' Simon said, looking rather bemused.

'My sister has three children and a lovely house-husband back home, who bakes the lightest scones in Ireland,' she informed him. 'Not that that louse cares.'

Simon assessed the situation. 'I can see your point,' he said reasonably. 'But with all due respect, it looks like there's a pair of them in it.'

He was right. Oona wasn't fighting Christian off. Far from it. Instead she was snuggling into him and even letting her head rest upon his shoulder. Cosy wasn't in it.

'Do you want me to intervene?' Simon said manfully. 'I haven't picked a fight in twenty years, and I might be a little rusty, but I can certainly have a go if you like.'

'It's all right. You don't have to impress me.'

He looked relieved. 'To be honest, I probably wouldn't have.'

'I think it's best if I deal with this on my own.'

But Simon seemed anxious to help. 'I'm sure I saw a bucket out by the pool. I could go and fill it with cold water.'

It was tempting, but a bucket of cold water would only turn Christian into a walking wet T-shirt competition, and Oona might bed him on the spot.

'Look,' she admitted to Simon, 'she's having a bit of trouble at home.'

'Ah,' he said.

'I'm not sure what she thinks she's up to tonight, but I probably need to talk her out of it.'

Preferably before Christian's hand worked its way down to her bottom. It was already halfway down her back. She seemed to be laughing hard at something he was saying. Her shoulders were shaking, at any rate. So he was a wit as well as a little brat.

As for Oona . . . well, Millie would save that one until she got her back to the apartment. But she wasn't above taking out from her purse the photo of Gary, Aoifa and Chloe and waving it under their mother's nose whilst repeating mournfully, 'Look at their little faces.'

'I'd better leave you to it so,' Simon said.

He didn't want to go. That much was plain. And Millie didn't want him to leave. It had been such a perfect evening that she wanted it to go on and on. She had banked on a drink and some more intimate conversation, and then maybe even another kiss like the one they'd just had on the beach.

Or was she being woefully misguided? Maybe he had planned on buying her a 7Up before heading swiftly for his own apartment, and the lads.

'I know it sounds like a cliché, but I've had a lovely evening,' he said warmly.

He hadn't planned the swift getaway. Phew.

'Me too.'

'And there's nothing I'd like more than to kiss you again, but in the circumstances . . .'

'Wink at me instead,' Millie said happily.

'What?' He looked rather startled.

'The way you did in our apartment.'

He thought hard for a bit. Then his face cleared. 'I wasn't actually winking. I had something in my eye.'

'Oh!' said Millie. Her cheeks exploded with shame. She might as well have confessed that her favourite programme was *Benny Hill*.

'But I certainly can if you want,' he said gamely. 'If that's what turns you on.'

'Stop,' she begged. 'I'm embarrassed enough.'

'Will I see you tomorrow?' he asked.

She didn't even hesitate: no decorum whatsoever. 'Yes!' she said.

He left the bar still laughing at the idea of being a winker. Millie looked after him until he had disappeared out the door. She gave a blissful little sigh.

But now to the pair at the bar. She made sure she had her purse at the ready in case it became necessary to whip out the family photo sooner than anticipated. She didn't know what she was going to say to them. 'A-ha!' maybe, or 'Gotcha!' What did one say in these situations?

Perhaps she would tap them on the shoulder instead. That would certainly put a swift stop to all the laughing and giggling that was going on.

Either way she was ready for them. Simon had left her feeling confident, assertive, attractive, and not to be messed with. She was also fuelled up on two hefty glasses of red wine and a pre-dinner cocktail.

But then Christian looked over his shoulder and spotted her approach. Instead of jumping guiltily off the stool as though his arse were scalded, he remained exactly where he was, with his arm still hooked around Oona as though she was his moll.

'Hi,' Millie ended up saying, rather flatly.

'Hi,' said Christian back. He looked strangely excited. His face was all flushed – probably from Oona crawling all over him – and his hair tumbled becomingly into his eyes.

Oona didn't register Millie at all. But then again her head was buried so far into Christian's shoulder that all light and sound may very well have been blocked out.

'Gin,' Christian said succinctly.

'Sorry?'

'Your sister has been at the gin.'

And Millie saw that Oona wasn't laughing her head off at all, but was in fact crying. Pitifully. Little gin-soaked sobs escaped onto Christian's bare skin, and her body gave the odd, wretched twitch.

'I found her like this,' he told Millie, lest she accuse him of wilfully pouring it down her sister's neck.

Millie sliced him with a look. He gave her one back as though to say, 'What? I'm the good guy in all this.'

Which Millie very much doubted. He looked like he was enjoying himself far too much to be entirely innocent. Look at him now, patting Oona's shoulder intimately and murmuring something in Spanish that Millie couldn't understand – but, rest assured, would look up in her phrasebook the moment she got back to the apartment. The name Millie was mentioned and eventually Oona lifted her sodden head.

Oooh. She was a sight: swollen eyes, big red nose, skin raised and blotchy the way it always was under an onslaught of gin. Her sundress was lovely, though, and her breasts oozed out becomingly over the top. Something that hadn't eluded Christian, Millie was sure.

'Sorry about this,' she hiccuped to Millie.

'Oh, Oona.'

'Christian has been very kind,' she said pitifully.

'It was nothing,' Christian said, in a rather deep voice that Millie suspected was put on. God love him, it was a wet dream come true – the woman he madly fancied he was getting to *save*. Only from the clutches of a gin bottle, but still . . .

'I thought you were going to stay at home with Dad?'

Millie was only saying this because she felt guilty for having gone out with Simon when Oona so clearly had things on her mind. And had already started drinking.

Millie was a bad sister. Or at least not a great one.

'Look, do you want to talk?' she asked.

Christian stirred masterfully. 'I think it might be best if she just sat here quietly for a bit—'

'Shut up,' Millie told him.

Oona rubbed her eyes with the balls of her hands. She was wearing mascara, wet mascara to boot, and when she was finished she looked like an inebriated panda. 'OK,' she said.

Christian wasn't going to shift, that much was obvious. In the end, Millie had to say to him, 'I would like to order two coffees. Are you, or are you not, the barman here?'

He glared. 'I'm overworked,' he spat, before giving up his stool reluctantly. He paused long enough to murmur to Oona, 'My shift ends at midnight, if you feel you need to talk some more—'

'Now,' said Millie. 'If you can find a kettle that works.'

He gave her another black look before going off behind the bar.

'And, Christian?' said Oona. 'Thanks for listening to me.'

She offered him a very sweet smile, which of course he took completely to heart. Eyes shining with devotion, he disappeared off into the back, presumably in search of the Nescafé.

Millie sat up on his vacated stool. It was roasting hot from his bottom, the little pup. Beside her, Oona sniffled into a tissue.

'Oona, do you not think it's time to talk to Brendan about Nancy?'

Oona immediately looked more sober. 'Nancy?' she said in great surprise.

Millie wondered whether she was being a bit naïve. Or maybe she just didn't want to face it. 'Look, everything's been a big change for Brendan in the last year. He goes from working in a garage with a gang of lads to being at home with three kids on his own.' She added delicately, 'A man who wasn't all that progressive to begin with.'

'God, no,' Oona agreed with a sigh. 'When I married him he couldn't boil an egg. Mind you, neither could I. I think we had to buy a book in the end.'

'The thing is, maybe he can't handle it,' Millie suggested simply. 'Maybe all his talk about men being just as satisfied in the home is just that – talk. Underneath it all, he might feel wildly jealous of you. He might feel powerless, penniless, crushed, emasculated!'

'I doubt it. Did I tell you he's setting up an Irish branch of SAHPs? They're going to have golf weekends away and everything, in between lobbying for the signs on baby-changing facilities to be made unisex.'

Millie was a bit cross at her theory being dismissed so casually. 'None of that means anything. It might just be a cover for how miserable he really is. And I'm absolutely sure that I read somewhere that men who feel inferior to their wives often look elsewhere to boost their flagging egos.'

She thought it might have been in a fashion magazine in the dental surgery, but the point wasn't lost on Oona.

'He's not having an affair with Nancy,' she said steadily.

'How can you be so sure? There must be *some* reason the sex has dried up.' Now they were getting to the nub of the argument. But just to be sure, she enquired delicately, 'I'm gathering it *has* dried up?'

'Like the Sahara Desert,' Oona confirmed.

'You need to talk to him. Demand some answers. *I* would.'

But Oona just looked tired. 'Millie, I appreciate what you're trying to say. But this is not about Brendan. It's me.'

'What?'

'I just don't fancy him any more,' she said simply.

'But . . . but . . .' Millie closed her mouth again. She didn't know what to say. All her great theories were dust in her mouth.

'It's hard to get your head around, isn't it?' Oona agreed. 'On the surface, he's perfect. Good-looking, fantastic around the house, great with the kids but not too great – as in, they still prefer me. What's there *not* to fancy?' She looked completely miserable. 'Yet the minute he takes his clothes off, I feel absolutely nothing.'

Millie had a brief, disturbing, image of Brendan with his clothes off.

'How long has this been going on?' she asked.

Seeing as they had produced three children, then the problem couldn't be that entrenched.

'Since shortly after he gave up his job.'

It didn't take a genius to see the link.

'Does he know?'

Oona looked at her darkly. 'Over the last three months I've pleaded exhaustion, drunkenness, headaches, and never-ending periods. Why do you think I wanted to go to Spain for the week, only to get out of sex? I'd say he's got a fair idea.'

'I think he's worried you're a bit depressed.'

Oona groaned. 'I'm a total bitch. Wouldn't you think I could just close my eyes and think of Ireland?'

Millie didn't know what to say. She was still trying to adjust to the fact that it was Brendan who was rebuffed and neglected and going around bursting with sexual frustration.

'It's not your fault,' she told Oona consolingly. Well, she was her sister. Naturally it wasn't her fault, even if it was.

But, surprisingly, Oona was taking this one on the chin. 'I was the one who suggested that he give up on his career and stay at home. I thought it was a great idea. It was *him* I was worried about – an Arsenal fan stuck in the kitchen all day long?' She concluded gloomily, 'But far from being emasculated, I'd go so far as to say that he's randier than ever.'

That was probably more information than Millie needed.

Oona, meanwhile, was holding her glass up to the light in the vain hope that it contained another drop of gin. It didn't. She was reduced to sucking the piece of lemon dry.

'Oh, it's just shite!' she burst out. 'And we always had such great sex too – it's OK, there's no need to put your hand over your mouth, I won't go into detail. But back when he worked in the garage we couldn't keep our hands off each other. He'd come home in the evenings, after selling some flash sports car or taking delivery of a batch of Italian four-by-fours, and I'd be mad for him.'

'So what are you saying – he's just not manly enough any more?'

'You make it sound like I'm back in the Dark Ages.'

'Maybe you are.'

Oona considered this for a bit. 'All right, maybe I *can't* handle it. Maybe this role-swapping thing isn't for everybody, but we're too afraid to say it because we'll be accused of holding back the progress of the flipping human race.'

'You and Brendan? I doubt it.'

'I've tried my best,' she said mournfully. 'But I'm just not sophistic-ated enough, or progressive enough, or whatever it takes. I just can't fancy a man that goes around like he's Housewife of the Year, and I'm sorry if that makes me shallow.'

She didn't need to put it any plainer than that.

There was a little silence as they both contemplated the situation. 'You need to tell him, Oona.'

She was looking more and more sober by the minute. 'I can't tell him that I don't *fancy* him any more.'

'I mean the role-swapping thing. You'll have to tell him it's not working out and that you'll have to swap back.'

Oona looked more upset. 'But he loves staying at home! Only the other day he was saying that he'd never go back to work again. And it's done wonders for the kids. I can't suddenly say, hey, I've changed my mind. It wouldn't be fair on them.'

'And what about you?' Millie challenged. 'What are you going to do for the next ten years? Invent headaches and exhaustion? Give in to sex twice a year, on his birthday and at Christmas?'

'And maybe Hallowe'en too?' Oona suggested hopefully, like she was trying to cut a deal.

'This thing is not going to just go away,' Millie said sternly. 'You owe it to him. You owe it to *yourself*.' She had to swallow hard. 'Unless, of course, you plan on cosying up to nineteen-year-olds.'

Oona had the good grace to look embarrassed. 'He's twenty-one.'

'And that makes it OK?'

'We haven't done anything.' She sounded a bit sulky.

'I should hope not.'

'All right, so maybe I was flirting a bit. But it's his fault for going around the place in those tight clothes and with his nipples on show!'

'Oona.'

'Oh, shut up. I'm frustrated, OK? Can you blame me? It was just a bit of fun, that's all.'

'That's how these things start,' Millie lectured. She was quite enjoying herself. It wasn't often she was in position to give Oona advice on such matters. 'And I think Christian might think it's more than fun.'

'Christian?' Oona laughed. 'I'd imagine he has a new girl every time that coach pulls up.'

'What I'm saying is that a holiday fling isn't going to sort out your problems.'

'It won't sort out yours either.'

'What?'

'Why didn't you tell me you were going to a fertility clinic?'

Millie jumped guiltily. Why did feelings of guilt always accompany any mention of the clinic?

'How did you know?'

'Because I'm your sister,' Oona said baldly. 'We spent eighteen years together in the same house. You can't hide anything from me. No matter what you do, no matter how well you try to hide it, I will just *know*.' Then she said, 'Oh, all right, ever since we had that conversation about you having a baby on your own, I've had my suspicions. So I went through your stuff when you sneaked off yesterday and I saw the emails.'

'How dare you?' Millie spluttered.

Oona was completely unrepentant. 'I was worried about you. Fertility treatment is a serious business, Millie. I wanted to be sure you weren't putting yourself in any harm. I'd expect you to do the same for me.'

'Well!' Millie huffed again. Then she deflated. Feck it, at least it was out in the open now. And it was kind of nice that Oona had been looking out for her, even if it had been in an underhand way.

'Dad doesn't—'

'God, no.' She gave Millie an evil little smile. 'I figured I'd let you break the news to him and Mum. In your own time, of course.'

Millie coloured.

'You should have told me,' Oona said, serious now. 'I might have been able to help.'

'Sorry. I was just having such a hard time getting my *own* head around it. I was afraid you'd think I was foolish. Or wrong.'

Oona looked exasperated. 'Jesus, Millie, even if I did, I'd have the wit to keep it to myself.'

Well, of course she would have. Millie couldn't think now why she *hadn't* told her.

Oona was great. She didn't even ask for all the gory details. There was no interrogation about clinics or sperm or how Millie's baby would cope without a father.

Instead she just said, 'You haven't . . . done it already, have you?' She looked down at Millie's stomach, as though expecting her to be already bursting out of her clothes.

'I have to come back in a month or two to have the procedure.'

'OK,' said Oona. 'I'll come with you.'

Millie suddenly came over all tearful. Weren't sisters great?

'You'd want to run it past Brendan first.'

'Oh, he won't mind. He's great like that.' Then the gin kicked in again, because she got all choked up too. 'And the poor man hasn't had sex in ages! Not so much as a sniff of it!'

Millie was feeling so benign that she too began to shed a tear for Brendan, although normally the problem of men going without sex didn't concern her too much. In fact, it very often served them right.

But tonight she had a fabulous, supportive sister, not to mention being fresh from a date with a wonderful man. All was right with her world.

'Tell him you love him,' she sniffed. 'And that you're sorry things have been a bit shaky recently.'

'Do you think?' Oona sobbed.

'Tell him that you have things to sort out. That the two of you can't go for weeks without sex.'

'It's been more like three months,' Oona admitted.

Millie stopped crying. 'You haven't had sex in three *months*?'

There was a little silence after this.

'And just to clarify – you left him at home with Nancy?'

Chapter Twenty-Three

Nuala was on hunger strike back in Dublin.

This was no mean feat for a woman who loved her food. Auntie June had relented the previous night and taken her up a tray of food. But she was too late. Nuala's position was entrenched: no matter what Auntie June baked, cooked, fried or flambéed, Nuala was having none of it.

This news came through the next morning, just as Millie was up for the day. Oona was sleeping off her hangover. Dad had already been down to the local supermarket for bread and milk and was still holding them, white-knuckled, as Auntie June relayed the sorry tale down Oona's mobile phone.

'She's got a stash of biscuits up there, and some bananas, and she's getting water from the bathroom when I'm not looking.' Her voice was thin and high, totally unlike her usual cheery self. 'I can't cope with her at all.'

Even Dennis was a bit shocked.

'You must have done something else to upset her,' he insisted.

'I did not!' Auntie June spluttered. 'The TV thing was two days ago. How long can she keep it up?'

It was anybody's guess. It wasn't as though there was precedent already set of Mum deciding to go on hunger strike. But then she hadn't been given to drifting off mid-sentence before either, or mislaying basic household goods.

It was all new and strange, and it gave Millie an anxious feeling in her stomach.

'I've tried to talk to her. I've tried to reason with her. I've told her she can have anything she wants – she can have the bloody TV on twenty-four hours a day if she wants, I don't care! But she won't listen to me. Dennis, I hate to say this, but I just don't think she's herself.'

But of course Dennis had known that for ages; he just hadn't let on. Millie had known it too, but she had failed to follow it up.

At least Auntie June had the nerve to come out and say it.

But Millie found that she didn't like her any better because of it.

'How is she now?' Dennis demanded.

'Asleep,' Auntie June said with great relief. 'By the time she wakes up Neville should be here.'

'Neville?' Dad enquired.

'He's on his way up as we speak.'

Neville was Auntie June's husband. He was a bit canine-looking too, and had a reputation in the family for being a bit nosy. He was always asking about people's salaries and pension plans, and he had once opened all of Mum's kitchen presses just to see what was in them.

Millie and Dennis looked at each other, thinking the same thing: there was poor Mum, upstairs in her nightie, hungry (well, not that hungry), while Neville went through her drawers downstairs.

'I don't think that's a good idea,' Dennis said.

'It's just until you get back on Saturday.'

Dennis was impatient. 'You don't have to go near her. Just leave her be. That's probably the best thing. She'll come round in her own time.'

Millie could tell he thought Auntie June was getting a bit too much mileage out of this; you would think Mum was somehow upstairs on the landing shrieking abuse and hurling old copies of celebrity magazines.

'There's something else,' Auntie June said at last.

Millie's heart sank. Surely it couldn't be too bad. Yet all kinds of scenarios ran through her head; the smell in the room had become overpowering, for example, and Neville was needed to power-wash it down.

'What are you talking about?' Dennis asked at last. He was obviously dreading it too.

'I didn't want to tell you,' Auntie June said. 'I didn't want to spoil your holiday.'

As though the fact that Mum was barricaded in her room, not speaking and on a hunger strike hadn't already done the trick.

'She hit me, all right?'

'*What?*'

She mistook Dennis's horror to be concern about herself.

'I'm fine,' she assured him. 'She didn't get a good swing at me.'

More likely Auntie June's padded little body had cushioned the blow.

'How did this happen?' Dennis enquired, his voice shaking.

'I was trying to change her duvet cover,' Auntie June said bossily.

'She'd spilt something down it. I told her she couldn't sit there in her own filth. But she wouldn't give the thing to me so I had to take it from her. And that's when she lashed out. Gave me a right slap across the arm.'

There was no doubt in her head as to the victim of the piece.

'So Neville is coming up tonight,' she finished up defiantly, daring Dennis to disagree.

As if he were in any position to. He just closed his eyes for a brief moment, and then he was in control again.

'Sit tight,' he told Auntie June. 'We're coming home.'

Just like that the holiday was over.

When Oona emerged from her bedroom, looking like a creature from the swamp, and heard that Dennis was flying home, she announced that she was going too.

She was upset when she heard what had happened with Mum. 'And I know this sounds terrible, but I'm more upset at the thought of Nancy straddling Brendan,' she confessed.

'I'm sure she's not. He wouldn't do something like that. Anyway, they'll never get the chance, not with all the other mums around.'

'All the same, I kind of want to get home to him,' she said. 'And the kids – the little pets! If I don't get my arms around Gary's chubby little waist this minute . . . You don't mind, do you?'

What could Millie say? Oona was going home to try to save her marriage, and who could blame her?

And it was probably best to get her away from Christian. Millie believed her when she had said that nothing had happened between them, but there was no sense in leaving her in the way of temptation, especially with hefty doses of sunshine and gin thrown in.

'Of course not.'

'Thanks.' Then she declared, 'I can't wait to get out of here. I don't think I've ever had a worse holiday in my life.'

Millie let this ingratitude pass.

And now that Dad and Oona were going, it seemed odd that Millie would stay. For what, exactly? She had no further business at the clinic. And she had already filled her prescription at the local pharmacy. The pills were safely zipped up in her make-up bag, all ready for when she chose to use them. Even the sun had gone in today, with rain forecast for the rest of the week.

So that left what?

Simon.

A man she barely knew but had stayed awake half the night thinking about. A man she wished she had met years ago, not at the age of thirty-nine and on the brink of fertility treatment in a desperate attempt to have a baby before it was too late. And that was the thing: time.

If only she had the luxury of seeing where things with Simon might lead. Oh, to have weeks and months of wooing each other, of moonlight walks and candlelit dinners (interrupted by the occasional row, of course, because they wouldn't be able to stop themselves). Who knows, they might be perfect for each other. He might be the man she had waited her whole life for.

Or he might not. She didn't know a single thing about him, not really. He seemed normal enough on the surface, but who knew what lurked underneath? He might turn out to be as big a toad as Andrew, or even worse.

And where would Millie be then? Single again, still childless, and with her poor old eggs that much nearer their expiry date. She'd be back at the clinic, begging on her hands and knees for sperm, and they would probably tell her that she was too ancient and foolish to get any.

It was just too risky. There were too many unknowns.

Except for one – she wanted a baby. And she had this great chance, here in Spain, which she might regret not taking for the rest of her life.

'They have three seats left on a flight at two p.m.,' Dennis shouted excitedly from the living room, where he was on the phone to the travel agent. 'If we don't take them now they'll be gone.'

You'd think he was escaping Beirut.

'You're going to stay on, though, Millie, aren't you?' Oona said. 'There's no reason for you to go home.'

'Thanks very much.'

'You know what I mean. It's your holiday, you might as well finish it out. And there's that nice Simon . . .' She raised an eyebrow archly. 'I saw the way he was looking at you last night.'

'I thought you were too drunk to notice.'

'You never told me how your date went, anyway.'

Millie couldn't bear to get into an account of it. Not when it was all over now. She fudged it by saying, 'Fine.'

Oona pulled a little face. 'He's not worth sticking around for then?'

He was, very much so, but not at the expense of other things.

'Look, he's lovely. But I have a lot to think about, especially if I'm back here in a couple of months' time. I'd quite like to get home and sort some things out.'

Oona nodded sagely. 'That's not a bad idea. Romance is probably the last thing on your mind.'

'Hm,' said Millie, thinking of Simon's hot lips and lovely thighs. But her mind was made up. She would go home today with Oona and Dad and prepare herself for her future as a donor sperm recipient and single mother.

She was sure that it would turn out to be more glamorous than it sounded.

Chapter Twenty-Four

C hristian announced that the bus wouldn't take them to the airport. He said that it was due to come on Saturday morning, but seeing as they were leaving two days early they would have to make their own way back. They could get a taxi maybe. Or walk if they had the energy. It wasn't his business, and if Millie didn't mind he had to go and dredge the pool now because some joker from the stag party had thrown in a pair of ladies' underwear that had got snagged in the filter.

'They aren't mine,' Millie felt compelled to state, feeling guilty by association.

Not that Simon would do something like that, even if he'd got anywhere near her knickers. It was probably Jamie.

Christian wasn't appeased. He was in a terrible mood. But he did it beautifully. His dark eyes flashed all over the place and his jaw was clenching and unclenching like he was in the movies. His hair, gelled to within an inch of its life, quivered stiffly with outrage. And why not? To his mind he was a man – boy – spurned.

'I think Oona wants to drop by later and say goodbye,' Millie mumbled.

Oona hadn't said anything of the sort. She was back at the apartment merrily firing things into her suitcase, planning her outfit for the trip home, and not giving Christian a thought in the world – and after all that flirting too.

Millie didn't want to go making excuses for her, but at the same time Christian was so obviously put out by her early flight home to her husband that she felt she should say *something*.

It was in vain, because Christian just gave an elaborately casual shrug of his shoulders. 'I probably won't be here myself.'

'Oh.' Millie tried to sound suitably disappointed on Oona's behalf.

'But you can tell her from me to have a nice life.'

'I will,' Millie assured him.

Christian glowered. 'I suppose you think this is funny.'

'Me? Not at all.'

'Silly boy, no doubt you're thinking. Getting a crush on your sister.'

Millie said honestly, 'If you want to know, I'm more amazed than amused.' She added hastily, 'Not that there's anything wrong with Oona. She's great. She's terrific. It's just, well, you could have anyone you wanted.' No offence to Oona, of course.

'Of course I could,' Christian said impatiently. 'You should see this place in high season. Girls swarming around the place. Hundred of them, *thousands*, with spray-on tans and hair down to their waists. They come in gangs, and rent apartments, and lie out by the pool all day long in the tiniest bikinis you've ever seen.'

'I can imagine,' Millie sympathised.

'And they're not shy, either,' he said grimly. 'Oh, no. They catch one glimpse of me and that's it. For the next two weeks they hang around reception like flies. Asking me out, buying me drinks. Sidling up to me and pretending their kettles are broken.' He looked indignant. 'I have to beat them off with a stick.'

'Quite right too.'

'Irish girls are the worst,' he said, as though getting one back on Oona and Millie. 'And the amount they can drink! My God.'

Millie felt she should defend her countrywomen but then remembered that Oona had been at the bottom of a bottle of gin last night, and she herself had been squiffy on wine, so silence might be the best option.

'They come here year after year,' Christian went on, in a very jaded voice. He was all washed up at the age of twenty-one. 'Nothing on their minds except drinking and clubbing and having a good time.'

He had missed out a whole category of women who came for fertility treatment, she noticed.

'And they stay for two weeks, and they sleep with me, and then I pack them off home without a backwards glance.' He was sounding tragic now. 'But your sister,' he said. 'She looked so sad.'

Ah, yes – Oona, with her large breasts, sat by the pool like a long streak of misery, and unwittingly stoking Christian's rather torrid romantic interest. If she'd been all dolled up and sipping a multicoloured cocktail like the usual holiday set he wouldn't have given her a second glance.

He didn't want sex at all, Millie suddenly realised. In fact, it was far too much sex he was getting, and from an international selection of undoubtedly experienced beauties hellbent on having a great time.

What he was after was a meaningful relationship. Oona, with her sad eyes (Millie wanted to snicker) and her marital problems must have seemed like something to get his teeth into.

'She's not always sad, you know,' she said. 'In fact, usually there's nothing she likes better than drinking and clubbing and having a good time, only she's getting on a bit now and the bouncers don't let her in as much.' It might be best to burst his bubble once and for all. He would recover from his brief infatuation that much quicker. 'And while she might look very appealing and tragic out here, at home she's a bit of a slob. Brendan will testify to that.'

She shouldn't have mentioned Brendan.

Christian's nostrils flared magnificently. 'You mean the husband who neglects her?'

'Actually, he doesn't. They're just having a few problems right now,' Millie said neutrally. She wasn't about to break Oona's confidences, although she suspected that Christian's passion might swiftly wither if he knew it was Brendan going without, and not the tragic, untouched Oona.

'She is not a happy woman,' he said stubbornly.

'And you think you could make her happy?' she asked, but in a nice way.

Christian didn't like that. Probably because he knew how daft it sounded.

'She's going home to her husband and her three children, Christian.'

And that was that. Oona had never been going to do anything else, no matter how many more days she stayed. Even Christian could see that.

He gave a sigh. His lower lip quivered appealingly. There was a very distinct possibility that he was thoroughly enjoying all this. No doubt he would spend some private time in the apartment after they had gone, tenderly sniffing Oona's pillow, unaware that she had been dribbling on it the previous night.

'I wonder should you lay off the tourists?' Millie suggested tentatively.
'What?'

'There must be some nice local girls around here you could date.'

He'd surely have a better chance of a relationship with those than the likes of the two girls Millie could now see laying themselves out carefully by the pool, the better to show off their oiled bodies and startling fake tans.

'I'll bear your advice in mind,' Christian said nicely, already eyeing up the girls by the pool. Then he conceded, 'I might be here later. If Oona wants to say goodbye.'

'I'll tell her,' Millie promised him.

*　*　*

She found Simon on a sun lounger by the pool with a newspaper.

Thankfully he was wearing some clothes. Right now Millie didn't need the distraction.

'Hi.'

His whole face lit up when he saw her approaching. He looked, quite simply, delighted to see her. His lovely brown eyes locked on to hers warmly and he got eagerly to his feet.

Oh God. This was going to be harder than she had thought. Especially as she was delighted to see him too.

'I was going to knock on your door but I thought it was still a bit early,' he told her.

It was nine a.m. And he was already waiting to see her. Even his sun lounger was angled optimistically towards her apartment.

Was she mad? Telling a man like Simon that she was off home three days earlier than expected, thanks a million, don't-call-me-I'll-call-you? Was she *insane*?

And all for what – a fertility treatment that had only a fifteen per cent chance of working, and came riddled with all kinds of difficult questions?

If only he would stop smiling at her like that. It made her great decision look like a piece of singular foolishness.

'Where are the gang?' she said, just to buy time. The one time you'd want them around they wouldn't be there, of course.

'They went to that lap-dancing club last night behind my back,' Simon said. He confided, 'To honest I think they were so shocked by it all that they came home to bed early and are tucked up still. Underneath it all they're very innocent, you know.'

Millie grinned back but it felt fake. *She* felt fake, standing there chatting and smiling as if everything was OK.

'I've told them that I might tell Sandra. That should keep them in line for the rest of the week,' he said with satisfaction.

Just tell him, she urged herself.

But then he reached out to touch her arm intimately. She jumped like she was burnt.

'So, what do you want to do today?' he asked. 'I thought we might pack up a picnic and go sightseeing if the rain holds off.'

It sounded lovely; a whole day with Simon, perched on some hill somewhere, swigging white wine and flirting like mad.

Before her lily-livered resolve could weaken any further she blurted out, 'I can't.'

'Oh?'

'I'm going home, Simon. Mum's . . . well, she's not well.' There was no sense in getting into hunger strikes. 'Dad wants to get back to her, and Oona and I are going with him.'

He took a moment to digest this. 'OK,' he said slowly. 'I guess that knocks a picnic on the head.' He looked disappointed.

'I'm sorry, Simon.'

But he bucked up a bit and said, 'It's OK. You can't help it. Your mum is sick. If you have to go, then you have to go.'

The thing was, she didn't. But there was no point in complicating matters. It wouldn't change anything.

'When are you flying out?' he asked.

'This afternoon. We're leaving soon. I just came to say goodbye.'

She must have looked totally woebegone because he gave a little laugh and said, 'It's not the end of the world, Millie. We would both have been going home on Saturday anyway.'

'I suppose.' She was a bit miffed at his pragmatism. A tiny part of her had hoped that he would throw himself into the pool in anguish.

'Anyway,' he said softly, 'we can always see each other in Dublin.'

And he gave her another smile that nearly undid her altogether. For two pins now she would wrap her arms around him and kiss him hard.

But this was the real world. And she had made her decision.

And so, with great regret, she looked him straight in his lovely brown eyes and, 'I don't think that's a good idea.'

He jerked away as though he had been slapped.

'Right,' he said. 'That's fine.'

'Simon—'

'It's no problem, Millie. Really.'

He recovered quickly but not before she saw his hurt and confusion. She couldn't blame him. After such a lovely evening, no doubt he had thought they might continue on.

'It's not anything to do with you, Simon.'

'Phew,' he said. 'No foul breath, then. That's a relief.'

She ignored his sarcasm. 'It's me.'

'Millie. For God's sake. We had one date. You don't have to trot out the whole "it's not you, it's me" routine. So you don't want to meet me again. I'm completely fine with that – honestly.'

His brown eyes didn't look so lovely any more. They were impatient and pissed off. And she was the cause of it. She felt worse.

'Can I please just explain?'

He gave a sigh. 'It's not necessary.'

'I know, but it would make me feel better.'

Now he gave a short laugh.

'Which is selfish but at least I'm admitting it,' she added.

He wasn't keen. But at least he remained standing there, even if he was tapping his newspaper against his thigh as though he were extremely pressed for time.

'I'm going ahead with the fertility treatment,' she told him quietly.

He shrugged, not understanding. 'I had assumed you were. I didn't think you'd have changed your mind after one date with me. I'm hot, but I'm not that hot.'

She gave a little smile. He didn't return it, but he didn't look so cross either.

'I had a lovely evening with you yesterday,' she told him. Then, in case he was in any doubt, she emphasised, 'A *really* lovely evening. And there's nothing I'd like better than to take things up again in Dublin.'

He looked slightly more appeased now. At any rate he had stopped bashing the newspaper against his thigh.

'But I can't, not if I'm going to be coming back here in a month or two's time. I can't undergo fertility treatment while carrying on with you at the same time. I just can't hedge my bets like that.'

She had hoped that maybe he would praise her honesty, her forthrightness. He might recognise that, really, she was quite a principled person.

But he just raised an eyebrow and queried, 'Carrying on?'

'You know what I mean.'

'We don't have to have sex, if that would, you know, um, interfere with . . .' He gave a rather embarrassed nod towards her stomach area.

'It's not about sex,' she said – a statement that went against everything she'd ever been taught about conception and having a baby. 'Come on, you don't even agree with what I'm doing.'

'You're right,' he said stoutly. 'I don't.'

'Well, then! Would you be comfortable with that? Me nipping back to Spain for donor sperm?'

'I wouldn't like it, but I wouldn't stop you.'

His lofty tone grated on her.

'How kind.'

He looked annoyed again. 'I've said it from the start – it's your own business, Millie. It's nothing to do with me.'

'Even if you were going out with me? I think you'd find you'd feel a little differently then.'

'Please don't tell how I would or would not feel.'

'All right, then – I'll speak for myself. And I don't think I could be with someone who didn't support me one hundred per cent,' she said primly.

'Good luck to you so,' he snapped. 'Because I don't think too many men would be queuing up to take you on if they knew about your fertility treatment.'

'Take me on!' She was open-mouthed now. 'So, what, now I'm supposed to be *grateful* to you?'

Somehow this conversation had got a bit out of control. A simple goodbye had turned into a heated debate about the very subject they had been avoiding for all they were worth.

Now she knew why.

'Can you just think past yourself for one moment?' he said loudly. 'What?'

'What about your child, if you succeed in having one? I would have thought it would be great to have a man's influence in your child's life, even if he wasn't the father. I would have thought it was pretty darned essential.' He looked at her in a way she didn't like. 'But I suppose if men aren't necessary for conception, then they're certainly not needed for parenting, are they? Just so much dead wood.'

Millie felt a bit sick. 'Don't you dare put words in my month. Do you think I chose for things to be this way? I would *love* my child to have a father in his or her life! I'd give anything!'

'So why are you doing what you're doing? Why are you here at a clinic in Spain?'

'Because it's the only way. It's the only way I'm going to have a baby! And yes, maybe it *is* the most selfish thing I could do – but I've already owned up to that.' She was red-faced and on the verge of tears when she finished.

Simon saw it. He stopped. After a minute he said, more softly, 'I'm sorry.'

'It's all right.'

'You're not selfish, Millie.'

'Maybe I am! Maybe this whole thing is wrong.'

'Stop. I just said those things because I was angry. And disappointed.'

'So am I. But I can't split myself. And if I'm going to go down this road, then I owe it to this baby to do it properly.'

Simon didn't try to argue her out of it. Part of her was glad. Another part of her wished he would rush to put his arms around her and insist that she was wrong; that somehow, donor IUI was completely compatible with starting a new relationship.

But he must have come to the same realisation as her because he just said, 'If that's what you want.'

She didn't at all. But that was neither here nor there.

'It is,' she said, with as much conviction as she could muster.

Things were awkward now. There were no more smiles. Just a sense of formality and a rush to get away.

'I hope it works out for you, Millie.'

'Thanks. Me too.'

'Have a good flight.'

He nodded quickly at her, then turned round and walked out of her life.

Chapter Twenty-Five

Jaz said that it had rained non-stop for the days that Millie was in Spain. Lashed. You never saw anything like it. At one point she had been trapped in the doorway of Debenhams for a whole fifteen minutes on her lunch break, with a flipping river flowing past that posed serious consequences for her new shoes.

'And look at the tan on you, you lucky duck,' she marvelled. 'Here, doesn't she look great, girls?'

Great might be pushing it, but Millie definitely had a bit of colour in her cheeks as well as five days' worth of freckles across her nose. Undoubtedly the whole lot would have disappeared by the weekend, especially under the blinding fluorescent lights and airless atmosphere of the ALP claims department.

She handed out the big bars of Toblerone chocolate she had bought them all in the airport on the way home.

'Keep that thing away from me,' Jaz ordered fiercely. She was on some new diet. Nobody had really bothered to enquire what.

'So what's the news while I've been away?' Millie asked.

'Sure we've nothing to tell at all,' Yvonne said, looking baffled.

It was true. Nobody wanted to talk about petty claims or the new rule that you had to log in and out whenever you went to toilet, and which Jaz was drawing up a petition against at that very moment. She went roughly fifteen times a day herself, spending an average of ten minutes there each time. It helped the day pass.

'We want to hear about *you*,' she said now with relish, and they all dragged their swivel chairs into a cosy circle around Millie. 'Tell us everything before we burst.'

Millie didn't really want to. Spain seemed like a hundred years ago now, even though she was only back two days. The thoughts of going through the whole thing now with the girls required the kind of energy and enthusiasm that she just didn't have that morning.

She was annoyed with herself. She should be as excited as the girls – she had stage one of the process under her belt, no matter what else had happened in Spain.

'Don't leave anything out,' Yvonne ordered excitedly.

She could see that they were expecting a blood-and-guts account of the whole trip. They had earned it, with their unstinting support. She couldn't let them down.

And so she summoned a cheery smile and began her tale with Maria and the cappuccino maker and the biscuits. ('*That's* how you run an office,' Jaz commented approvingly.) She told them all about her meeting with Dr Costa, and the hundreds of photos of babies on the walls – the clinic's success stories.

'You'll have a photo up there soon,' Deirdre said encouragingly.

'That Dr Costa sounds marvellous,' Yvonne chipped in approvingly.

They weren't so certain about the student sperm donors, no more than herself.

'Are they even old enough to sign a consent form?' Jaz said bluntly.

'They're probably mature students,' Yvonne said. Millie knew that she was trying to make her feel better. 'At least twenty-two or twenty-three.'

'They might even be older than that,' Deirdre said very kindly.

Millie outlined the insemination procedure, which set Jaz off crossing her legs. She detailed the success rates, and they were kind about that too.

'Fifteen per cent! That's pretty good, isn't it?' said Yvonne, even though it wasn't.

'Not bad at all,' Jaz said stoutly. 'And you've always been lucky, haven't you, Millie?'

She said this only because Millie had won a giant Easter egg in the office raffle two years ago. She had put on five pounds eating the thing, so any good luck in winning it was questionable.

Finally, as an authentic touch, she produced a copy of the prescription for the ovulatory drugs.

They were delighted with it, and passed it gingerly around between them.

'My cousin was on those,' Yvonne said. 'She was like a weasel.' But then she said, 'She ended up having twins.'

Twins! It was just the right thing to have said. Everybody immediately forgot about the meagre success rates, and started to surmise about Millie having twins. Deirdre hoped she'd get one of each, a boy and a girl. Jaz worried about the stretch marks.

'Imagine if you *did* have twins – you'd get two photos put up on the clinic wall,' said Yvonne, only half joking.

And Millie let her spirits be lifted by the wild speculation. She needed some hope. Otherwise she had landed back in cold, wet Ireland with nothing except a dream of having a baby, after jettisoning a relationship that might actually have had a future.

'When are you flying back for the treatment?' Deirdre enquired. She nearly said 'twins'.

Millie didn't know. She hadn't even unpacked her suitcase yet. It had been late when she had finally staggered in home last Wednesday night and she had thrown it in the corner and not gone back to it since.

Instead she had spent all of Thursday mourning Simon.

He was due to fly back in on Saturday. That was about all she knew about him. She had no address for him, no telephone number. She hadn't a clue where he worked, or where he hung out at the weekends. He didn't know the first thing about her either, except that she worked in the claims department of an insurance company. He didn't even have her mobile number.

So there was no way at all of them contacting each other. Not that either of them wanted to, but she found the finality of it very upsetting, and she had gone around in her dressing gown all day when she should have been jogging, or eating lentils, or doing something else worthy to prepare her body for a possible pregnancy. She still had two days left of her holiday.

On Friday morning she couldn't bear her own company any more and had gone into work. It hadn't helped: she was still miserable, when the girls understandably expected her to be raring to go back to Spain.

'I don't know,' she answered, rather evasively. 'Maybe in a couple of months.'

'What?' Jaz cried, obviously disgusted by this lack of urgency. 'You have the drugs. The clinic is on red alert. What's stopping you?'

She didn't want to tell them about Simon. The whole thing would sound silly. A holiday romance! they would say, whilst exchanging indulgent smiles. The sun, they would tell her – it does odd things to people. They would advise her that it probably wouldn't have lasted, not once they both got back home on solid ground. These things never did.

But why then was Millie's head full of Simon? When would it fade? At the same time as the freckles?

'Nothing,' she said.

Well, it was true. She had seen to that.

'I'll probably wait one cycle,' she told them, trying to look and feel a bit more motivated. 'Just to be sure of my dates. Then I'll start the drugs and make an appointment to go back to Spain.'

'Good for you. If you're going to go through with it, then there's no sense in hanging around,' Jaz said in approval.

'No,' Millie agreed heartily, even though she felt as flat as a pancake inside.

Nuala was mortified about the whole thing with June.

'I never hit either of you when you were children, did I?' she said anxiously.

'Oh, you were always lashing out,' Oona assured her. 'We used to try and hide the rolling pin from you, didn't we, Millie? Miss Whiplash, that's what we used to call you behind your back.'

'Stop,' Nuala cried, hands flying to her face in shame even though she knew Oona was only joking.

It was Saturday afternoon and they were sitting around the kitchen table with big mugs of tea. Auntie June was long gone, even if there was a pair of mucky wellie boots by the door as a grim reminder of her visit.

Mum had abandoned her 'hunger strike' within five minutes of them arriving home from Spain on Wednesday night. Millie and Oona had gone straight upstairs from the taxi to her room, leaving Dennis to deal with Auntie June. He didn't elaborate on what was said, but voices were raised. At one point a dog had started barking outside, and Mum, in an unexpected quip, said, 'That'll be Neville,' and a moment later the doorbell had rung, sending the three of them into fits of nervous laughter.

There was no laughter this afternoon. Or not much, anyway.

'I just lost control,' Nuala said simply, as though she couldn't quite believe it. 'I snapped.'

Yes. Nobody wanted to come out and say, 'Well, you've obviously gone completely barmy.' But at the same time, having shirked the issue so beautifully for so long, it was time finally to face it.

'Is there any chance at all it could be to do with Omega 3?' Oona said at last. 'Could you be taking too much?'

Dennis stirred hopefully. He had said very little so far.

But Nuala shook her head. 'I don't think so.' She looked at Dennis. 'Tell them about the driving, Dennis.'

Dennis didn't want to. It was probably ingrained in him at this stage to cover these things up. He should have had a job in Scotland Yard.

But Nuala kept looking at him insistently.

He gave a deep sigh. 'She took the side out of Bob Murphy's car back in May.'

'What?' said Oona in delight.

Bob Murphy up the road had gone and bought a brand-new executive Rover with his lump-sum retirement plan, which he had bored everybody about for years. The Rover was all leather and chrome and big alloy wheels, and he spent the whole day long driving around in it, waving out at the common folk from behind the wheel.

According to Dennis, Bob had pulled up beside Mum at the traffic lights last May and done his waving bit. Not only had she not waved back, but when the lights went to green she had also merrily veered over into his lane and ripped the side out of his brand-new car.

'I didn't see him,' she said, when Dennis finished up. 'I just didn't see him.'

It was another frozen peas moment. Millie didn't think she'd ever be able to look at one again.

'That wasn't the start of it, though,' Nuala said.

'You mean there's *more*?' Oona groaned.

'Oh, yes,' said Nuala. She looked like she was only warming up. It was possible that she was glad finally to get it all off her chest. 'You know the way we've been calling Eamon Jenkins a fecker for years now?'

Of course they did. They had practically dined out on it. It was great to have a good, old-fashioned family villain.

'He's not,' Nuala declared. 'Me losing my job wasn't his fault. I was making a lot of mistakes. In the end he had to let me go.'

The image of Eamon Jenkins as an unlikely stud in hot pursuit of Tracey around the office in her miniskirts was finally put to rest.

They were all a bit disappointed.

Especially Dennis, it seemed. He said accusingly, 'You never told me that.'

'I was too embarrassed. And anyway, you didn't really want to know.'

'What? That's ridiculous.'

'You'd just have kept telling me I was fine. And feeding me flipping fish.'

Well, if that wasn't the height of ingratitude . . . And after all Dennis had done for her too!

He blinked angrily across the table at her now. 'You agreed with me. You were the one who said don't tell the girls. That they'd only be looking at you like you'd lost your marbles.'

Nuala looked tired. 'I know, Dennis. I know. But maybe we shouldn't have.'

They sat there for a bit in the knowledge that there was something wrong with Nuala.

'What'll we do?' Millie asked at last.

Nuala looked a bit frightened. Millie didn't blame her. She was the one it was happening to, after all.

It was Dennis who decided. 'We'll go back to the GP. We'll tell him everything this time. About the car crash and the job and everything.'

He looked at Nuala.

She nodded.

'Come on,' he said. 'We'll go and ring him now.'

And they went out of the kitchen together.

'God, I hope she's not going to go around belting people the whole time,' Oona said. 'Our own mother, turning into a thug.'

'I'm sure it's probably something minor,' said Millie, even though she was sure it wasn't.

'I hope you're right.' And Oona gave a deep sigh.

She had her own troubles that day, most notably a husband who was still going on about the marvellous meal Nancy had cooked while Oona was away – so much for Nancy being a crap cook. Nancy's house was also the kind of place after Brendan's own heart – all bleached wood and neatly folded piles of ironing, and the whole place so clean that it was like something from a gravy ad.

'The kids got on great too,' Brendan had declared when Oona first arrived back. 'They didn't want to come home at all.'

The kids, of course, rubbished this claim by clinging to Oona like a pack of rabid monkeys, only breaking off every now and again to give the piñatas a violent blow with one of Brendan's golf clubs.

'Don't ever leave us again, Mammy,' Aoifa had said tearfully.

Oona had been in floods too. 'I won't. I promise.'

If only things with Brendan were that easy. When he wasn't going on about Nancy's cookery skills – Oona wondered fearfully to Millie whether she would have to take up a cookery course in order to compete – he was planning the next jaunt with the other mums from the mother and toddler group.

'I think I've left it too late,' she blurted to Millie now. She looked miserable. 'I've ignored him for too long, and now Nancy's got her foot in the door while I was off sunning myself in Spain.'

And flirting madly with Christian, but there was no need to mention that.

'Don't be silly.'

'He didn't even make a pass at me when I got home. He's gone without sex for so long now that it's normal. In the end *I* had to seduce *him*.'

Millie wasn't sure she had heard right. 'You had . . . sex?'

244

'Well, yes. It's the only way. Otherwise I might as well hand him to Nancy on a plate.'

'And how was it?' Millie bit down the urge to close her eyes tight squeamishly.

'Awful,' Oona said flatly. 'I didn't feel a thing. All I could think of was that he smelled of pull-ups and Rice Krispie buns.' She gave herself a bit of a shake. 'Still, I'm sure I'll get used to it. And I might buy him some dress-up clothes for Christmas to try and spice things up. A fireman's outfit or something, or a leather thong.'

Mentally Millie just couldn't go there.

'And what are you going to be wearing?' she asked. 'Some ridiculous French maid's uniform, with your bum hanging out?'

Oona considered this. 'I'd better make sure to put a lock on the door just in case the kids walk in.'

'Listen to yourself. You never needed any of that kind of stuff before.'

'Things aren't like before.'

'That's for sure,' Millie said, watching Brendan out the window happily plucking some apples from Dennis's tree for a crumble later on. 'I thought you were going to talk to him about going back to work?'

'Sssh,' said Oona, in case he might hear through the double-glazing. 'I can't ask him to do that. Look at him! Happy as anything.'

'So you'll just buy a couple of saucy outfits and it'll be fine?'

Oona rubbed her eyes tiredly. 'I just don't want to rock the boat. Not when we've spent so long putting the whole thing in place.'

'There's no shame in admitting failure, Oona.' And Millie should know. 'And how do you know he's happy? Just because you're going to give him grudging sex every now and again you think he won't notice any change? If you'd like the old Brendan back, then maybe he'd like the old Oona back too.'

Oona clamped her hands over her ears. 'Shut up. I've already ordered a whole load of stuff from Ann Summers. The best thing you could do is take the kids off some afternoon so that we can use it.'

It mightn't do Millie a bit of harm. An afternoon in the company of Oona's children might finally spur her on to Phase 2 of her master plan: the popping of the pills and the making of the appointment. Aoifa, Gary and Chloe's sweet little faces could be all the inspiration that she needed.

Unfortunately right now they were beating the stuffing out of each other in the garden. Brendan was trying to separate them.

'Do that one more time, young man, and you'll go on the naughty chair,' he told Gary sternly.

'All right,' Gary said, smiling, knowing full well that there was no naughty chair at Granddad's.

The naughty chair had never really worked anyway, even though Brendan had persisted with it. The children tended to just have a nice sit down on it, and recharge their batteries for the next pitched battle.

Brendan grew redder in the face as Gary launched himself at Aoifa again. 'I'm going to count to five!' he warned ominously.

Oona reached over promptly and threw the kitchen window open. 'Stop that right now, you little brat, or I'll give you a wallop across the arse!' she bellowed at Gary.

Gary stopped in his tracks. His hand fell timidly. Aoifa stopped crying. Chloe gurgled happily at the sound of her mother's voice. Peace was restored.

Brendan turned slowly and glared.

'I've done it again, haven't I?' Oona sighed.

Millie just eyed her meaningfully.

'Maybe you're right,' said Oona. 'Maybe it's time we talked.'

Chapter Twenty-Six

Two weeks later Millie began the course of ovulatory drugs. Maybe it was the rude reminder of her mother's mortality that finally propelled her in the direction of her bedroom drawer in search of them. Who knew what was around the corner for any of them? She had come this far; she might as well get on with it.

Today was the moment of truth. Today she would find out just how well the drugs had worked. The clinic where she was booked in for a scan would tell her whether or not she could proceed with her planned trip to Spain on Friday for her donor IUI.

She was shaking with nerves as she climbed up on the examining table and pulled up her top. At least it took her mind off Mum; Mum, who was undergoing her own battery of medical investigations.

At least Millie's news was good: the technician who scanned her ovaries seemed pleased.

'You have two follicles on your right ovary, one at 15 millimetres and one at 17 millimetres,' she announced, looking at the ultrasound screen.

Millie didn't dare to get excited. 'Is that good?'

'Anything over fifteen is considered ripe,' the technician confirmed. 'And as you're only on cycle Day ten, they'll have another two or three days to mature. Follicles grow an average of one to two millimetres per day.'

Millie began to worry. Now they were starting to sound huge. She turned her head to look at the screen, expecting to see things the size of clementine oranges. But she couldn't really make out much at all, just shades of grey and black.

'Big follicles generally means they're better developed,' the technician reassured her. 'We like to see them about 18 millimetres.'

Millie quickly did the maths in her head. That meant that by the time they were triggered in three or four days' time, both of her follicles would be mature.

More than mature, in fact. Maybe a little on the aged side.

'They don't go off, do they?'

The technician smiled. 'No.'

At last Millie let herself relax. She had hoped for one decent follicle. But *two*. Still, she didn't want to get too excited. A lot could happen between now and Friday. One of them might inexplicably burst, if such a thing could happen. Or go missing in there, or something.

At the same time two mature follicles surely meant that her chances were at least fifty per cent better, right?

The technician seemed to think so. 'You're doing really well,' she praised her.

Millie felt she couldn't take all the credit. 'I took ovulatory drugs.'

'Well, of course,' the technician said, as though everybody did, whether they were trying to get pregnant or not.

But being unsurprised was part of her job. She looked at people's ovaries all day long. Millie's weren't anything special, whether they were plumped up on hard drugs or not.

They certainly felt plumped up. They felt huge. Yesterday she had dropped a biro on the floor at work but had been too scared to bend over and pick it up in case she ruptured something inside.

It wasn't just her ovaries either. Her whole stomach felt bloated. Jeans that had fitted her comfortably couldn't even be buttoned up with a squeeze. And as for the spots . . . She had broken out in a horrible rash all over her chin two days into the drug regime.

'It looks like acne,' Jaz had said immediately upon examining it. She had a teenage son.

Acne! At Millie's age. But apparently skin problems were one of the side effects.

There were many others. She hadn't had any psychotic episodes yet, but it was probably only a matter of time. She'd had pretty much every-thing else, including the aforementioned bloatedness, bad sleep, skin breakouts and raging headaches. The leaflet that had come with the pills had also warned that she might experience 'mood disturbances', which was worrying, and she had been reluctant to go to the super-market all week in case she unexpectedly experienced one by the cold counter. Could they be a precursor to the psychotic episodes?

The girls in work didn't notice anything different about her, of course.

'I think you look great,' Deirdre had gone so far as to say. But maybe she was just being kind.

'Except for the pimples,' Jaz qualified, confirming Millie's suspicions.

Probably she was too aware of everything. But she had never taken anything stronger than an aspirin in her life, and certainly not something aimed at revving up her ovaries to do several times the work they normally did, and naturally she was a little apprehensive.

'It'll all be worth it in the end,' Maria had said reassuringly in an email. She would be delighted with the news of the two follicles. The scan today, which Millie was having done in a private clinic out of her own pocket ('How much?' Jaz had screeched incredulously. 'For five minutes' work?'), would copper-fasten arrangements. Had Millie had no decent follicles, or only one immature one, then all the careful planning made over the past month would come to nothing.

In other words, cancellation.

It was the dirty word of fertility treatment (although Millie was sure there were plenty more).

It always meant that something had gone wrong: follicles had refused to grow, or too many had grown at once in over-stimulation, or some other gloomy variation that inevitably led to cancellation, financial pain and utter heartache.

'It isn't your month,' the treatment providers generally said consolingly, because they had to say something.

Millie had dreaded hearing those words from Maria. In fact she had planned to get in there first with, 'It wasn't my month,' just so she wouldn't have to hear Maria say it.

Happily, instead Maria would be telling her to confirm her flight and accommodation, and that she would see her Thursday afternoon for the trigger shot, followed by the actual insemination on Friday.

Millie was fine when she thought about it like that. She had no bother at all dealing with practicalities such as flight arrangements, and what time she would need to be at the clinic. For whole hours at a time she could distance herself by planning what to pack, and who to ask to water her basil plant while she was gone.

When she *really* thought about it – the reality of getting inseminated on Friday with donor sperm in the hope of getting pregnant with a son or daughter – she wanted to fall down on the ground with nerves. In some ways she could hardly believe it. For all the planning and research and that first trip out to Spain, some part of her had always doubted that she would actually go through with it. She would make all the right noises, she would even buy the drugs, but in the end she would bottle out.

Or else someone would stop her – who, she wasn't sure. Some stern guardian of morals and ethics, maybe, who worked at a fertility watchdog-type organisation behind a big black desk. Someone she imagined would look like a head teacher and who would catch wind of Millie's plans and phone her up, yelling, 'Just what the *hell* do you think you're doing, young lady?'

Dorothy almost fit the bill. Dorothy disapproved, didn't she? Millie had thought she saw her bless herself last week when Millie had crossed her path to get to the coffee machine. Surely she would corner Millie and advise her that she was cracked and to forget the whole thing. But she didn't. She had just kept quiet in the corner all week, damn her.

Millie wished that someone else would take responsibility. That way, if it all went wrong, if her son or daughter wasn't that happy with how they'd come about, then it wouldn't entirely be Millie's fault.

'They'll be delighted they were born in the first place,' Jaz assured her. 'Supposing you hadn't bothered your barney going to Spain at all to look for a father for them? Where would they be then? Not even a twinkle in your eye, that's where. You just tell them that if they ever get stroppy.'

Millie wasn't sure about the logic of that at all. But then Roma from Accounts downstairs pitched in with reassuring stories about various neighbours on her estate who were successfully rearing broods of children with no father on the scene at all.

'There's not one of those children a drug addict,' she declared, which seemed to be the litmus test.

'But they know who their father is, right?' Millie had clarified. There was a difference.

'Yes. Well, most of them anyway.'

Yvonne had seen the worry on her face and had given her a squeeze. 'Once you love that child with your heart and soul he or she will be fine.'

That chestnut again. Millie just wasn't sure she believed it. But at the same time she was grateful for their support. They couldn't be more positive about the whole thing, and had even had a heated argument about who would get to drive her to the airport on Thursday morning.

Jaz had won, until she discovered that Millie's check-in time was ten minutes to six.

'I'll get a taxi,' Millie had assured her.

'Ring us when you get there, though, won't you? We'll want to know how you got on.'

Their focus was Millie, bless them. They just wanted whatever would make her happy. Little Bonita in their minds would arrive on this planet wrapped in a fluffy pink blanket with the sole purpose of fulfilling

Millie's maternal desires. It wasn't for them to worry about Bonita's lack of a traceable father.

No, that was Millie's job, usually in the dead of night, with her ovaries throbbing like a toothache. She would weigh up her own desires against the consequences for Bonita. There were never any winners in this nightly tussle, and eventually she would tell Bonita sleepily, 'Oh, we'll talk about it in the morning.'

'Right,' said the technician, switching off the machine and handing Millie a bundle of tissues to wipe the sticky ultrasound goo off her tummy. 'You're done.'

'Oh.' Millie had been quite enjoying lying there, with somebody else in charge. It saved her the bother.

'When are you having the treatment?'

'Friday.'

'Good luck,' said the technician. She looked like she meant it.

'Thank you.'

Five minutes later Millie was dressed, had paid, and was standing outside the clinic.

She took a deep breath.

There was no going back now. She was on a regime, a protocol. her ovaries were primed. The clinic in Spain was expecting her. Whatever misgivings remained, she was now being borne along by pharmaceuticals and arrangements and a batch of donor sperm that had been earmarked for her, and that they would be defrosting in readiness.

She was going it alone.

Oona was delighted about the two follicles.

'We should celebrate. Crack open a bottle of champagne.'

'I can't drink,' said Millie regretfully. Well, she probably could – the instructions that came with the pills hadn't said anything about avoiding alcohol – but she was far too scared to introduce anything else into the mix. God knows what effect fizzy champagne might have on things. She might have to be taken into the garden and let off or something.

'A cup of tea then,' Oona said.

Millie automatically looked towards the kitchen. Brendan was bound to be in there, with the kettle primed and ready.

But he wasn't. And Oona was getting up with a heavy sigh, as though she actually intended to make the tea herself.

Millie grimaced. Oona's tea was always horrible – a thin, tepid, grey substance, and she never thought to offer any biscuits, never mind a nice warm scone with jam and cream like Brendan would have done.

Maybe he was busy outside. He had laid down a herb garden during the spring, apparently, and the place was now coming down with rosemary and parsley and thyme. 'I didn't even know you could eat chervil,' Oona had marvelled to Millie.

She was banging about the place now, getting mugs and spoons and concocting her grey brew. 'Are you sure you don't want me to fly out with you on Thursday?'

'Quite sure,' said Millie firmly.

'I'd have to ask Brendan, but I'm sure it'd be no problem.'

'I'm only staying two nights, Oona. I'll be fine.'

There would be no holiday this trip: no stretching by the pool and trying to learn the language. It was strictly Thursday to Saturday and she would be back in her own bed for the weekend.

She wasn't staying in a holiday complex either. This time it was a budget hotel Maria had recommended a few streets away from the clinic.

'What about emotional support?' Oona asked. 'It's a very big step, Millie. You might need a shoulder to cry on.'

'I won't be crying,' Millie promised her. 'Thanks, anyway.'

'Well, if you're sure,' Oona said. She looked slightly relieved. 'To be honest, I think I'd find it hard to get away anyway. It depends on how things pan out.'

She was being cryptic. Millie wondered whether she was talking about sex again, and had earmarked this week for another conjugal attempt.

Aoifa came running into the room from upstairs, followed by Gary and Chloe.

'Daddy's after shouting out his bedroom door at us for making too much noise,' Gary relayed excitedly.

'He used a bad word too,' Aoifa said, delighted. 'A *really* bad word, Mammy.'

'Don't mind him,' Oona said hastily, lest she repeat it now. 'He's just nervous.'

Millie was confused. Could he actually be upstairs waiting for sex with Oona at this moment? The prospect of a liaison with a blatantly unwilling wife might be enough to bring on a fit of bad temper.

But no. She heard him coming down the stairs now. His steps were rather laboured and unenthusiastic.

'Don't say anything, OK?' Oona urged Millie.

As if she would. She hadn't a clue what was going on. All she hoped was that he had all his clothes on.

'Just pretend like it's normal,' Oona hissed.

There was a pause by the door and then Brendan walked in.

For a minute Millie didn't recognise him.

He was squashed into a suit – a big grey serious-looking suit with a blinding white shirt and a tie wrapped firmly around his massive neck. His shoes were black and so shiny that Millie had to avert her eyes. Gone was his cool man-about-the-house stubble, and his square chin was red and freshly shaven. He'd had a haircut too – a very recent and quite severe one – and he looked a bit naked and startled.

He looked, well, exactly like he used to look before any of this had happened.

'You look great!' Oona cried in encouragement. 'Doesn't he, kids?'

The kids were hanging back, eyes like saucers, staring up at him like they'd never seen him before. Their memories were short, bless them, and Daddy was the guy who wore jeans and an apron, and Mammy was the one in the grey suits.

'Are you going to a funeral, Daddy?' Gary enquired tentatively.

'No, pet,' said Oona gently. 'He's going to a job interview.'

The statement settled over the room like dirty words. Brendan seemed torn between nerves and embarrassment at this turn of events. Oona, in contrast, determinedly looked cheery and optimistic.

Millie didn't know how to look, or where. Clearly there were issues going on here that she knew nothing about, except that sex was in there somewhere, or rather the lack of it.

'Who's the lucky firm then?' she asked lightly.

Brendan stiffly said, 'Some motor company out in Dundrum. Oona found it for me on the Internet.'

He didn't look particularly grateful.

'They sell huge big flashy cars,' Oona assured Millie.

'And she sent my CV and letter of application in,' Brendan added pointedly, not being bought off for a second by the prospect of big flashy cars.

'Well, you're so busy with the kids, I just thought I'd help . . .' Then, in a clear attempt to shift the focus off herself, she announced, 'Millie has two follicles!'

'That's great, Millie,' Brendan said, taking great care not to look anywhere in the direction of her ovaries. He wasn't really able for the finer points of Millie's fertility treatment and tended to shy away from in-depth discussions of anything too graphic. But he had been very supportive of her venture otherwise. He had even put himself forward as a potential male role model in her child's life.

'I think I'd be quite a good one,' he had said earnestly. 'As a kind of non-conformist man. It's very important that children don't grow up with stereotypical notions about men and women – particularly in your case, when you'll be a non-conventional family anyway, won't you?'

'Yes,' said Millie, hoping that she didn't look hopelessly confused. She really must bone up on all the new lingo. Only last week she had discovered on a parenting site on the Internet that, if successful, she would be an 'alternative parent' in a 'one-parent household' whose main social outlet may well be a 'donor conception network' that she just might have to set up herself. Oh, couldn't she just go to the play-ground with Bonita like everybody else?

But Brendan had seemed delighted that Millie would be joining him in being slightly odd.

'Don't worry,' he'd said with relish. 'You'll soon get used to it. To hell with the begrudgers!'

But of course that had been last week. This week he was being sent on job interviews. He couldn't very well be an alternative parent in a car showroom in Dundrum.

He looked slightly bemused now by the rapid turn of events.

'Do you want a cup of tea before you go?' Oona asked kindly.

He cast a look at the mugs of thin, barely steaming liquid that she was pouring. His gullet worked. 'No, thanks.'

'You'll be fine,' she reassured him.

'It's probably a waste of time even going there anyway,' he said grouchily. 'I've been out of work for months. I'm rusty, out of the loop.'

'Just say you've been at home with the kids.'

'And what, that I couldn't hack it and had to go back to work? That I missed the laddish banter so much that I threw in the tea towel?'

He wanted to say more, Millie knew. He was dying to say that his wife was refusing to have sex with him unless he went out and earned a pay packet and proved his masculinity, but he couldn't in front of Millie. Really, he wanted to call Oona a dinosaur, and probably had already in the privacy of their bedroom, dozens of time. It was unfair, and they all knew it, but what there was to be done?

'Just give it a go,' Oona pleaded. 'If you really don't want the job, then we'll talk again.'

But they probably wouldn't have sex. Or only very unsatisfactory sex. That fact was hanging over them like a hatchet, and was probably what propelled Brendan, reluctantly, to the worktop for his keys.

They all gathered around to see him off.

'Go get them, Daddy,' Gary said. Aoifa hugged him, and Chloe left a jammy fingerprint on his suit trouser leg.

'Damn,' said Brendan, trying to scrub it off.

Oona stepped forward to give him a little kiss on the cheek. 'Good luck,' she said.

He went off looking like a man condemned.

Chapter Twenty-Seven

The phone rang that night as Millie was dragging out her suit-case and pondering what to take to Spain. It was only for two days. Did she even need a suitcase? A change of knickers would nearly do. And a book to take her mind off things. If she was diligent she would take the Spanish-English dictionary that she had bought a couple of weeks back in a fresh burst of determination to acquire the language.

Naturally, she hadn't opened it since.

She chucked it into the suitcase anyway, as punishment, and reached for the phone. 'Hello?'

'Millie? It's Simon.'

She nearly dropped the receiver. She didn't say anything at all. She *couldn't*.

He must have taken this as a deep unwelcome, because he said, 'All right, look, I know you told me to bugger off.'

Finally she found her voice. Unfortunately it came out as a bit of a squeak. 'I did not tell you to bugger off.'

'You more or less did. You told me you didn't want to see me again. Which is actually worse when you think about it.'

'I didn't say I didn't want to see you again. I said I *couldn't* see you again.'

'I think that's called splitting hairs.'

She wasn't going to take that lying down. Especially when she had agonised good and proper about the whole thing. She wouldn't have her soul-searching dismissed so casually.

'There's a very big difference,' she pointed out snootily.

'Believe it or not, I didn't actually ring you up to argue with you. But if that's what keeps you happy . . .'

'It's not,' she assured him.

Hearing his voice was wonderful. She might as well admit it. She was smiling rather foolishly all over her face.

This was not good. She had been doing so well these past few weeks too, hardly thinking about him at all, except for the odd indulgent and rather heated fantasy of him in his swimming trunks. But otherwise she had prided herself on moving on. Any time he'd popped into her head she had pushed him firmly out, and focused instead on Spain.

When Oona had asked after him the other day Millie had even pretended that she found it hard to place the name. 'Oh, you mean the guy I met on holidays?' she had said with magnificent vagueness. 'No, that wasn't going anywhere.'

And now here he was, ringing her up out of the blue, and she was actually *fixing her hair in the mirror*, as though he could see her.

Something occurred to her.

'How did you even get my number?'

They'd exchanged nothing, scarcely even pleasantries in the end. He might have gone to great lengths to track her down. Her mind raced ahead to private detectives and extensive Internet searches. Could he have had her followed? It was all rather flattering, and not a little dramatic.

'You're in the phone book.'

Oh. She had forgotten about that. She deflated.

'Mind you, I had to phone up three other Millicent Dorans and ask them whether they were having fertility treatment in Spain first.'

'You did not.' She was horrified.

'I got some pretty colourful responses.'

She was chuckling now, even though she tried to stop herself. She was enjoying herself far too much for someone who had already said her goodbyes to this man.

'I didn't expect to hear from you,' she admitted.

'I know,' he said. 'I didn't really expect to be ringing you.'

There was a little warm pause.

'Especially as you were so stern with me the last time we met,' he said, only half joking.

'I wasn't! I just . . . I did what I had to do.' That came out sounding very stiff and, frankly, stupid.

'I know,' he said. 'And I'm not asking you to go back on all that.'

'You're not?'

Some part of her had hoped that he was ringing her up to beg her to reconsider. That he hadn't been able to eat or sleep or shave since he'd last clapped eyes on her, and that he was now only a shadow of his former self, but had a horrible long beard as well, and could she

please find it in herself to reconsider her decision and give him a
. another chance?

He didn't say any of this, of course. And anyway, he sounded far too
robust to have gone without food or sleep for six weeks. Health and
vigour came off him in waves. She couldn't tell whether he'd grown
a beard or not, but the chances are he hadn't.

'I'm ringing you up to invite you to Jamie's wedding,' he said.

She certainly hadn't expected that.

'What?'

'I know it's very short notice. But it's taken me two weeks to build
up my nerve, OK? In fact I was going to go on my own. I'm too old
to care if people think I'm a sad loser, and anyway, I figured one of the
bridesmaids might take pity on me – hope springs eternal and all that.'

Millie tried to process his request. Jamie's wedding? *Her*? And Simon?

'It's probably going to be awful,' he went on quickly, as if bracing
himself for her immediate rejection. 'Sandra's lost the run of herself a bit
and they're arriving in a horse-drawn carriage, and there's going to be
a ten-piece band and a DJ who's going to play ABBA the whole night
long. And instead of the traditional first dance at the reception, they're
going to get up and sign a duet – "I've Got You Babe", even though
Jamie hasn't a note in his head and he's so nervous about it that he's
been having panic attacks all week.'

Millie thought it sounded rather wonderful. She could imagine
Sandra, whom she had never meant, but who would undoubtedly arrive
in the most appalling over-the-top dress and proceed to thoroughly
enjoy her own wedding day. And Jamie, big and bluff and probably half
drunk, trying to be Sonny to her Cher.

'Even worse,' Simon admitted, 'I'm the best man. Again. For some
reason everybody thinks that because I'm single, I'd be delighted to be
asked to be best man. Like it'll cheer me up or something.'

'Poor you,' Millie commiserated, smiling.

'And I'll have to make a speech, and try to be funny, and to be
honest the only way to make it better would be if I had somebody to
bring to it,' he said. Then added hastily, 'You, I mean. I don't mean just
anybody off the street.'

She opened her mouth to say something, but he was off again. He
was, she realised, nervous.

'I know it's very short notice. I know there are certain things like
outfits and shoes and accessories to be considered – very serious things
that take more than four days to source. I've done my research.'

Millie could just imagine him diligently consulting a plethora of
women's magazines.

'So I'm sorry to be asking you so late in the day. But if you'd consider coming with me, well, I'd really like that,' he finished up simply.

She should say no, of course. It would be starting the whole thing up again, wouldn't it? It would be going back on her decision.

But he had come seeking her out despite that. He had put his pride on the line. She couldn't remember the last time any man had done that for her.

She felt all her resolve go out the window, like so much hot air. Going to a wedding with Simon, even an awful one, was one of the things she would most like to do in this world, she realised.

And so began the sneaky, internal bargaining all over again. One date couldn't hurt, could it? It wouldn't *corrupt* her. It didn't mean she had to commit to every wedding he asked her to in the future. She would still proceed with her treatment and all that.

In fact, a wedding – better still, an awful wedding – could be the very thing to take her mind off the waiting afterwards.

That clinched it. A date with Simon wouldn't compromise things, and it might actually do her good. Armed with this flabby self-justification, she asked giddily, 'When is it?'

'Friday,' he said.

Friday. Her stomach dropped with disappointment.

'Like I said, it's very short notice.'

'Simon, I can't,' she blurted.

There was a little pause, then he said, 'Whew! You're never one to let a guy down gently, Millie, I'll give you that much.'

She had done it again. Put her big foot in it and hurt his feelings unnecessarily.

'I'm in Spain on Friday for my fertility treatment.'

At about the time Sandra and Jamie were exchanging vows, Millie would very likely be in a white gown and reclining on a table in a room in the clinic.

'Oh,' he said. 'That's a shame.'

It was hard to read that. Was he disappointed that she couldn't go to the wedding with him, or that she was going ahead with Spain?

She hoped it was the former. She was afraid of his disapproval, she realised. She actually cared what this guy thought, a guy she had known for all of five days on a sun holiday in Spain.

'I can't postpone it at this stage,' she said. 'Everything is in place.'

There was no need to go into drugs, or mature follicles or any of that. Hopefully he would understand.

'Of course,' he said. 'Like I said, it was very short notice. I didn't really expect that you'd be able to come.'

But he had hoped she would. Otherwise he wouldn't have gone ringing her up.

'I'm really, really sorry.'

'It's fine.' His voice was very neutral. 'You don't even know Jamie that well, anyway. You'd probably have been bored stiff.'

She wouldn't have been. She'd have been with Simon – how could she have been bored stiff? But there was no point in saying that. It would sound like she was placating him.

There was a funny little silence now. He had put himself on the line twice and been rejected twice. And both times for reasons that had nothing to do with not liking him enough, or not wanting to see him again.

Once again it was her fertility issues that were getting in the way.

As if on cue, her ovaries gave a nasty little throb. They had been particularly painful the last couple of days, as if bitching heartily about the strain they were being put under. And all for two miserable follicles! She had come across other women on the Internet who were producing twenty-five. So, right now, she had no sympathy whatsoever for her ovaries. Throb on, she told them viciously.

Meanwhile Simon was on the end of the phone, hurt, rejected and fed up all over again. She was developing a worrying talent for this.

'Maybe we could meet up when I get back?' she suggested impulsively.

Now, why hadn't she thought of that before? The whole thing didn't have to revolve around Jamie's wedding. What was to stop them arranging something post-Spain? Nothing too heavy. Just a coffee or something.

She began to feel excited now at the prospect of seeing him again. She had missed his lovely brown eyes, and his brown hair, and his brown skin. Mind you, his skin might not be so brown now that he was six weeks out of the sun. But then her freckles had disappeared too. And the little bit of colour in her legs. Would he even recognise her on home ground?

Fake tan, she decided. A little bit wouldn't hurt. He might even be thinking the same thing.

But he wasn't. 'I think maybe you were right, Millie. You need to go and do this thing for yourself.'

'What?'

'Your fertility treatment. I don't think there's an awful lot of room in your life for anything else.'

She wanted to tell him that she had been wrong; that there was. She just hadn't realised it until he had phoned tonight.

'Let's not do anything rash here,' she said, trying to keep it light. 'All right, so I've got a few things on my mind at the moment—'

'You're trying to have a baby, Millie.'

'Well, yes, but I don't have to *choose* between the two things, do I? We can talk about this. See if we can work something out.'

He said, gently but firmly, 'Go to Spain, Millie. It's what you want to do.'

And he hung up.

Chapter Twenty-Eight

Nuala got her diagnosis the day before Millie went back to Spain. The GP had referred her to a neuro-consultant in one of the big hospitals who saw her the following week on a cancellation.

'It'll probably be a waste of time,' she said, on going. She was feisty because she hadn't mislaid so much as an orange in the supermarket that week.

They had gone in expecting him to shine a penlight into her eyes and make her say 'Aaah', or something harmless like that. Instead he performed an MRI, a vascular brain scan and a series of psychometric tests. After all of these he brought her back in again, and sat her and Dad down, and told her in the nicest way possible that while he couldn't be one hundred per cent sure, he was fairly certain that she had fronto-temporal dementia, otherwise known as Pick's disease.

'What?' She and Dennis looked at each other in great astonishment. The only person they knew with dementia was Great-Auntie Brid, but she was ninety-four, and all bent over in an S shape, and hadn't been out of a nursing home in ten years. There was no way Mum was like that.

'My wife is only sixty-four,' Dennis informed the consultant rather loftily.

The consultant told them that, unlike Alzheimer's, it was a disease that struck at the relatively young. It was also a progressive, degenerative disease for which he could give her no cure.

'I'm an optimist,' she assured him kindly.

She didn't have Alzheimer's. That was the main thing. They knew about that and it didn't look very nice: those poor souls who couldn't remember their own names, never mind those of their extended family. People whose pasts were nothing but a series of gaping big holes that nothing would ever fill again.

Nuala had never forgotten anything in her life. She could tell you the year and the month Prince Andrew and Fergie got married, because she still had the special edition of *Hello!* No, all in all, this Pick's disease thing sounded like a breeze in comparison.

But then the consultant began to go on about its progression, and how she would have to put some management techniques in place.

'Sorry?' said Nuala, worried that he would make her give up tea.

Driving was out. One of the features of the disease was sometimes an inability to heed things in the peripheral vision, hence Bob Murphy's car and the frozen peas. She was clearly a danger to herself and to others.

Nuala took it on the chin. She'd never been that fond of driving anyway. She much preferred to look out the window at the shops while Dennis did the dirty work.

'Is there anything else?' she asked in rather cavalier fashion. Bring it on.

'The best thing you can do now is go and do your own research,' the consultant advised her. 'There's plenty of information out there and the more you know the better.'

He explained that the disease was caused by the shrinking of the cells due to a build-up of protein in the affected areas of the brain.

Dennis jerked upright at this. So protein was the culprit! If he'd known that, he'd said afterwards, he'd have been cutting *back* on the bloody fish.

'So my brain is getting smaller?' Nuala enquired. She was taking notes now. She wanted him to see that she was perfectly capable of writing things down.

'It's atrophying. It's wasting away.'

Oooh. There was no need for that.

'But obvious mental impairment and memory loss occur later.'

As if that were supposed to cheer her up.

Beside her Dennis looked crushed.

They didn't really want to know any more. But he told them anyway. He went on about personality changes. She might be displaying a tendency towards lack of empathy with others. She might feel more tiredness than usual, and get a bee in her bonnet about certain things. It was possible that she got irritated easily. This could spill over into aggression. She might start to over-eat and develop a tendency to booze.

She and Dennis looked at each other in alarm.

Alzheimer's was starting to look rather attractive in comparison.

'Oh, look, will I know I'm going mad?' she butted in at last (displaying some of the aforementioned irritability). 'Or will I just drift off pleasantly some day in front of the telly?'

The consultant looked rather startled. But she just wanted to know.

He told her that it wasn't a question of madness but rather deterioration. But he assured her that with proper care, she had years of quality life yet. And that when the disease eventually progressed, they would make proper plans for her future care.

Dennis had been silent so far, each new symptom hitting him like a little missile. But he sat up now. 'What do you mean, her future care?'

The consultant reasonably pointed out that at some point her dependency would increase.

As Dennis told it afterwards, he had weighed in magnificently at that point, and given the consultant a piece of his mind. He said there was no question of 'care' for her, that she would be looked after at home by him, thanks very much, and the consultant could prescribe her all the expensive drugs that he wanted, but that in the meantime Dennis was going to keep on buying the fish oil.

'Don't mind him, I'd say he was like a lamb,' Oona had said on the phone to Millie.

Oona wasn't at the house on The Night of the Diagnosis, as it was to become known. She'd wanted to be, given the news, but Brendan had got a second interview at the garage through no fault of his own. She wasn't able to get a babysitter at such short notice, and so it was just Millie, Mum and Dad sitting around the kitchen table over strong tea and a plate of bourbon biscuits.

These family conferences, Millie thought, were becoming a worryingly regular affair.

By rights she should be hosting a conference of her own. Mum and Dad still didn't know that she was going to Spain at first light. They hadn't the faintest idea.

'You can't keep putting it off,' Oona had warned her. 'Tell them tonight. Before you go.'

But how could she? Look at them! Dad kept gazing over at the phone longingly as though willing it to ring with the news that they'd mixed up the lab results and that really, Nuala was fine after all, and they should just cut down on her magazine consumption.

Mum, meanwhile, was looking at the bourbon creams as though they were poison. The over-eating thing had really struck a chord, especially as she'd put on five pounds in hospital from pigging out. As she'd said to Millie earlier, what joy would there be left in shopping and fashion if she let herself go to a size eighteen? No, her brain could go to pot but she'd be damned if her waistline did.

Millie would be doing them no favours at all by landing the idea of Bonita on them tonight.

She would tell them when she came back.

Honestly, she would.

Anyway, the treatment mightn't even work. She would have gone and upset them for nothing.

Then she wondered why she'd automatically assumed they would be upset. They might be delighted. They might be completely sanguine about the prospect of an unknown father, and tell her it was the best thing she'd ever done.

She could always hope.

Nobody had said anything at all yet about Nuala's diagnosis. Nuala herself finally put down her cup of tea, and announced, 'Well, it's not terminal.'

'No,' Dennis agreed.

'Not very anyway,' she amended. 'Although I suppose I won't care much towards the end.'

They pondered this for another long, gloomy minute.

'I certainly don't feel like I'm going demented.' She was getting quite chatty now. But Oona had said it was only a matter of time before she began to enjoy her notoriety. 'Do I *look* demented?'

'No, but you could do with a clean blouse,' Millie said bluntly.

Lack of interest in personal hygiene and appearance was apparently a feature of the disease. They had found that out from some literature the consultant had given them. That symptom had got Nuala early. It was quite ironic, given her interest in shopping.

'He was a very nice man,' Nuala went on, although nobody had disputed the fact. 'It's not his fault that he has to give out bad news to people every day of the week. People who aren't as used to dealing with the medical profession as me.'

She meant her hospital stay. Millie wondered whether the nurses had recovered yet.

'So what happens next?' she enquired.

'I'm not sure,' Nuala mused 'Apparently I might end up mute. Didn't he say that, Dennis? We must buy some writing pads.'

'No, I mean, is there any help out there? Support groups, that kind of thing. Did he give you any advice on where to go?'

'Oh, Dennis wrote all that down.'

Dennis managed to lift his head from his mug of tea. 'I have it there somewhere,' he said.

Mum seemed to be coping a lot better with the news than he was. He wasn't following his usual pattern, which would be to immediately look up protein-free meals upon his arrival home.

But of course it was a big shock to him. Mum might have the

diagnosis, but he was the one who'd ultimately have the responsibility for her. Naturally he'd be thinking of the future. He might be casting his mind ahead to the day when Nuala would be mute, but still thinking that she'd be capable of jotting her thoughts down on a pad instead.

'I feel bad even saying it, but thank God he's retired and can look after her,' Oona had confessed on the phone earlier. 'Otherwise it'd be you or me. Could you imagine?'

They'd have to pitch in, of course. But there was no question that it would be Dennis who would primarily be living with the disease.

'I can look up things on the Internet tomorrow,' Millie assured him now. 'Support groups and the rest.' She didn't want him thinking that he was entirely on his own with this. 'We'll do a fact-finding mission between us, how about that?'

'Yes,' he said.

He didn't look that enthused.

She tried again. 'And then, next week, when it's sunk in a bit better, we'll all meet up. Do up some kind of plan. I just bet there are loads of other people out there coping with this. If there isn't a support group, then we'll start our own one!'

Steady on, she told herself.

But Nuala liked the sound of this. 'Oh, yes. We could have coffee mornings. Or go shopping together. That's if we all don't get lost.'

Wandering off was another symptom of the disease.

Nuala and Millie laughed. It probably wasn't the time or the place, but hang it.

To their utter surprise, and his, Dennis started to cry. Right there at the kitchen table. Not hysterically or anything, just a couple of low sobs that he tried to choke back.

Millie had never seen him cry before, except the time when his brother, her uncle Tom, had died from cancer. She'd only been about fifteen at the time, and she'd found him in the darkened living room, hunched over in his chair with tears coursing down his face. She hadn't known what to do. She was too young. She had offered no comfort, just slipped out of the room like she hadn't noticed. She'd felt a bit ashamed afterwards.

Nuala seemed a bit like that today. Instead of reaching across to him, she looked at him as though she couldn't quite understand his upset. *She* hadn't even cried over it yet, nor did she look likely to.

It was Millie who said, 'Dad? Dad, are you all right?'

He recovered quickly. He wiped the sleeve of his cardi across his face roughly, and lifted his head. 'Sorry.'

'It's all right, it's fine. Will I get you a whiskey or something?'

She could do with one herself. Dad didn't cry. He bitched, and gave advice when it wasn't needed, and had the odd controlling turn, but he didn't cry. Especially not now, not when he was needed the most.

'No,' he said. 'No thanks. I'm all right now.' He raised red, tired eyes to Nuala's. 'We should have done something sooner. We might have been able to nip it in the bud before it went too far.'

Millie's heart went out to him. 'There was nothing you could have done, Dad.'

'How do you know? There might be treatments, drugs.'

'There isn't. You heard the consultant.'

'There are other consultants out there. Loads of them! Who's to say he's the best one?'

'Dad . . .'

'But instead we sat here and we ignored it. And now look where we are!'

He glared at Nuala angrily as though the whole thing were her fault.

She looked hurt, and under attack, even though it was himself he was really angry at.

Then just as quickly it was gone. 'Sorry. Sorry,' he said. He rubbed his eyes hard again, and when he looked up, he was fine.

'It's a lot to take in,' he told Nuala. 'We'll have a sleep on it tonight. It'll look a lot better in the morning.'

Nuala was reassured again. Normal service had resumed. 'It will. And, you know, it could be a lot worse.'

It couldn't really. But because she was the one who said it, and looked like she genuinely believed it, then they did too, a bit.

Millie didn't want to leave them, but it was getting late. Mind you, she had such an early start that it was scarcely worth her while going to bed at all.

This time tomorrow night she would be in Spain, in bed in her little hotel. She'd have had her trigger shot at the clinic earlier and, with luck, her poor, swollen ovaries would pop out those eggs and find some release. She could lie there and try to feel them floating down, in readiness for the great egg-meets-sperm plan.

She could lie there and think about Simon.

As though she hadn't stopped thinking about him all week.

This time it really was over, not that it had started in any great way to begin with.

But the line in the sand had been drawn, and by him this time. She couldn't blame him.

And maybe it was for the best. It had all got very complicated in the end. And who was to say it would have worked out anyway?

No more than the blooming IUI. That might take two or three attempts, or more.

'Will we see you tomorrow?' Nuala asked anxiously, as Millie stood to go.

'No, Mum. I'm busy for the next couple of days. Something's come up. But I'll pop over Saturday evening to say hello.'

On Saturday evening she'd be back and the deed would be done.

She felt all funny and emotional now as she kissed Nuala's downy, innocent cheek.

Nuala thought the tears were for her. And of course they were, mostly. 'Don't worry about me,' she said stoutly. 'I'll be absolutely fine.'

'Of course you will be, Mum.'

Chapter Twenty-Nine

M illie was in what was called the Two-Week Wait. The term
sounded witty and cute, dreamt up maybe by an advertising
executive somewhere on his lunch break. There were entire sites on
the Internet devoted to the concept, with pink backgrounds, and jolly
logos and lists of appealing-looking links to click on. The Two-Week
Wait sounded like, well, fun.

In fact it referred to the most excruciating, stressful, sleepless, para-
noid fourteen days of Millie's life as she waited to discover whether
she was pregnant or not. It was those two long, long weeks that spanned
from the day of the IUI in Spain to the day she could officially take
a pregnancy test, and it was killing her.

'Don't test before the two weeks is up,' Maria had warned her sternly.
'We know all about those early pregnancy tests that are out there, and
we strongly advise you not to go rushing out to buy them.'

Millie, of course, had immediately galloped out upon her arrival home
and stocked up on a handful. She had tried to deflect attention from them
by buying a tube of toothpaste too, but the shop assistant wasn't fooled.

They sat in her bedroom drawer now, along with the lubricant and
the thermometer and Robitussin Expectorant and all the other para-
phernalia of her previous attempts. She had buried them at the very
bottom of the drawer and tried to ignore them, but they called out to
her, mostly at night, and she knew she would end up eventually tearing
the shiny plastic off one of them, hands shaking, before making a beeline
for the bathroom.

But not yet. It was only six days since her return from Spain. Six
days and nineteen hours and fifteen minutes to be precise. She was
counting. Well, what else was she supposed to do, for the love of God?
Forget that she had flown halfway across Europe, pumped up on drugs,
for a fertility cycle?

269

There should be more drugs, she decided darkly. Hallucinatory ones, maybe, that let you pass the two weeks oblivious and high as a kite. Or else something to put you to sleep. The clinic should have little warm rooms at the back, like incubators, where they could pop women who'd had treatment into beds, and leave them there, sleeping peacefully, until it was time to find out whether the thing had worked or not. They would wake you up gently with the words, 'Time to test!'

But mental torture was all part of the plan, it seemed. And having too much time on her hands; time that she should no doubt be spending productively, like weeding the garden, or getting through all that pesky back filing in work. But she didn't, naturally. She sat there looking at her ankles, wondering if it were possible that they were a tad swollen. And was that a tiny wave of nausea she'd felt a moment ago?

Yesterday she had burped. Just once, after her dinner. Nothing too remarkable about that. But straightaway she had gone galloping off to the Internet to read other women's experiences. 'I'm SO gassy!' (The Americans were the best – it was no holds barred.) 'And guess what – I discovered this morning I'm pregnant!' Gas was good, it seemed. Or else bad, because she then came across a woman from Arkansas who had burped and broke wind throughout her entire Two-Week Wait before discovering that she was flatly not pregnant.

The list of symptoms was bewildering: cramps, hiccups, hot flushes, strange smells, tingling nipples, household pets suddenly behaving strangely – all these could be symptoms of being up the duff. Or not, of course, depending on who was describing them and which state in America they were from.

'Do you smell something funny?' Millie asked Oona hopefully. She was sitting in her kitchen Friday evening after work, drinking greyish tea. 'Something kind of metallic?'

Surely Oona wouldn't. And that would prove that Millie was pregnant, right? Metallic smells were common in early pregnancy, she had read. Allegedly, anyway.

Oona looked at her very sternly. 'Go for a walk or something, Millie. Or to the cinema. Buy a good book. *Please.*'

You couldn't blame her. She had been on the receiving end of many of Millie's 'symptoms' in the last week.

'I can't read at a time like this.'

Even the kids were fractious today. They all had hideous head colds, with green stuff coming out of their noses, and Millie was desperately trying not to breathe in the same air as them just in case she did happen to be pregnant.

Oona looked like she was trying to avoid them too. 'Ah, Gary, pet!

Don't wipe it there! Get a tissue!' In the end she had to go over and do the job for him. 'I'd better get them cleaned up a bit before Brendan gets home,' she fretted. 'I don't want him thinking the place has fallen apart his very first week back at work.'

She was deluding herself. The kitchen was like a bombsite, and had been since about five minutes after he'd walked out the door on Monday morning. The rest of the house wasn't any better, so much so that when Millie had called by, Oona had made her stand on the front step while she had rushed around closing all the doors. Then she had warned Millie that under no circumstances was she to venture into the bathroom. 'You'll have to go in the bushes out the back,' she'd said. She'd meant it too.

Brendan was loving it, of course. According to Oona, there was nothing he liked better than to walk in from his new, enforced place of employment and find Oona elbow-deep in dinner – usually something like macaroni cheese that you simply couldn't go wrong with, but which she would anyway, and badly.

'Smells interesting,' he would say, eyebrows raised sarcastically, knowing damned well it would be a takeout from the Chinese again later on.

Then he would do a slow walk around the house – his victory lap, Oona termed it – picking up school uniforms, bits of half-eaten food, and empty DVD cases off the floor, while the children scrabbled about in the dirt, usually barefoot and unfed.

'How's that festering sore?' he had asked Gary sympathetically yesterday. It wasn't even a sore, Oona maintained. It was just a scratch that had got a bit infected. 'Did Mammy not put a fresh plaster on it? Dear, oh dear. We'd better do something about that before you get gangrene and it falls off.'

Gary, of course, loved the attention, and had played up a bit, clutching his leg and groaning.

'Maybe you could lay the table,' Oona had asked Brendan stiffly, trying to get back some control of the situation.

'Ah, if only I could find it,' he had murmured.

In the end he had taken a giant black refuse sack and swept everything off the table top into it, to be sorted later. By him. Properly. Oona had fumed. Then after tea he would change out of his smart suit and into his jeans and apron and put in a couple of hours' housework. Oona's pride wouldn't let her flop down on the couch as usual with a glass of wine and so she would have to work too, and they would sweat it out in silence in the kitchen, careful not to brush against each other.

'He never did help out after work before,' Oona said to Millie

271

viciously now. 'He'd be in on that couch beside me, drinking beer and swearing at Arsenal on the television. He's just doing it to prove a point, the pig.'

Needless to say, brilliant sex had yet to materialise. But he was only a week at his new job. And Oona hadn't managed to cut back her office hours yet, even though she had applied. It was probably just a question of them both settling back into their old roles, Millie consoled her, and then they would be leaping on each other just like old times.

'I'd rather drive over him with the car,' Oona had said flatly.

On reflection it might take a little longer than anticipated.

The extra work wasn't suiting her either. With no more leisurely trips to the hairdresser's courtesy of Brendan, her hair was a frizzy fright, and her roots were at least an inch long. There were no more new clothes either, or facials, and her hands were two big red work-worn lumps. Even if by some miracle she suddenly felt like mad, crazy sex with Brendan, it was debatable whether she'd be able to tempt him.

The children weren't over the moon either. They didn't like their new childminder. She was Mrs Malone, and she was a large, unsmiling woman who served them up big doorsteps of bread and butter, and appeared to have no sense of humour whatsoever. Gary had tried winking, grinning and flirting with her, but she was unmoved by his charms.

'I hate her, she's horrible, she's a witch,' he had screamed only that morning as Oona had dropped them all off before dashing to work.

'Don't be silly, Gary.'

'I hate her too,' Aoifa had said defiantly.

Chloe just cried and cried.

'Oh, for feck's sake!' Oona had shouted.

This had brought Mrs Malone running from the house, her lips thinning in disapproval.

'I think I hate her too,' Oona had muttered to the children, and for some reason they found this hilarious and they'd all cheered up.

She had told Millie that she was going to look into a new child-minder. Mrs Malone had been recommended by Nancy, of all people. Which probably explained why she was such a bitch.

There had been no word from Nancy. Or, at least, not that Oona knew. Maybe she was still ringing Brendan on his mobile at work. The worst thing was that Oona hadn't the energy to care.

Millie was sure she felt another little wave of nausea pass over her now at the kitchen table.

'Does it smell that bad?' said Oona in alarm, looking into the casserole she was trying to cobble together for dinner.

'No, it's nothing,' said Millie. It was too early for nausea, anyway. She was deluding herself. She would shut up.

The real problem was that she had no one to bore. Oona was great, and very patient with her, but she hadn't been in Spain with Millie last week, and she wouldn't be there tonight when Millie settled in for an evening of phantom pregnancy symptoms on her own. There was no husband or partner to clutch the arm of and say, 'I think I'm having a hot flush. Go look up the Internet, quick.'

Spain had been OK. There had been so much to do that it wasn't possible to feel lonely. And Maria had been there, encouraging and kind, and nearly more excited about Millie's two lovely big follicles than she had been herself. 'He's delighted, delighted,' she kept saying, referring to Dr Costa. Millie had nearly expected them to throw a party for her.

Between popping in and out of the clinic, and walking back and forth to the hotel, the two days had flown. Maria and Dr Costa had waved her off with optimistic words and exhortations to let them know, and Millie's lovely soft security blanket wasn't really ripped away from her until she stepped into Arrivals in Dublin Airport, and there was nobody to meet her, and she had to drive home alone with a stranger's sperm inside her.

But she had known it would be like that. It wasn't as though she had entered into it under any illusions. Doing things that way was tough. There were consequences for everybody, including herself.

But right now there might be a tiny life tenuously growing inside her; just a little ball of tissue nestled tight, busily dividing and trying to find a foothold in the dark. She could hardly bear to think about it, yet ended up thinking of nothing else. It would be a blastocyst by now, if it existed at all: a few cells that formed the very foundations of her baby.

Stop it now, she told herself sternly. In a minute she would have a name picked out and chosen a school.

But just as soon as she managed to put it out of her mind for two minutes, somebody would ask about it.

'Well?' the girls would demand nosily upon her arrival into work every morning. And Millie would have to list off any new 'symptom' or lack thereof.

'You just can't tell at this stage,' Yvonne would end up saying authoritatively. But that didn't stop them asking the next morning, and the next. They would be basket cases the day Millie actually had to test.

'Do it in work,' Jaz had already begged.

Millie could just imagine it: the entire office standing outside the ladies' holding their breaths while she tried to pee on a stick. And what if the test was negative? She would have to walk back out into the middle of them all, and probably apologise.

'No,' she had said.

'We'll come to your house then.'

'No!'

'Do you want to stay for dinner?' Oona asked now.

Millie cast a very brief look in at the casserole. 'No, thanks' she said.

'What are you going to do on your own for the evening? Look at the four walls?'

'I have plenty of things to do,' Millie said loftily. After she had looked at the four walls, she would probably go on the Internet and compare her non-symptoms with those of other women who had subsequently discovered, after two weeks of no symptoms, that they were pregnant.

'You only have a one-in-six chance, Millie,' Oona said suddenly. 'I'm sorry if that sounds harsh.'

Millie gave a little laugh. 'It does a bit. Aren't you supposed to be supporting me, and telling me to hope for the best?'

'I *am* supporting you. You know that I think that what you're doing is very brave, and independent, and . . . oh, all that crap. But I just don't want you pinning all your hopes on it, that's all. Because it mightn't happen for you.'

'I know that. The clinic was very clear about the success rates. I know myself that the odds are against me. So thanks for your concern, but you've nothing to worry about.'

Oona looked relieved. 'I've wanted to say that all week, but you've been so excited. I don't want to come over all gloomy.'

'I know,' said Millie. 'But I'm fine. Honestly.'

But the gloss had gone off things a bit. It was probably just as well. Now she really might go out and buy a good book, instead of wasting another evening in a quandary of 'what ifs?'. She would go to the shops right now, and pick up a Jaz special – something with oodles of sex and glamour and no babies whatsoever. It was worth a shot.

'Will you see Mum tomorrow?' Oona asked.

They had been taking it in turns to pop over, just for moral support.

Actually, Nuala was getting a bit fed up of it. While it was nice to have the attention, it was interrupting her routine. 'I'm not going down the pan just yet,' she had said when Millie was over last.

'I'll see.' It was Saturday tomorrow, and she was dying for a rest after the week.

'Did you know that in forty per cent of cases it's hereditary?' Oona said rather suddenly. 'Pick's disease.'

274

Millie had known. The genetics of the disease was something that neither of them had been keen on discussing up to now.

'Nobody on Mum's side has ever had it,' Millie pointed out. Although there was some great-uncle way back who used to do strange things to himself in public, and they'd had to keep him indoors in the end.

Please God Millie wouldn't end up like that. And now that she was single, there wouldn't even *be* anybody to keep her indoors. She'd be wandering about the streets embarrassing herself without even knowing it, until someone came and mercifully sectioned her. Bonita probably, God love her.

Oona seemed to be having the same gloomy thoughts. 'I don't think that's any guarantee we'll be spared. On the bright side, statistically only one of us will get it. To be honest, I hope it's you.'

'Thanks, Oona.'

'Still, I suppose give it another twenty years and we'll know one way or the other.'

On that cheery note Millie went home.

Chapter Thirty

There was a light on in the living room when she drew up.
She was so used to coming back to a dark house that the sight gave her quite a fright.

She turned the car engine off silently and sat there, saucer-eyed.

Her first thought was that Mum had been right: word had somehow leaked out that she was a woman on her own now, a woman with unprotected treasures such as a DVD player and a digital camera, and who habitually forgot to put her house alarm on.

And there was an unscrupulous burglar inside right this minute, or even a whole gang of them, loading up her stuff into bin liners, and excitedly on their mobile phones trying to find a way of offloading two dozen early pregnancy tests – 'unused and still in their original wrappings'.

Actually, probably not.

She had most likely left the light on herself. She had been known to do it in the past.

She was about to get out of the car when a light went on upstairs. In her bedroom. Her heart constricted. Those damn burglars were leaving no stone unturned.

She would ring the guards. This was their area of expertise, surely. But then she immediately wondered whether she had left any off-white underwear strewn across the floor, and that might eventually turn up in a court of law to embarrass her.

As her finger dithered over her phone, she noticed a car sitting outside the drive. It was a black, shiny, phallic-looking number.

It was Andrew's car.

Andrew, who should be in Germany. Andrew, whom she'd last spoken to weeks and weeks ago in a shopping centre in Spain.

But somehow he was back and in their house.

Her house, she grimly reminded herself. He didn't live there any more.

She was over the shock now. Anger slowly grew. How dare he let himself in as though he had every right? Without even a courtesy phone call in advance? She bitterly rued her laziness in not changing the locks.

But it had hardly seemed necessary. After their last conversation it seemed unlikely she'd ever see sight or sound of him again, except maybe via his solicitor.

And now he was in her house. Poking around. Going through her things. Had he seen the giant Galaxy bar that she had been eating last night in front of the telly? Oh, Millie! he might be saying to himself, perhaps with a knowing little smile. And there were other, more awful, things lying around too − like that book on surviving crap relationships that Jaz had given her, and her black female gangsta rap CDs, and four boxed sets of *Sex and the City* (Oh, Millie!). He would know immediately that she'd had no social life whatsoever since he'd left.

Her anger waned, to be placed by abject mortification instead.

But the real horror story was a pregnancy book that she was pretty sure she had left on the coffee table. In full view. It was Oona's, and it was open on the page that listed possible pregnancy symptoms. She might have written little notes in the margin too, such as 'Strange, queasy feeling around lunchtime . . . !' All right, she definitely had. Oh God.

And now he was upstairs, in the bedroom, where she kept her most private things. Her emails from the clinic. The unfinished box of ovulatory drugs. The flipping early pregnancy tests, which she now heartily wished some burglar *had* stolen.

She felt like she had been laid bare in front of the very person who had forced her down that road.

She felt like vomiting.

The light went off in the bedroom now. He hadn't spent much time there. Not enough to have read emails or examined in amazement a packet of ovulatory drugs, anyhow.

Millie felt braver now. Then bolshy. Then downright mad again.

And what the hell was she doing cowering outside her own house, while that lily-livered commitment-phobe enjoyed the heat inside?

She lifted her house keys grimly. She was going in.

But hang on. What did he *want*? What had brought him all the way over from Germany on a chilly Friday night? There was no sense in barging in there completely unprepared.

Perhaps he had come to confront her in person over the money.

But what was he going to do – wrestle her to the ground and refuse to let her go until she handed over the joint credit card and cheque-book? Or else grab a pair of scissors and cut up all their cash cards in front of her, shouting victoriously, 'Take that!'

He needn't worry. She hadn't touched a penny of their joint funds since that phone call all those weeks ago. He would know that from the statements that came from the bank. So he couldn't have come to accuse her of further theft.

What then?

Barbara had taken his clothes. So he hadn't come back for those.

Another possibility, not entirely pleasant, landed in the equation: reconciliation.

Millie's stomach churned a little sourly. Out popped her second burp of the week, only this time it was unrelated to pregnancy symptoms.

And to think that she'd once dreamt of such a thing! In those early days after the break-up she would have taken him back on any terms at all if he would just give her a baby. Pathetic, but true. He could have announced that he intended to take two more wives, and a permanent suite in the Hilton, and she would have considered it had he agreed to try to conceive. Oh, she might have sung along with the rap sisters, but one crook of his finger and she would probably have gone.

But now?

She imagined him waiting inside, bent double under the weight of an enormous bouquet of red roses. He would rush forward upon hearing her key in the door, crying and keening, 'Millie, take me back! I've been so damned foolish!'

And she would say, 'Really? You're too late. There's every chance I'm pregnant by some chap I've never met.'

Well, only a fifteen per cent chance, but he wasn't to know that.

It would certainly wipe the amorous smile off his face, wouldn't it? He'd be on the next return flight to Germany.

But she was being facetious now. If reconciliation was what he was here for, then she should at least consider her options. She was, after all, a woman of a certain age, with no guarantees that she would ever get pregnant, no matter how many cycles of donor IUI she under-went. If she still wanted a baby, then Andrew probably remained her best bet.

But she'd have to have sex with him again. Every second day. Which would be difficult when she actually couldn't stand him.

Not right now anyway. It was possible that, with the passage of time, years and years of it, she might look upon his weak, betraying, cowardly face and love him all over again, and call him Huggle Buggle (she was embarrassed even remembering that) and want to spend the entire of Saturday in bed with him. Unlikely, but possible.

But right now he was too late. She was in a different place. She was in the Two-Week Wait, a.k.a. the land of phantom pregnancy symptoms. Her heart was in Spain, and her body in limbo. She didn't even want to clap eyes on him again, never mind daydream about Saturdays in bed with him.

No, that honour went to Simon.

Ah, there he came again, rushing into her head.

He was always doing it, usually when she was least expecting it. She would be innocently contemplating what to get in the Spar for lunch, or whether the tax on her car was due, when up he would pop, making her stomach melt with longing. No matter how many times she reminded herself that it was over, he just kept coming back.

There had been no word from him, of course. No little phone call to see how she'd got on in Spain. As if there would have been. But some little part of her had prayed that maybe he would rethink her coffee invitation, and they would meet for a cappuccino in a cosy little café somewhere, and flirt and pretend that she hadn't had IUI at all.

But Simon didn't really do pretending, worst luck.

Also, he might have struck lucky at Jamie's wedding after all. One of Sandra's strapping bridesmaids had probably known a good thing when she saw one. Millie was tortured with images of him under a banquet table, smothered between the witch's bosoms and loving every minute of it.

At that point, she would usually jack-knife up in the bed in the small hours and wonder whether she had the done the right thing after all.

Too late now. She had made her choice.

Back to the matter at hand: her estranged husband, who was now in the kitchen because the light had just gone on in there. What was he doing – making himself a cup of tea?

She let herself in quietly.

Maybe she would wait till he came out of the kitchen and jump out at him and give him a fright. But that would just be childish.

Instead she called, 'Andrew?'

He walked out into the hall.

They stood in silence for a moment, looking at each other.

Millie's first thought was that he had got fat again.

'Millie,' he said, rather carefully, as though preparing himself for attack.

As so he should.

'You should have phoned to let me know you were coming by,' she said coldly.

'Yes, I know. Sorry. I waited outside for ages, but when you didn't come home . . .'

'I was at Oona's. You could have phoned my mobile.'

'I know. But I had some things to collect. I thought I'd make a start.'

Millie saw that he had a mug in his hand that usually sat at the back of the kitchen press: a Liverpool mug with a chip in the side. He also had an olive-stoner that he'd once brought back from Greece.

'It must have been hard to manage without those,' she said.

His chin rose defensively. There were two other, smaller chins, underneath. She wondered what had happened that he had let himself go again.

But that was for later.

Right now one thing was clear: whatever he had come back for, it wasn't reconciliation.

Luckily, she wasn't disappointed. In fact she felt surprisingly little for someone whose marital break-up was so fresh. A couple of short months ago she had loved this man. Now she was wondering how soon she could get rid of him so that she could have her dinner.

He didn't seem in any hurry. He even went so far as to offer her a tentative smile. It only made her suspicious.

'So!' he said. 'You look well.'

He sounded surprised. He knew how she turned to food when times got tough. No doubt he'd expected her to run to Lidl the minute he'd left the country, and that he would find her in outsize stretch pants and clutching a Big Mac.

No chance of that. Millie was back on the lentils again. The Galaxy bar last night had been a minor aberration.

'Yes,' she agreed.

She didn't return the compliment. It would be lying. Instead she let her eyes drift none-too-subtly down his front. He was wearing one of his old stretchy jumpers and a pair of shapeless jeans. He tried to pull in his belly but it only worked for a second before it flopped back out. What a porker, she thought in childish delight. And where were the sharp suits gone? And the cool seventies haircut?

He looked just like the old Andrew, back when he'd been in the bank. Perhaps they hadn't been ready for him in Germany.

'Anyway!' he said, obviously unable to bear her scrutiny any longer. 'How have you been?'

'Me? Super. Never been better.'

'Millie. Please.'

'Please, what? Be nice? The last time we spoke you threatened me over money.'

He managed to scrape together enough decency to look embarrassed. 'Yes. I'm sorry about that.'

She just folded her arms and looked at him.

'What do you want, Andrew? Apart from your stuff.'

There was a holdall at the bottom of the stairs. It had some books he'd left behind and a desk planner. She saw a spare asthma inhaler he'd left in the bathroom, and a ratty old pair of runners that he wore at the weekends. He didn't amount to much at the end of the day.

'All right,' he said, looking defensive again, 'I called around because I think it's time we regularised things.'

She didn't bother to hide her distaste. '*Regularised* things?'

He reached into his back pocket and took out a white envelope. 'I didn't want you to get this in the post. I wanted to give it to you myself.' He held it out. 'It's a draft separation agreement. I think it's time, don't you?'

She realised that he had his mature voice on, the one he used to use when talking to her parents and people he was trying to impress in the pub. It had always made Millie want to giggle.

She didn't feel much like laughing now.

She took the envelope. It felt heavy and portentous. No doubt he had hired the kind of lawyers that spent the equivalent of Ghana's national budget on embossed, headed notepaper, the kind that was so thick you could barely squeeze it into a printer.

'You came all the way from Germany just to deliver this?' Her scepticism was clear.

He looked a bit embarrassed. 'Actually, I'm not in Germany any more.'

She was completely taken back. Germany was the promised land; the very reason he had left Millie. And now he was announcing that he wasn't there any more?

She didn't know how she felt.

'The job didn't suit you?'

Oh, how she hoped he had been fired. Embarrassingly. In front of the entire office. And preferably for some misdemeanour that involved the female staff toilets and that somebody had recorded on their mobile phone and posted on the Internet.

'The job was fine,' he assured her. 'I just decided to leave.'

She could feel anger build in her now, warming her cheeks.

'Just like you decided to go in the first place?'

He looked pained. It was plain he didn't want to revisit all that. Well, tough. 'I'm sorry about that.'

Obviously he was hoping that a short apology would do the trick.

'You walked out on our marriage for a job in Germany, and then you didn't even have the decency to *stay*?' Her voice had gone up a bit. She didn't give a hoot.

Andrew, meanwhile, was looking out the glass panel by the side of the front door. Millie looked too. His interior car light was on. It snapped off again.

'Loose wire,' he said.

'Don't try and change the subject,' she said coldly.

He looked like a rat backed into a corner. 'Oh, look, Millie, I didn't leave you for Germany, I left you because you were gone cracked.'

Here they went again.

'I was not gone cracked.' She shot a quick look into the living room. The pregnancy book was not on the coffee table. She must have put it away, thank God.

He was looking at her in a manner she wasn't keen on. Like he was superior or something. 'All right,' he said. 'Take your bedroom drawer up there.'

'You didn't look in it, did you?' she blurted.

He looked offended. 'I most certainly did not.'

She sent more gratitude heavenwards.

'Most people keep their clothes in it. But not you. My God, I didn't even know what half that stuff was for.'

Well, of course he hadn't. All he'd had to do was perform, which he'd refused to do half the time. It was left squarely to Millie to effect a successful conception. Besides, all those things were just aids. A little help along the way, if you like. How else did he think people got pregnant, for God's sake? By just having sex?

'Here, do you remember that microscope thing you bought?' he said suddenly.

'The Fertility Monitor,' Millie said thinly.

It had been an American gadget complete with an actual microscope and slides.

'We spent two days trying to figure out which bit of you to try to squeeze into the slides.' He was looking at her in some amusement now.

Even she rustled up a smile. The thing had come with a fifty-page instruction manual that left them no wiser when they'd finished it.

'And what about the time you made me change all my Y-fronts to boxer shorts so that I could "breathe"?'

OK, it was all getting just a bit too chummy now.

'Yes, well,' she said briskly, 'that's all behind us now.'

'I suppose,' he said. What little warmth there had been between them fizzled out. 'I don't suppose you bother with all that now,' he said.

Little did he know. The bedroom drawer was fuller than ever. Her latest purchase was fish oil. She'd read that it thinned the blood, which might help with implantation of embryos, hence she popped a couple of pills every night before bed, even though they gave her horrible indigestion and even worse breath. And she could swear that she was growing little folds of flesh that resembled gills.

There were probably a couple of other new things in the drawer too — vitamins and herbs and other so-called miracle cures that she'd fallen for on the Internet. If she could have bought an actual man and stuffed him in the drawer too, then she probably would have.

The thing had been so full that she'd had difficulty opening it last night. She may have to resort to using one of the tubes of lubricant on the castors in an effort to ease its passage in and out.

But was she obsessed? No. Not her, no matter what Andrew said.

He was looking past her to the car again. The interior light was on again.

'Andrew,' she said, 'who's in your car?'

Perhaps it was a dog. A clever one, who could reach buttons.

But he looked so shifty that she knew immediately it wasn't a dog. Or, at least, not the canine kind.

'Look, you might as well know. I've met someone else.'

Well. She hadn't been expecting that. He might have had the decency to let the embers of their marriage grow stone cold before he hopped on someone else.

'I see.' She kept her voice as emotionless as possible. She wouldn't let him think that she cared. 'What's her name? Helga?'

She knew that was childish and low but she couldn't help herself.

'She's Irish. I met her on a flight to Frankfurt one day.'

How romantic. A rendezvous in the business class.

'She's the reason I've come back.'

Now, that hurt.

He didn't have to say it like that. He didn't have to point out his new girlfriend's pulling power to his ex-wife who had driven him away in the first place with her incessant demands for a baby.

Millie kept her face pleasantly blank. 'Are you sure she doesn't want to come in for a cup of tea?'

He thought she was serious, the big thick. 'Thanks, anyway, but I don't think that would be appropriate in the circumstances,' he said.

Millie had no desire at all to meet his new squeeze. All right, maybe a tiny part of her was curious. She looked out at the car now, trying to see in the passenger window. Hopefully she was some big tank with a plain, spotty face. She already had a strange interest in interior lights. He didn't deserve anything more. He didn't deserve anybody at all.

'But you understand now why I want to, well, wrap things up.' He nodded towards the separation agreement.

'I understand perfectly,' Millie assured. 'Rest assured you don't want them wrapped up any faster than I do.'

Then she blurted, purely in a tit-for-tat, 'Anyway, I met someone too.'

He wasn't to know that it was on a package holiday to Spain. She wasn't going to stand there like some factory reject while his new girlfriend sat outside her house ruining the electrics on his car.

'Really?' he said. He even managed to look pleased about it, the oaf.

'His name is Simon. He's lovely.' But she stopped at that. She felt too dishonest. Simon wouldn't be a bit impressed at being used as leverage against her ex.

But it didn't matter because she would never see him again.

Every time she thought that, she had a hollow feeling inside.

Andrew, oblivious to her mood, was going for a joke now. 'I thought there was something different about you all right. A glow.'

Millie wasn't sure how to take this. Either she was pregnant, or she was in love with Simon.

Oh, why couldn't she have both?

Because she had a drawer full of fertility aids upstairs in her bedroom, that was why. The minute any man was in danger of entering her life, she was sure to chase them away by brandishing an ovulation predictor stick at them.

She might as well face it, Andrew was right – she was a loon. But hopefully a pregnant loon. Then it would be worth it – right?

'I'd better go,' Andrew said.

'Great,' said Millie, rather too enthusiastically. But she was desperate to be shot of him. She wanted to eat chocolate. Or drink wine. Something, anything, that might block out the dawning suspicion that she may have made a mistake.

Chapter Thirty-One

Millie never got to use any of her early pregnancy tests. She began to bleed four days later, eleven days after the IUI. It was all over before it had even started.

At least she was at home when it happened. It was a Tuesday evening and she had just finished dinner. Television beckoned, and her fish oil pills, and an early night. She had been exhausted that week, and crampy, and sure that something was afoot. Best to look it up on the Internet and see what the ladies from Arkansas thought. Either she was pregnant, or she'd eaten something that disagreed with her.

And then the bleeding had begun.

She didn't know what to do for a minute. Her immediate reaction was panic. It was too early, her period wasn't even due yet.

Her next thought was to ring Maria. She would give her some advice, wouldn't she? She would tell her how to stop it and make things OK. There must be something she could take – a vitamin pill or a cup of herbal tea or something. Maria would know exactly what to do.

But it was eight o'clock in Spain. The clinic was shut for the day. Maria and Dr Costa and everyone else had gone home.

She decided to ring Oona. Oona had been pregnant three times; she would know what was normal, wouldn't she? Perhaps this bleeding was something to do with the embryo settling in. It might be good news, not bad.

Oona's tone didn't give her any hope. 'I don't know, Millie,' she said at last. 'It didn't happen with any of mine.' She added hastily, 'Everyone's different, though.'

But there was no sense in fooling herself. She felt the last of her hope die hard.

'I'll come over,' Oona said.

'No, don't. I'm fine.'

'It's no problem. Brendan's home, I can be over in five minutes.'

'Really, Oona. I'm just going to see how the night goes. I'll ring you in the morning.'

The bleeding got heavier. Millie curled up on the sofa with a cushion pressed to her stomach protectively even though she knew it was too late. Her little baby, if it had existed at all, was gone.

The tears came then. She howled like she had never done in her life before, not even when Andrew had left all those weeks ago. For a whole hour she rocked back and forth on the sofa, tears streaming down her face. She didn't even care if the neighbours heard.

And the cramps had started in earnest now. She was in for the worst period of her life, she knew. In a minute she'd have to take some painkillers and check that she wasn't out of tampons.

Finally she stopped crying. She felt dull and flat, like her whole life was grey.

She only had herself to blame for setting her expectations so high. She had known there was only a fifteen per cent chance. Hadn't they warned her at the clinic? Hadn't Oona said it only last week? She herself had been repeating it in her head like a mantra: don't get your hopes up; it'll only end in disappointment.

But she hadn't really believed it.

No, deep down she had been sure her number would come up. Well, she'd had such a run of bad luck lately, hadn't she? To be looking forty in the face was bad enough, but then for her husband to have scarpered practically mid-bonk must surely qualify her for some kind of compensation. Maybe some little part of her had believed that the person in charge of the odds, whoever they were, was bound to take pity on her and say, 'Oh, stick her in the fifteen per cent – everything else about her life is crap.'

And she had wanted this baby so much. Nobody could have wanted it more than she did. Look at the lengths she had gone to! She had wrestled with her conscience over donor sperm. She had gone all the way to Spain and back, twice. She had been through a marriage break-up for the sake of this baby, for heaven's sake. No, there wouldn't have been a child more loved and cosseted and treasured than little Bonita. Didn't *that* entitle her to a place in the fifteen per cent?

Apparently not.

She sat there and she hated them: those women who had made it in. The ones who were now looking at a positive pregnancy test while she was left with the other eight-five per cent, heartbroken and bitter and spent.

But that passed quickly, thankfully. It was nobody's fault.

Or was it?

She was thirty-nine after all; maybe her uterus was dodgy. Or it could have been her eggs; her FSH might have sneaked up overnight. And what about that glass of wine she'd had at Oona's last week, which she knew she shouldn't have drunk but had been too weak-willed to resist? Stupid, stupid.

She knew it was silly, trying to find something to blame. As if she could ever know for sure anyway.

She would ring Maria in the morning, but she already knew what she would say: 'It wasn't your month. Take a few days out, see how you feel, and we can start again next month.'

Start again? Millie couldn't imagine it. She didn't know how people did it, cycle after cycle. How did they scrape together all that energy and emotional commitment, not to mention money, to go through the whole process again, only to face possible failure at the end of it all?

Millie didn't think she was strong enough. Right now, she could never see herself going back to Spain.

She began to cry again. The house was so silent that the noise seemed very loud. It made her all the more aware of how alone she was in her wretchedness.

But hadn't she chosen it that way? Hadn't she pushed away her chance of happiness with Simon in her hunger for a baby?

At the thought of Simon her sobs geared up a notch, coloured with horrible self-pity now. Even her louse of a husband had somebody to cuddle up to tonight. What had she? A box of tissues and a bar of bloody Galaxy.

There was a tap on the window.

Dennis peered in owlishly at her.

He often didn't bother with the doorbell; heedless of her privacy, he just came right up to the window and looked in.

'Some day I'll be doing something horribly embarrassing and you'll fall over with the fright,' she often warned him.

That day had come, it seemed.

His grin froze as he registered that she was bawling her eyes out. For a second he faltered, as though tempted to nip away unseen. This was far worse than the time Andrew had scarpered, and he'd had to console her with two sugars in a cup of tea. Those were real tears she was shedding. This was *serious*.

He didn't sidle away. Instead he called, 'You'd better let me in.'

★   ★   ★

She told him everything. It was time.

Anyway, she couldn't have stopped herself if she'd tried. She was too upset. The minute she opened her mouth it all came tumbling out: Spain, the IUI, the donor sperm, the fake pregnancy symptoms and finally the bleeding.

Dennis sat on the edge of the sofa throughout, still in his coat, and with his car keys in his hand.

So far he had said nothing, although he had given a little involuntary jerk at the word sperm.

'Sorry,' she ended up eventually, dabbing at her eyes with a fresh tissue. 'I should have told you before now. But it never seemed like the right time.'

Also, she was far too cowardly, but there was no need to go beating herself up about that now.

He still said nothing. She sneaked a look at him. He looked petrified. All this stuff was firmly Mum's department. It was all very well filling the maternal void every now and again, but it was obvious that he felt he had drawn the short straw tonight.

And Mum wasn't even languishing in hospital this time. No, she was gone shopping. And with Auntie June, of all people, who had greeted Nuala's diagnosis cautiously. She'd never heard of Pick's disease before, and had assumed that it would eventually turn Nuala into some benign soul who was a bit batty and forgetful but otherwise as happy as Larry. Surely regular meals and fresh air and a few butterscotches every now and again would suffice in the care of such a person.

But Nuala was still mad to go shopping. Auntie June had suggested she travel up from Wexford to meet Nuala for a nice meal in a restaurant, but Nuala was having none of it. Why sit in some boring eaterie when there was a mid-season sale on in Brown Thomas? She was determined to get a raincoat at half-price if it killed her, and Auntie June was just the person to accompany her.

'If you don't, I'll take another swipe at you,' she said.

Auntie June had reared away, not realising at first that she was joking.

'There's nothing wrong with her at all,' she had said to Dennis rather accusingly, as though the two of them were making it up. Indeed Neville had muttered that they could now blame all kinds of bad behaviour on it, and that Dennis would reveal that he was suffering from it too.

Auntie June and Mum had set off hours ago in the direction of the shops. They hadn't been seen since.

But the truth was that Millie – and Dad – had better get used to Mum not being fully present. She was still fine, of course. Most days you'd hardly notice any change in her. She herself remained strangely detached from her diagnosis, and would explain to people at length all about the disease as though it were happening to someone else entirely.

'It's when the front temporal lobe basically goes into meltdown,' she had chattily informed a group of Dennis's ex-work colleagues at a recent drinks do. 'Right about here.' And she tapped on her forehead like she was knocking on wood. 'It's not like Alzheimer's, where memory is the first thing to go, although I was in the lingerie department of Marks & Spencer's last week and I couldn't remember my bra size. Mostly, though, I'm suffering from personality changes and a lack of social skills.' She had been oblivious to the looks being exchanged between the rather startled guests. 'Of course they won't be able to tell for sure until I actually die, and they take out my brain and do a post-mortem on it. I'd imagine it'll be like mince meat.'

Well, that had put everybody right off their cocktail sausages.

'I thought she was supposed to go demented?' Oona would complain. 'But all she's done is bitch about the cup of tea I brought her in. I'm telling you, they've misdiagnosed her. I'm madder than she is.'

And she did appear normal most of the time, if somewhat less decisive and a good bit grumpier.

Dennis was well able for her, though. After his initial shock he had rallied and begun to view the whole thing as a challenge.

'It's something to get our teeth into,' they had heard him tell Nuala one day rather excitedly.

Within a week he had done hours of research on Millie's computer, and gone and rearranged the entire kitchen to be more user friendly. His next mission was the remote control. He labelled all the TV channels on it in big red pen so that she could easily find *Judge Judy* without first stumbling inadvertently across *Extreme Fetishes*. He happily kept a diary of her appointments and her medication, and what she should be eating. He even sourced a CD of 'music therapy' off the Internet and the house would be filled with the sounds of Bach and Beethoven all day long.

'You'll have to speak up,' Nuala had said last week when Millie had phoned. 'I can't hear you over the flipping racket.'

And they had laughed at him.

The laughing always stopped very quickly when he brought out her medication. She was on an unnatural number of pills in various psychedelic shades. It took her nearly ten minutes in the morning to choke them all down. Just last week they had given her a new one – a super pill, the size of a small rugby ball, and all the colours of the rainbow. It'd nearly blind you before you ever got it into your mouth. Dennis always stood behind her in the mornings while she took it in case he had to perform the Heimlich manoeuvre.

Nothing would cure the disease, of course, only slow it down. Nuala would never get better, only worse. And subconsciously they were all starting to adjust to that. Oona didn't visit any more without ringing to give some notice first, for instance.

And Millie was telling Dad about the IUI, not Mum.

'You weren't expecting that, were you?' she finished up shakily.

'No,' he agreed.

An unplanned pregnancy, of course, was what he'd actually been expecting for the past twenty-five years. From the time Oona and Millie had begun to sidle past him at the front door in their miniskirts and hooker boots he had more or less expected such a disaster to happen. Whenever Nuala would greet him upon his arrival home from work with the words, 'Millie has some news for you,' his whole face would lock in an expression of pain and resignation. So sure was he that one day he would be babysitting an illegitimate grandchild that, for many years, he would usually greet such an announcement by asking Millie straight out, 'Whose is it?'

It had never occurred to him that one of his daughters would wilfully *plan* a pregnancy, via a fertility clinic in Spain, father unknown.

'Would you like a cup of tea?' he asked eventually.

Tea was good. Tea was safe. Maybe with a couple of chocolate biscuits on the side.

'It'd make you feel better,' he advised.

And him too. That way he could hide in the kitchen for half an hour making it, and hopefully when he came back in Millie would have pulled herself together and they could watch *Fair City* on the telly.

'That'd be nice,' she said, letting him off the hook. He was only a man after all, as Oona would say. He couldn't really be expected to fill Mum's shoes, no matter how much they might all try.

But he stayed put, even if he was about to topple off the edge of the sofa at any moment.

'Are you sure?' he said.

'Yes, with two sugars.'

'No, I meant, are you sure that you're not . . . pregnant?'

It cost him a lot to choke the word out. He had similar difficulty with words like 'sex'. Millie was quite proud of him.

'I am, Dad.'

'Right,' he said, nodding furiously. Then: 'I'm very sorry, Millie.'

She hadn't expected that. 'Thanks, Dad.'

'Oh, now,' he said fretfully, as she started to cry again.

'Sorry,' she said. But there was no stopping the tears – just when she thought she hadn't a single drop left too. 'I'm just so upset!' she bawled.

Dennis rose to the challenge. Undoubtedly it would have been better had Nuala been there, but he had learned a thing or two from her over the years. And so he made a cup of tea, with two sugars, and opened a fresh box of tissues, and tucked a blanket in around her legs.

He even borrowed a few of Nuala phrases: 'Let it all out, you'll feel better for it,' and, 'Things won't look so bad in the morning.'

'They will,' said Millie, unwilling to be appeased so easily. 'They'll look shite.'

'Yes, but tomorrow's another day,' Dennis said, more insistent.

'And Andrew's got a new girlfriend.'

That cut him off mid-cliché. 'What?'

'Some Irish girl. He came back from Germany for her.' And she had a good cry over that too. She hadn't let herself before; it would have seemed like defeat or something. But seeing as she was already crying, it didn't feel so pathetic.

'That fellow was an awful yoke,' Dennis said grimly, and gratifyingly.

'He was, wasn't he?' she sobbed. 'He didn't even have the decency to wait.'

For what, she wasn't sure. For her to get pregnant? That would have been nice. Then she wouldn't have given two hoots.

But she wasn't pregnant, and he was with somebody new, and she only had her father for company.

He was sweetly patting her head now, as though she were five, and handing her another fistful of tissues. 'Blow,' he said.

She did. 'We're having a separation agreement.' Her voice was so thick that it sounded like it was coming from underwater.

'It's probably for the best, Millie,' he said gently. 'Draw a line under things.'

Well, yes, but somehow she'd thought that *she* would be the one issuing agreements and legal documents. Not him. Instead he swans up out of the blue with a new girlfriend and a whole new life, and where was the bloody justice in that?

There wasn't any. Not for Millie, anyhow.

Dennis was still doing his level best to cheer her up. 'At least that clinic place will be open in the morning and you can ring them for advice.'

'They'll only tell me to give it another go.' She felt sour and churlish now.

'And when you get your energy back, you will.'

'I won't. I've had enough.'

'You're not a quitter, Millie Doran.' He looked quite cross now.

'I am, I'm a total quitter and loser.' She stopped crying long enough to peer at him. 'Are you actually *encouraging* me to go to Spain for donor sperm?'

He jumped nervously at the word sperm again. 'I'm supporting you in your attempts to have a baby,' he said, hedging his bets.

'Which means donor sperm, Dad. And me becoming a single mother. That was always your worst nightmare.'

'It certainly was not.'

'It was, along with oil prices going up.'

He smiled at that. The central heating bill had always been one of his primary concerns. 'Silly really, wasn't it?' he said. 'Worrying about things before they'd even happened. And now look at Mum – the whole thing out of the blue.'

Yes.

'Are you feeling better?' he enquired.

'A bit.' She actually was, which was surprising. Maybe Dad had been right about letting it all out. 'You'd better go. Mum will be home soon.'

He didn't like Nuala being in the house on her own since her diagnosis. But surprisingly, he didn't spring from the couch and race for the door.

'Oh, they won't be back for hours yet,' he said with magnificent carelessness, although the shops closed at nine. 'And then they'll drag out everything they've bought, and try it on, and to be honest, I'd just as soon not be there.'

He was lying. He would love it: the discussion of a skirt's length, the examination of the fabric, the checking that there was a spare button attached just in case. Then the fashion parade, with Mum marching up and down the hall in her new raincoat while he commented loudly on the shoulder width. He was a big girl's blouse only he wouldn't admit it.

But he wasn't going to rush home, however much he wanted to. He was going to stay for Millie's sake.

And she was going to let him.

'Now,' he said, 'how about another cup of tea?'

Chapter Thirty-Two

Millie didn't ring the clinic the following morning. Or the morning after that. She figured she'd wait until she felt a little less emotional and then she'd ring. Then it was so busy in work that she forgot, and suddenly it was the weekend, and the clinic was closed again.

Eventually Maria tracked her down at the end of the following week. 'I'm just checking in with you, that's all.'

'I'm not pregnant,' Millie said immediately. Before Maria could get a word in, she said, 'It just wasn't my month. Still, these things happen. It was only a fifteen per cent chance after all.'

Maria was quiet for a bit, probably because Millie had stolen all her lines.

'Are you OK?' she said then, sympathy bubbling down the phone. She really was lovely.

'I am,' Millie assured her.

At least, she was now. It had been the roughest week of her life, but she had got through it, and now at least she could talk about it without bursting into tears.

And the girls in work had been great. They had instinctively known that she didn't want to discuss it, and they had shown their empathy in other ways: the bar of Galaxy she found left on her desk, for instance, and the way they took more than their share of calls so as to spare her someone whinging down the phone about a burst pipe.

Even Dorothy had been sweet, insisting that Millie take an extra half-hour for her lunch break yesterday. And nobody, but nobody, was so tactless as to mention their own children all week, even though Jaz's daughter Cleo had gone and got her tongue pierced on the sly behind her back.

Maria was no daw either. 'You probably don't want to think about another cycle just yet,' she said diplomatically.

'No. Not just yet.'

'That's perfectly understandable. We'll leave it up to you. You take a bit of time off, and when you feel up to trying again, then give me a call.'

Her warmth nearly set Millie off crying again.

'I'll pass on the news to Dr Costa. You mind yourself now, do you hear?'

Millie duly promised that she would, and she thanked Maria for all her help before hanging up.

Millie let a cycle pass. But at the beginning of the next cycle, she didn't feel ready either. The ovulatory drugs lay in her drawer gathering durt. She knew that time wasn't on her side, but even that thought wasn't enough to spur her on.

'You will, though, won't you?' Oona said now. 'Have another go.'

They were in her kitchen again drinking gin and tonics. It was a Friday night, The place was in total chaos. Oona was still in her work clothes, while Brendan wasn't even home yet. Gary, Aoifa and Chloe tore around the place, shrieking and unwashed. Chloe had no nappy on as she was being toilet-trained, but not very successfully judging by the puddles dotted around the floor. Gary had a white sliced loaf under his arm from which he periodically took a slice of bread and stuffed it into his mouth. It was, Millie deduced, dinner.

'I don't know,' she said. 'I'll have to see.'

'You're only saying that because it's still a bit fresh. Give it another month and you'll be raring to go again.'

But Millie felt strangely apathetic about the prospect of returning to Spain. All the excitement and anticipation of that first time had dissipated. Now when she thought about going through it all again she felt only lethargy and disinterest.

She wasn't quite sure what had changed. Her desire for a baby was as strong as ever. Yesterday on her extended lunch break she had gone into Mothercare, as she had done so many times previously. They had new stock in the newborn section: little pink and blue sleepsuits with teddy bears embroidered on the front, and matching hats and bootees. She had stood there for ages fingering them, pretending that she was trying to choose. She got such a pain of longing in her chest that eventually she'd had to run out of the place.

No, she still wanted to be a mother. Desperately. But somehow Spain no longer seemed like the answer.

And some of it was to do with Dennis.

Foolishly, she mentioned this to Oona.

'I knew it,' said Oona grimly. 'He said something to you, didn't he?

Something embarrassingly backward. Don't take any notice of him, Millie. He's an awful old goat. I could have told you that he'd faint at the very mention of donor IUI.'

'He didn't faint at all. He was great about it.'

'Oh,' said Oona, surprised and a bit grumpy.

He had stayed until nearly eleven o'clock that Tuesday night, until eventually Millie could drink no more tea and had practically had to shoo him out the door. Then he had phoned first thing the following morning to make sure that she was all right.

He'd never have done that had Mum been well. He wouldn't have needed to, because she'd have done it instead.

Maybe Mum's illness had a silver lining after all.

'I want my baby to have a father,' she told Oona simply. 'And I don't just mean in a test tube. I want her to have a living, breathing father that she can recognise in a crowd. I want her to have someone who'll teach her how to ride a bike, and do her homework with her occasionally, and be there if she needs to ring him in the middle of the night.'

'I'd never ring Dad in the middle of the night,' Oona said, looking alarmed.

'Well maybe you should.'

Oona just remained dubious at the very idea.

'That's a big turnaround, Millie,' she said at last.

'I know.'

'It pretty much knocks Spain on the head, doesn't it?'

Millie thought for a minute. Then she gave a shaky sigh. 'Yes. I guess it does.'

And that was that. There would be no more phone calls to Maria, ever.

Oona reached for the gin bottle. 'I think we need a top-up after that.'

They had a big drink of their gin. Millie wasn't sure how she felt; all the agonising and the tussles with her conscience now seemed in vain. It was an awful lot of effort for nothing at the end of the day. She wondered was she giving up too easily.

Oona piped up, 'I've just had an idea.'

'What?' Millie hoped she was going to suggest they ring out for a curry. Maybe that might fill the hole inside her.

'We'll get you a known donor.'

'Pardon?'

'I read about it once. You can find them on the Internet.' She was excited now. 'I don't know why we didn't think of it before. We'll do an advertisement – "Single woman seeks broody man" or something like that – and put it up on one of those singles chatrooms. You'll probably get a load of replies. We'll pick out the best ones, you exchange a few emails with them, and then you can meet up with the successful candidate and do the business with a turkey baster.'

'Forgive me if I'm not jumping up and down.'

'What?' It's the ideal solution. You get exactly what you want – a baby, but with a father attached. You don't have to marry him or anything. He just gets some weekend visits.'

Millie turned the idea over in her head. It sounded horribly businesslike and unromantic. But hardly any less so than lying spread-eagled on a trolley in Spain.

And her child would know its father. There would be no questions over biology, or heritage or background. As Oona said, wasn't it the perfect solution?

But the idea left her as flat as the prospect of another cycle in the clinic. There would be a father all right, but one who would have as little true connection to Millie as a faceless student in Spain. Instead of picking him from a freezer, he would be plucked off a singles' website.

'I don't think so,' she said.

Oona was a bit put out that her marvellous idea was getting so little hop. 'I don't know what's wrong with you tonight at all, Millie.'

Millie didn't either.

Actually she did.

Simon was what was wrong with her, and had been for weeks. He was the reason she didn't want some bloke off the Internet, even if he was very nice and produced oodles of top-quality sperm.

Whenever she thought of babies now, she thought of Simon.

It was all horribly confusing.

She wanted a baby, but she also wanted Simon. And she wanted Simon to be the father of her baby.

Undoubtedly he would have something to say about that.

Although probably not. He may well be on a hot date with that heifer of a bridesmaid right now. He mightn't have given Millie a thought since he'd phoned her nearly two months ago.

It was all too late. She'd had her chance, and she'd blown it. Not once, not twice, but *three times*. That must be some kind of record.

And even if by some remote chance he hadn't hooked up with Sandra's bridesmaid, he would still never contact Millie again. There were only so many rebuffs a man could take.

It would be up to Millie, but she didn't have his number. Or his address. She didn't know where he worked, or where any of his friends lived, or indeed the first thing about him. He wasn't in the phone book, because she'd already sneakily checked.

Now that she *couldn't* contact him, she desperately wanted to, of course. Oh, what kind of a fool had a holiday romance yet failed to get their paramour's number!

Gin, she decided. It was the only solution tonight. And lots of it.

Gary trundled in from upstairs now. He had been suspiciously absent for the past ten minutes.

'Mammy,' he said, 'what's this?'

And he held up a condom. A used condom.

'Oh my God.' Oona whipped it from him fast.

Gary was hurt. 'I found it in the bin. I was going to tie them together and make a catapult.' And he held up another condom. It too was used.

'Gary!' Oona snatched that one off him too. Her cheeks looked as hot as furnaces. 'Go and play with your sisters.' She thrust a whole packet of chocolate biscuits at him. 'Share those out, it'll keep you going till dinner.'

'Yeah!' said Gary, running off.

Millie looked on with great interest, and raised eyebrows, as Oona went to the bin in the corner to dispose of the offending condoms. She was avoiding Millie's eye, and no wonder too.

'I take it they're yours and Brendan's?' Millie enquired archly.

Oona tried to look coy but failed hopelessly. 'Oh, all right. We've had sex, yes.'

'More than once, obviously.'

Oona went and closed the living-room door on the children. 'I don't want to corrupt them. Or at least any more than they already are.'

'So,' said Millie, 'was it Brendan's birthday or something?'

'No,' admitted Oona. 'We've been at it all week.'

And she beamed happily. Now that Millie took a good look at her, there was a glow about her – the glow of someone who had been awake until two a.m. shagging. Her hair had a suspicious matted lump at the back too, and Millie was sure that her polo-neck jumper was to hide more unsightly evidence of a jolly good night.

'So you're back on track?'

'Yes,' she declared delightedly. 'We can't keep our hands off each other. It's just like old times.'

Millie was very surprised. They had barely been on speaking terms the last time she'd seen them. 'That's great, Oona.'

'I know. I was worried there for a while.'

She looked relieved. And completely wrecked.

'I told you him going back to work was the best thing all round,' Millie couldn't resist saying. It wasn't often she was right.

'Oh, it wasn't anything to do with that,' Oona said. 'We've been having even less sex since he started work at that garage. No, this is what did it.'

And she took a postcard from a kitchen drawer and put it down on the table. It had a picture on the front of a couple on a beautiful moonlit beach. They were scantily clad, and entwined in an impossibly romantic position, and snogging the faces off each other. Her hands were caressing his bottom, while his hovered suggestively around her knockers. There was hair and teeth and acres of brown skin everywhere. In another minute they would be having sex.

Millie turned the postcard over. In cheeky red pen were the words, 'Love, Christian.'

'Oh my God.'

The little pup. Talk about stirring up trouble.

'I know,' said Orla.

'You gave him your *address*?'

'I had to! It was the only way he'd let me leave that day.'

'And you didn't think to give him a false one?'

'Millie! I am shocked at you.'

'Why? You've done it loads of times before with other men.'

Unless, of course, Oona had *wanted* Christian to contact her.

But she was throwing up her hands in complete innocence 'I presumed he'd forget all about me. And then this arrived in the post out of the blue. I wasn't even here. Brendan got it. He went mad.'

'I'm not surprised.'

'You should have heard him – ranted and raved around the place, accusing me of all sorts of things. And the language out of him! We were all shocked – he's been so squeaky clean lately.'

She was remarkably cheerful about the whole thing.

'But did he not think you were after having an affair?'

'Oh, he did, yeah,' she confirmed sunnily. 'I think that's why he wanted Dad to go with us to Spain in the first place. He knew there was something up since I'd stopped having sex with him. Christian sending the postcard only confirmed his suspicions.'

'So what happened?'

'There was murder,' Orla said excitedly. 'He threw accusations at me about Christian. I threw it right back at him about Nancy and her gazebo. A few plates were thrown. Then we both realised how much we loved each other, so we went upstairs and had fantastic sex.' She looked misty-eyed at the memory. 'Twice.'

Millie would bet that when Christian had sent that meddlesome postcard, he had never envisaged that he would become a marital aid in Oona's troubled home. Seeing as he had been so concerned about Oona going 'untouched', it was poetic justice in a way.

'So Brendan could have stayed at home after all then,' she said.

'Oh, no,' Oona said grimly. 'That was never going to work out. He was *mothering* me, Millie. Did you not notice? All that pampering and fussing and sending me out to get my hair done. He even ironed my underwear, did I tell you that?' She shuddered in distaste. 'I could never fancy a man like that. But the whole thing wasn't wasted − he still does loads of housework when he gets home in the evenings, and the ironing at the weekends. How many other men do that?'

'He's a treasure,' Millie agreed. 'But everybody knew that except you.'

'I know.' The gin was obviously kicking in because she got a bit teary-eyed. 'I feel bad for making him go so long without sex. I even asked him whether he was tempted by Nancy. But he said no, that she has a touch too much hair on her upper lip.' And she hooted in delight.

Two headlights swept across the drive outside. Brendan, Durex's best customer again, was home.

'Hadn't you better throw that postcard out?' Millie worried.

She didn't want another row to start, and spoil everything.

But Oona just smiled and tucked it safely back into the drawer. 'I'm going to take it out whenever things get a bit slow in the sack. Even the mention of it is enough to bring on a burst of testosterone.'

And she smiled smugly at the prospect.

'Daddy!' the children shouted in delight as Brendan arrived in carrying four boxes from Pizza Express.

'Dinner!' Oona shouted in relief.

'I knew you wouldn't get a chance to make anything,' Brendan said, eyeing the bottle of gin. But he was only joking.

Oona simpered back in a most disgusting way, before floating over to give him a big kiss on the lips.

'Baby,' he said, delighted.

Millie and the children were left looking at each other in embarrassment as wet kissing noises filled the kitchen.

'They're always doing that now,' Gary said to her, shaking his head in despair.

Eventually Chloe, the baby, piped up, 'I'm hungry.'

Oona managed to extricate herself from Brendan, who was looking ruddy in the face. 'Pet!' she said, scooping her up. 'Of course you are. You've only had a packet of crisps all day. Come on, Brendan, let's get them fed and then it's time for a bath and bed.'

And then it was on to a new box of condoms, by the looks of things.

'Millie, you'll stay for pizza, won't you?' said Brendan. He could afford to be generous. He was going off to work every morning with a big smile on his face.

Although she was delighted for them, Millie didn't think she could bear to watch them pawing each other all evening.

Especially as she had nobody to paw. Somewhere in this city, the love of her life was lost, with no way of contacting him. Well, he wasn't the love of her life – she didn't know him well enough for that – but she fancied him like hell, and there was nothing she would rather do right now than get him in a clinch.

But there was no point even thinking like that. Not only had she spurned him repeatedly, but she also had no idea in this world how to contact him. Short of wandering the streets like some sad sicko in the unlikely hopes of running into him, she was doomed to suffer from unrequited love well into old age.

'Thanks anyway,' she told Brendan rather tragically, 'but I think I'll go home.'

There was a bottle of white wine in the fridge – she was already half-pissed on gin, she might as well go the whole way. Then she would fall into bed and hopefully not dream about either babies or Simon.

'Are you sure?' said Oona, eyeing up Brendan's bottom and not paying any proper attention to Millie at all.

They didn't even notice her leave, and it was up to Gary to see her off with a wink at the door, a slice of greasy pizza in his hand. 'Good night, luv.'

Once home, Millie made immediate headway into the bottle of white wine. Then she started wishing she'd stayed for pizza after all, because she couldn't stop thinking about one now. A large ham and pepperoni with extra cheese to be exact.

In fact she'd order one. She deserved it. (You go, girl!)

The pizza company promised to have it at her door in thirty minutes, along with a two-litre bottle of Coke (she deserved it) and a tub of Ben & Jerry's ice cream (she didn't deserve that, but nobody else did either).

She was about to replace the phone when she had a eureka moment. She'd only had about two of them in her entire life before, so it was significant.

This one was to do with the phone. 'We have an incoming call log!'

Actually, those had been Andrew's exact words when they had bought the new phone last year. He had a typical male fascination with buttons and manuals and had spent a blissful two nights 'setting the phone up'. Millie had been happy enough just to learn how to make and answer a call, but was forced all the same to sit through a tedious tutorial by Andrew on how to store and retrieve numbers, how to redial the last dialled number (why?) and even how to send a text.

Now she wished to God she had paid more attention when he had been droning on about the incoming call log. If she could work it out, then she would find out Simon's number.

She had a couple of false starts as she struggled with the functions, and then Dad's number came up from when he had called yesterday.

Hurrah!

Then Dad's number again.

And again. Oh, for God's sake. The man had no life. (She conveniently forgot that he still thoughtfully rung up to see how she was, even all these weeks later.)

She went back some more. Thankfully, most people phoned her on her mobile: twenty numbers later and Simon's number finally came up. At least she hoped it was his. It could well be some telemarketing number, but she didn't think so. She would save it to the address book straightaway and then she would sit and plan her strategy. This would require careful thought and consideration before she took her next step.

But she must have skipped that bit too in Andrew's tutorial, because instead of saving the number she ended up dialling it instead.

Oh, shit.

What was she going to do now?

Hang up, quickly.

But that was just childish. And she wanted to talk to Simon, didn't she?

She just wished she were a bit more sober, that was all.

Quaking, she pressed the phone to her ear. Half of her hoped he wasn't home. The other half hadn't time to feel anything because suddenly he was on the other end.

'Hello?'

At least, it sounded like him. She had better just be sure, though. 'This isn't a telemarketing company, is it?'

'Who is this?' he asked suspiciously.

OK, it definitely was Simon. 'Me,' she said. 'I mean, Millie.'

There was a big long silence. He was probably trying hard to remember who the hell she was. Millie? Millie who? Oh yes, that strange bird he met on holidays in Spain, who kept turning him down.

Or else the silence was due to the fact that she had interrupted him mid-sex with the bridesmaid, and he was busy pulling his trousers up.

But apparently she was wrong on both counts because then he said, very warmly, 'Hi, Millie.'

She was gratified. Surely he wouldn't sound so pleased if he didn't care – right?

'I was just ringing . . .' Why *was* she just ringing? Because she liked him a lot and wanted to have his babies? That might be a bit too much to land on him in an initial phone call.

'I just wanted to say hello, really,' she ended up saying, a bit limply.

He didn't mind her lack of direction at all. 'It's really good to hear from you.'

She was more confident now that there was no bridesmaid in the background, or even on the scene at all. He'd never be so accommodating otherwise, would he?

All the same she couldn't resist asking, 'How was Jamie's wedding?'

'Great,' he said. 'As in, they enjoyed the day. I did my best man bit, and got very drunk.'

She smiled, her heart lifting.

He didn't ask about Spain. And she didn't mention it. It was as though neither of them wanted to spoil things.

Then, very bravely for a man who had been knocked back repeatedly, he said, 'Look, you're obviously not doing anything tonight. Neither am I. Do you want to meet for a drink?'

Her heart rose. And then fell again. She felt like a broken record. 'I can't,' she said miserably.

'Right,' he said, with a little sigh.

'It's not like that. It's just that I'm waiting for a pizza to arrive.' She was mortified saying it.

'Ah,' he said, very kindly not passing any kind of judgement. He sounded relieved.

She took a breath and spoke fast. 'It's very embarrassing to admit this, but it's a sixteen-inch pizza, and I got a tub of ice cream as well, so if you haven't had dinner yet, then you're very welcome to come and share mine.'

Now he must really think she was a hog. He had probably gone right off her, and he would hang up at any moment.

Instead he said, 'I'm on my way.'

Chapter Thirty-Three

It was a terrible race around the place tidying up before he arrived. She abandoned it halfway, realising that she should be spending the time on herself. It wasn't like he was going to run his finger around the skirting board, was he?

She gave the nearest skirting board a quick flick of her duster just in case, before hurling it down and racing upstairs for a two-minute shower, and then into something flattering.

If only she *had* something flattering. Why was every single nice thing in the wash just when you needed it? Well, all two of them?

By the time she had finished rifling through her wardrobe for an alternative, and tried on five different pairs of shoes, the bedroom was like a hurricane had passed through it.

Luckily he wouldn't see it. They were just having a pizza, for heaven's sake, not hot sex. Right?

All the same there was no doubt that there was a sense of rekindling in the air. Otherwise he wouldn't be coming around. Or have sounded so warm and eager on the phone. Supposing the rekindling went so well that they burst into flames later on, only to be confronted by three-week-old sheets on her bed? One of which had a hole in it?

Time wise, she had a stark choice to make: she could put on make-up before he arrived, or she could change the sheets.

Oh, hell. She would change the sheets.

But that didn't meant she was expecting sex. Absolutely not. The very idea sent her stomach into somersaults. It was just a contingency plan, that was all.

By the time she'd finished putting on the expensive linen sheets that they'd received as a wedding present (take that, Andrew), she was in need of another shower. But the bedroom looked OK once she'd picked up all her work clothes off the floor and shoved them into a press, and placed a couple of literary books on the nightstand. In the unlikely event that they would end up in the bedroom, naked, there wasn't really anything else that he might stumble across that would embarrass her.

Except for the drawer.

The flipping drawer with all her fertility aids.

If he went in there he'd die with the shock. It was like an Aladdin's Cave for the conceptionally challenged.

She opened it up. It was so full that she had to brace herself, and use two hands. Finally it sprung out, disgorging its array of strange goodies.

Looking in, Millie realised that her entire life for the past year could be traced through its contents. There at the very back was the jolly little book on the birds and the bees that she had bought months and months ago when she had first thought they had better get on with having a baby (if only it had been that simple). The book had innocently assumed, like Millie, that it was simply a question of time – and sexual intercourse, naturally – before a baby would come along, possibly dropped by a stork, and everything would be rosy in the garden.

Towards the front of the drawer was the harder stuff. She reached in and took out the Fertility Monitor, complete with slides, which Andrew had found so amusing when he had called around that night. He hadn't found it amusing when they'd been trying to use the damn thing, no more than herself. But then again any sense of humour had gone from their sexual relationship at that point.

Ah, there was her trusty thermometer, looking a bit rusty around the tip now. And all her charts, neatly catalogued and held together with a paperclip. Mention must be made too of her selection of vitamin supplements and her lubricant and her fish oil and a copy of *Taking Charge of Your Reproductive Cycle*, thoroughly thumbed through.

Finally at the front was her latest endeavour: Spain. She found all her emails to Maria, neatly printed out and folded into an envelope. Directly under them were all her early pregnancy tests, still waiting optimistically to be used.

Millie wished she could look upon all these things with nostalgia. Or a sense of closure. But they just reminded her of all the heartache and pain. In that drawer lay the tatters of her marriage, not to mention her unfulfilled baby hopes.

There was nothing in it that brought her any happiness or sense of achievement.

She went and got the bin from the corner of the bedroom and she began to empty the contents of the drawer into it. She didn't even think about it too much. She just knew that she wanted to be rid of everything in that drawer.

The bin got full halfway through, and she had to go into the spare bedroom for reinforcements.

Finally the drawer was empty, except for a few pairs of winter socks. Which were actually in their rightful place, as the drawer had started out life as her sock drawer.

She felt peculiarly calm when she had finished. She would never give up on having a baby – well, maybe when she was fifty she would – but she was done with the weird stuff.

Downstairs the doorbell rang.

She slammed the empty drawer shut and ran down the stairs.

Simon looked gorgeous.

That was Millie's first thought upon seeing him. It was shallow, but true.

There he stood on her doorstep, in more clothes than she'd ever seen him in, carrying a sixteen-inch pizza, a tub of Ben & Jerry's, a two-litre bottle of Coke, and a bunch of flowers.

'I met the pizza guy on the way in,' he explained. He added hastily, 'He didn't bring the flowers.'

Millie accepted them. 'They've lovely,' she said.

'Actually, they're only from the local garage, but it was the best I could do at such short notice.'

The romantic gesture suddenly made Millie feel a bit awkward and embarrassed. It put an expectation on the evening, or something. Was he anticipating dim lights and scented candles, and then terrific sex?

He seemed a bit nervous too. Well, they hadn't seen each other since Spain, where it had been sunny and warm, with beautiful scenery, and where everybody had looked gorgeous, including themselves – or at least passable, anyway.

It was a damn sight different on her doorstep on a chilly Friday evening with lukewarm pizza, and with her wearing no make-up (bad decision).

What if it really *had* been a holiday romance? Tonight might end up being a total disaster, with neither of them quite able to recapture that Spanish magic.

He was probably thinking the same – at any rate he cast a little look over his shoulder as though wondering whether he could hitch a lift out of the place with the pizza guy.

And to think that she had changed the *sheets*?

'Anyway, come in,' she mumbled.

'Um, thanks.'

Things got worse in her tiny hallway. He was all elbows as he tried to take off his coat whilst balancing the pizza. Meanwhile she flapped about with the flowers and the tub of Ben & Jerry's ice cream.

'Nice house,' he said, gamely ignoring the messy pile of takeaway leaflets on the hall table and the red wine stain on the carpet.

She had decided that they would eat in the living room on the couch. It would be less formal.

But she had forgotten that the middle of the couch had a big dip in it, and the minute they sat down on it she practically tumbled onto his lap.

'Sorry about that,' she said, leaping off him, mortified.

'No problem,' he said. 'I quite enjoyed it.'

She laughed. The ice was broken, and they smiled at each other.

Oh, what lovely brown eyes he had. They were even browner than she remembered. And his tan was just as healthy-looking. How could that be? Did he loofah and moisturise and all that carry-on?

Whatever he did it worked. All she could think of was the clean sheets again. Shame on her.

It was going to be OK. It hadn't just been a holiday romance. There was still something there. Something wonderful.

'I suppose we're on a date, are we?' he asked cautiously.

'I suppose we are.' Then she was suddenly anxious. 'Are you OK with that?' Maybe he really *had* just come over for his dinner.

'Absolutely. God knows I've been trying to get a date with you for a good while now.'

She blushed. 'I didn't mean to turn you down so many times.'

'My ego is in tatters,' he assured her.

'I was worried that I might have driven you into the arms of Sandra's bridesmaid,' she confessed, seeing as they were being so honest.

He blinked a bit at that. 'No,' he assured her. 'Anyway, didn't I tell you that I was very choosy?'

And he gave her a look that sent her heart into meltdown. They sat there for another while, just smiling at each other. Honestly, this was getting silly.

She cleared her throat sternly. Someone would have to bring this meeting to order.

'Thanks for coming over,' she said rather formally.

'Thanks for inviting me,' he said, rather amused.

She wasn't quite sure what to say next. She didn't want to come right out and start talking about 'them'. Especially as she didn't even know if there *was* a them. There had been in Spain. But a lot had happened since Spain, including her failed fertility treatment.

He must have been thinking along the same lines, because he used the momentary gap in the conversation to jump in.

'Millie, it's lovely to see you again. Really lovely. But before we go any further with this thing – this date, or whatever we're on – we need to talk about your fertility treatment.'

Her back was immediately up. Honestly, could the guy not get down off his soapbox for one single evening?

'Look,' she said abruptly, 'it didn't work, OK?'

'What?'

'My treatment. I had the IUI, but I didn't get pregnant.'

'Oh.'

'So there you go.'

He took a moment to absorb this. 'But you can try again, can't you?'

'Sorry?'

'The success rates are so low. What, about fifteen to twenty per cent? A lot of people take three or more attempts.'

She looked at him suspiciously. 'You seem to know an awful lot about it.'

He helped himself to a slice of pizza. 'Yes,' he said. 'I've been doing some research.'

'Research?'

He saw her surprise. 'I didn't know hardly a thing about it until I met you. So I thought I'd better educate myself.'

She still wasn't sure where this was leading – unless his 'research' had been to store up fresh ammunition with which to attack her.

'Why?' she asked.

She might as well hear him out. If she was going to continue to see him – and she very much wanted to – then she supposed she would have to come to terms with his position. Just as he would have to come to terms with hers. She might have decided to give up on her treatment, but the fact was that she had gone through one cycle of it, and she didn't want to be judged on it for the duration of their relationship.

If there was going to be a relationship, that was, and right now from his tone it was looking iffy.

'I haven't changed my mind, if that's what you're wondering,' he said.

No surprises there then.

'I still think that a child needs a father.'

'You're not going to get any arguments there. And could you sound just a little less pompous?'

'I didn't mean to sound pompous at all.' He looked taken aback. 'What I wanted to say was that, if we . . .' he hunted around for words, 'if you and I continue to . . . see each other . . .'

'If we don't kill each other first,' she supplied tartly. But inside she felt all happy and light. He thought they had a future too.

'Could you not interrupt?'

'Sorry.'

'If we got together, then I would support you if you wanted to go again.'

'Where?'

'To Spain.'

She certainly hadn't expected that.

She just looked at him, not sure what to say.

'It's what you wanted, wasn't it?' he said, looking a bit disappointed that she wasn't grinning in delight. 'You said you couldn't be with somebody if they didn't stand by you.'

'I know . . .'

'Mind you,' he said, 'there's a bit of a flaw in your argument. I mean, why would you want to go to Spain for donor sperm in the first place if you were with somebody?'

'True,' she said.

'It might be overkill on the sperm front,' he advised her.

And she snickered, even though this was no laughing matter at all.

She got serious again. He had made a very big offer. She knew how strongly he felt about the whole donor thing, so it was a big deal for him to say that.

'Thank you,' she said sincerely. 'But I won't need to take you up on it. Because I'm not going back to Spain.'

'You're not?'

'No. I've kind of decided it's not for me.'

'Oh.' He clearly hadn't been expecting that either. No doubt he had thought she'd invited him around tonight in the hopes of doing some kind of balancing act between him and donor IUI in Spain.

Not that she hadn't considered it. Strongly.

But, honestly, life was complicated enough.

'So . . . um . . . what does that actually mean?' Clearly he was struggling to get a handle on the whole situation.

'It means I still want a baby while I have time,' she said. 'But I thought I'd go for it the natural way.'

Oops. She hadn't quite meant to put it so bluntly.

Or maybe she had. After the whole experience with Andrew she had learned a thing or two. If Simon wanted out, then he had better do so now, and not a year down the line when her FSH had gone through the roof.

'I see,' he said. Then he enquired delicately – hopefully? – 'Am I in the picture anywhere?'

'If you want to be.'

He thought about it for a while. But not for too long, thank God. 'Yes,' he said. 'I do.'

Then, just in case he thought they were going to get down to it on the couch the minute the pizza was finished, she said, 'But I don't think we know each other well enough just yet to have a baby.'

It killed her to say it. There, two feet away from her, was a man – a lovely, kind, sexy man – who wanted babies. *Babies.* And she had changed her sheets. The old Millie would have grabbed him by the scuff of the neck and taken him upstairs immediately, and stripped him down. Then, after a quick check of her temperature, she would have slapped him across the arse, and ordered, 'Go for it, boy!'

But the new Millie, the one who had emptied her drawer in a fit of therapeutic zeal, was going to be sensible and not rush into things. She wasn't going to make the fatal mistake of putting her desire for motherhood ahead of what could be the best relationship of her life.

Besides, how long did it take to get to know each other well enough? A month? Two months?

She would apply her entire energy to knowing Simon inside out. She would make it her life's mission.

There were still a few bits of the old Millie left in the new Millie. But that was OK too.

'I agree,' Simon said. 'Besides, we want to be able to have some fun first, don't we?'

And he winked at her.

Millie laughed her head off.

He looked offended. 'I've been practising that all week.'

Then the sagging couch dipped further as he moved closer. 'I'd better change tactics,' he said.

Millie tumbled happily on to his lap again. He felt lovely and solid under her. She hoped she wasn't too heavy.

But he didn't give any indication that he was in pain. Instead he pulled her close and kissed her.

The pizza was forgotten. And the ice cream, merrily melting on the table. The white wine grew warmer, but who cared?

Millie herself was getting dangerously warm too. But everything about Simon just felt so good, from his lovely firm lips to his broad shoulders and his silky brown hair.

God, were her hands *really* in his hair? She'd better get a grip right now or next thing they really would be availing themselves of those clean sheets.

She broke away, murmuring virtuously, 'The pizza will get cold.'

He was looking rather warm too. If she hadn't thrown out her trusty thermometer she'd bet it would register in the high nineties.

Now that things were under control again, she had a bone to pick.

'You sent me away the last time we spoke on the phone. You told me to go have my treatment. What if I hadn't phoned you tonight? I might never have heard from you again!'

'You would have. I was going to give it a month or two, and then I was intending to phone you again. Round about now, in fact.'

He was telling the truth. She was completely flattered.

'Look,' she said, 'do you want to eat this pizza or not?'

'Yes,' he confessed, 'but I'm too distracted.'

'Me too.'

She wasn't sure who began the kissing again. Probably her, don't you know it. But there was nobody keeping scores here, and she closed her eyes and held him tight.

She became vaguely aware of a dull, rather fast thudding, and she thought, 'Damn that biological clock!' But then, with a rush of relief, she realised that it was Simon's heart, and it was beating for her.